Dark Princess

Dark Princess

W.E.B. Du Bois

MINT EDITIONS

Dark Princess was first published in 1928.

This edition published by Mint Editions 2024.

ISBN 9798888971024 | E-ISBN 9798888971055

Published by Mint Editions®

MINT EDITIONS

minteditionbooks.com

Publishing Director: Katie Connolly
Design: Ponderosa Pine Design
Production and Project Management: Micaela Clark
Typesetting: Westchester Publishing Services

To

Her High Loveliness
TITANIA XXVII

BY HER OWN GRACE
QUEEN OF FAERIE,

Commander of the Bath; Grand Medallion of Merit;
Litterarum Humanarum Doctor;
Fidei Extensor; etc., etc.

OF WHOSE FAITH AND FOND AFFECTION
THIS ROMANCE
WAS SURELY BORN

Contents

PART I
THE EXILE

AUGUST, 1923

Summer is come with bursting flower and promise of perfect fruit. Rain is rolling down Nile and Niger. Summer sings on the sea where giant ships carry busy worlds, while mermaids swarm the shores. Earth is pregnant. Life is big with pain and evil and hope. Summer in blue New York; summer in gray Berlin; summer in the red heart of the world!

I

Matthew Towns was in a cold white fury. He stood on the deck of the *Orizaba* looking down on the flying sea. In the night America had disappeared and now there was nothing but, waters heaving in the bright morning. There were many passengers walking, talking, laughing; but none of them spoke to Matthew. They spoke about him, noting his tall, lean form and dark brown face, the stiff, curled mass of his sinewy hair, and the midnight of his angry eyes.

They spoke about him, and he was acutely conscious of every word. Each word heard and unheard pierced him and quivered in the quick. Yet he leaned stiff and grim, gazing into the sea, his back toward all. He saw the curled grace of the billows, the changing blues and greens; and he saw, there at the edge of the world, certain shining shapes that leapt and played.

Then they changed—always they changed; and there arose the great cool height of the room at the University of Manhattan. Again he stood before the walnut rail that separated student and Dean. Again he felt the bewilderment, the surge of hot surprise.

"I cannot register at all for obstetrics?"

"No," said the Dean quietly, his face growing red. "I'm sorry, but the committee—"

"But—but—why, I'm Towns. I've already finished two years—I've ranked my class. I took honors—why—I—this is my Junior year—I must—"

He was sputtering with amazement.

"Hell! I'm not asking your pity, I'm demanding—"

"I'm sorry."

The Dean's lips grew thin and hard, and he sent the shaft home as if to rid himself quickly of a hateful task.

"Well—what did you expect? Juniors must have obstetrical work. Do you think white women patients are going to have a nigger doctor delivering their babies?"

Then Matthew's fury had burst its bounds; he had thrown his certificates, his marks and commendations straight into the drawn white face of the Dean and stumbled out. He came out on Broadway with its wide expanse, and opposite a little park. He turned and glanced up at the gray piles of tan buildings, threatening the sky, which were the University's great medical center. He stared at them. Then with bowed head he plunged down 165th Street. The gray-blue Hudson lay beneath his feet, and above it piled the Palisades upward in gray and green. He walked and walked: down the curving drive between high homes and the Hudson; by graveyard and palace; tomb and restaurant; beauty and smoke. All the afternoon he walked, all night, and into the gray dawn of another morning.

II

In after years when Matthew looked back upon this first sea voyage, he remembered it chiefly as the time of sleep; of days of long, long rest and thought, after work and hurry and rage. He was indeed very tired. A year of the hardest kind of study had been followed by a summer as clerical assistant in a colored industrial insurance office, in the heat of Washington. Thence he had hurried straight to the university with five hundred dollars of tuition money in his pocket; and now he was sailing to Europe.

He had written his mother—that tall, gaunt, brown mother, hard-sinewed and somber-eyed, carrying her years unbroken, who still toiled on the farm in Prince James County, Virginia–he had written almost curtly: "I'm through. I cannot and will not stand America longer. I'm off. I'll write again soon. Don't worry. I'm well. I love you." Then he had packed his clothes, given away his books and instruments, and sailed in mid-August on the first ship that offered after that long tramp of tears and rage, after days of despair. And so here he was.

Where was he going? He glanced at the pale-faced man who asked him. "I don't know," he answered shortly. The good-natured gentleman stared, nonplused. Matthew turned away. Where *was* he going? The ship was going to Antwerp. But that, to Matthew, was sheer accident. He was going *away* first of all. After that? Well, he had thought of France. There they were at least civilized in their prejudices. But his French was poor. He had studied German because his teachers regarded German medicine as superior to all other. He would then go to Germany. From there? Well, there was Moscow. Perhaps they could use a man in Russia whose heart was hate. Perhaps he would move on to the Near or Far East and find hard work and peace. At any rate he was going somewhere; and suddenly letting his strained nerves go, he dragged his chair to a sheltered nook apart and slept. To the few who approached him at all, Matthew was boorish and gruff. He knew that he was unfair, but he could not help it. All the little annoyances, which in healthier days be would have laughed away, avoided, or shortly forgotten, now piled themselves on his sore soul. The roommate assigned him discovered that his companion was colored and quickly decamped with his baggage. A Roumanian who spoke little English, and had not learned American customs, replaced him.

Matthew entered the dining room with nerves a-quiver. Every eye caught him during the meal—some, curiously; some, derisively; some, in half-contemptuous surprise. He felt and measured all, looking steadily into his plate. On one side sat an old and silent man. To the empty seat on the other side he heard acutely a swish of silk approach—a pause and a consultation. The seat remained empty. At the next meal he was placed in a far corner with people too simple or poor or unimportant to protest. He heaved a sigh to have it over and ate thereafter in silence and quickly.

So at last life settled down, soothed by the sea—the rhythm and song of the old, old sea. He slept and read and slept; stared at the water; lived his life again to its wild climax; put down repeatedly the cold, hard memory; and drifting, slept again.

Yet always, as he rose from the deep seas of sleep and reverie, the silent battle with his fellows went on. Now he yearned fiercely for someone to talk to; to talk and talk and explain and prove and disprove. He glimpsed faces at times, intelligent, masterful. They had brains; if they knew him they would choose him as companion, friend; but they did not know him. They did not want to know him. They glanced at him momentarily and then looked away. They were afraid to be noticed noticing him.

And he? He would have killed himself rather than have them dream he would accept a greeting, much less a confidence. He looked past and through and over them with blank unconcern. So much so that a few—simpler souls, themselves wandering alone hither and thither in this aimless haphazard group of a fugitive week-ventured now and then to understand: "I never saw none of you fellers like you—" began one amiable Italian. "No?" answered Matthew briefly and walked away.

"You're not lonesome?" asked a New England merchant, adding hastily, "I've always been interested in your people."

"Yes," said Matthew with an intonation that stopped further conversation along that line.

"No," be growled at an insulted missionary, "I don't believe in God—never did—do you?"

And yet all the time he was sick at heart and yearning. If but one soul with sense, knowledge, and decency had firmly pierced his awkwardly hung armor, he could have helped make these long hard days human. And one did, a moment, now and then a little tow-haired girl of five or six with great eyes. She came suddenly on him one day: "Won't you play ball with me?" He started, smiled, and looked down. He loved children. Then he saw the mother approaching—typically Middle-West American, smartly dressed and conscious of her social inferiority. Slowly his smile faded; quickly he walked away. Yet nearly everyday thereafter the child smiled shyly at him as though they shared a secret, and he smiled slowly back; but he was careful never to see the elaborate and most exclusive mother.

Thus they came to green Plymouth and passed the fortress walls of Cherbourg and, sailing by merry vessels and white cliffs, rode on to the Scheldt. All day they crept past fields and villages, ships and windmills, up to the slender cathedral tower of Antwerp.

III

Sitting in the Viktoria Café, on the Unter den Linden, Berlin, Matthew looked again at the white leviathan—at that mighty organization of white folk against which he felt himself so bitterly in revolt. It was the same vast, remorseless machine in Berlin as in New York. Of course, there were differences — differences which he felt like a tingling pain. He had on the street here no sense of public insult; he was treated as he was dressed, and today he had dressed carefully, wearing the new suit made for the opening school term; he had on his newest dark crimson tie that burned with the red in his smooth brown face; he carried cane and gloves, and he had walked into this fashionable café with an air. He knew that he would be served, politely and without question.

Yes, in Europe he could at least eat where he wished so long as he paid. Yet the very thought made him angry; conceive a man outcast in his own native land! And even here, how long could he pay, he who sat with but two hundred dollars in the world, with no profession, no work, no friends, no country? Yes, these folks treated him as a man—or rather, they did not, on looking at him, treat him as less than a man. But what of it? They were white. What would they say if he asked for work? Or a chance for his brains? Or a daughter in marriage? There was a blonde and blue-eyed girl at the next table catching his eye. Faugh! She was for public sale and thought him a South American, an Egyptian, or a rajah with money. He turned quickly away.

Oh, he was lonesome; lonesome and homesick with a dreadful homesickness. After all, in leaving white, he had also left black America—all that he loved and knew. God! He never dreamed how much he loved that soft, brown world which he had so carelessly, so unregretfully cast away. What would he not give to clasp a dark hand now, to hear a soft Southern roll of speech, to kiss a brown cheek? To see warm, brown, crinkly hair and laughing eyes. God—he was lonesome. So utterly, terribly lonesome. And then—he saw the Princess!

Many, many times in after years he tried to catch and rebuild that first wildly beautiful phantasy which the girl's face stirred in him. He knew well that no human being could be quite as beautiful as she looked to him then. He could never quite recapture the first ecstasy of the picture, and yet always even the memory thrilled and revived him. Never after that first glance was he or the world quite the same.

First and above all came that sense of color: into this world of pale yellowish and pinkish parchment, that absence or negation of color, came, suddenly, a glow of golden brown skin. It was darker than sunlight and gold; it was lighter and livelier than brown. It was a living, glowing crimson, veiled beneath brown flesh. It called for no light and suffered no shadow, but glowed softly of its own inner radiance.

Then came the sense of the woman herself: she was young and tall even when seated, and she bore herself above all with a singularly regal air. She was slim and lithe, gracefully curved. Unseeing, past him and into the struggling, noisy street, she was looking with eyes that were pools of night—liquid, translucent, haunting depths—whose brilliance made her face a glory and a dream.

Matthew pulled himself together and tried to act sensibly. Here—here in Berlin and but a few tables away, actually sat a radiantly beautiful woman, and she was colored. He could see the faultlessness of her dress. There was a hint of something foreign and exotic in her simply draped gown of rich, creamlike silken stuff and in the graceful coil of her hand-fashioned turban. Her gloves were hung carelessly over her arm, and he caught a glimpse of slender-heeled slippers and sheer clinging hosiery. There was a flash of jewels on her hands and a murmur of beads in half-hidden necklaces. His young enthusiasm might overpaint and idealize her, but to the dullest and the oldest she was beautiful, beautiful. Who was she? What was she? How came this princess (for in some sense she must be royal) here in Berlin? Was she American? And how was he—

Then he became conscious that he had been listening to words spoken behind him. He caught a slap of American English from the terrace just back and beyond.

"Look, there's that darky again. See her? Sitting over yonder by the post. Ain't she some pippin? What? Get out! Listen! Bet you a ten-spot I get her number before she leaves this café. You're on! I know niggers, and I don't mean perhaps. Ain't I white. Watch my smoke!"

Matthew gripped the table. All that cold rage which still lay like lead beneath his heart began again to glow and burn. Action, action, it screamed—no running and sulking now—action! There was murder in his mind-murder, riot, and arson. He wanted just once to hit this white American in the jaw—to see him spinning over the tables, and then to walk out with his arm about the princess, through the midst of a gaping, scurrying white throng. He started to rise, and nearly upset his coffee cup.

Then he came to himself. No—no. That would not do. Surely the fellow would not insult the girl. He could count on no public opinion in Berlin as in New York to shield him in such an adventure. He would simply seek to force his company on her in quite a natural way. After all, the café was filling. There were no empty tables, at least in the forward part of the room, and no one person had a right to a whole table; yet to approach any woman thus, when several tables with men offered seats, was to make a subtle advance; and to approach this woman?—Puzzled and apprehensive, Matthew sat quietly and watched while he paid his waiter and slowly pulled on his gloves. He saw a young, smooth-faced American circle carelessly from behind him and saunter toward the door. Then he stopped, and turning, slowly came back toward the girl's table. A cold sweat broke out over Matthew. A sickening fear fought with the fury in his heart. Suppose this girl, this beautiful girl, let the fresh American sit down and talk to her? Suppose? After all, who—what was she? To sit alone at a table in a European café—well, Matthew watched. The American approached, paused, looked about the café, and halted beside her table. He looked down and bowed, with his hand on the back of the empty chair. The lady did not start nor speak. She glanced at him indifferently, unclasped her hands slowly, and then with no haste gathered up her things; she nodded to the waiter, fumbled in her purse, and without another glance at the American, arose and passed slowly out. Matthew could have shouted.

But the American was not easily rebuffed by this show of indifference. Apparently he interpreted the movement quite another way. Waving covertly to his fellows, he arose leisurely, without ordering, tossed a bill to the waiter, and sauntered out after the lady. Matthew rose impetuously, and he felt that whole terrace table of men arise behind him.

The dark lady had left by the Friedrichstrasse door, and paused for the taxi which the gold-laced porter had summoned. She gave an address and already had her foot on the step. In a moment the American was by her side. Deftly he displaced the porter and bent with lifted hat. She turned on him in surprise and raised her little head. Still the American persisted with a smile, but his hand had hardly touched her elbow when Matthew's fist caught him right between the smile and the ear. The American sat down on the sidewalk very suddenly.

Pedestrians paused. There was a commotion at the restaurant door as several men rushed out, but the imposing porter was too quick; he had caught the eye and pocketed the bill of the lady. In a moment, evidently thinking the couple together, he had handed both her and Matthew into the taxi, slammed the door, and they had whirled away. In a trice they fled down the Friedrichstrasse, left across the Französische, again left to Charlotten, and down the Linden. Matthew glanced anxiously back. They had been too quick, and there was apparently no pursuit. He leaned forward and spoke to the chauffeur, and they drove up to the curb near the Brandenburg Gate and stopped.

"*Mille remerciements, Monsieur!* " said the lady. Matthew searched his head for the right French answer as he started to step out, but could not remember: "Oh—oh—don't mention it," he stammered.

"Ah—you are English? I thought you were French or Spanish! She spoke clear-clipped English with perfect accent, to Matthew's intense relief. Suppose she had spoken only French! He hastened to explain: "I am an American Negro."

"An American Negro?" The lady bent forward in sudden interest and stared at him. "An American Negro!" she repeated. "How singular—how very singular! I have been thinking of American Negroes all day! Please do not leave me yet. Can you spare a moment? Chauffeur, drive on!"

IV

As they sat at tea in the Tiergarten, under the tall black trees, Matthew's story came pouring out:

"I was born in Virginia, Prince James County, where we black folk own most of the land. My mother, now many years a widow, farmed her little forty acres to educate me, her only child. There was a good school there with teachers from Hampton, the great boarding-school not far away. I was young when I finished the course and was sent to Hampton. There I was unhappy. I wanted to study for a profession, and they insisted on making me a farmer. I hated the farm. My mother finally sent me North. I boarded first with a cousin and then with friends in New York and went through high school and through the City College. I specialized on the pre-medical course, and by working nights and summers and playing football (amateur, of course, but paid excellent expenses in fact), I was able to enter the new great medical school of the University of Manhattan, two years ago.

"It was a hard pull, but I plunged the line. I had to have scholarships, and I got them, although one Southern professor gave me the devil of a time."

The lady interrupted. "Southern?" she asked. "What do you mean by 'Southern'?"

"I mean from the former slave States although the phrase isn't just fair. Some of our most professional Southerners are Northern-born."

The lady still looked puzzled, but Matthew talked on.

"This man didn't mean to be unfair, but he honestly didn't believe 'niggers' had brains, even if he had the evidence before him. He flunked me on principle. I protested and finally had the matter up to the Dean; I showed all my other marks and got a re-examination at an extra cost that deprived me of a new overcoat. I gave him a perfect paper, and he had to acknowledge it was 'good,' although he made careful inquiries to see if I had not in some way cribbed dishonestly.

"At last I got my mark and my scholarship. During my second year there were rumors among the few colored students that we would not be allowed to finish our course, because objection had been made to colored students in the clinical hospital, especially with white women patients. I laughed. It was, I was sure, a put-up rumor to scare us off. I knew black men who had gone through other New York medical schools which had become parts of this great new consolidated school. There had been no real trouble. The patients never objected—only Southern students and the few Southern professors. Some of the trustees had mentioned the matter but had been shamed into silence.

"Then, too, I was firm in my Hampton training; desert and hard work were bound to tell. Prejudice was a miasma that character burned away. I believed this thoroughly. I had literally pounded my triumphant way through school and life. Of course I had met insult and rebuff here and there, but I ignored them, laughed at them, and went my way. Those black people who cringed and cowered, complained of failure and 'no chance,' I despised—weaklings, cowards, fools! Go to work! Make a way! Compel recognition!

"In the medical school there were two other colored men in my class just managing to crawl through. I covertly sneered at them, avoided them. What business had they there with no ability or training? I see differently now. I see there may have been a dozen reasons why Phillips of Mississippi could neither spell nor read correctly and why Jones of Georgia could not count. They had had no hardworking mother, no Hampton, no happy accidents of fortune to help them on.

"While I? I rose to triumph after triumph. Just as in college I had been the leading athlete and had ridden many a time aloft on white students' shoulders, so now, working until two o'clock in the morning and rising at six, I took prize after prize—the Mitchel Honor in physiology, the Welbright medal in pathology, the Shores Prize for biological chemistry. I ranked the second-year class at last commencement, and at our annual dinner at the Hotel Pennsylvania, sat at the head table with the medal men. I remember one classmate. He was from Atlanta, and he hesitated and whispered when he found his seat was beside me. Then he sat down like a man and held out his hand. 'Towns,' he said, 'I never associated with a Negro before who wasn't a servant or laborer; but I've heard of you, and you've made a damned fine record. I'm proud to sit by you.'

"I shook his hand and choked. He proved my life-theory. Character and brains were too much for prejudice. Then the blow fell. I had slaved all summer. I was worked to a frazzle. Reckon my hard-headedness had a hand there, too. I wouldn't take a menial job-Pullman porter, waiter, bell-boy, boat steward good money, but I waved them aside. No! Bad for the soul, and I might meet a white fellow student."

The lady smiled. "Meet a fellow student—did none of them work, too?"

"O yes, but seldom as menials, while Negroes in America are always expected to be menials. It's natural, but—no, I couldn't do it. So at last I got a job in Washington in the medical statistics department of the National Benefit. This is one of our big insurance concerns. O yes, we've got a number of them; prosperous, too. It was hard work, indoors, poor light and air; but I was interested—worked overtime, learned the game, and gave my thought and ideas.

"They promoted me and paid me well, and by the middle of August I had my tuition and book money saved. They wanted me to stay with them permanently; at least until fall. But I had other plans. There was a summer school of two terms at the college, and I figured that if I entered the second term I could get a big lead in my obstetrical work and stand a better show for the Junior prizes. I had applied in the spring for admission to the Stern Maternity Hospital, which occupied three floors of our center building. My name had been posted as accepted. I was tired to death, but I rushed back to New York to register. Perhaps if I had been rested, with cool head and nerves-well, I wasn't. I made the office of the professor of obstetrics on a hot afternoon, August 10, I well remember. He looked at me in surprise. 'You can't work in the Stern Hospital—the places are all taken.'

"'I have one of the places,' I pointed out. He seemed puzzled and annoyed.

"'You'll have to see the Dean,' he said finally.

"I was angry and rushed to the Dean's office. I saw that we had a new Dean—a Southerner.

"Then the blow fell. Seemingly, during the summer the trustees had decided gradually to exclude Negroes from the college. In the case of students already in the course, they were to be kept from graduation by a refusal to admit them to certain courses, particularly in obstetrics. The Dean was to break the news by letter as students applied for these courses by applying early for the summer course, I had been accepted before the decision; so now he had to tell me. He hated the task, I could see. But I was too surprised, disgusted, furious. He said that I could not enter, and he told me brutally why. I threw my papers in his face and left. All my fine theories of race and prejudice lay in ruins. My life was overturned. America was impossible—unthinkable. I ran away, and here I am."

V

They had sat an hour drinking tea in the Tiergarten, that mightiest park in Europe with its lofty trees, its cool dark shade, its sense of withdrawal from the world. He had not meant to be so voluble, so self-revealing. Perhaps the lady had deftly encouraged confidences in her high, but gracious way. Perhaps the mere sight of her smooth brown skin had made Matthew assume sympathy. There was something at once inviting and aloof in the young woman who sat opposite him. She had the air and carriage of one used to homage and yet receiving it indifferently as a right. With all her gentle manner and thoughtfulness, she had a certain faint air of haughtiness and was ever slightly remote.

She was "colored" and yet not at all colored in his intimate sense. Her beauty as he saw it near had seemed even more striking; those thin, smooth fingers moving about the silver had known no work; she was carefully groomed from her purple hair to her slim toe-tips, and yet with few accessories; he could not tell whether she used paint or powder. Her features were regular and delicate, and there was a tiny diamond in one nostril. But quite aside from all details of face and jewels—her pearls, her rings, the old gold bracelet—above and beyond and much more than the sum of them all was the luminous radiance of her complete beauty, her glow of youth and strength behind that screen of a grand yet gracious manner. It was overpowering for Matthew, and yet stimulating. So his story came pouring out before he knew or cared to whom he was speaking. All the loneliness of long, lonely days clamored for speech, all the pent-up resentment choked for words.

The lady listened at first with polite but conscious sympathy; then she bent forward more and more eagerly, but always with restraint, with that mastery of body and soul that never for a moment slipped away, and yet with so evident a sympathy and comprehension that it set Matthew's head swimming. She swept him almost imperiously with her eyes—those great wide orbs of darkening light. His own eyes lifted and fell before them; lifted and fell, until at last he looked past them and talked to the tall green and black oaks.

And yet there was never anything personal in her all-sweeping glance or anything self-conscious in the form that bent toward him. She never seemed in the slightest way conscious of herself. She arranged nothing, glanced at no detail of her dress, smoothed no wisp of hair. She seemed at once unconscious of her beauty and charm, and at the same time assuming it as a fact, but of no especial importance. She had no little feminine ways; she used her eyes apparently only for seeing, yet seemed to see all.

Matthew had the feeling that her steady, full, radiant gaze that enveloped and almost burned him, saw not him but the picture he was painting and the thing that the picture meant. He warmed with such an audience and painted with clean, sure lines. Only once or twice did she interrupt, and when he had ended, she still sat full-faced, flooding him with the startling beauty of her eyes. Her hands clasped and unclasped slowly, her lips were slightly parted, the curve of her young bosom rose and fell.

"And you ran away!" she said musingly. Matthew winced and started to explain, but she continued. "Singular," she said. "How singular that I should meet you; and today." There was no coquetry in her tone. It was evidently not of him, the hero, of whom she was thinking, but of him, the group, the fact, the whole drama.

"And you are two—three millions?" she asked.

"Ten or twelve," he answered.

"You ran away," she repeated, half in meditation.

"What else could I do?" he demanded impulsively. "Cringe and crawl?"

"Of course the Negroes have no hospitals?"

"Of course, they have—many, but not attached to the great schools. What can Howard (rated as our best colored school) do with thousands, when whites have millions? And if we come out poorly taught and half equipped, they sneer at 'nigger' doctors."

"And no Negroes are admitted to the hospitals of New York?"

"O yes—hundreds. But if we colored students are confined to colored patients, we surrender a principle."

"What principle?"

W.E.B. DU BOIS

"Equality."

"Oh—equality."

She sat for a full moment, frowning and looking at him, Then she fumbled away at her beads and brought out a tiny jeweled box. Absently she took out a cigarette, lighted it, and offered him one. Matthew took it, but he was a little troubled. White women in his experience smoked of course—but colored women? Well—but it was delicious to see her great, somber eyes veiled in hazy blue.

She sighed at last and said: "I do not quite understand. But at any rate I see that you American Negroes are not a mere amorphous handful. You are a nation! I never dreamed—but I must explain. I want you to dine with me and some friends tomorrow night at my apartment. We represent—indeed I may say frankly, we are a part of a great committee of the darker peoples; of those who suffer under the arrogance and tyranny of the white world."

Matthew leaned forward with an eager thrill. "And you have plans? Some vast emancipation of the world?"

She did not answer directly, but continued: "We have among us spokesmen of nearly all these groups—of them or for them—except American Negroes. Some of us think these former slaves unready for cooperation, but I just returned from Moscow last week. At our last dinner I was telling of a report I read there from America that astounded me and gave me great pleasure—for I almost alone have insisted that your group was worthy of cooperation. In Russia I heard something, and it happened so curiously that—after sharp discussion about your people but last night (for I will not conceal from you that there is still doubt and opposition in our ranks)—that I should meet you today.

"I had gone up to the Palace to see the exhibition of new paintings you have not seen it? You must. All the time I was thinking absently of Black America, and one picture there intensified and stirred my thoughts—a weird massing of black shepherds and a star. I dropped into the Viktoria, almost unconsciously, because the tea there is good and the muffins quite unequaled. I know that I should not go there unaccompanied, even in the day; white women may, but brown women seem strangely attractive to white men, especially Americans; and this is the open season for them.

"Twice before I have had to put Americans in their place. I went quite unconsciously and noted nothing in particular until that impossible young man sat down at my table. I did not know he had followed me out. Then you knocked him into the gutter quite beautifully. It had never happened before that a stranger of my own color should offer me protection in Europe. I had a curious sense of some great inner meaning to your act—some world movement. It seemed almost that the Powers of Heaven had bent to give me the knowledge which I was groping for; and so I invited you, that I might hear and know more."

She rose, insisted on paying the bill herself. "You are my guest, you see. It is late, and I must go. Then, tomorrow night at eight. My card and address—oh, I quite forgot. May I have your name?"

Matthew had no card. But he wrote in her tiny memorandum book with its golden filigree, "Matthew Towns, Exile, Hotel Roter Adler."

She held out her hand, half turning to go. Her slenderness made her look taller than she was. The curved line of her flowed sinuously from neck to ankle. She held her right hand high, palm down, the long fingers drooping, and a ruby flamed dark crimson on her forefinger. Matthew reached up and shook the hand heartily. He had, as he did it, a vague feeling that he took her by surprise. Perhaps he shook hands too hard, for her hand was very little and frail. Perhaps she did not mean to shake hands—but then, what did she mean?

She was gone. He took out her card and read it. There was a little coronet and under it, engraved in flowing script, "H.R.H. the Princess Kautilya of Bwodpur, India." Below was written, "Lützower Ufer, No. 12."

VI

Matthew sat in the dining room of the Princess on Lützower Ufer. Looking about, his heart swelled. For the first time since he had left New York, he felt himself a man, one of those who could help build a world and guide it. He had no regrets. Medicine seemed a far-off, dry-as-dust thing.

The oak paneling of the room went to the ceiling and there broke softly with carven light against white flowers and into long lucent curves. The table below was sheer with lace and linen, sparkling with silver and crystal. The servants moved deftly, and all of them were white save one who stood behind the Princess' high and crimson chair. At her right sat Matthew himself, hardly realizing until long afterward the honor thus done an almost nameless guest.

Fortunately he had the dinner jacket of year before last with him. It was not new, but it fitted his form perfectly, and his was a form worth fitting. He was a bit shocked to note that all the other men but two were in full evening dress. But he did not let this worry him much.

Ten of them sat at the table. On the Princess' left was a Japanese, faultless in dress and manner, evidently a man of importance, as the deference shown him and the orders on his breast indicated. He was quite yellow, short and stocky, with a face which was a delicately handled but perfect mask. There were two Indians, one a man grave, haughty, and old, dressed richly in turban and embroidered tunic, the other, in conventional dress and turban, a young man, handsome and alert, whose eyes were ever on the Princess. There were two Chinese, a young man and a young woman, he in a plain but becoming Chinese costume of heavy blue silk, she in a pretty dress, half Chinese, half European in effect. An Egyptian and his wife came next, be suave, talkative, and polite—just a shade too talkative and a bit too polite, Matthew thought; his wife a big, handsome, silent woman, elegantly jeweled and gowned, with much bare flesh. Beyond them was a cold and rather stiff Arab who spoke seldom, and then abruptly.

Of the food and wine of such dinners, Matthew had read often but never partaken; and the conversation, now floating, now half submerged, gave baffling glimpses of unknown lands, spiritual and physical. It was all something quite new in his experience, the room, the table, the service, the company.

He could not keep his eyes from continually straying sidewise to his hostess. Never had he seen color in human flesh so regally set: the rich and flowing grace of the dress out of which rose so darkly splendid the jeweled flesh. The black and purple hair was heaped up on her little head, and in its depths gleamed a tiny coronet of gold. Her voice and her poise, her self-possession and air of quiet command, kept Matthew staring almost unmannerly, despite the fact that he somehow sensed a shade of resentment in the young and handsome Indian opposite.

They had eaten some delicious tidbits of meat and vegetables and then were served with a delicate soup when the Princess, turning slightly to her right, said:

"You will note, Mr. Towns, that we represent here much of the Darker World. Indeed, when all our circle is present, we represent all of it, save your world of Black Folk."

"All the darker world except the darkest," said the Egyptian.

"A pretty large omission," said Matthew with a smile.

"I agree," said the Chinaman; but the Arab said something abruptly in French. Matthew had said that he knew "some" French. But his French was of the American variety which one excavates from dictionaries and cements with grammar, like bricks. He was astounded at the ease and the fluency with which most of this company used languages, so easily, without groping or hesitation and with light, sure shading. They talked art in French, literature in Italian, politics in German, and everything in clear English.

"M. Ben Ali suggests," said the Princess, "that even you are not black, Mr. Towns."

"My grandfather was, and my soul is. Black blood with us in America is a matter of spirit and not simply of flesh."

"Ah! Mixed blood," said the Egyptian. "Like all of us, especially me," laughed the Princess.

"But, your Royal Highness—not Negro," said the elder Indian in a tone that hinted a protest.

"Essentially," said the Princess lightly, "as our black and curly-haired Lord Buddha testifies in a hundred places. But"—a bit imperiously—"enough of that. Our point is that Pan-Africa belongs logically with Pan-Asia; and for that reason Mr. Towns is welcomed tonight by you, I am sure, and by me especially. He did me a service as I was returning from the New Palace."

They all looked interested, but the Egyptian broke out:

"Ah, Your Highness, the New Palace, and what is the fad today? What has followed expressionism, cubism, futurism, vorticism? I confess myself at sea. Picasso alarms me. Matisse sets me aflame. But I do not understand them. I prefer the classics."

"The Congo," said the Princess, "is flooding the Acropolis. There is a beautiful Kandinsky on exhibit, and some lovely and startling things by unknown newcomers."

"*Mais*," replied the Egyptian, dropping into French—and they were all off to the discussion, save the silent Egyptian woman and the taciturn Arab.

Here again Matthew was puzzled. These persons easily penetrated worlds where he was a stranger. Frankly, but for the context he would not have known whether Picasso was a man, a city, or a vegetable. He had never heard of Matisse. Lightly, almost carelessly, as he thought, his companions leapt to unknown subjects. Yet they knew. They knew art, books, and literature, politics of all nations, and not newspaper politics merely, but inner currents and whisperings, unpublished facts.

"Ah, pardon," said the Egyptian, returning to English, "I forgot Monsieur Towns speaks only English and does not interest himself in art."

Perhaps Matthew was sensitive and imagined that the Egyptian and the Indian rather often, if not purposely, strayed to French and subjects beyond him.

"Mr. Towns is a scientist?" asked the Japanese.

"He studies medicine," answered the Princess.

"Ah—a high service," said the Japanese. "I was reading only today of the work on cancer by your Peyton Rous in Carrel's laboratory."

Towns was surprised. "What, has he discovered the etiological factor? I had not heard."

"No, not yet, but he's a step nearer."

For a few moments Matthew was talking eagerly, until a babble of unknown tongues interrupted him across the table.

"Proust is dead, that 'snob of humor'—yes, but his *Recherche du Temps Perdu* is finished and will be published in full. I have only glanced at parts of it. Do you know Gasquet's *Hymnes*?"

"Beraud gets the Prix Goncourt this year. Last year it was the Negro, Maran—"

"I have been reading Croce's *Aesthetic* lately—"

"Yes, I saw the Meyerhold theater in Moscow-gaunt realism— *Howl China* was tremendous."

Then easily, after the crisp brown fowl, the Princess tactfully steered them back to the subject which some seemed willing to avoid.

"And so," she said, "the darker peoples who are dissatisfied—"

She looked at the Japanese and paused as though inviting comment. He bowed courteously.

"If I may presume, your Royal Highness, to suggest," he said slowly, "the two categories are not synonymous. We ourselves know no line of color. Some of us are white, some yellow, some black. Rather, is it not, your Highness, that we have from time to time taken council with the oppressed peoples of the world, many of whom by chance are colored?"

"True, true," said the Princess.

"And yet," said the Chinese lady, "it is dominating Europe which has flung this challenge of the color line, and we cannot avoid it."

"And on either count," said Matthew, "whether we be bound by oppression or by color, surely we Negroes belong in the foremost ranks."

There was a slight pause, a sort of hesitation, and it seemed to Matthew as though all expected the Japanese to speak. He did, slowly and gravely:

"It would be unfair to our guest not to explain with some clarity and precision that the whole question of the Negro race both in Africa and in America is for us not simply a question of suffering and compassion. Need we say that for these peoples we have every human sympathy? But for us here and for the larger company we represent, there is a deeper question—that of the ability, qualifications, and real possibilities of the black race in Africa or elsewhere."

Matthew left the piquant salad and laid down his fork slowly. Up to this moment he had been quite happy. Despite the feeling of being out of it now and then, he had assumed that this was his world, his people, from the high and beautiful lady whom he worshiped more and more, even to the Egyptians, Indians, and Arab who seemed slightly, but very slightly, aloof or misunderstanding.

Suddenly now there loomed plain and clear the shadow of a color line within a color line, a prejudice within prejudice, and he and his again the sacrifice. His eyes became somber and did not lighten even when the Princess spoke.

"I cannot see that it makes great difference what ability Negroes have. Oppression is oppression. It is our privilege to relieve it."

"Yes," answered the Japanese, "but who will do it? Who can do it but those superior races whose necks now bear the yoke of the inferior rabble of Europe?"

"This," said the Princess, "I have always believed; but as I have told your Excellency, I have received impressions in Moscow which have given me very serious thought—first as to our judgment of the ability of the Negro race, and second"—she paused in thought—"as to the relative ability of all classes and peoples."

Matthew stared at her, as she continued:

"You see, Moscow has reports—careful reports of the world's masses. And the report on the Negroes of America was astonishing. At the time, I doubted its truth: their education, their work, their property, their organizations; and the odds, the terrible, crushing odds against which, inch by inch and heartbreak by heartbreak, they have forged their unfaltering way upward. If the report is true, they are a nation today, a modern nation worthy to stand beside any nation here."

"But can we put any faith in Moscow?" asked the Egyptian. "Are we not keeping dangerous company and leaning on broken reeds?"

"Well," said Matthew, "if they are as sound in everything as in this report from America, they'll bear listening to."

The young Indian spoke gently and evenly, but with bright eyes.

"Naturally," he said, "one can see Mr. Towns needs must agree with the Bolshevik estimate of the lower classes."

Matthew felt the slight slur and winced. He thought he saw the lips of the Princess tighten ever so little. He started to answer quickly, with aplomb if not actual swagger.

"I reckon," he began—then something changed within him. It was as if he had faced and made a decision, as though some great voice, crying and reverberating within his soul, spoke for him and yet was him. He had started to say, "I reckon there's as much high-born blood among American Negroes as among any people. We've had our kings, presidents, and judges—" He started to say this, but he did not finish. He found himself saying quite calmly and with slightly lifted chin:

"I reckon you're right. We American blacks are very common people. My grandfather was a whipped and driven slave; my father was never really free and died in jail. My mother plows and washes for a living. We come out of the depths—the blood and mud of battle. And from just such depths, I take it, came most of the worthwhile things in this old world. If they didn't—God help us."

The table was very still, save for the very faint clink of china as the servants brought in the creamed and iced fruit.

The Princess turned, and he could feel her dark eyes full upon him.

"I wonder- –I wonder," she murmured, almost catching her breath.

The Indian frowned. The Japanese smiled, and the Egyptian whispered to the Arab.

"I believe that is true," said the Chinese lady thoughtfully, "and if it is, this world is glorious."

"And if it is not?" asked the Egyptian icily. "It is perhaps both

W.E.B. DU BOIS

true and untrue," the Japanese suggested. "Certainly Mr. Towns has expressed a fine and human hope, although I fear that always blood must tell."

"No, it mustn't," cried Matthew, "unless it is allowed to talk. Its speech is accidental today. There is some weak, thin stuff called blood, which not even a crown can make speak intelligently; and at the same time some of the noblest blood God ever made is dumb with chains and poverty."

The elder Indian straightened, with blazing eyes.

"Surely," he said, slowly and calmly, "surely the gentleman does not mean to reflect on royal blood?"

Matthew started, flushed darkly, and glanced quickly at the Princess. She smiled and said lightly, "Certainly not," and then with a pause and a look straight across the table to the turban and tunic, "nor will royal blood offer insult to him." The Indian bowed to the tablecloth and was silent.

As they rose and sauntered out to coffee in the silk and golden drawing room, there was a discussion, started of course by the Egyptian, first of the style of the elaborate piano case and then of Schönberg's new and unobtrusive transcription of Bach's triumphant choral Prelude, "Komm, Gott, Schöpfer."

The Princess sat down. Matthew could not take his eyes from her. Her fingers idly caressed the keys as her tiny feet sought the pedals. From white, pearl-embroidered slippers, her young limbs, smooth in pale, dull silk, swept up in long, low lines. Even the delicate curving of her knees he saw as she drew aside her drapery and struck the first warm tones. She played the phrase in dispute—great chords of aspiration and vision that melted to soft melody. The Egyptian acknowledged his fault. "Yes—yes, that was the theme I had forgotten."

Again Matthew felt his lack of culture audible, and not simply of his own culture, but of all the culture in white America which he had unconsciously and foolishly, as he now realized, made his norm. Yet withal Matthew was not unhappy. If he was a bit out of it, if he sensed divided counsels and opposition, yet he still felt almost fiercely that that was his world. Here were culture, wealth, and beauty. Here was power, and here he had some recognized part. God! If he could just do his part, any part! And he waited impatiently for the real talk to begin again.

It began and lasted until after midnight. It started on lines so familiar to Matthew that he had to shut his eyes and stare again at their swarthy faces: Superior races—the right to rule—born to command—inferior breeds—the lower classes-the rabble. How the Egyptian rolled off his tongue his contempt for the "r-r-rabble!" How contemptuous was the young Indian of inferior races! But how humorous it was to Matthew to see all tables turned; the rabble now was the white workers of Europe; the inferior races were the ruling whites of Europe and America. The superior races were yellow and brown.

"You see," said the Japanese, "Mr. Towns, we here are all agreed and not agreed. We are agreed that the present white hegemony of the world is nonsense; that the darker peoples are the best— the natural aristocracy, the makers of art, religion, philosophy, life, everything except brazen machines."

"But why?"

"Because of the longer rule of natural aristocracy among us. We count our millenniums of history where Europe counts her centuries. We have our own carefully thought-out philosophy and civilization, while Europe has sought to adopt an ill-fitting mélange of the cultures of the world."

"But does this not all come out the same gate, with the majority of mankind serving the minority? And if this is the only ideal of civilization, does the tint of a skin matter in the question of who leads?" Thus Matthew summed it up.

"Not a whit—it is the natural inborn superiority that matters," said the Japanese, "and it is that which the present color bar of Europe is holding back."

"And what guarantees, in the future more than in the past and with colored more than with white, the wise rule of the gifted and powerful?"

"Self-interest and the inclusion in their ranks of all really superior men of all colors—the best of Asia together with the best of the British aristocracy, of the German Adel, of the French writers and financiers—of the rulers, artists, and poets of all peoples."

"And suppose we found that ability and talent and art is not entirely or even mainly among the reigning aristocrats of Asia and Europe, but buried among millions of men down in the great sodden masses of all men and even in Black Africa?"

"It would come forth."

"Would it?"

"Yes," said the Princess, "it would come forth, but when and how? In slow and tenderly nourished efflorescence, or in wild and bloody upheaval with all that bitter loss?"

"Pah!" blurted the Egyptian—"pardon, Royal Highness—but what art ever came from the canaille!"

The blood rushed to Matthew's face. He threw back his head and closed his eyes, and with the movement he heard again the Great Song. He saw his father in the old log church by the river, leading the moaning singers in the Great Song of Emancipation. Clearly, plainly he heard that mighty voice and saw the rhythmic swing and beat of the thick brown arm. Matthew swung his arm and beat the table; the silver tinkled.

Silence dropped on all, and suddenly Matthew found himself singing. His voice full, untrained but mellow, quivered down the first plaintive bar:

"When Israel was in Egypt land—"

Then it gathered depth:

"Let my people go!"

He forgot his audience and saw only the shining river and the bowed and shouting throng:

"Oppressed so hard, they could not stand,
Let my people go."

Then Matthew let go restraint and sang as his people sang in Virginia, twenty years ago. His great voice, gathered in one long deep breath, rolled the Call of God:

> *"Go down, Moses!*
> *Way down into the Egypt land,*
> *Tell Old Pharaoh*
> *To let my people go!"*

He stopped as quickly as he had begun, ashamed, and beads of sweat gathered on his forehead. Still there was silence—silence almost breathless. The voice of the Chinese woman broke it.

"It was an American slave song! I know it. How—how wonderful."

A chorus of approval poured out, led by the Egyptian.

"That," said Matthew, "came out of the black rabble of America." And he trilled his "r." They all smiled as the tension broke.

"You assume then," said the Princess at last, "that the mass of the workers of the world can rule as well as be ruled?"

"Yes—or rather can work as well as be worked, can live as well as be kept alive. America is teaching the world one thing and only one thing of real value, and that is, that ability and capacity for culture is not the hereditary monopoly of a few, but the widespread possibility for the majority of mankind if they only have a decent chance in life."

The Chinaman spoke: "If Mr. Towns' assumption is true, and I believe it is, and recognized, as sometime it must be, it will revolutionize the world."

"It will revolutionize the world," smiled the Japanese, "but not—today."

"Nor this *siècle*," growled the Arab.

"Nor the next—and so in saecula saeculorum," laughed the Egyptian.

Well," said the little Chinese lady, "the unexpected happens."

And Matthew added ruefully, "It's about all that does happen!"

He lapsed into blank silence, wondering how he had come to express the astonishing philosophy which had leapt unpremeditated from his lips. Did he himself believe it? As they arose from the table the Princess called him aside.

VII

I trust you will pardon the interruption at this late hour," said the Japanese. Matthew glanced up in surprise as the Japanese, the two Indians, and the Arab entered his room. "Sure," said he cheerily, "have any seats you can find. Sorry there's so little space."

It was three o'clock in the morning. He was in his shirt sleeves without collar, and he was packing hastily, wondering how on earth all these things had ever come out of his two valises. The little room on the fifth floor of the Roter Adler Hotel did look rather a mess. But his guests smiled and so politely deprecated any excuses or discomfort that he laughed too, and leaned against the window, while they stood about door and bed.

"You had, I believe," continued the Japanese, "an interview with her Royal Highness, the Princess, before you left her home tonight."

"Yes."

"I—er—presume you realize, Mr. Towns, that the Princess of Bwodpur is a lady of very high station—of great wealth and influence."

"I cannot imagine anybody higher."

The elder Indian interrupted. "There are," he said, "of course, some persons of higher hereditary rank than her Royal Highness, but not many. She is of royal blood by many scores of generations of direct descent. She is a ruling potentate in her own right over six millions of loyal subjects and yields to no human being in the ancient splendor of her heritage. Her income, her wealth in treasure and jewels, is uncounted. Sir, there are few people in the world who have the right to touch the hem of her garment." The Indian drew himself to full height and looked at Matthew.

"I'm strongly inclined to agree with you there," said Matthew, smiling genially.

"I had feared," continued the younger Indian, also looking Matthew squarely in the eye, "that perhaps, being American, and unused to the ceremony of countries of rank, you might misunderstand the democratic graciousness of her Royal Highness toward you. We appreciate, sir, more than we can say," and both Indians bowed low, "your inestimable service to the Princess yesterday, in protecting her royal person from insufferable insult. But the very incident illustrates and explains our errand.

"The Princess is young and headstrong. She delights, in her new European independence, to elude her escort, and has given us moments of greatest solicitude and even fright. Meeting her as you did yesterday, it was natural for you to take her graciousness toward you as the camaraderie of an equal, and—quite unconsciously, I am sure—your attitude toward her has caused us grave misgiving."

"You mean that I have not treated the Princess with courtesy?" asked Matthew in consternation. "In what way? Tell me."

"It is nothing—nothing, now that it is past, and since the Princess was gracious enough to allow it. But you may recall that you never addressed her by her rightful title of 'Royal Highness'; you several times interrupted her conversation and addressed her before being addressed; you occupied the seat of honor without even an attempted refusal and actually shook her Highness' hand, which we are taught to regard as unpardonable familiarity."

Matthew grinned cheerfully. "I reckon if the Princess hadn't liked all that she'd have said so—"

The Japanese quickly intervened. "This is, pardon me, beside our main errand," he said. "We realize that you admire and revere the Princess not only as a supremely beautiful woman of high rank, but as one of rare intelligence and high ideals."

"I certainly do."

"And we assume that anything you could do—anyway you could cooperate with us for her safety and future, we could count upon your doing?"

"To my very life."

"Good—excellent—you see, my friends," turning to the still disturbed Indians and the silent, sullen Arab, "it is as I rightly divined."

They did not appear wholly convinced, but the Japanese continued: "In her interview with you she told you a story she had heard in Moscow, of a widespread and carefully planned uprising of the American blacks. She has intrusted you with a letter to the alleged leader of this organization and asked you to report to her your impressions and recommendations; and even to deliver the letter, if you deem it wise.

"Now, my dear Mr. Towns, consider the situation: First of all, our beloved Princess introduces you, a total stranger, into our counsels and tells you some of our general plans. Fortunately, you prove to be a gentleman who can be trusted; and yet you yourself must admit this procedure was not exactly wise. Further than that, through this letter, our reputations, our very lives, are put in danger by this well-meaning but young and undisciplined lady. Her unfortunate visit to Russia has inoculated her with Bolshevism of a mild but dangerous type. The letter contains money to encourage treason. You know perfectly well that the American Negroes will neither rebel nor fight unless put up to it or led like dumb cattle by whites. You have never even heard of the alleged leader, as you acknowledged to the Princess."

"She is evidently well spied upon."

"She is, and will always be, well guarded," answered the elder Indian tensely.

"Except yesterday," said Matthew.

But the Japanese quickly proceeded. "Why then go on this wild goose chase? Why deliver dynamite to children?"

"Thank you."

"I beg your pardon. I may speak harshly, but I speak frankly. You are an exception among your people."

"I've heard that before. Once I believed it. Now I do not."

"You are generous, but you are an exception, and you know you are."

"Most people are exceptions."

"You know that your people are cowards."

"That's a lie; they are the bravest people fighting for justice today."

"I wish it were so, but I do not believe it, and neither do you. Every report from America—and believe me, we have many—contradicts this statement for you. I am not blaming them, poor things, they were slaves and children of slaves. They can not even begin to rise in a century. We Samurai have been lords a thousand years and more; the ancestors of her Royal Highness have ruled for twenty centuries—how can you think to place yourselves beside us as equals? No—no—restrain your natural anger and distaste for such truth. Our situation is too delicate for niceties. We have been almost betrayed by an impulsive woman, high and royal personage though she be. We have come to get that letter and to ask you to write a report now, to be delivered later, thoroughly disenchanting our dear Princess of this black American chimera."

"And if I refuse?"

The Japanese looked pained but patient. The others moved impatiently, and perceptibly narrowed the circle about Matthew. He was thinking rapidly; the letter was in his coat pocket on the bed beyond the Japanese and within easy reach of the Indians if they had known it. If he jumped out the window, he would be dead, and they would eventually secure the letter. If he fought, they were undoubtedly armed, and four to one. The Japanese was elderly and negligible as an opponent, but the young Indian and the Arab were formidable, and the older Indian dangerous. He might perhaps kill one and disable another and raise enough hullabaloo to arouse the hotel, but how would such a course affect the Princess?

The Japanese watched him sadly.

"Why speak of unpleasant things," he said gently, "or contemplate futilities? We are not barbarians. We are men of thought and culture. Be assured our plans have been laid with care. We know the host of this hotel well. Resistance on your part would be absolutely futile. The back stairs opposite your entrance are quite clear and will be kept clear until we go. And when we go, the letter will go with us."

Matthew set his back firmly against the window. His thoughts raced. They were armed, but they would use their arms only as a last resort; pistols were noisy and knives were messy. Oh, they would use them—one look at their hard, set eyes showed that; but not first. Good! Then first, instead of lurching forward to attack as they might expect, he would do a first-base slide and spike the

Japanese in the ankles. It was a mean trick, but anything was fair now. He remembered once when they were playing the DeWitt Clinton High—but he jerked his thoughts back. The Japanese was nearest him; the fiery younger Indian just behind him and a bit to the right, bringing him nearer the bed and blocking the aisle. By the door was the elder Indian, and at the foot of the bed, the Arab.

Good! He would, at the very first movement of the young Indian, who, he instinctively knew, would begin the mêlée, slide feet forward into the ankles of the Japanese, catching him a little to the right so that he would fall or lurch between him and the Indian. Then he would with the same movement slide under the low iron bed and rise with the bed as weapon and shield. But he would not keep it. No; he would hurl it sideways and to the left, pinning the young Indian to the wall and the Japanese to the floor. With the same movement he would attempt a football tackle on the Arab. The Arab was a tough customer—tall, sinewy, and hard. If he turned left, got his knife and struck down, quick and sure, Matthew would be done for. But most probably he would, at Matthew's first movement, turn right toward his fellows. If he did, he was done for. He would go down in the heap, knocking the old Indian against the door.

Beside that door was the electric switch. Matthew would turn it and make a last fight for the door. He might get out, and if he did, the stairs were clear. The coat and letter? Leave them, so long as he got his story to the Princess. It was all a last desperate throw. He calculated that he had good chances against the Japanese's shins, about even chances to get under the bed unscathed, and one in two to tackle the Arab. He had not more than one chance in three of making the door unscathed, but this was the only way. If he surrendered without a fight—that was unthinkable. And after all, what had he to lose? Life? Well, his prospects were not brilliant anyhow, And to die for the Princess-silly, of course, but it made his blood race. For the first time he glimpsed the glory of death, Meantime he said—be sensible! It would not hurt to spar for time.

He pretended to be weighing the matter.

"Suppose you do steal the letter by force, do you think you can make me write a report?"

"No, a voluntary report would be desirable but not necessary. You left with the Princess, you will remember, a page of directions and information about America to guide her in the trip she is preparing to make and from which we hope to dissuade her. You appended your signature and address. From this it will be easy to draft a report in handwriting so similar to yours as to be indistinguishable by ordinary eyes."

"You add forgery to your many accomplishments."

"In the pursuit of our duty, we do not hesitate at theft or forgery."

Still Matthew parried: "Suppose," he said, "I pretended to acquiesce, gave you the letter and reported to the Princess. Suppose even I told the German newspapers of what I have seen and heard tonight."

There was a faraway look in the eyes of the Japanese as he answered slowly: "We must follow Fate, my dear Mr. Towns, even if Fate leads to murder. We will not let you communicate with the Princess, and you are leaving Berlin tonight."

The Indians gave a low sigh almost like relief.

Matthew straightened and spoke slowly and firmly.

"Very well. I won't surrender that letter to anybody but the Princess—not while I'm alive. And if I go out of here dead I won't be the only corpse."

Every eye was on the Japanese, and Matthew knew his life was in the balance. The pause was tense; then came the patient voice of the Japanese again.

"You—admire the Princess, do you not?"

"With all my heart."

The Indians winced.

"You would do her a service?"

"To the limit of my strength."

"Very well. Let us assume that I am wrong. Assume that the Negroes are worth freedom and ready to fight for it. Can you not see that the name of this young, beautiful, and highborn lady must under no circumstances be mixed up with them, whether they gain or lose? What would not Great Britain give thus to compromise an Indian ruler?"

"That is for the Princess to decide."

"No! She is a mere woman—an inexperienced girl. You are a man of the world. For the last time, will you rescue her Royal Highness from herself?"

"No. The Princess herself must decide."

"Then—"

"Then," said the Princess' full voice, "the Princess will decide." She stood in the open doorway, the obsequious and scared landlord beside her with his pass-keys. She had thrown an opera cloak over her evening gown, and stood unhatted, white-slippered, and ungloved. She threw one glance at the Indians, and they bowed low with outstretched hands. She stamped her foot angrily, and they went to their knees. She wheeled to the Arab. Without a word, he stalked out. The Japanese alone remained, calm and imperturbable.

"We have failed," he said, with a low bow.

The Princess looked at him. "You have failed," she said. "I am glad there is no blood on your hands."

"A drop of blood more or less matters little in the great cause for which you and I fight, and if I have incurred your Royal Highness' displeasure tonight, remember that, for the same great cause, I stand ready tomorrow night to repeat the deed and seal it with my life."

The Princess looked at him with troubled eyes. Then she seated herself in the only and rather rickety chair and motioned for her two subjects to arise. Matthew never forgot that scene: he, collarless and in shirt sleeves, with sweat pouring off his face; the room in disorder, mean, narrow, small, and dingy; the Japanese standing in the same place as when he entered, in unruffled evening dress; the Indians on their knees with hidden faces; the Princess, disturbed, yet radiant. She spoke in low tones.

"I may be wrong," she said, "and I know how right, but infinitely and calmly right, you usually are. But some voice within calls me. I have started to fight for the dark and oppressed peoples of the world; now suddenly I have seen a light. A light which illumines the mass of men and not simply its rulers, white and yellow and black. I want to see if this thing is true, if it can possibly be true that wallowing masses often conceal submerged kings. I have decided not simply to send a messenger to America but shortly to sail myself—perhaps this week on the *Gigantic*. I want to see for myself if slaves can become men in a generation. If they can—well, it makes the world new for you and me." The Japanese started to speak, but she would not pause:

"There is no need for protest or advice. I am going. Mr. Towns will perform his mission as we agreed, if he is still so minded, and as long as he is in Europe, these two gentlemen," she glanced at the Indians, "will bear his safety on their heads, at my command. Go!"

The Indians bowed and walked out slowly, backward. She turned to the Japanese. "Your Highness, I bid you goodnight and goodbye. I shall write you."

Gravely the Japanese kissed her hand, bowed, and withdrew. The Princess looked at Matthew. He became acutely conscious of his appearance as she looked at him almost a full minute with her great, haunting eyes.

"I thank you, again," she said slowly. "You are a brave man—and loyal." She held out her hand, low, to shake his. But the tension of the night broke him; he quivered, and taking her hand in both his, kissed it.

She rose quickly, drew herself up, and looked at first almost affronted; then when she saw his swimming eyes, a kind of startled wonder flashed in hers. Slowly she held out her hand again, regally, palm down and the long fingers drooping.

"You are very young," she said.

He was. He was only twenty-five. The Princess was all of twenty-three.

*Fall. Fall of leaf and sigh of wind. Gasp of the world-soul
before, in crimson, gold, and gray, it dips beneath the snows.
The flame of passing summer slowly dies in the looming
shadow of death. Fall on the vast gray-green Atlantic,
where waves of all waters heave and groan toward bitter
storms to come. Fall in the crowded streets of New York.
Fall in the heart of the world.*

I

Matthew was paring potatoes; paring, paring potatoes. There was a machine in the corner, paring, too. But Matthew was cheaper than the machine and better. It was not hard work. It was just dull—idiotic, dull. He pared mechanically, with humped shoulders and half-closed eyes. Garbage lay about him, and nauseating smells combined of sour and sweet, decay and ferment, offal and delicacy, made his head dizzy and his stomach acrid. The great ship rose, shivered and screamed, dropped in the gray grave of waters, and groaned as the hot hell of its vast belly drove it relentlessly, furiously forward. The terrible, endless rhythm of the thing—paring, rising, falling, groaning, paring, swaying, with the slosh of the greasy dishwater, in the close hot air, set Matthew to dreaming.

He could see again that mother of his—that poor but mighty, purposeful mother—tall, big, and brown. What hands she had— gnarled and knotted; what great, broad feet. How she worked! Yet he seemed never to have realized what work was until now. On the farm—that little forty acres of whitish yellow land, with its tiny grove and river; its sweep of green, white cotton; its geese, its chickens, the cow and the old mule; the low log cabin with its two rooms and wide hall leading to the boarded kitchen behind—how he remembered the building of that third room just before his father went away—work? Work on that curious little hell in paradise had not been work to him; it had been play. He had stopped when he was tired. But mother and the bent old father, had it been work for them-hard, hateful, heavy, endless, uninteresting, dull, stupid? Yes, it must have been like this, save in air and sun; toil must have dulled and hardened them. God! What did this world—

"That-a nigger did it—I know!—That-a-there damn nigger!"

The Italian bent over him. Matthew looked up at him without interest. His soul was still dreaming far away—rising, falling, paring, glowing. Somebody was always swearing and quarreling in the scullery. Funny for him to be here. It had seemed a matter of honor, life, death, to sail on this particular ship. He had, with endless courtesy and with less than a hundred dollars in his pocket, assured the Princess that he needed nothing. And then—fourth class to Hamburg, standing! And the docks. The *Gigantic* was there. Would she sail on it? He did not know. He approached the head steward for a job.

"No—no more work." He stood hesitating. A stevedore who staggered past, raining sweat, dropped his barrow and hobbled away. Matthew left his bags, seized the heavy barrow, and trundled it on the ship. It was not difficult to hide until the boat had swung far down the channel. Then he went to the head steward again.

"What the hell are you doing here? Just like a damn nigger!"

Here again it came from the lips of the fat, lumbering Italian: "—damn-a nigger." And Matthew felt a flat-handed cuff beside his head that nearly knocked him from the stool. He arose slowly, folded his arms, and looked at the angry man. The Italian was a great baby whom the men picked on and teased and fooled—cruel, senseless sport for people who took curious delight in tricking others of their kind.

It was to Matthew an amazing situation—one he could not for the life of him comprehend. These men were at the bottom of life—scullions. They had no pride of work. Who could have pride in such work! But they despised themselves. God was in the first cabin, overeating, guzzling, gambling, sleeping. They despised what He despised. He despised Negroes. He despised Italians, unless they were rich and noble. He despised scullion's work. All these things the scullions despised.

Matthew and the Italian were butts—the Italian openly, Matthew covertly; for they were a little dashed at his silence and carriage. But they sneered and growled at the "nigger" and egged the "dago" on. And the Italian—big, ignorant moron, sweet and childish by nature, wild and bewildered by his strange environment, despised the black man because the others did,

This time their companions had slyly slipped potatoes into the Italian's pan until he had already done twice the work of the others. But the last mess had been too large—he grew suspicious

W.E.B. DU BOIS

and angry, and he picked on Matthew because he had seen the others sneer at the dark stranger, and he was ready to believe the worst of him.

Matthew stood still and looked at the Italian; with a yell the irate man hurled his bulk forward and aimed a blow which struck Matthew's shoulder. Matthew fell back a step and still stood looking at him. The scullery jeered:

"Fight—the nigger and the dago."

Again the fist leaped out and hit Matthew in the nose, but still Matthew stood and did not lift his hand. Why? He could not have said himself. More or less consciously he sensed what a silly mess it all was. He could not soil his hands on this great idiot. He would not stoop to such a brawl. There was a strange hush in the scullery. Somebody yelled, "Scared stiff!" But they yelled weakly, for Matthew did not look scared. He was taller than the Italian, not so big, but his brown muscles rippled delicately on his lithe form. Even with his swelling nose, he did not look scared or greatly perturbed. Then there was a scramble. The kitchen steward suddenly entered, one of the caste of stewards—the visible revelation of God in the cabin; a splendid man, smooth-coated, who made money and yelled at scullions.

"Chief!"

The Italian ducked, ran and hid, and Matthew was standing alone.

The steward blustered: "Fighting, hey?"

"No."

"I saw you!"

"You lie!"

The scullery held its breath. The steward, with purple face, started forward with raised fist and then paused. He was puzzled at that still figure. It wouldn't do to be mauled or killed before scullions..

"All right, nigger—I'll attend to you later. Get to work, all of you," he growled.

Matthew sat down and began paring, paring, again. But now the dreams had gone. His head ached. His soul felt stripped bare. He kept pondering dully over this room, glancing at the shifty eyes, the hunches and grins; smelling the smells, the steam, the grease, the dishwater. There was so little kindness or sympathy for each other here among these men. They loved cruelty. They hated and despised most of their fellows, and they fell like a pack of wolves on the weakest. Yet they all had the common bond of toil; their sweat and the sweat of toilers like them made one vast ocean around the world. Waves of world-sweat droned in Matthew's head dizzily, and naked men were driven drowning through it, yet snapping, snarling, fighting back each other as they wallowed. Well, he wouldn't fight them. That was idiotic. It was human sacrilege. If fight he must, he would fight stewards and cabin gentry-lackeys and gods.

He walked stiffly to his berth and sat half-dressed in a corner of the common bunk room, hating to seek his hot, dark, ill-ventilated bunk. The men were growling, sprawling, drinking, and telling smutty stories. They had, it seemed to Matthew, a marvelous poverty of capacity to enjoy—to be happy and to play.

The door opened. The kitchen steward came in, followed by a dozen men and women, evidently from the first cabin—fat, sleek persons in evening dress, the women gorgeous and bare, the men pasty-faced and swaggering. All were smoking and flushed with wine. Towns started and stared—my God! If one face appeared there—if the Princess came down and saw this, saw him here! He groaned and stood up quickly, with the half-formed design of walking out.

"A ring, men!" called the steward. The scullery glowered, smirked, and shuffled; backed to one side, torn by conflicting motives, hesitating.

"These ladies and gentlemen have given a purse of two hundred dollars to have this fight out between the darky and the dago. Strip, you—but keep on your pants. This gentleman is referee. Come, Towns. Now's the chance for revenge."

The Italian rose, lounged forward, and looked at Towns truculently, furtively. His anger was gone now, and he was not sure Towns had wronged him. Towns looked at him, smiled, and held out his hand. The Italian stared, hesitated, then almost ran

W.E.B. DU BOIS

and grabbed it. Towns turned to the steward, still watching the door:

"We won't fight," he said.

"We ain't gonna fight," echoed the Italian.

"Throw them into the ring."

"Try it," cried Towns.

"Try it," echoed the Italian.

The steward turned red and green. He saw a fat fee fading.

"So we can't make you rats fight," he sneered.

"Oh, yes, we'll fight," said Matthew, "but we won't fight each other. If rats must fight they fight cats—and dogs—and hogs."

"Wow!" yelled the scullery, and surged.

"Home, James," squeaked a shrill voice, "they ain't gonna be no fight tonight." She had the face of an angel, the clothes of a queen, and the manners of a prostitute. The guests followed her out, giggling, swaying, and swearing.

"S'no plash f'r min'ster's son, nohow," hiccoughed the youth in the rear.

The steward lingered and glanced at Matthew, teetering on heel and toe.

"So that's your game. Trying to stir up something, hey? Planning Bolshevik stuff! D'ye know where I've half a mind to land you in New York? I'll tell you! In jail! D'ye hear? In jail!"

The room was restless. The grumbling stopped gradually. The men looked as though they wanted to talk to him, but Matthew crept to his bunk and pretended to sleep. What was going to happen? What would they do next? Were they going to make him fight his way over? Must he kill somebody? Of all the muddles that a clean, straight life can suddenly fall to, his seemed the worst. He tossed in his narrow, hot bed in an agony of fear and excitement. He slept and dreamed; he was fighting the world. Blood was spurting, heads falling, ghastly eyes were bulging, but he slew and slew until his neighbor yelled:

"Who the hell you hittin'? Are youse crazy?" And the man fled in fear.

Matthew rose early and went to his task-paring, peeling, cutting, paring. Nothing happened. The steward said no further word. The scullery growled, but let Matthew alone. The Italian crept near him like a lost dog, trying in an inarticulate way to say some unspoken word.

So Matthew dropped back to his dreams. He was groping toward a career. He wanted to get his hand into the tangles of this world. He wanted to understand. His revolt against medicine became suddenly more than resentment at an unforgivable insult—it became ingrained distaste for the whole narrow career, the slavery of mind and body, the ethical chicanery. His sudden love for a woman far above his station was more than romance—it was a longing for action, breadth, helpfulness, great constructive deeds.

And so, rising and falling, working and writhing, dreaming and suffering, he passed his week of days of weeks. He hardly knew when it ended. Only one day, washing dishes, he looked out of the porthole; there was the Statue of Liberty shining.

And Matthew laughed.

II

There is a corner in High Harlem where Seventh Avenue cuts the dark world in two. West rises the noble façade of City College—gray and green. East creeps the sullen Harlem, green and gray. There Matthew stood and looked right and left. Left was the world he had left—there were some pretty parlors there, conventional in furniture and often ghastly in ornament, but warm and homelike in soul. There was his own bedroom; Craigg's restaurant with its glorious biscuit; churches whose music often brushed his ears sweetly, afar; crowded but neat apartments, swaggering but well-dressed lodgers, workers, visitors. He turned from it with a sigh. He had left this world for a season—perhaps forever. It would hardly recognize him, he was sure, for he was unshaven and poorly clothed.

He turned east, and the world turned too—to a more careless and freer movement, louder voices, and easier camaraderie.

By the time Lenox Avenue was reached, the world was gay and vociferous, and shirt sleeves and overalls mingled with tailored trousers and silk hosiery. But Matthew walked on in the gathering gloom: Fifth Avenue—but Fifth Avenue at 135th Street; he knew it vaguely—a loud and unkempt quarter with flashes of poverty and crime. He went on into an ill-kept hall and up dirty and creaking stairs, half-lighted, and knocked on a door. There were loud voices within—loud, continuous quarreling voices. He knocked again.

"Come in, man, don't stand there pounding the door down."

Matthew opened the door. The room was hot with a mélange of smoke, bad air, voices, and gesticulations. Groups were standing and sitting about, lounging, arguing, and talking. Sometimes they shouted and seemed on the point of blows, but blows never came. They appeared tremendously in earnest without a trace of smile or humor. This puzzled Matthew at first until he caught their broad a's and curious singing lilt of phrase. He realized that all or nearly all were West Indians. He knew little of the group.

They were to him singular, foreign and funny. He had never been in a group of them before. He looked about.

"Is Mr. Perigua in?"

Someone waved carelessly toward the end of the room without pause in argument or gesture. Matthew discovered there a low platform, a rickety railing, and within, a table and several men. They were talking, if anything, louder and faster than the rest. With difficulty he traced his way toward them.

"Mr. Perigua?"

No response—but another argument of which Matthew understood not a word.

"May I speak with Mr. Perigua?"

A man whirled toward him.

"Don't you see I'm busy, man? Where's the sergeant-at-arms? Why can't you protect the privacy of my office whenI'm in conference?"

A short, fat, black man reluctantly broke off an intense declamation and hastened up.

"What can I do for you? Are you a member?" He seemed a bit suspicious.

"I don't know—I have a message for Mr. Perigua."

"Give it to me."

"It is not written—it is verbal."

"All right, tell me; I'm Mr. Perigua's representative—official sergeant-at-arms of this—" he hesitated and looked suspiciously at Matthew again—"club."

Perigua had heard his name repeated and turned again. He was a thin, yellow man of middle size, with flaming black hair and luminous eyes. He was perpetual motion, talking, gesticulating, smoking.

"What?" he said.

"A message."

"From where?"

"From—abroad."

Perigua leaped to his feet.

"Get out," he cried to his fellows—"State business. Committee will meet again tomorrow night—what? Then Tuesday—No?

Well, then tomorrow at noon—you can't—well, we'll meet without you. Do you think the world must stand still while you guzzle? Come in. Sergeant, I'm engaged. Keep the gate. Well?"

Matthew sat down within the rail on a chair with half a back. The black eyes blazed into his, and the long thin fingers worked. The purple hair writhed out of place.

"I've been in—Berlin."

"Yes?"

"And certain persons—"

"Yes, yes, man. My God! Get on with it."

"—gave me a message—a word of greeting for Mr. Perigua."

"Well, what is it?"

"Are you Mr. Perigua?"

"My God, man—don't you know me? Is there anybody in New York that doesn't know Perigua? Is there anybody in the world? Gentlemen"—he leaped to the rail—"am I Perigua?" A shout went up.

"Perigua-P-erigua forever!" And a song with some indistinguishable rhyme on "Perigua forever" began to roll until he stopped it with an impatient shout and gesture.

"Shut up. I'm busy."

Matthew whispered to him. Perigua listened and rose to his feet with transfigured face.

"Man—my God! Come!" He tore toward the door.

"*Le jour de gloire est arrivé!* Come, man," he shouted, and dragging Matthew, he reached the door and turned dramatically:

"Men, I have news great news—the greatest! Salute this Ambassador from the World—who brings salvation. There will be a plenary council tomorrow night. Midnight. Pass the word. Adieu." And as they passed out, Matthew heard the song swell again—"Perigua, Perigua, Per—"

They passed upstairs to another room. It was a bedroom, dirty, disheveled, stuffed with furniture and with stale smells of food and tobacco. A scrawny woman, half-dressed, rose from the bed, and at an impatient sign from Perigua went into the next room and closed the door.

Perigua grasped Matthew by both hands and hugged him.

"Man," he gasped, "man, God knows you're welcome. I am on my last legs. I don't know where to turn. The landlord has dispossessed us, bills are pouring in, and over the country, the world, the brethren are clamoring. Now all is well. We are recognized—recognized by the great leaders of Asia and Africa. Pan-Africa stands at last beside Pan-Asia, and Europe trembles."

Matthew felt his spirits droop. This man was no leader, he was too theatrical. Matthew felt that he must get at the facts before he took any steps.

"But tell me—all about your plans," he said.

"Who are you?" countered Perigua.

Matthew answered frankly.

"I am a Pullman porter. I was a student in medicine, but I quit. I went to Europe and there by accident met people who had heard of you and your plans. They were not agreed, I must say plainly, as to their feasibility, but they commissioned me to investigate."

"Did they send any money?"

"None at present. Later, if my reports are satisfactory, they may."

"And you are a porter? How long have you been in service?"

Matthew answered: "Since this morning. You see, I came back as a scullion. Had some trouble on the boat because I was a stowaway, but despite all, they gave me fifty dollars for my work and offered to hire me permanently. I took the money, bought some clothes, and applied for a Pullman job. It seemed to me that it offered the best opportunity to see and know the Negroes of this land."

"You're right, man, you're right. Have any trouble getting on?"

"Not much."

Perigua pondered. "See here," he said, "I'll make you Inspector of my organization and give you letters to my centers. Travel around as porter. Sound out the country-test out the organization. Make your report soon and get some money. Something must happen, and happen soon."

"But what—" began Matthew. Matthew never forgot that story. Out of the sordid setting of that room rose the wild head of Perigua, haloed dimly in the low-burning gas. Far out in street and alley groaned, yelled, and sang Harlem. The snore of the woman came fitfully from the next room, and Perigua talked.

Matthew had at first thought him an egotistic fool. But Perigua was no fool. He next put him down as an ignorant fanatic—but he was not ignorant. He was well read, spoke French and Spanish, read German, and knew the politics of the civilized world and current events surprisingly well. Was he insane? In no ordinary sense of the word; wild, irresponsible, impulsive, but with brain and nerves that worked clearly and promptly.

He had a big torn map of the United States on the wall with little black flags clustered over it, chiefly in the South.

"Lynchings," he said briefly. "Lynchings and riots in the last ten years." His eyes burned. "Know how to stop lynching?" he whispered.

"Why—no, except—"

"We know. Dynamite. Dynamite for every lynching mob."

Matthew started and grew uneasy. "But," he objected, "they occur sporadically—seldom or never twice in the same place."

"Always a half dozen in Mississippi and Georgia. Three or four in South Carolina and Florida. There's a lynching belt. We'll blow it to hell with dynamite from airplanes. And then when the Ku Klux Klan meets sometime, we'll blow them up. Terrorism, revenge, is our program."

"But—" began Matthew as sweat began to ooze.

Perigua waved. He was a man difficult to interrupt. "We've got to have messengers continuously traveling to join our groups together and spread news and concert action. The Pullman porters have a new union on old-fashioned lines. I'm trying to infiltrate with the brethren. See? Now you're going to take a job as Inspector and run on a key route. Where are you running now?"

"New York to Atlanta."

"Good! Boys don't like running south. You can do good work there."

"But just a moment—are the Negroes back of you ready for this—this—"

"To a man! That is, the real Negroes—the masses, when they know and understand—most of them are too ignorant and lazy—but when they know! Of course, the nabobs and aristocrats, the college fools and exploiters—they are like the whites."

Matthew thought rapidly. He did not believe a word Perigua said, but the point was to pretend to believe it. He must see. He must investigate. It was wild, unthinkable, terrible. He must see this thing through.

III

G eorge!"
Inherently there was nothing wrong with the name. It was a good name. The "father" of his country and stepfather of Matthew had rejoiced in it. Thus Matthew argued often with himself.

"George!"

It was the name that had driven Matthew as a student away from the Pullman service. It was not really the name—it was the implications, the tone, the sort of bounder who rejoiced to use it. A scullion, ennobled by transient gold and achieving a sleeping-car berth, proclaimed his kingship to the world by one word:

"George!"

So it seemed at least to oversensitive Matthew. It carried all the meaner implications of menial service and largess of dimes and quarters. All this was involved and implied in the right not only to call a man by his first name, but to choose that name for him and compel him to answer to it.

So Matthew, the porter on the Atlanta car of the Pennsylvania Railroad, No. 183, and Southern Railroad, No. 33, rose in his smart and well-fitting uniform and went forward to the impatiently calling voice.

The work was not hard, but the hours were long, and the personal element of tact and finesse, of estimate of human character and peculiarities, must always be to the fore. Matthew had small choice in taking the job. He had arrived with little money and almost ragged. He had undertaken a mission, and after Perigua's amazing revelation, he felt a compelling duty.

"Do you belong to the porters' union?" asked the official who hired him.

"No, sir."

"Going to join?"

"I had not given it a thought. Don't know much about it."

"Well, let me tell you, if you want your job and good run, keep out of that union. We've got our own company union that serves all purposes, and we're going to get rid gradually of those radicals and Bolsheviks who are stirring up trouble."

Matthew strolled over to the room where the porters were resting and talking. It was in an unfinished dark corner of the station under the stairs, with few facilities and no attempt to make it a club room even of the simplest sort.

"Say," asked Matthew, "what about the union?"

No one answered. Some glanced at him suspiciously. Some went out. Only one finally sidled over and asked what Matthew himself thought of it, but before he could answer, another, passing, whispered in his ear, "Stool pigeon—keep your mouth." Matthew looked after the trim young fellow who warned him. It was Matthew's first sight of Jimmie.

THE DAY HAD BEEN TRYING. A fussy old lady had kept him trotting. A woman with two children had made him nurse; four Southern gentlemen gambling in the drawing room had called him "nigger." He stood by his car at Washington at nine-thirty at night, his berths all made. To his delight Jimmie was on the next car, and they soon were chums. Jimmie was Joy. He was not much over twenty-five and so full of jokes and laughter that none, conductors, passengers, or porters, escaped the contagion of his good cheer. His tips were fabulous, and yet he was never merely servile or clownish. He just had bright, straight-eyed good humor, a quick and ready tongue; and be knew his job down to z. He was invaluable to the greenness of Matthew.

"Here comes a brownskin," he whispered. "Hustle her to bed if she's got a good berth in the middle of the car, else they'll find a 'mistake' and put her in Lower One," and he sauntered whistling away as the conductor stepped out. The conductor was going in for the diagram.

"Wait till I get back," he called, nodding toward the coming passenger.

The young colored woman approached. She was well dressed but a bit prim. She had Lower Six. Matthew sensed trouble, but remembering Jimmie's admonition, he showed her to her berth. She did not look at him, but he carefully arranged her things.

The conductor came back. "What did you put her there for?" he asked.

"She had a ticket for Six," Matthew answered. Both he and the conductor knew that she had not bought that ticket in person. In Washington, they would never have sold a colored person going south Number Six—she'd have got One or Twelve or nothing. The conductor was mad. It meant trouble for him all next day from every Southerner who boarded the train.

"Tell her there's some mistake—I'll move her later." But Matthew did not tell her. On the contrary, he suggested to her that he make her berth. She knew why he suggested it, and she resented it, but consented without glancing at him. He sympathized even with her resentment. The conductor swore when he came through with the train conductor and found her retired, but he could do nothing, and Matthew merely professed to have misunderstood.

In the morning after an almost sleepless night and without breakfast, Matthew took special care of the dark lady, and when she was ready, carried her bag to the empty drawing room and let her dress there in comfort. There again he felt and understood the resentment in her attitude. She could not be treated quite like other passengers. Yet she must know it was not his fault, and perhaps she did not know that the extra work of straightening up the drawing room at the close of a twenty-four-hour trip was no joke. Still, he smiled in a friendly way at her as he brought her back to the seat which he had arranged first, so as to put her to the least unpleasantness from sitting in someother berth. A woman flounced up and away as the girl sat down.

She thanked Matthew primly. She was afraid to be familiar with a porter. He might presume. She was not pretty, but round-faced, light brown, with black, crinkly hair. She was dressed with taste, and Matthew judged that she was probably a teacher or clerk. She had a cold half-defiant air which Matthew understood. This class of his people were being bred that way by the eternal conflict. Yet, he reflected, they might say something pleasant and have some genial glow for the encouragement of others caught in the same toils.

Then, as ever, his mind flew back to Berlin and to the woman of his dreams and quest. He wondered where she was and what she was doing. He had searched the newspapers and unearthed but one small note in the *New York Sunday Times*, which proved that the Princess was actually on the *Gigantic*: "Her Royal Highness, the Princess of Bwodpur, has been visiting quietly with friends while en route from England to her home in India, by way of Seattle." He smiled a bit dubiously; what had porters and princesses in common?

He came back to earth and began the daily struggle with the brushing and the bags through narrow aisles out to the door; to collect the coats and belongings and carefully brush the clothes of twenty people; to wait for, take, and appear thankful for the tip which was wage and yet might be thrown like alms; to find lost passengers in the smoking-car, toilet, or dining room and lost hats, umbrellas, packages, and canes—Matthew came to dread the end of his journeys more than all else.

His colored passenger did "not care" to be brushed. As they rolled slowly through the yards, he glanced at her again.

"Anything I can do for you?" he asked.

"Aren't you a college man?" she asked, rather abruptly.

"I was," he answered, wiping the sweat from his face.

She regarded him severely. "I should think then you'd be ashamed to be a porter," she said.

He bit his lips and gathered up her bags.

"It's a damned good thing for you that I am," he wanted to say; but he was silent. He only hoped desperately that she would not offer to tip him. But she did; she gave him fifteen cents. He thanked her.

IV

With a day off in Atlanta, Matthew and Jimmie looked up Perigua's friends. Jimmie laughed at the venture, although Matthew did not tell him much of his plans and reasons.

"Don't worry," grinned Jimmie; "let the white folks worry; it'll all come out right."

They had a difficult time finding any of the persons to whom Perigua had referred Matthew. First, they went down to Decatur Street. It was the first time Matthew had been so far south or so near the black belt. The September heat was intense, and the flood of black folk overwhelmed him. After all, what did he know of these people, of their thoughts, ambitions, hurts, plans? Suppose Perigua really knew and that he who thought he knew was densely ignorant? They walked over to Auburn Avenue. Could anyone tell them where the office of the *Arrow* was? It was up "yonder." Matthew and Jimmie climbed to an attic. It was empty, but a notice sent them to a basement three blocks away—empty, too, and without notice. Then they ran across the editor in a barber shop where they were inquiring—a little, silent, black man with sharp eyes. No, the *Arrow* was temporarily suspended and had been for a year. Perigua? Oh, yes."

"Well, there could be a conference tonight at eight in the Odd Fellows Hall—one of the small rooms."

"At what hour?"

"Well, you know colored people."

If he came at nine he'd be early. Yes, he knew Perigua. No, he couldn't say that Perigua had much of a following in Atlanta, but Perigua had ideas. Perigua had—yes, ideas; well, then, at nine. Jimmie said he'd leave him at that. He had a date, and he didn't like speeches anyhow. They parted, laughing.

Nobody came until nine-thirty; by ten there was the editor, an ironmolder, a college student, a politician, a street cleaner, a young physician, an insurance agent, and two men who might have been idlers, agitators, or plain crooks. It was an ugly room, incongruously furnished and with no natural center like a fireplace, a table, or a rostrum. Some of the men smoked, some did not; there was a certain air of mutual suspicion. Matthew gathered quickly that this was no regular group, but a fortuitous meeting of particles arranged by the editor, Instead of listening to a conference, he found himself introduced as a representative of Mr. Perigua of New York, and they prepared to hear a speech. Matthew was puzzled, nonplused, almost dumb. He hated speech-making. His folk talked too easily and glibly in his opinion. They did not mean what they said—not half—but they said it well. But he must do something; he must test Perigua and his followers. He must know the truth. So Matthew talked—at first a little vaguely and haltingly; and then finally he found himself telling them almost word for word that conversation about American Negroes in Berlin. He did not say who talked or where it took place; he just told what was said by certain strangers. They all listened with deep absorption. The student was the first to break out with:

"It is the truth; we're punk—useless sheep; and all because of the cowardice of the old men who are in the saddle. Youth has no recognition. It is fear that rules. Old slipper is afraid of missing his tea and toast."

The editor agreed. "No recognition for genius," he said. "I've published the *Arrow* off and on for three years."

"Usually off," growled the politician.

"And a damn poor paper it is," added the ironmolder. "I know it, but what can you expect from two hundred and fifty-eight paid subscribers? If I had five thousand I'd show you a radical paper."

"Aw, it's no good—niggers won't stay put," returned the politician.

"You mean they won't stay sold," said someone.

"We're satisfied—that's the trouble," said the editor. "We're too damn satisfied. We've done so much more with ourselves than we ever dreamed of doing that we're sitting back licking our chops and patting each other on the back."

"Well," said the young physician, "we *have* done well, haven't we?"

"*You* has," growled the ironmolder. "But how 'bout us? You-all is piling up money, but it don't help us none. If we had our own foundries, we'd get something like wages 'stead of scabbing to starve white folks."

"Well, you know we are investing," said the insurance agent. "Our company—"

"Hell! That ain't investment, it's gambling."

"That's the trouble," said the scavenger. "We'se strivers; we'se climbing on one another's backs; we'se gittin' up—some of us— by trompin' others down."

"Well, at any rate, some do get up."

"Yes, sure—but the most of us, where is we going? Down, with not only white folks but niggers on top of us."

"Well, what are we going to do about it?"

"What can we do? Merit and thrift will rise," said the physician.

"Nonsense. Selfishness and fraud rise until somebody begins to fight," answered the editor.

"Perigua is fighting."

"Perigua is a fool—Negroes won't fight."

"*You* won't."

"Will *you*?"

"If I get a chance."

"Chance? Hell! Can't any fool fight?" asked the editor.

"Sure, but I ain't no fool—and besides, if I was, how'd I begin?"

"How!" yelled the student. "Clubs, guns, dynamite!"

But the politician sneered. "You couldn't get one nigger in a million to fight at all, and then they'd sell each other out."

"You ought to know."

"I sure do!" And so it went on. When the meeting broke up, Matthew felt bruised and bewildered.

V

Matthew walked into the church about noon. Jimmie positively refused to go. "Had all the church I need," he said. "Besides, got a date!" The services were just beginning. It was a large auditorium, furnished at considerable expense and with some taste. It gave a sense of space and well-being. The voices of the surpliced choir welled up gloriously, and the tones of the minister rolled in full accents.

Matthew particularly noticed the minister. He remembered the preacher at his own home—an old, bent man, outlandish, with blazing eyes and a fire of inspiration and denunciation that moved every auditor. But this man was young-not much older than Matthew—good-looking, intelligent and educated This service of mingled music and ceremony was attractive, and the sermon-well, the minister did not say much, but he said it well; and if conventionally and with some tricks of the orator, yet he was pleasing and soothing. His Death was an interpretation of Fall—the approach of looming Winter and the test of good resolutions after the bursting Spring and fruitful Summer.

The audience listened contentedly but with no outbursts of enthusiasm. There were a few "amens" from the faithful near the pulpit, but they followed the cadence of the beautiful voice rather than the impact of his ideas. The audience looked comfortable, well fed and well clothed. What were they really thinking? What did the emancipation of the darker races mean to them?

Matthew lingered after the service, and his tall, well-clad figure attracted attention. A deacon welcomed him. He must meet the pastor; and at the door in his silk robe he did meet him. They liked each other at a glance. The minister insisted on his waiting until most of the crowd had passed. Matthew ventured on his queries.

"I've just returned from Germany—" he began.

The minister beamed: "Well, well! That's fine. Hope to take a trip over myself in a year or two. My people here insist. May get a Walker popularity prize. Now what do people over there think of us here? I mean, of us colored folk?"

It was the opening. Matthew explained at length some of the opinions he had heard expressed. The minister was keen with intelligent interest, but just as he was launching out in comment, they were interrupted.

"Brother Johnson, we're ready now and dinner will be on the table. Mustn't keep the old lady waiting."

The speaker was a big, dark man, healthy-looking and pleasant, carefully tailored with every evidence of prosperity. His car and chauffeur were at the curb—a new Cadillac sedan.

The minister hesitated. "My friend, Mr. Towns—just from Germany—" he began.

"Delighted, I'm sure."

"Yes, this is Brother Jones, president of the Universal Mutual— you've heard, I know, of our greatest insurance society. Mr. Towns is just from Germany. I'll—"

"Bring him along—bring him right along and finish your talk at the table. Always room in the pot for one more. Germany? Well! Well! Are they still licked over there? Been promising the old lady a trip for the last ten years—Germany, France, Italy and all. Like to take in Africa too. But you know how it is— business—" And they were packed into the big car and gliding away.

There was no chance to finish the talk with the young minister. The host started off talking about himself, and nothing could stop him. His home was big and costly—too overdone to be beautiful, but with a good deal of comfort and abundant hospitality. He served a little whiskey to Matthew upstairs with winks and asides about the minister; and then, downstairs and everywhere he talked of himself. He was so naïve and so thoroughly interested in the subject that none had the heart to interrupt him, although his wife, as she fidgeted in and out helping the one rather unskillful maid, would say now and then:

"Now, John—stop boasting!"

John would roar good-naturedly—hand around another helping of chicken or ham, pass the vegetables and hot bread, and begin just where he left off: "And there I was without a cent, and four hundred dollars due. I went to the bank—the First National—old man Jones was my people, his grandfather owned mine. 'Mr. Jones,' says I, 'I want five hundred dollars cash today!'

"'Well, John,' says he, 'what's the security?'

"'I'm the security,' says I, and, sir, he handed me the cash! Well, he wasn't out nothing. My check in five figures goes at the bank today—don't it, Reverend?" And so on, and so forth. It was frank, honest self-praise, and his audience hung on his words, although most of them had heard the story a hundred times.

"So you've been to Germany? Well, well! Have they got them radicals in jail yet? Italy's got the dope. Old Moso—what's his name? Mr. Jones was saying the last time I was in the bank, making my weekly deposit—what was it? About six thousand dollars, as I remember—says he, 'John, we need a Mosleny right here in America!'"

"You're not against reform, are you, Mr. Jones?"

"No; no, sir, I'm a great reformer. But no radical. No anarchist or Bolshevik. We've got to protect property."

There was an interruption from some late arrivals.

"What boat did you return on?" asked somebody.

Matthew smiled and hesitated. "The *Gigantic*," he said, and he wanted to add, "In the scullery." Could they stand the joke? He looked up and decided they couldn't, for he was looking into the eyes of the latest arrival, and she was the prim young person who had tipped him fifteen cents yesterday morning!

"Mr. Towns, who has just returned from a trip to Germany, Miss Gillespie. Miss Gillespie is our new principal of the recently equipped Jones school—named after the President of the First National."

Matthew smiled, but Miss Gillespie did not. She frankly stared, bowed coldly, and then, after a small mouthful or two, whispered to her neighbor. The neighbor whispered, and then slowly the atmosphere of the table changed. Matthew was embarrassed and amused, and yet how natural it all was—that unfortunate smile of his—that unexplained trip to Germany, and the revelation evidently now running around that he was a Pullman porter.

They thought him a liar through and through. It was not simply that he was a railway porter—no, no! Mr. Jones was democratic and all that; but after all one did not make chance porters guests of honor; and Mr. Jones, when the whispering reached him, grew portentously and emphatically silent.

Matthew, now thoroughly upset, rose with the others and made his way straight to the minister.

"Say, I seem to have cut a hog," he said. The minister smiled wanly and said, "I'm afraid I'm to blame—I—"

"No, no," said Matthew, and then tersely he told of his rebuff and flight to Europe and his return to "begin again." "I did not mean really to sail under false colors, and I did come home on the *Gigantic*. I pared potatoes all the way over."

The minister burst into a laugh. They shook hands, and with a hurried farewell to a rather gruff host, Matthew slipped away. But he left fifteen cents for Miss Gillespie. Jimmie roared when Matthew told him.

VI

In October, Matthew wrote his first report for the Princess. He wrote it on his knee and in his one chair, sitting high up in the narrow furnished bedroom which he had hired in New York on West Fifty-Ninth Street. It was a noisy and dirty region, but cheap and near his work. There was a bed, a chair, and a washstand, and he had bought a new trunk, in which he locked up his clothes and few belongings.

YOUR ROYAL HIGHNESS:

I have at your request made a hasty but careful survey of the attitude of my people in this country, with regard to the possibility of their aid to a movement looking toward righting the present racial inequalities in the world, especially along the color line.

My people are increasing in material prosperity. A few are even accumulating wealth; large numbers own their homes and live in cleanliness and a fair degree of comfort. Extreme poverty and crime are decreasing, while intelligence is increasing. There is still oppression and insult, some lynching, and much caste and discrimination; but on the whole the Negro has advanced so rapidly and is still advancing at such a rate that he is more satisfied than complaining. He is astonished and gratified at his own success, and while he knows that he is not treated quite as a man and lacks the full freedom of a white man, he believes that he is daily approaching this goal.

This main movement and general feeling is by no means shared by all. There is. bitter revolt in the hearts of a small intelligentsia who resent color-caste, and among those laborers who feel in many ways the pinch of economic maladjustment and see the rich Negroes climbing on their bowed backs. These classes have no common program, save complaint, protest, and inner bickering; and only in the case of a small class of immigrant West Indians has this complaint reached the stage that even contemplates violence.

Perigua is a man of intelligence and fire—of a certain honesty and force; but he is not to be trusted as a leader. His organization is a loose mob of incoherent elements united only by anger and poverty. They have their reasons. I first thought Perigua a vain and egotistic fool. But the other night sitting in his dirty flat—a furious, ragged figure of bitter resentment—he told me part of his story; spat it out in bits: of the beautiful wife whom an Englishman seduced; the daughter who became a prostitute; of the promotion refused him in the railroad shops because of color, and his fight with the color line in the army; of his prosecution for 'inciting to riot'; his conviction and toil in jails and chain gangs, with vermin and disease; and of his long, desperate endeavor to stir up revolt in America. Perigua and those whom he represents have a grievance and a remedy, but he will never accomplish anything systematic. Do not think of contributing to his organization. I still have your envelope unopened. He has no real organization. He has only personal followers.

On the other hand, the Negroes are thick with organizations they are threaded through with every sort of group movement; but their organizations so far chime and accord with the white world; their business organizations, growing fast, have the same aims and methods as white business; their religion is a replica of white religion, only less snobbish because less wealthy. Even their labor movement is the white trade union, hampered by the fact that white unions discriminate and that colored labor is the wage-hammering adjunct of white capital.

Your Highness and the friends whom I had the honor of meeting may then well ask, 'Are these folk of any possible use to a movement to abolish the present dictatorship of white Europe?' I answer, yes, a hundred times. American Negroes are a tremendous social force, an economic entity of high importance. Their power is at present partly but not wholly dissipated and dispersed into the forces of the overwhelming nation about them. But only in part. A tremendous striving group force is binding this group together, partly through the outer pounding of prejudice, partly by the growth of inner ideals. What they can and will do in the rebuilding of a better, bigger world is on God's knees and not now clear; but clarity dawns, and so far as we gain self-consciousness today we can be a force tomorrow.

The burning question is: What help is wanted? What can we do? What are your aims and program? I know well from your own character and thought that you could not encourage mere terrorism and mass murder. The very thought of ten million grandchildren of slaves trying to wrest liberty from ten times their number of rich, shrewder fellows by brute force is, of course, nonsense. On the other hand, with intelligence and forethought, concentrated group action, we can so align ourselves with national and world forces as to gain our own emancipation and help all of the colored races gain theirs.

Frankly then, what is the Great Plan? How and when can we best cooperate? What part can I take? I am eager to hear from you.

I am, your Royal Highness—

There came a knock on the door, and Matthew opened it. A young Japanese stood there who politely asked for Mr. Keswick. No, Mr. Keswick was not here and did not live here. In fact, Matthew had never heard of Mr. Keswick. The Japanese was sorry—very, very sorry for the intrusion. He went softly down the stairs.

VII

There was no answer to Matthew's report. He had given the Princess a temporary address at Perigua's place, and in this report he enclosed this room as a permanent one. He had sent the Princess' letter to her bankers, as agreed on. Still there was no word or sign. Matthew was at first patient. After the second week, he tried to be philosophical. At the end of a month, he was disappointed and puzzled. By the first of December the whole thing began to assume a shape grotesque and unreal. They over there had perhaps succeeded in changing her mind. Perhaps she herself, coming and seeing with her own eyes, had been disillusioned. It would be hard for a stranger to see beneath the unlovely surface of this racial tangle. But somehow he had counted or this woman—on her subtlety and vision; on her own knowledge of the color line.

He did not know what to do. Should he write again? His pride said no, but his loyalty and determination kept him following up Perigua and remaining in touch with him. At least once a week they had conferences and Matthew reported. This week there was, as usual, little to report. He had seen a dozen men—three crazy, three weak, three dishonest, three willing but bewildered, dazed, lost. Broken reeds all. Perigua listened dully, hunched in his chair, chewing an unlit cigar—unkempt, unshaven, ill. His eyes alone lived and flamed as with unquenchable fire.

"Any money yet from abroad?" he asked.

"No."

"Have you asked for any?"

"No."

"So," said Perigua. "You think it useless?" Hitherto Matthew had tried to play his part—to listen and study and say little as to his own thought. Suddenly, now, a pity for the man seized him. He leaned forward and spoke frankly:

"Perigua, you're on the wrong tack. First of all, these people are not ready for revolt. And next, if they were ready, it's a question if revolt is a program of reform today. I know that time has been when only murder, arson, ruin, could uplift; when only destruction could open the path to building. The time must come when, great and pressing as change and betterment may be, they do not involve killing and hurting people."

Perigua glared. "And that time's here, I suppose?"

"I don't know," said Matthew. "But I hope, I almost believe it is. It must be after that hell of ten years ago. At any rate, none of us Negroes are ready for such a program against overwhelming odds—"

"No," yelled Perigua. "We're tame tabbies; we're fawning dogs; we lick and growl and wag our tails; we're so glad to have a white man fling us swill that we wriggle on our bellies and crawl. We slave that they may loll; we hand over our daughters to be their prostitutes; we wallow in dirt and disease that they may be clean and pure and good. We bend and dig and starve and sweat that they may sit in sweet quiet and reflect and contrive and build a world beautiful for themselves to enjoy.

"And we're not ready even to protest, let alone fight. We want to be free, but we don't dare strike for it. We think that the blows of white men—of white laborers, of white women—are blows for us and our freedom! Hell! You damned fool, they have always been fighting for themselves. Now, they're half free, with us niggers to wait on them; we give white carpenters and shop girls their coffee, sugar, tea, spices, cotton, silk, rubber, gold, and diamonds; we give them our knees for scrubbing and our hands for service—we do it and we always shall until we stand and strike."

And Perigua leaped up, struck the table until his clenched hand bled.

Matthew quailed. "I know—I know," he said. "I'm not minimizing it a bit. In a way, I'm as bitter about it all as you— but the practical question is, what to do about it? What will be effective? Would it help, for instance, to kill a couple of dozen people who, if not innocent of intentional harm, are at least unconscious of it?"

"And why unconscious? Because we don't make 'em know. Because you've got to yell in this world when you're hurt; yell and swear and kick and fight. We're dumb. We dare not talk, shout, holler. And why don't we? We're afraid, we're scared; we're congenital idiots and cowards. Don't tell me, you fool—I know you and your kind. Your caution is cowardice inbred for ten generations; you want to talk, talk, talk and argue until somebody in pity and contempt gives you what you dare not take. Go to hell—go to hell—you yellow carrion! From now on I'll go it alone."

"Perigua—Perigua!"

But Perigua was gone.

Matthew was nonplused. All his plans were going awry. Still no word or sign from the Princess, and now he had alienated and perhaps lost touch with Perigua. What next? He paused in the smoky, dirty club rooms and idly thumbed yesterday morning's paper. Again he inquired for mail. Nothing. He stood staring at the paper, and the first thing that leaped at him from a little inconspicuous paragraph on the social page was the departure "for India, yesterday, of her Royal Highness, the Princess of Bwodpur."

He walked out. So this was the end of his great dream—his world romance. This was the end. Whimsically and for the last time, he dreamed his dream again: The Viktoria Café and his clenched fist. The gleaming tea table, the splendid dinner. Again he saw her face—its brave, high beauty, its rapt interest, its lofty resolve. Then came the grave face of the Japanese, the disapproval of the dark Indians, the contempt of the Arab. They had never believed, and now he himself doubted. It was not that she or he had failed—it was only that, from the beginning, it had all been so impossible—utterly unthinkable! What had he, a Negro, in common with what the high world called royal, even if he had been a successful physician—a great surgeon? And how much less had Matthew Towns, Pullman porter!

A dry sob caught in his throat. It was hard to surrender his dream, even if it was a dream he had never dared in reality to face. Well, it was over! She was silent—gone. He was well out of it, and he walked outdoors. He walked quickly through 135th Street, past avenue and park. He climbed the hill and finally came down to the broad Hudson. He walked along the viaduct looking at the gray water, and then turned back at 133rd Street. There were garages and old, decaying buildings in a hollow. He hurried on, past "Old Broadway" and up a sordid hill to a still terrace, and there he walked straight into the young Atlanta minister.

"Hello! I *am* glad to see you."

For a moment Matthew couldn't remember—then he saw the picture of the church-the dinner and the Joneses.

He greeted the minister cordially. "How is Miss Gillespie?" be asked with a wry grin.

"Married—married to that young physician you met at the radical conference. Oh, you see we followed you up. They have gone to Chicago. Well, here I am in New York on a holiday. Couldn't get off last summer and thought I'd run away just before the holidays. Been here a week and going back tomorrow. Hoped I might run across you. I feel like a man out of a strait-jacket. I tell you this being a minister today is—is—well, it's a hard job."

"My experience is," said Matthew, "that life at best is no cinch."

The minister smiled sympathetically. "I tell you," he said, "let's have a good time. I want to go to the theater and see movies and hear music. I want to sit in a decent part of a good theater and eat a good dinner in a gilded restaurant, and then"—he glanced at Matthew—"yes, then I want to see a cabaret. I've preached about ballrooms and 'haunts of hell," he said with a whimsical smile, "but I've never seen any."

Matthew laughed. "Come on," he said, "and we'll do the best we can. The first balcony is probably the best we can do at a theater, and not the best seats there; but in the movies where 'all God's chillun' are dark, we can have the best. That gilded restaurant business will be the worst problem. We'd better compromise with the dining room at the Pennsylvania station. There are colored waiters there. At the Grand Central we'd be fed, but in the side aisles. But what of it? I'm in for a lark, and I too have a day off.—In fact, it looks as though I had a life off."

They visited the Metropolitan Art Museum at the minister's special request; they dined about three at the Grand Central station, sitting rather cosily back but on one side, at a table without flowers. Matthew calculated that at this hour they would be better received than at the more crowded hours. Then they went at six to the Capitol and sat in the great, comfortable loge chairs.

The minister was in ecstasy. "White people have everything, don't they?" he mused, as they walked up the Great White Way slowly, looking at the crowds and shop windows. "These girls, all dressed up and painted. They look—but—are many of them for sale?"

"Yes, most of them are for sale—although not quite in the way you mean. And the men, too," said Matthew.

The minister was a bit puzzled, and as they went into the Guild Theater, said so. It was an exquisite place and they had fairly good seats, well forward in the first balcony.

"What do you mean—'for sale'?" he asked.

"I mean that in a great modern city like New York men and women sell their bodies, souls, and thoughts for luxury and beauty and the joy of life. They sell their silences and dumb submissions. They are content to do things and let things be done; they promise not to ask just what they are doing, or for whom, or what it costs, or who pays. That explains our slavery."

"This is not such bad slavery."

"No—not for us; but look around. How many Negroes are here enjoying this? How many can afford to be here at the wages with which they must be satisfied if these white folks are to be rich?"

"You mean that all luxury is built on a foundation of poverty?"

"I mean that much of the costliest luxury is not only ugly and wasteful in itself but deprives the mass of white men of decent homes, education, and reasonable enjoyment of life; and today this squeezed middle white class is getting its luxuries and necessities by inflicting ignorance, slavery, pow erty, and disease on the dark colonies of European and American imperialism. This is the New Poverty and the basis of armies, navies, and war in Nicaragua, the Balkans, Asia, and Africa. Without this starvation and toil of our dark fellows, you and I could not enjoy this."

The minister was silent, for the play began. He only murmured, "We are consenting too," and then he choked—and half an hour later, as the play paused, added, "And what are we going to do about it? That's what gets me. We're in the mess. It's wrong—wrong. What can we do? I can't see the way at all."

Then the play swung on: beautiful rooms; sleek, quiet servants; wealth; a lovely wife loving another man. The husband kills him; the curtain leaves her staring at a corpse with horror in her eyes.

The minister frowned. "Do they always do this sort of thing?" he asked.

"Always," Matthew answered; and the minister added:

"Why can't they try other themes—ours for instance; our search for dinner and our reasons for the first balcony. Good dinner and good seats—but with subtle touches, hesitancies, gropings, and refusals that would be interesting; and that woman wasn't interesting."

They rode to Harlem for a midnight lunch and planned afterward to visit a cabaret. The minister was excited. "Don't flutter," said Matthew genially; "it'll either be tame or nasty."

"You see," said the minister, "sex is curiously thrust on us parsons. Men dislike us—either through distrust or fear. Women swarm about us. The Church is Woman. And there I am always, comforting, advising, hearing tales, meeting evil—ducking, dodging, trying not to understand—not understanding— that's the trouble. Towns, what the devil should I know of the temptations—the dirt—the—"

"Look here!" interrupted Towns. They were in a restaurant on Seventh Avenue. It was past midnight. The little half-basement was tasteful and neat, but only a half dozen people were there. The waffles were crisp and delicious. Matthew had bought a morning paper. Glancing at it carelessly, as the minister talked, he shouted, "Look here!" He handed the paper to the minister and pointed to the headlines. The Ku Klux Klan was going to hold a great Christmas celebration in Chicago.

"In Chicago?"

"Yes."

"But Chicago is a stronghold of Catholics."

W. E. B. DU BOIS

"I know. But watch. The Klan is planning a comeback. It has suffered severe reverses in the South and in the East; I'll bet a dollar they are going to soft-pedal Rome and Jewry and concentrate on the new hatred and fear of the darker races in the North and in Europe. That's what this meeting means."

The minister frowned and read on. . . Klansmen from the whole country will meet there. The grand officers and Southern members will go from headquarters at Atlanta on a luxurious special train and meet other Klansmen and foreign guests in Chicago; there they will discuss the repeal of the Fifteenth Amendment, and prepare for a great meeting on the Rising Tide of Color, to be called later in Europe.

"And we sit silent and motionless," said the minister.

"That's it; not only injustice, oppression, insult, a lynching now and then—but they rub it in, they openly flout us. Is there any group on earth, but us, who would lie down to it?"

The minister was silent.

Then he said, "They may be rallying against Rome and liquor rather than against us."

"Nonsense," said Matthew, and added, "What do you think of violence?"

"What do you mean?"

"Suppose Negroes should blow up that convention or that fine de luxe Special and say by this bloody gesture that they didn't propose to stand for this sort of thing any longer?"

The minister quailed. "But what good? What good? Murder, and murder mainly of the innocent; revenge, hatred, and a million 'I told you so's.' 'The Negro is a menace to this land!'"

"Yes, yes, all that; but not simply that. Fear; the hushing of loose slander and insult; the curbing of easy proposals to deprive us of things deeper than life. They look out for the Indian's war whoop, the Italian's knife, the Irishman's club; what else appeals to barbarians but force, blood, war?"

The minister answered slowly: "These things get on our nerves, of course. But you mustn't get morbid and too impatient. We've come a long way in a short time, as time moves. We're rising—we're getting on."

But Matthew brooded: "Are we getting on so far? Aren't the gates slowly, silently closing in our faces? Isn't there widespread, deep, powerful determination to make this a white world?"

The minister shook his head; then he added: "We can only trust in Christ—"

"Christ!" blurted Matthew.

VIII

The cabaret was close, hot, and crowded. There was loud music and louder laughter and the clinking of glasses. More than half the patrons were white, and they were clustered mostly on one side. They had the furtive air of fugitives in a foreign land, out from under the eyes of their acquaintances. Some were drunk and noisy. Others seemed looking expectantly for things that did not happen, but which surely ought to happen in this bizarre outland! The colored patrons seemed more at home and natural. They were just laughing and dancing, although some looked bored.

The minister stared. "Are they having a good time, or just trying to?"

"Some of them are really gay. This girl here—"

The minister recoiled a little as the girl reached their table. She was pale cream, with black eyes and hair; and her body, which she was continuously raising her clothes to reveal, had a sinuous, writhing movement. She danced with body and soul and sang her vulgar "blues" with a harsh, shrill voice that hardly seemed hers at all. She was an astonishing blend of beauty, rhythm, and ugliness. She had collected all the cash in sight on the white side and now came over to the Negroes.

"Come on, baby," she yelled to the minister, as she began singing at their table, and her writhing body curled like a wisp of golden smoke. The minister recoiled, but Matthew looked up and smiled. Some yearning seized him. It seemed so long since a woman's hand had touched him that he scarce saw the dross of this woman. He tossed her a dollar, and as she stooped to gather it, she looked at him impishly and laughed in a softer voice.

"Thanks, Big Boy," she said.

The proprietor with his half-shut eyes and low voice strolled by. "Would you boys like a drop of something or perhaps a little game?"

The minister did not understand.

"Whiskey and gambling," grinned Matthew. The minister stirred uneasily and looked at his watch. They stayed on, ordering twenty-five-cent ginger ale at a dollar a bottle and gay sandwiches at seventy-five cents apiece, and a small piece at that.

"Honest," said the minister, "I'm not going to preach against cabarets and dance halls anymore. They preach against themselves. There's more real fun in a church festival by the Ladies' Aid!" Then he glanced again at his watch. "Good Lord, I must go—it's three o'clock, and I must leave for Philadelphia at six."

Matthew laughed and they arose. As they passed out, the dancing girl glided by Matthew again and slipped her hand in his.

"Come and dance, Big Boy," she said. Her face was hard and older than her limbs, but her eyes were kind. Matthew hesitated.

"Goodbye," he said to the minister, "hope to see you again sometime soon." He went back with the girl.

IX

That trip in his Pullman seemed Matthew's worst. Sometimes as he swung to Atlanta and back he almost forgot himself in the routine, and Jimmie's inexhaustible humor always helped. He became the wooden automaton that his job required. He neither thought nor saw. He had no feelings, no wishes, and yet he was ears and voice, swift in eye and step, accurate and deferential. But at other times all things seemed to happen and he was a quivering bundle of protests, nerves—a great oath of revolt. It seemed particularly so this trip, perhaps because he was so upset about the Princess' departure.

Besides that, Jimmie left him at Atlanta. He had taken a few days off. "Got a date," he grinned.

Matthew was lonesome and tired, and his return trip began with the usual lost article. People always lose something in a Pullman car, and always by direct accusation, glance, or innuendo the black porter is the thief. This time a fat, flashily dressed woman missed her diamond ring.

"—a solitaire worth five hundred dollars. I left it on the window-sill—it has been stolen."

She talked loudly. The whole car turned and listened. The whole car stared at Matthew. It is no pleasant thing to be tacitly charged with theft and to search for vindication under the accusing eyes of two dozen people. Matthew took out the seats, raised the carpet, swept and poked. Then he went and dragged out all the dirty bed-linen from the close-packed closet and went over it inch by inch. He searched the women's toilet room. Then coming back with growling conductor and whispering passengers, he found the ring finally in the spittoon. He got little thanks—indeed he knew quite well that some would think he had concealed it there. The woman gave him fifty cents. Also he missed his breakfast, and his head ached.

The inevitable woman with the baby was furious, for in his search he had forgotten to get the hot milk from the diner, and the cook had used it. A man passed his station because the train conductor had not been notified of the extra stop. The Pullman conductor placed the blame on the porter.

"Damn niggers are good for nothing," said the angry man.

Of course Matthew was supposed to be a walking encyclopedia of the country they were traversing:

"What town is this?"

"Greensboro, madam."

"What mountains are those?"

"The Blue Ridge, sir."

"What creek are we crossing?"

"I don't know, madam."

"Well, don't you know anything?" Matthew silently continued his dusting.

"Is that the James River?"

"It's a portion of it, madam."

"Is that darky trying to be smart?" The bell rang furiously. To Matthew's splitting head it seemed always angry. He brought cup after cup of ice water to people too lazy to take a dozen steps.

"Why the hell don't you answer the bells when they ring?" growled the poker gambler who had the drawing room. "Bring us some C. & C. ginger ale and be quick about it."

"Sorry, but the—"

"Don't answer me back, nigger."

Matthew went and brought Clicquot Club, the only kind they carried. Apparently the passenger did not know the difference.

It was dinner time and he got a moment to sit down in the end section and dozed off.

"Do you hear?" an elderly man was yelling at him. "Which way is the diner?"

"Straight ahead, sir, second car."

The man looked at him. "Asleep at your post is not the way to get on in this world," he said. Matthew looked at him. His patience was about at an end, and the man saw something in his eye; he added as he turned away: "Young man, my father fought and died to set you free."

"Well, he did a damned poor job," said Matthew, and he went into the smoking room and into the toilet and shut and locked the door.

It was nearly ten at night when dinner for the porters was ready, for the passengers had stuffed themselves at lunch and were not hungry until late; the food left was cold and scarce, and the cooks too tired to bother. He was greeted by a chorus when he returned to the car. It began as he passed the drawing room:

"Where's that porter—George!"—"Can you get me some liquor—any fly girls on the train—how about that one in Lower 5? Then outside: "Porter, will *you please* make this berth—you've passed it repeatedly. These colored men are too presuming."—"Water!"—"—When do we get to?"—"What station was that?"—"Please hand me my bag."—"How can I get into that upper? Haven't you a lower?"—"Where's the conductor?"—"What connections can I make?"—"How late are we?"—"When do we change time?"—"When is breakfast?"—"That milk for baby, and right off!"—"Ice water."—"Shoes!"

Matthew left the train with a gasp and took the subway to Harlem. It was after midnight and clear and cold. He wanted warmth and company, and he went straight to the cabaret. He knew he was going, and all day long the yearning for some touch of sympathy and understanding had been overpowering. He wanted to forget everything. He was going to get drunk. He walked by Perigua's place from habit. It was closed and vacant. No one whom he saw could tell him where Perigua was. Matthew turned and walked straight to the cabaret.

"Hello, Big Boy."

He gripped the girl's hand. It was the only handclasp that seemed even friendly that he had had for a long time. She curled her arm about his neck. "What do you say to a drink?" she asked. He drank the stuff that burned and rankled. He danced with the girl, and all the time his head ached and whirled. What could he do? What should he do?

He went out with her at four o'clock in the morning; he scarcely knew when or why. He wanted to forget the world. They whirled away in a taxi, and stumbled up long stairs, and then with a sigh he slipped his clothes off, and clasping his arms around her curving form, fell into dreamless sleep.

X

At the head of the stairs next morning Matthew met Perigua. The girl had looked at his haggard face with something like forgotten shame.

"Goodbye, Big Boy," she said, "you ain't built for the sporting game. I wish"—she looked at him uncertainly, her face drawn and coarse in the morning light, her body drooping—"I wish I could help some way. Well, if you ever want a friend, come to me."

"Thank you," he said simply, and kissing her forehead, went. For a long time she stood with that kiss upon her brow.

Then he met Perigua coming out of the door opposite. Was he in Perigua's building? He had been too drunk the night before to notice. No, this was too narrow for 135th Street. He met Perigua, and Perigua blazed at him:

"You're having a hell of a time, ain't you! Prostitutes instead of patriotism." Then he snarled, "Wake up! The time is come! Have you seen this?"

It was an elaborate account of the coming meeting of the Klan in Matthew looked at him sharply. Something else was wrong; he looked hungry and wrought up with drink or excess. Matthew glanced at the paper. The great Klan Special was leaving Atlanta for Chicago three days later at three-forty in the afternoon. Special cars with certain high guests would join them at various points and from various cities.

"I'm going to Chicago," said Perigua.

Matthew seized him by the shoulders.

"All right," he said, "but first come and have breakfast."

Perigua hesitated and then morosely yielded. They ate silently and then smoked.

"Perigua," said Matthew, suddenly, "have you got money to go to Chicago?"

"Is that any of your damned business?"

"Yes, it is. If you are going to Chicago to look over the situation, consult with your lieutenants, and lay plans for future action, you need money. You ought to buy some clothes and stop at a good hotel."

Matthew knew perfectly well that Perigua was going on some hare-brained mission and that he might in desperation do actual harm. He knew, too, that Perigua would like to go, or to imagine he was going, on some such mission as Matthew had sketched. Suddenly, Matthew was thinking of that unopened envelope given him by the Princess. Perhaps there lay the answer to her silence and departure as well as money. The envelope was to go to Perigua only in case he was found trustworthy. But in case he was not and the envelope could not be returned, what then?

He took a quick resolve. "Come by my room—it's on the way to the train."

Silently Perigua followed. They went down by Elevated and soon were sitting in that upper room. Matthew went to his trunk. It was unlocked. He was startled. He did not remember leaving it unlocked; he searched hurriedly. Everything seemed intact, even his bank book and especially the sealed letter at the bottom, hidden among books. Matthew did not touch the envelope, but took out his savings bank book, and said:

"I'm going to give you one hundred and fifty dollars to get some clothes and go to a good hotel in Chicago. Try the Vincennes— I'll write you there."

They went out together to the bank. Matthew returned feeling that he had done a wise thing. He had a string on Perigua and could keep in touch with him. Now for that envelope. The more he thought of it, the more he was sure that it would throw light on the situation. It was careless of him to have left his trunk unlocked. The landlady was all right, but the other lodgers! He drew out the letter and paused. What did he mean to do? He tore the letter open.

A piece of paper fluttered out. He searched the envelope. Nothing more. He looked at the paper.

Sir:

In unwavering determination to protect the name of a certain high personage, we have taken the liberty to abstract her letter and draft. All her letters to you and yours to her will come to us. Will you not believe this is all for the best and that we remain, with every assurance of regard,

Your Obedient Servants

Matthew stared. When and where had it been possible? He could not conceive. Then he remembered that polite little Japanese's visit. The Princess had never heard a word from him. She never would. Then his heart leapt. The Princess had not deliberately neglected or deserted him! She simply had not heard from him and could not find him! He had blamed the Princess for her apparent neglect, when in reality she knew nothing. He was ashamed of himself. He had yielded to debauchery and drunkenness. Well, he would atone and get back to his job. Should he write the Princess again? No. The Japanese and Indians were intercepting his letters. He started. Perhaps they had given her forged reports and sent her home disillusioned. Never mind. Even then, it would be on his report, or supposed report, that she was acting. He must get to work. He must think and plan.

XI

Matthew arose next day saner and clearer-headed and much less sanguine. It was December fifteenth. The Princess, had she been in earnest and remembered their meeting, would surely have insisted on seeing him in person and at least greeting him. It must have been curiously easy to make her lose faith. She had in all probability quite forgotten him and his errand. White America had flattered her wealth and beauty. Well, what then? Why, then it was for him to show her and her colleagues that black America counted in the world. But how? How? Then came illumination. He might himself go to Chicago! Without the slightest doubt other observers of the darker world would be on hand. He might go and curb Perigua and watch this meeting.

All the way down to Atlanta he pondered and fidgeted, and decision did not come until, to his great joy, he met Jimmie with his cheerful smile.

"Where've you been, you old cheat?" he cried.

Jimmie laughed. "Running to Chicago now."

"What? Changed your run? Why?"

"Two reasons. First: it's a good run; second-well, that I'll show you later. Come on now and sign up for the Klan Special."

"For the what?"

"The Klan Special. It's on my run, and they want porters. Come and try it."

Matthew stood still. It was just the thing. He'd go to Chicago as a porter and watch. Yes—this was precisely what he would do. With Jimmie he went to the harassed Pullman manager, who was only too glad to get so good a porter on such a train as the Klan Special.

"Had a hell of a time. Boys don't want to wait on the Klan. Damned nonsense. The Klan don't amount to anything. Chiefly a social stunt and gassing for effect. I will put you Car X466 near the end of the train, between Jimmie's compartment car and the observation coach. You are bound to make a pile in tips. So long."

Matthew and Jimmie went out together. Both were overjoyed to see each other. Matthew forgot all about Jimmie's second reason until he noticed that Jimmie was bubbling over with some secret of his own.

"Have dinner with me," Jimmie said. "Got something to show you."

They took the Hunter Street car and rode across town past the quiet old campus of Atlanta University and through it and then away out by the new Booker Washington High School. Jimmie stopped at a pretty little cream and green cottage. It was tiny, but neat, and there was a yard in front with roses still blooming. Before Matthew could ask what it all meant, out of the house came a girl and the tiniest of babies. Jimmie set up a shout of explanations.

"Been married a year," he said. "Married before I knew you, but the wife was working in Chicago and wouldn't come until I could set up a regular home. But the baby brought her, and I got the home."

She was a little black, sweet-faced girl with lovely skin, crisp hair, and great black eyes—very practical and very loving, and her earth was quite evidently bounded by Jimmie and the baby. Matthew had never seen so small a baby. It was amorphous and dark red-brown and singularly cunning. They had a hilarious dinner, and Jimmie was at the best of his high humor.

He whispered all his romance to Matthew, while his wife washed the dishes.

"Never thought of marrying a black girl," he explained. "I was spending all I could make on a 'high yaller' in Harlem; when she heard I wasn't a banker, merchant, or doctor, she cut me so clean, I fell in two pieces and one landed in Chicago. I met Dolly, and gosh! I couldn't leave her; innocent, sweet, and with sense. O boy, but I got some wife! And that kid!"

Matthew was troubled. Suppose something happened in Chicago or to this train; to this boy with his soul full of joy, and to this sweet-faced little black wife?

The next few days the Klan delegates gathered in Atlanta on special trains from New Orleans and other cities. Jimmie, looking the crowd over with practised eye, prophesied a "hot time," plenty of gambling and liquor and good tips. Matthew was still disturbed, but Jimmie pooh-poobed.

"They're all right. Just don't let yourself get mad. Remember that, for the trip, you are just a machine, a plow or a mule, and I—I'm a savings bank for the kid."

"Jimmie," said Matthew suddenly, "suppose somebody tried to get back at these Klansmen somehow in Chicago."

"Nonsense," said Jimmie carelessly, "niggers dassn't, Catholics and Jews are too long-headed, and the Klan is too well guarded. Just heard them talking about extra police protection." He was off before Matthew could say more.

Then the rush began. The train was to leave on the twentieth at three-forty, over the Louisville and Nashville, and for the last half hour before, Matthew had hardly time to think. His and Jimmie's cars were at the end of the train; other Pullmans followed. In the middle of the train was the diner, and the club car and smoker was far forward.

It was nearly ten o'clock at night before Matthew got his berths made down and came into Jimmie's car. They started for the diner. Just as they were passing out of the car, a bell rang, but Jimmie paid no attention.

"Come on," he said, "there's a flash dame in D who wants too much attention; I don't trust her. Her husband, or the man she's with, is up ahead, drunk and gambling. Let her wait."

In the diner with the other porters, they had a gay time. Jimmie winked at the steward and soon produced a mysterious flask; immediately they were all drinking to "The Baby" and listening to some of the choicest of Jimmie's stories.

"Let's go up and see the bunch in the smoker," said Jimmie when dinner was over. "I hear there's a big game on."

Matthew and Jimmie went forward. They were surely having a wild time in the smoker. The drinking and gambling were open, and one could see the character of the crowd-business men, Rotarians, traveling salesmen, clerks—a cross section of American middle-class life.

"I am going back," said Matthew at last, for he was tired and not particularly interested.

"Be with you in just a minute," said Jimmie. "I must see this poker hand through. My God, do you see this flush? Glance at my car as you go through and see if it is all right; I'll be back in a jiffy. That fly dame will be yelling for something. Her daddy's in here linin' his grave with greenbacks."

Matthew walked back thinking of Jimmie. That baby! That mother's face! There were, after all, some strangely beautiful things in life. He walked through Jimmie's compartment car and saw that all was quiet. Just as he was leaving, however, he heard the bell and saw that, sure enough, Compartment D had rung again. He walked back and knocked lightly.

"Porter!"

Matthew entered.

"It is stifling in here," came a voice from the berth. "Please open the window."

It was warm in Georgia, but the train would soon be in the cooler mountains; nevertheless, Matthew without argument started to open the window at her feet.

"No, this one at my head," insisted the woman, "and for mercy's sake, close the door behind you."

He closed the door softly and then bent over her to raise the window. There came over him at the moment a subtle flash of fear. She was a large woman—opulent and highly colored, and she lay there on her back looking straight up into his eyes. Her breasts were half-covered—one scarcely at all. He could not raise the sash with his hands unaided. He braced his knee on the berth and, using the metal handle for unlocking the upper berth, he bent down hard. The window flew up, but his hand came down lightly on the woman's bosom. Again came that gust of fear. He glanced down. She did not stir, but looked up at him with slightly closed eyes. For a moment, he caught his breath and his heart hammered. Then suddenly the door behind was flung violently open. The woman's face changed in a flash. She screamed shrilly as Matthew started back and drew the sheet close about her:

"Get out of here, you black nigger! How dare you touch me! I asked you to raise the window!"

Matthew, terrified, turned, and with one sweep of his arm fiercely pushed aside the man who was entering. The man went down in a heap, and quickly Matthew passed out into the corridor. He started forward to tell Jimmie, but he heard oncoming footsteps and an opening door. Turning, he ran into his own car, got his pistol from the clothes closet, and stepped into the toilet.

There was a long silence, then a cry, a rush of feet, and hurried voices. Then came a tense quiet. Matthew waited and waited until he could bear it no longer. He stepped out into the washroom and listened. Somewhere he could hear a thump-thump-thump. He raised the window and looked out. Something was dragging and bumping beside the car ahead. He heard a noise behind and turned quickly. A porter staggered in. Matthew recoiled, on guard.

"Anything wrong?" he said, thickly.

"They've lynched Jimmie," said the porter.

Matthew sank suddenly to the lounge. My God! It was Jimmie he had heard coming. He sat down and vomited. He stood up again, staggered to the door, and fainted away.

XII

It was morning. Matthew opened his eyes slowly and stared at the high white walls. There were two blurs before him, one on either side. Gradually, as he shut his eyes and opened them again, they resolved themselves into two faces. Then he knew them. One was Perigua; the other was Jimmie's little black wife. Where was he? He strove to sit up. He was in a hospital. He wanted to rage. He wanted to tell Perigua and everybody that he was a murderer. Poor Jimmie, poor little wife and baby! Perigua—revenge! All these things he strove to say, but the nurse glided by and stopped him. She gave him something to drink, and he fell asleep.

Three days later he left the General Hospital, and he and Perigua and Jimmie's wife met together in a big brown house on Fourth Street. He poured out his story, and they listened. Perigua said nothing. But the little wife put her hand timidly in his and said: "You are not to blame. It was not your fault." And then she added: "We had the funeral here in Cincinnati. I wish you could have been there. There were beautiful flowers. But they would not open the coffin. They would not let me see his face." And she repeated, looking up at Matthew:

"They did not let me see his face."

Then Perigua said:

"He didn't have no face."

There rose a shriek in Matthew's throat. It struggled and surged, and broke to horrid silence within him. The hot tears burned in his eyes. Something died in Matthew that day. He put all his savings into the little mother's hand and pushed her gently out the door.

"Goodbye," he said, and "God forgive me!"

Perigua sat down and smoked, and silently showed him newspaper clippings.

Christmas had passed. The Klan was holding its great meeting in Chicago, and the papers were full of news about it and of pictures of the members. They seemed to be making a new campaign against the Catholic Church; they had apparently dropped the fight on Jews; but they were concentrating on a campaign against colored peoples throughout the world, and the world was listening to them. Moreover, they were adroitly seeking to pit the dark peoples against each other—Japanese against Chinese; Indians against Negroes; Negroes against Arabs; Mulattoes against Blacks. They even had certain Japanese and other Asiatic guests!

"That special train will return in triumph next Monday," said Perigua finally, looking at Matthew, gloomily.

Matthew brooded. "We must do something, Perigua," he said; "we *must* do something—something startling."

Perigua bent forward and glowed. "Something to make the world sit up!"

"Yes," said Matthew, "and my plan is this: I'm going to write and demand a meeting of the national officers of the Porters' Union in Chicago. I'll attend and tell my story of Jimmie's lynching and demand a nationwide strike of porters until somebody is arrested for this crime."

Perigua's face fell. "Hell!" he said.

XIII

Worn and nervous, Matthew went to the Chicago meeting of the porters. He talked as he had never talked before, in that room with barred doors. With streaming eyes he told the story of Jimmie, of the little black wife, of the baby. He went over the events of that terrible night. He offered to testify in court, if called upon. The porters listened, tense and sympathetic; but they were silent and uneasy over the strike. It was "too risky"; they would "lose their jobs"; "Filipinos would be imported"; white men "at a living wage and no tips" would replace them: the nation would not stand being "held up" by Negroes, and white labor would not back them. "Do you think the white railway unions would raise a finger? I guess not!" said one.

No—a general Pullman strike would never do. Public opinion among Negroes, however, forced them to some action. While the white newspapers had said little about the gruesome lynching, and that little dismissed and excused it because of "an atrocious attack upon a woman," the colored world knew of it to its farthest regions. Once the matter had come up in the Klan Convention and a brazen-throated orator had declared that this was the punishment which would always be meted out to the "black wretches who dared attack Southern womanhood!"

The plan finally agreed on was the utmost Matthew could extract from the union. It confined itself to a porters' strike on the Klan Special. The train was to arrive in Cincinnati at eight at night on the thirtieth of December and leave at eight forty-five. Before the train came in and while it was in the station, the porters were to make up all the berths they could; at eight-forty all the porters were to leave their cars and march out of the train shed to the main waiting room; there they were to declare a strike, refusing to accompany farther a train on which one of their number, an innocent man, had been lynched, under atrocious circumstances.

Matthew hurried back to Cincinnati to perfect the plans there. Perigua had been in Chicago, but he kept out of the way. No one seemed to know him there, but in his two or three fugitive visits to Matthew he assured him that he was working underground and making sure that none of the porters should see him. He promised to meet Matthew in Cincinnati.

With great fanfare of trumpets and waving of flags, the Klan Special started south. The porters were grim and silent. One of the organizers of the union had a hurried meeting with them just as they left, and on the way down, there were frequent conferences. The train was to leave Cincinnati without a single porter. There was little porter's work to be done at night except making the remaining berths, and this would have to be done by the conductors and the passengers themselves.

It was not, after all, a very bold scheme, or one calling for great courage. Matthew felt how small a gesture it was, and yet just now any protest was something; he knew that even this might not have been feasible, had it not been helped by the fact that none of the porters wanted to go south on this train. Fear, therefore, pushed them to strike for principle when under other circumstances many might have refused. It was extremely unlikely, too, that any porters who were laying over in Cincinnati, or who lived there, would volunteer to take the strikers' places. As the diner was detached at Cincinnati, the waiters would not have to take a stand. They were to disappear quietly, so as not to be asked to serve as porters.

Perigua arrived in Cincinnati three hours before the Klan Special was due. He and Matthew sat again in the big gloomy room on Fourth Street.

Matthew looked strained and thin, but he was sanguine. He detailed his activities.

"Everything's all right here," he said. "I think it's going to make a big sensation. Newspapers will eat it up, and the whole of colored Cincinnati is whispering."

Perigua listened in silence and then laughed aloud. "Well, what's the matter?" asked Matthew, testily.

"They've double-crossed you, you boob," said Perigua at last. "Nonsense they can't as long as the men stick."

"Sure 'as long as.' Know what I've been doing in Chicago?"

"No—what?"

"Working for the Klan. Private messenger and stool pigeon for Green, the Grand Dragon. Know all the big ikes—Therwald, Bates, Evans. Say, they knew of this strike from a dozen pigeons before it was planned. They passed the word to Uncle George. It'll never come off."

"But, say—"

"Shut up—come with me."

Matthew was disturbed but walked silently with Perigua along Fourth and then over and west on Carlisle Avenue a couple of blocks, past old brick buildings, smoke-grimed over the tawdry decorations of a rich, dead generation. Perigua pointed out a certain large house.

"Go in," he said. "You'll find forty porters lodging there. 'Strike' is the password. They're new men gathered quietly from all over the South, expenses paid, ready to scab at a moment's notice. Tell 'em you're inspecting the bunch and flash this badge on them."

It was as Perigua said. Matthew almost staggered out of the house, with tears in his eyes.

"I don't care," he cried to Perigua. "We'll strike anyhow. The men will stick, I know. Let the scabs come—they'll get one beating!"

"Piffle! They'll never strike. Not a man will budge when they hear of that bunch waiting for their jobs, and they'll hear of it before they are well out of Chicago, Uncle George will see to that."

"But what can we do, Perigua?" We must do something—God! We *must*!"

"Sure. Listen. Two can play at double-crossing. I brought Green news of the strike—"

"You?"

"Yes—he heard it from a dozen others. And then, for full measure, I lied about how Chicago Negroes planned a riot as the Klan left. He swallowed both tales and gave me a thousand dollars to push both schemes along; then he tipped off the Pullman Company and the police."

"But it wasn't true about the riot?"

"Of course it wasn't."

"What did you do?"

"Hung around, filled him with tips and fairy tales, and finally beat it here!"

"What for?"

Ferigua quickly straightened up. "Goodbye," he said, holding out his hand.

"Where are you going?" Matthew asked. Perigua glared. "I will tell you. I'm taking the next train south," he said with blazing eyes. Matthew stared.

"But—" he expostulated. "The Klan train will not arrive for two hours yet!"

"I shall need those hours," said Perigua.

"And you will not see the strike?"

"No—because there won't be no strike."

Matthew gripped Perigua's arm with his own nervous, shaking fingers.

"What's your plan, Perigua?"

Perigua faced him, speaking slowly and distinctly: "I used to run on this route from Chicago to Florida through Cumberland Gap. Did you see the Gap when you came up?"

Matthew shook his head.

"Well, you come down the valley from Winchester and Richmond and rush into the hills; suddenly you meet the mountains, and diving through one great crag, the tunnel emerges as from a rock wall on to a high trestle which spans the Powell River! Hm! Great sight! All right. Now for the great Pullman strike!"

"But Perigua—what have we to do with—with scenery? And suppose the cowards don't strike?"

Matthew knew the answer before he asked. He saw the heavy black bag which Perigua carried so carefully. He knew the answer. Perigua's mind was made up. He was mad—a desperate fanatic. What—

"Scenery!" laughed Perigua. "Listen, fool: we're mocked, betrayed and double-crossed, your race are born idiots and cowards! Well, I'm going this alone. Get me? Alone! When the Klan Special sees that scenery—when it reaches that trestle, the trestle ain't going to be there!"

"What is going to become of it?" Matthew asked slowly, talking against time and trying to think.

"I am going to blow it up," said Perigua.

"But how can you do it? Where can you stand? How can you fire any charge without elaborate wiring to get yourself far enough away?"

"I am not going to get away," said Perigua. "I am going to sit right on that trestle, and I am going to hell with it."

They looked each other straight in the eye.

"What are you going to do about it?" whispered Perigua.

Matthew hesitated. "Nothing—" he answered slowly.

Perigua approached Matthew, and there was danger in his eyes.

"You'll peach?" he whispered.

"I'll never betray you, Perigua."

"Well, what will you do?"

Matthew was silent.

"Well, speak, man," growled Perigua.

"I'll keep still," said Matthew. "All right, keep still. But listen, man. It's going to be done, and if you can't be a man, don't be a damned tale-bearing dog!"

He started away. Matthew's thoughts raced. Here was the answer to that sneer of the Japanese. The world would awaken tomorrow to the revolt of black America. His head swam.

He ran after Perigua and gripped his arm. He was all atremble. He whispered in Perigua's ear.

"I don't believe what you have said. I don't believe the porters will back down before the scabs, but if they do—"

"Well, if they do, what?" asked Perigua.

"Wait," said Matthew. "How will the world know that this wasn't an accident rather than—revenge?"

"I've got posters that I printed myself."

"Give them to me."

"What for?"

"If the porters strike, I'll destroy them. But if they don't strike, I'll scab with them on the Klan Special—and I'll go to hell with you."

"By the living Christ," said Perigua, "you've got guts!"

"No," said Matthew, "I am a coward. I dare not live."

Perigua gripped his hand. "I've searched through ten millions," he said, "and found only one who dared. Now I am going. Here! I'll give you half the handbills."

He thrust a bundle into Matthew's hand. "Placard the cars with these after midnight. And, say—oh, here it is—here's a letter."

XIV

The porters' strike was over before it began. The officials had early wind of the plan, and by the time the Special reached Indianapolis, rumors of the host of strike breakers, ready and willing to work, reached the porters' ears and were industriously circulated by the conductors and stool-pigeons. There was a moment of strained expectancy as the train drew into the depot. Reporters came rushing out, and numbers of colored people who had learned of something unusual stood about. In the waiting room stood a crowd of porters in new uniforms, together with several Pullman officials, and an unusual number of policemen who bustled about and scattered the crowds.

"Come—clear the way—move on!"

"Where are you going?" one of them asked Matthew, suspiciously. Leaning by the grill and straining his eyes, Matthew had waited in vain for the porters to leave their cars and march out according to the plan agreed on. Not a porter stirred. He saw them standing in their places, some laughing and talking, but most of them silent and grim. Matthew went ashen with pain and anger. He beckoned to some of the men he knew and had talked to. They ignored him.

He leaned dizzily against the cold iron, then started for the gate. A policeman accosted him, roughly seizing his arm.

"I'm joining this train as porter," he explained. "I've been on sick leave." A Pullman official stepped forward.

"I don't know anything about this," he began. But Matthew spied his conductor.

"Reporting for duty, Cap," he said.

The conductor grinned. "Thought you were leading a strike," he sneered, and then turning to the official he said: "Good porter—came up with me. I was just coming to get an extra man for the smoker."

"All right."

And Matthew passed the gate. He spoke to not a single porter, and none spoke to him. All of them avoided each other. They had failed—they had been defeated without a fight.

"We're damn cowards," muttered Matthew as he climbed aboard.

"Any man's a coward in midwinter when he's got a wife, a mortgage, two children in school, and only one job in sight," answered the old porter who followed him.

"Good," growled Matthew. "Let's all go to hell."

An hour late the Klan Special crawled out of Cincinnati and headed South. The railroad and Pullman officials sighed in relief and laughed. The colored crowd faded away and laughed too, but with different tone.

Matthew donned his uniform slowly, as in a trance. He could not yet realize that his strike had utterly failed. He was numb with the day's experience and still weak from illness. He shrank from work in the smoker with that uproarious, drunken crowd of gamblers. The conductor consented to put him on the last car instead, bringing the willing man from that car to the larger tips of the smoker.

"We've dropped the observation," said the conductor, "and we've got a private car on the end with four compartments and a suite. They're mostly foreign guests of the Klan, and they keep pretty quiet. They are going down to see the South. Afraid you won't make much in tips—but then again you may." And he went forward.

Matthew went back and walked again through the horror of Jimmie's murder. He entered the private car. There was a reception room and a long corridor, but the passengers had apparently all retired. Matthew sat down in the lounge and took from his pocket the package which Perigua had given him; with it was the letter. He looked at it in surprise. He knew immediately whose it was; he saw the coronet; he saw the long slope of the beautiful handwriting; but he did not open it. Slowly he laid it aside with a bitter smile. It could have for him now neither good news nor bad, neither praise nor inquiry, neither disapproval nor cold criticism. No matter what it said, it had come too late. He was at the end of his career. He had started high and sunk to the depths, and now he would close the chapter.

In the first miles of the journey toward Winchester, Matthew was grim; cold and clear ran his thoughts.

"*Selig der, den Er in Siegesglänze findet.*"

He was going out in triumph. He was dying for Death. The world would know that black men dared to die. There came the flash of passing towns with stops here and there to discharge passengers; he helped the porter on the next car, which was overloaded; he was hurrying, helping, and lifting as was his wont. And hurrying, helping, and lifting, he flew by towns and lights. Then coming suddenly back from beneath this dream of loads—from the everyday things—he tried to remember the Exaltation—the Great Thing. What was the Great Thing? And suddenly he remembered. He was going to kill these people. Just a little while and they would be twisted corpses-dead-and some worse than dead—crippled, torn and maimed.

The dark horror of the deed fell hot upon him. He had not seen it before—he had not wholly realized it. Yet he must go on. He could not stop. What had other men thought when they murdered in a great cause? Suddenly he seemed to know. It was not the dead who paid—it was the living; not the killed, but the Killer, who knew and suffered. This was Hell, and he was in it. He must stay in it. He must go through with it. But, Christ! The horror, the infamy, the flaming pain of the thing!

And the world flew by—always, always the world flew by; now in a great blurred rush of sound; now in a white, soft sweep of space and flash of time. Darkness ascended to the stars, and distance that was sight became sound.

It was War. In all ages men had gone forth to kill. But never—never, from Armageddon to the Argonne, had they carried so bitter reasons, so bloody a guerdon. All the enslaved, all the raped, all the lynched, all the "jim-crowed" marched in ranks behind him, bloody with rope and club and iron, crimson with stars and nights. He was going to fight and die for vengeance and freedom. There would be no march of music and stream of banners and whine of vast-voiced trumpets, but it was war, *war*, War, and he the grim lone fighter.

But the pity of it—the crippled and hurt—the pain, the great pricks and flashes of pain, the wild screams in the night; the grinding and crushing of body and bone and flesh and limb—and his sweat oozed and dripped in the cold night. He cowered in that dim and swaying room and shook with ague. He was afraid. He was deathly afraid. If he could turn back! If he had but never fallen in with this crazy plan! If he could only die now, quickly and first! Yet he knew he would not flinch. He would go through with it all to the last horror. The cold, white thing within him gripped him—held him hard and fast with all his writhing. He would go through.

The outlines of mountains with snow lay sprinkled here and there. The lights on hill and hollow—on long shining rails and piling shadows paused, came back and forward, curved, and disappeared. He stood stiffly and heard the gay laughter of the smoker, and one shrill voice floated back with war of answering banter.

"Laugh no more!" he whispered, and then his thoughts went racing down to cool places, to summer suns and gay, gleaming eyes. The cars reeled forward, gathered themselves, became one great speeding catapult, and headed toward the last hills. Beside them a little river, silver, whistled softly to the night.

He collected his few pairs of shoes and set them carefully down before him, arranging them mechanically; he smiled—the shoes of the dead—and he strangled as he smiled; strong, big, expensive brogans; soft, sleek, slim calf; patent leather pumps with gaitered sides; slippers of gray suède.

Slowly he got out his shoe brushes, and then paused. His heart throbbed unmercifully and then was cold and still. It was ten o'clock. He put out his hand and felt the letter. Tomorrow she would hear from him. Tomorrow they would know that black America had its men who dared—whose faces were toward the light and who could pay the price.

He laid the letter on the table unopened and took up the rest of the package, the bundle of manifestoes which Perigua had prepared and printed himself. Slowly Matthew read the little six-by-eight poster. It was rhodomontade. It was melodrama, but it told its awful story. Matthew read it and signed his name beneath Perigua's.

The wreck tonight is to avenge the lynching
Of an innocent black man, jimmie giles, on this
Train, december 16, 1926, by men who seek our
Disfranchisement and slavery.

MURDER FOR MURDERERS
Miguel Perigua
Matthew Towns

Matthew folded the posters slowly and held them in his hands.

Murder and death. That was his plan. It did not seem so awful as he faced it. Except by the shedding of blood there was no remission of Sin. Despite deceptive advance, the machinery was being laid to strangle black folk in America and in the world. They must fight or die. There was no use in talk or argument. Here was the challenge. An atrocious lynching; an open, publicly advertised movement to take the first step back to Negro slavery. Kill the men who led it. Kill them openly, publicly, and spectacularly, and advertise the killing and tell why!

Only one thing else, and that was: he must die as they died. It must be no coward's act which brought death to others and escape to himself. He shifted his pistol and pulled it out. It was a big forty-five and loaded with five great bullets. If the wreck did not kill him, this would. He was ready to die. This was all he could do for the cause. He was not worth any other effort—he had tried and failed. He had once a great dream of world alliance in the service of a woman he had almost dared to love. He laughed aloud. She would not have looked twice even on Dr. Matthew Towns, world-renowned surgeon, save as she saw in him a specimen and a promise. And on a servant and a porter—a porter. He thought of the porters, riding to death. Let the cowards ride. Then he thought of their wives and babies, of Jimmie's wife and child. What difference? No—no—no! He would not think. That way lay madness. He rushed into the next car.

"Got—nothing to do," he stammered. "Will you lend me some shoes to black?"

"Will I?" answered the astonished and sweating porter. "I sure will! My God! Looks like these birds of mine was centipedes. Never did see so many shoes in mah life. Help yo'sell, brother, but careful of the numbers, careful of the numbers."

Matthew carried a dozen pairs to his car. He shuddered as he slowly and meditatively and meticulously sorted them for cleaning and blacking. They would not need these shoes, but he must keep busy; he must keep busy—until midnight. Then he would silently distribute his manifestoes throughout the train. At one o'clock the train would shoot from its hole to the high and narrow trestle. There was only one great deed that he could do for her, for the majority of men, and for the world, and that was to die tonight in a great red protest against wrong. And Matthew hummed a tune, "Oh, brother, you must bow so low!"

Then again he saw the letter lying there. Then again came sudden boundless exaltation. He was riding the wind of a golden morning, the sense of live, rising, leaping horseflesh between his knees, the rush of tempests through his hair, and the pounding of blood—the pounding and pounding of iron and blood as the train roared through the night. He felt his great soul burst its bonds and his body rise in the stirrups as the Hounds of God screamed to the black and silver hills. In both scarred hands he seized his sword and lifted it to the circle of its swing.

Vengeance was his. With one great blow he was striking at the Heart of Hell. His trembling hands flew across the shining shoes, and tears welled in his eyes. On, on, up and on! To kill and maim and hate! To throw his life against the smug liars and lepers, hypocrites and thieves, who leered at him and mocked him! Lay on—the last great whirling crash of Hell and then his heart stopped. Then it was that he noticed the white slippers.

He had seen them before, dimly, unconsciously, out at the edge of the circle of shoes, two little white slippers—two slippers that moved. He did not raise his eyes, but with half-lowered lids and staring pupils, he looked at the slippers—two slippers, far in the rear. They were two white slippers, and he could not remember bringing them in. They stood on the outermost edge of the forest of shoes—he had not seen them move, but he knew they had moved. He was acutely, fearfully conscious of their movement, and his heart stopped.

He saw but the toes, but he knew those slippers—the smooth and shining, high-heeled white kid, embroidered with pearls. Above were silken ankles, and then as he leaped suddenly to his feet and his brushes clattered down, he heard the thin light swish of silk on silk and knew she was standing there before him—the Princess of Bwodpur. His soul clamored and fought within him, raged to know how and where and when, and here of all wild places! He saw her eyes widen with curiosity.

"You—here—Mr. Towns," she said and raised half-involuntarily her jeweled, hanging hand. He did not speak—he could not. She dropped her hand, hesitated a moment, and then, stepping forward: "Have I—offended you in some way?" she said, with that old half-haughty gesture of command, and yet with a certain surprise and pain in her voice.

Matthew stiffened and stood at attention. He touched his cap and said slowly: "I am the porter on this car," and then again he stood still, silent and yet conscious of every inch of her, from her jeweled feet to the soft clinging of her dress, to the gentle rise of her little breasts, the gold bronze of her bare neck and glowing cheeks, and the purple of her hair. She could not be as beautiful as she always seemed to him-she could not be as beautiful to other eyes. But he caught himself and bit hard on his teeth. He would not forget for a moment that he was a servant and that she knew that he knew he was. But she only said, "Yes?" and waited.

He spoke rapidly. "Your Royal Highness must excuse any apparent negligence. I have received no word from you except one letter, and that only tonight. Indeed—I have not yet read that. I hope I have been of some service. I hope that you and his Excellency have learned something of my people, of their power and desert. I wish I could serve you further and—better, but I can not—"

W.E.B. DU BOIS

The Princess sat down on the couch and stared at him with faint surprise in her face. She had listened to what he said, never moving her eyes from his face.

"Why?" she said again, gently.

"Because," he said, "I am—going away."

"Have I offended you in some way?" she asked again.

"I am the offender," he said. "I am all offense. See," he said in sudden excitement, "this is my mission." And he handed her one of Perigua's manifestoes. The Princess read it. He looked on her as she read. As she read, wrinkling her brows in perplexity, he himself seemed to awake from a nightmare. My God! He was carrying the Princess to death! How in heaven's name had he landed in this predicament? Where was the impulse, the reasoning, the high illumination that seemed to point to a train wreck as the solution of the color problems of the world? Was he mad—had he gone insane?

Whatever he was, his life was done, and done far differently from his last wild dream. There was no escape. He must stop the train. Of course. He must stop it instantly. But how was he to explain to the world his knowledge? He could not pretend a note of warning without producing it, and even then they might ignore it. He could not give details to the con ductor lest he betray Perigua.

He did not consciously ask himself the one question: why not let the wreck come after all? He knew why. For a moment he thought of suicide and a dying note. No—they might ignore the warning and think him merely crazy. Already they were flying to make up lost time. No, he must live and spare no effort even to confession until he had stopped that train. First, warning—as a last resort, the bell-rope—and then—jail.

At any cost he must save the Princess and her great cause— God! They might even think her the criminal if anything happened on this train of death. And then he sensed by the silken rustle of garments that the Princess had finished reading and had arisen.

"Read my letter," she said.

His hands shook as he read. She had received and read his reports. They were admirable and enlightening. Her own limited experiences confirmed them in all essentials. The Japanese had joined her and was quite converted. They realized the tremendous possibilities of the American Negro, but they both agreed with Mr. Towns that there was no question of revolt or violence. It was rather the slow, sure, gathering growth of power and vision, expanding and uniting with the thought of the wider, better world.

But she could not understand why he did not answer her specific questions and refused her repeated invitations to call. She wanted to thank him personally, and she had so many questions— so many, many questions to ask. She had twice postponed her return home in order to see him. Now she must go, and curiously enough, she was going to the Ku Klux Klan meeting in Chicago at the invitation of the Japanese, and for reasons she would explain. Would Mr. Towns meet her there? She would be at the Drake and always at home to him. She sensed, as did the Japanese, subtle propaganda, to discount in advance any possible colored world unity, in this invitation to attend this meeting and ride on this special train. They were all the more glad to accept, as he would readily understand. Would he be so good as to wire, if he received this, to the New Willard, Washington?

Matthew was dumb and bewildered. He could not fathom the intricacies of the tactics of the Japanese. His reports had been passed to the Princess, and yet all her letters to him stopped save this. Or had it been Perigua who had rifled his mail? Or the Indians?

But what mattered all this now? It was too late. Everything was too late. Around him like a silent wall of earth and time ranged the symbolic shoes—big and little, slippers and boots, old, new, severe, elegant. He spoke hurriedly. There was no alternative. She had to know all. Time pressed. It was nearly one o'clock, and a cold tremor gripped slowly about his heart. He listened-glanced back at the door. God! If the conductor should come! Then he hurried on.

"I shall stop the wreck; then I am going—away!"

The Princess gave a little gasp and came toward him. He started nervously and listened.

"I must not stay," he said hurriedly, and in a lower voice: "This train will surely be wrecked unless I stop it. I did not dream you were aboard."

She made a little motion with her hands. "Wrecked? *This* train?" she said, and then more slowly, "Oh! Perigua's plan?" Then she stared at him. "And you—on it!"

He smiled. "Wrecked, and I—on it." Then he added slowly: "It was to be a proof—to his Excellency and you. And it was to be more than that: it was revenge." And he told her hurriedly of Jimmie's death.

"But you must stop it. It is a mad thing to do. There are so many sane, fine paths. I was so mistaken. I had thought of you as a nation of outcasts to be hurled forward as shock troops, but you are a nation of modern people. You surely will not follow Perigua?"

"No," he said quietly, "I will not. But let me tell you—"

Then she rose quietly and moved toward him. "And—Perigua must be—betrayed?"

"Never."

"And if—" She stared at him. "And if—"

"Jail," he said quietly, "for long years." She made a little noise like a sob controlled, but his quick ear caught another sound. "The conductor," he whispered. "Destroy these handbills for me." Quickly he stepped out into the corridor.

"Captain," he said hurriedly, "captain—this train mast be stopped—there is danger."

"What do you mean? Is it them damned porters again?"

"No—not they—but, I say—there is danger. Where's the train conductor?"

The Pullman conductor stared at him hard. "He's up in the third car," he said nervously, for it had been a hard trip.

"Come with me." Matthew followed.

They stepped in on the conductor in an empty compartment, where he was burrowing in a pile of tickets and stubs.

"Mr. Gray, the porter has a story for you."

"Spit it out—and hurry up," growled the conductor. The train flew on, and faster flew the time.

"You must stop the train," said Matthew.

The conductor glanced up. "What's the matter with you? Are you drunk?"

"I was never so sober."

"What the hell then is the matter?"

"For God's sake stop the train! There's danger ahead."

"Stop the train, already two hours late? You blithering idiot! Have all you black porters gone crazy?"

Matthew stepped out of the compartment and threw his weight on the bell-rope. The conductor swore and struck him aside, but there was a jolt, a low, long, grinding roar, and quickly the train slowed down. The conductor seized Matthew just as someone pounded on the window. A red light flashed ahead. Soon a sweating man rushed aboard.

"Thank God!" he gasped. "That was a narrow squeak. I was afraid I was too late to flag you. You must have got warning before my signal was lighted. There's been an explosion on the trestle. Rails are torn up for a dozen yards."

W.E.B. DU BOIS

XV

Matthew Towns blackened shoes. All night long he blackened shoes, cleaning them, polishing them very carefully, and arranging the laces. He was working in a standard Pullman at the forward end of the train, having been hurriedly transferred from the private car after the incident of the night. He gathered more shoes and blackened them, placing them carefully, in the graying dawn, under the appropriate berths. He arranged clean towels in the washrooms and tested the soap cocks. He saw that the toilets were clean and in order, and he carefully dusted the corridor and wiped the windows.

All the time there were two unobtrusive strangers who kept him always in sight. He paid no apparent attention to them but waited, watch in hand, as the train approached Knoxville. Someone asked the time.

"Six-thirty," he whispered.

"We're pretty late."

"Yes, on account of that delay on the road."

"When do we get in Knoxville?"

"About eight-thirty, I imagine. Breakfast will be served as soon as we arrive."

At last he went to some of the berths and pulled the lower sheet gently and then insistently.

"One hour to Knoxville," he said; and again and again. "One hour to Knoxville."

The car aisles began to fill with half-dressed travelers. He brought new bundles of towels and began to make up vacant berths. He worked rapidly and deftly. There was much confusion, and always the two unobtrusive men were near. Some of the returning passengers found their seats in order. Others did not and made sharp remarks, but Matthew pacified them, guided them to resting-places, and began to collect the luggage and to brush the clothes.

The sweat poured off him, but he worked swiftly. When they stopped in the depot, he was at the step in coat and cap, wooden, deferential: "Thank you, sir. All right here, Cap." They moved out for the swift three-hour run to Atlanta. He finished the other berths, brushed more passengers, stowed dirty linen, swept, dusted, and guided passengers to the dining car attached at Knoxville.

The train glided into the Atlanta station.

And then it came.

"Towns, step this way—gentleman wants to see you." He walked back through the train into the lounge of the private car again. On the table lay something under a sheet. About the door, several of the passengers were crowded.

As Matthew entered the car he saw in the vestibule, and for the first time since one awful night, a well-remembered figure—a woman, high-colored, big and boldly handsome, with her lowered eyelids and jeweled hands. Beside her was a weak-looking man, faultlessly tailored, with an old and dissipated face. They were in the waiting throng. The woman looked up. Her eyes widened suddenly, and then quietly she fainted away.

Matthew faltered but an instant and then walked steadily on. He entered the room. The conductor was there, the two quiet men, and a grave-faced stranger. And then came the Princess, the Japanese, and several other guests. They all sat, but Matthew stood silent, his uniform spotless, his head up. One of the strangers spoke.

"Your name is—"

"Matthew Towns."

"You are a porter?"

"Yes."

"The porters had planned a strike in Cincinnati?"

"Yes."

"Why didn't you strike?"

"I was going to, but I changed my mind."

"Why?"

"Because the others decided not to—and because I heard that this train was going to be wrecked."

"By the porters?"

"Certainly not!"

"By whom?"

"I cannot tell."

"Who told you?"

"I will not say."

"Did the other porters hear this?"

"No, I was the only one."

"How do you know?"

"I am sure."

"When did you hear this?"

"Just before the train started."

"From Chicago?"

"No, from Cincinnati."

"But you were in Chicago?"

"Yes."

"And planned the strike there?"

"Yes, I helped to."

"What did you do when you heard this rumor?"

"I offered to go as porter."

"You offered to go on a train that you knew was going to be wrecked?"

"Yes."

"Why?"

"Well—a porter-my friend—was lynched on this train a week ago. I urged the strike as a protest. When it failed—nothing mattered."

"Did you intend to stop the wreck?"

"At first, no."

"And you—you changed your mind?"

"Yes."

"Why?"

"I cannot tell."

"How did you think you could prevent it?"

"Well—I did prevent it."

"Who told you about this plot?"

"I will not tell."

"Did this man tell you?"

They drew the sheet from Perigua's dead face. Beneath the sheet his body looked queer, humped and broken. But his face was peaceful and smiling. Matthew's face was stone. "No."

"Do you know him?"

"No."

"Did you ever see him before?"

"Yes."

"Where?"

"In the office of the Grand Dragon of the Ku Klux Klan in the Sherman Hotel, Chicago."

There was a stir among the crowd. A big man with a flat, broad face and little eyes pressed forward and viewed the corpse.

"It may be Sam," he said. "Were any papers or marks found on him?"

"Nothing—absolutely nothing. Not even laundry marks."

"I'm almost sure that's Sam Johnson, who acted as messenger in our Chicago office. If it is," he spoke deliberately, "I'll vouch for him. Excellent character—wouldn't hurt a flea."

He glanced at Matthew.

The inquisitor turned back to Matthew.

"Who told you of this wreck?"

"I will not tell."

"Why not?"

"I take all the blame."

"Do you realize your position? You stand between high reward and criminal punishment."

"I know it."

"Who told you of the wreck?"

And then like sudden thunder came the low, clear voice of the Princess: "I told him!"

XVI

C ircuit Judge Windom, presiding over the criminal court of Cook County, Illinois, sat in his chambers with a frown on his face. Beside him sat his son, the gifted young medical student, home from the holidays.

"Certainly I remember Towns," said the younger man. "He was a fine fellow—first-rate brains, fine athlete, and a gentleman. If it had not been for his color, he'd have been sure to make a big reputation, but they drove him out of school. Somebody had kicked about Negroes in the women's clinics. Towns wouldn't beg—he slapped the Dean's face, I heard, and left."

"H'm—violent, even then."

"But, my God, father, Towns was a man—not just a colored man. Why, you remember how he beat me for the Mitchel Prize?"

"Yes, yes—but all that does not clear up this mystery. I can get neither head nor tail of it. Here is an atrocious railroad wreck planned on a leading railway. Half an hour more, and there would have been perhaps five hundred corpses strewn in the river. Awful! Dastardly! The explosion was bungled and premature. The trestle was left intact, but enough damage was done to have made the derailing of the train inevitable had it rushed through the tunnel unwarned. Section hands discovered at the last moment the broken rails and a dead man lying across them. They start to signal too late, but before they start Towns warns the conductor; when the conductor hesitates, Towns himself stops the train. Possibly the signal man might have stopped it eventually, but Towns actually stopped it.

"Now, how did Towns know? Was this the striking porters' plot? Towns and their leaders declare that, far from dreaming of this, they would not quit work for an ordinary strike, and certainly they would hardly have ridden on a train which they expected to be wrecked. An Indian Princess declares that she told Towns of the plot, and taking refuge in her diplomatic immunity, refuses to answer further questions. The English Embassy, which represents her country abroad, backs her reputation, vouches for her integrity, and promises her immediate withdrawal from the country. The dead Negro found on the trestle remains unidentified. Indeed there is no evidence of his connection with the wreck. The chief of the Klan thinks he recognizes the man as a former messenger, vouches for his character, and doubts his connection with any plot; he considers him a victim rather than a conspirator. Says, as of course we know, that Negroes never conspire. And now comes this extraordinary story of Towns himself."

"Well, at any rate, Towns wouldn't lie!" said the son. "But the point is, he won't tell the truth; and why? It looks dangerous, suspicious. Some red-handed rascals are going free."

"What does Towns say?"

"He says that he did not plan this outrage; that when he knew that it was planned he assented to it and determined to run on this train and to die in the wreck. Then, for some reason changing his mind and being unable to contemplate the death of all these passengers, he gave warning of the plot. He says that he had met the Princess abroad, had told her of his trouble in the medical school and elicited her sympathy and interest; that he had no knowledge that she was on the train, and no idea she was in the country. He then told her the danger of the train and his dilemma, and in generous sympathy, she had finally sought to direct the blame of guilty fore-knowledge to herself.

"In truth, and this he swears before God, the Princess of Bwodpur had not the faintest knowledge of the plot of wrecking the train until he himself told her five minutes before he stopped the train. He begs that she be entirely exonerated, despite her Quixotic attempt to save him, and that he alone bear the full blame and suffer the full penalty."

"Extraordinary—but if Towns says it's true, it's true. It may not be the whole truth, but it contains no falsehood."

"Well, it is full of discrepancies and suspicious omissions. Good heavens! A woman says she knew a train was to be wrecked, and yet rides on it, and tells the porter and not the conductor. The porter declares that she did not know or tell him, but that somebody else did; and yet *he* rides. A man found dead may be the wrecker, but the head of the Ku Klux Klan and one of the threatened party refuses to believe him guilty. The porter refuses to tell where he got his warning and prefers jail rather than reward."

"How did the case get to your court, father?"

"More complications. When Towns was arraigned at Atlanta, the passengers of the Klan Special came forward with a big purse to reward him for his services, and a sharp lawyer. Towns refused the money, but the court listened to the lawyer and held that no crime had been committed by Towns in its jurisdiction.

"Thereupon the District Attorney of this district sought indictment against Towns, charging that the Pullman porter strike was concocted in Chicago and that the wreck was part of the conspiracy. Towns denied this, but offered to come here without extradition papers. The District Attorney expected the help and support of the Pullman Company and the railroads. None of them lifted a finger.

"There is another curious and unexplained angle. You know there was a lynching on that Klan train. There was some dispute as to whether it took place in Georgia or Tennessee. Nothing was ever done about it, not even a coroner's inquest. Well, I have it on the best authority that when the woman who alleged the attack saw Towns face to face at the informal questioning on the train, she fainted away.

"I have tried to get in touch with her and her husband, who is Therwald, a high Klansman. They deny all knowledge and refuse to appear as witnesses. As residents of another state, I can't compel them. Moreover, I find that they have only recently been married, although the newspaper reports of the lynching refer to them as man and wife occupying the same compartment. Now what's behind all this?

"Well, he was indicted for conspiracy and pleaded guilty. He still declared that the porters' union and the Indian Princess knew nothing of the proposed wreck. He admitted that he did and further admitted that he consented to it and started on the journey determined not to betray the arch-conspirators, and then changed his mind and stopped the wreck. Now what can you make of such a Hell's broth?"

"I'm puzzled, father."

"The Princess of Bwodpur herself has come to me, stopping en route, as she explained, to Seattle and India. Evidently a great lady and extraordinarily beautiful, despite her color, which I was born to dislike. I pooh-poohed her story and showed her Towns' sworn confession. There is no doubt of her interest in him. She put up a strong plea, stronger than yours, son, but I was adamant. I had to be. I am not at all sure but that she is the guilty party and that Towns is shielding her. I don't know, my boy—I don't know where the truth lies. But there's more here than meets the eye. I scent a powerful, dangerous movement; and despite all you say, if Towns thinks that a plea of guilty and waiver of jury trial is going to get him mercy in my court, he is mistaken. I am sorry—I hate to do it; but he'll get the limit of the law unless he tells the whole truth." And the judge sighed wearily and gathered up his books.

XVII

Matthew sat in a solemn hall. It was "across the river"—north of the Loop and west of the Michigan Avenue bridge, in a region of vacant dilapidated buildings, of windows without panes and walls peeling and crumbling. A mighty, gray stone structure covered half the block. The front was wrinkled and uneven, with a shrunken door under an iron balcony. Three elevators with musty, clanking chains faced the door and rolled solemnly up five floors. The lobby was bordered with dark stone; the floor was white and gray and cold, and across one side was a huge sign—"Robert E. Crowe, State's Attorney, Office." Across the other side one read, "Criminal Court"

Within these doors, beyond a narrow, oak-paneled hall, tet Matthew Towns, in a high-ceilinged room. The long narrow windows, with flapping dirty green shades, admitted a fai light. The walls were painted orange-yellow. The lights were hanging from the ceiling in chandeliers of metal once brass colored, with each light socket in an ornamental cak-leat holder. The globes were of a bluish-yellow glass, pear-shaped The Bench, of polished oak, was at the rear of a circular oaken-railed enclosure. The enclosure had tables and chairs for lawyers, clients, and witnesses. Well to the front of this green-carpeted space was the desk of the clerk. To the rear, o a raised platform, were seats for the jury. Raised yet higher was the platform upon which rested the judge's bench; on either side of the bench were doors with signs, "Judge's Chambers," "Jury Rooms." Facing this circular enclosure were long seats in rows for the spectators. The floor here was the same dirty gray, much-worn tile, and the ceiling over the whole, while very high, was noticeable only because it was so soiled and stained.

Soft sunshine filtered in and lighted up the rich polish of the oak. Behind the high desk sat the judge—heavily silked, bis grave, gray face looking sternly out upon the world. The strained faces of that world, white, black, and brown, were crowded in the benches below, and some stood in babed silence. Policemen, bareheaded, moved silently about the throng, and two officials with silver and gilt stood just below the judge. There should have been music, Matthew thought, some slow beat like the Saul death march or the pulse of the Holy Grail. Then the judge spoke:

"Matthew Towns, stand up."

And Matthew rose and stood, center of a thousand eyes, and a sigh and a hiss went through the hall. For he was tall and impressive. The crisp hair curled on his high forehead. The soft brown of his eyes glowed dark on the lighter brown of his smooth skin. His gray suit lay smooth above the muscles and long bones of his close-knit body. He looked the judge full in the face. The eyes of the judge grew somber—but for a tint of skin, but for a curl of hair, but for a fuller curve of lip and cheek, this might have been his own son, this man whom his son had known and honored. "Matthew Towns," he said in low, slow tones, "you stand accused of an awful crime. With your knowledge and at least tacit consent, some person whom you know and we do not, planned to put a hundred, perhaps five hundred souls to torture, pain, and sudden death. At the last minute, when literally moments counted, you rescued these people from the grave. It may have been a brave—a heroic deed. It may have been a kind of deathbed repentance or even the panic of cowardice. In any case the guilt—the grave and terrible guilt hangs over you for your refusal to reveal the name or names of these blood-guilty plotters of midnight dread—of these enemies of God and man. With the stoicism worthy of a better cause and a cynical hardness, you let these men walk free and take upon yourself all the punishment and shame. It has a certain fineness of sacrifice, I admit; but it is wrong, cruel, hateful to civilization and criminal in effect and intent. There is for you no shadow of real excuse. You are a man of education and culture. You have traveled and read. I know that you have suffered injustice and perhaps insult and that your soul is bitter. But you are to blame if you have let this drown the heart of your manhood. You have no real excuse for this criminal and dangerous silence, and I have but one clear duty before me, and that is to punish you severely. I could pronounce the sentence of death upon you for deliberate conspiracy to maim and murder your fellow men; but I will temper justice with mercy so as still to give you chance for repentance. Matthew Towns, I sentence you to ten years at hard labor in the State Prison at Joliet."

The sun burst clear through the dim windows and lighted the young face of the prisoner.

Someone in the audience sobbed; another started to ap plaud. Matthew Towns followed the guard into the anteroom, and thither the Princess came, moving quietly to where he stood with shackled hands. The windows all about were barred, and at the farther end of the room stood the stolid officer with a pistol and keys. Down below hummed the traffic.

She took both his manacled hands in hers, and he steeled himself to look the last time at that face and into the deep glory of her eyes. She was simply dressed in black, with one great white pearl in the parting of her breasts.

"You are a brave man, Matthew Towns, brave and great. You have sacrificed your life for me."

Matthew smiled whimsically.

"I am a small man, small and selfish and singularly short of sight. I served myself as well as you, and served us both ill, because I was dreaming selfish little dreams. Now I am content; for life, which was twisting itself beyond my sight and reason, has become suddenly straight and simple. Your Royal Highness"— he saw the pain in her eyes, and he changed: "My Princess," he said, "your path of life is straight before you and clear. You were born to power. Use it. Guide your groping people. You will go back now to the world and begin your great task as the ruler of millions and the councilor of the world's great leaders.

"Your dream of the emancipation of the darker races will come true in time, and you will find allies and helpers everywhere, and nowhere more than in black America. Join the hands of the dark people of the earth. Discover in the masses of groveling, filthy, ignorant black and brown and yellow slaves of modern Europe, the spark of manhood which, fanned with knowledge and health, will light anew a great world-culture. Yours is the great chance—the solemn duty. I had thought once that I might help and in some way stand by the armposts of your throne. That dream is gone. I made a mistake, and now I can only help by bowing beneath the yoke of shame; and by that very deed I am hindered—forever—to help you or anyone—much. I—am proud—infinitely proud to have had at least your friendship."

The Princess spoke, and as she talked slowly, pausing now and then to search for a word, she seemed to Matthew somehow to change. She was no longer an icon, crimson and splendid, the beautiful perfect thing apart to be worshiped; she became with every struggling word a striving human soul groping for light, needing help and love and the quiet deep sympathy of great, fine souls. And the more she doffed her royalty and donned her sweet and fine womanhood, the further, the more inaccessible, she became to him.

He knew that what she craved and needed for life, he could not give; that they were eternally parted, not by nature or wealth or even by birth, but by the great call of her duty and opportunity, and by the narrow and ever-narrowing limit of his strength and chance. She did not even look at him now with that impersonal glance that seemed to look through him to great spaces beyond and ignore him in the very intensity and remoteness of her gaze. She stood with downcast eyes and nervous hands, and talked, of herself, of her visit to America, of her hopes, of him.

"I am afraid," she said, "I seem to you inhuman, but I have come up out of great waters into the knowledge of life." She looked up at him sadly: "Were you too proud to accept from me a little sacrifice that cost me nothing and meant everything to you?"

"It might have cost you a kingdom and the whole future of the darker world. It was just some such catastrophe that the Japanese and Indians rightly feared."

"And so, innocent of crime, you are going to accept the brand and punishment of a criminal?" "My innocence is only technical. I was a deliberate co-conspirator with Perigua. I—murdered Jimmie!"

"No—no—how can you say this! You did not dream of peril to your friend, and your pact with Perigua was a counsel of despair!"

"My moral guilt is real. I should have remembered Jimmie. I should have guided Perigua."

W.E.B. DU BOIS

"But," and she moved nearer, "if the dead man was—Perigua, what harm now to tell the truth?"

"I will not lay my guilt upon the dead. And, too—if I confessed that much, men might probe—further."

"And so in the end I am the one at fault!"

"No—no."

"Yes, I know it. But, oh, Matthew, are you not conscience mad? You would have died for your friend had you known, just as now you go to jail for me and my wild errand. But even granted, dear friend, some of the guilt of which you so fantastically accuse yourself—can you not balance against this the good you can do your people and mine if free?"

"I have thought of this, and I much doubt my fitness. I know and feel too much. Dear Jimmie saw no problem that he could not laugh off—he was valuable; indispensable in this stage of our development. He should be living now, but I who am a mass of quivering nerves and all too delicate sensibility I am liable to be a Perigua or a hesitating complaining fool untrained or half-trained, fitted for nothing but—jail."

"But—but afterward—after ten little years or perhaps less—you will still be young and strong."

"No, I shall be old and weak. My spirit will be broken and my hope and aspirations gone. I know what jail does to men, especially to black men—my father—"

"You are then deliberately sacrificing your life to me and my cause!"

"I am making the only effective and final atonement that I can to the Great Cause which is ours. I might live and work and do infinitely less."

"You have ten minutes more," said the guard.

"Is there nothing—is there not something I can do for you?"

"Yes one thing: that is, if you are able—if you are permitted and can do it without involving yourself too much with me and my plight."

"Tell me quickly."

"I would not put this request if I had any other way, if I had any other friend. But I am—alone." She gripped his hands and was silent, looking always straight into his eyes with eyes that never dropped or wavered. "I have a mother in Virginia whom I have forgotten and neglected. She is a great and good woman, and she must know this. Here is a package. It is addressed to her and contains some personal mementoes—my father's watch, my high-school certificate—old gifts. I want her to have them. I want her to see—you. I want you to see her—it will explain; she is a noble woman; old, gnarled, ignorant, but very wise. She lives in a log cabin and smokes a clay pipe. I want you to go to her if you can, and I want you to tell her my story. Tell her gently, but clearly, and as you think best; tell her I am dead or in a far country—or, if you will, the plain truth. She is seventy years old. She will be dead before I leave those walls, if I ever leave them. If she did not realize where I was or why I was silent, she would die of grief. If she knows the truth or thinks she knows it, she will stand up strong and serene before her God. Tell her I failed with a great vision—great, even if wrong. Make her life's end happy for her. Leave her her dreams."

"You have one minute more," said the guard.

The Princess took the package. The policeman turned, watch in hand. They looked at each other. He let his eyes feast on her for the last time—that never, never again should they forget her grace and beauty and even the gray line of suffering that leapt from nose to chin; suddenly she sank to her knees and kissed both his hands, and was gone.

Next day a great steel gate swung to in Joliet, and Matthew Towns was No. 1,277.

PART III

THE CHICAGO POLITICIAN

1924, JANUARY, TO APRIL, 1926

*Winter. Winter, jail and death, Winter, three winters long,
with only the green of two little springs and the crimson
of two short autumns; but ever with hard, cold winter in
triumph over all. Cold streets and hard faces; white death
in a white world; but underneath the ice, fire from heaven,
burning back to life the poor and black and guilty, the hopeless
and unbelieving, the suave and terrible. Dirt and frost, slush
and diamonds, amid the roar of winter in Chicago.*

I

Sara Andrews listened to the short trial and sentence of Matthew Towns in Chicago in early January, 1924, with narrowed eyelids, clicking her stenographer's pencil against her teeth. She was not satisfied. She had followed the Klan meeting with professional interest, then the porters' strike and Matthew's peculiar case. There was, she was certain, more here than lay on the surface, and she walked back to Sammy Scott's office in a brown study.

Sara Andrews was thin, small, well tailored. Only at second glance would you notice that she was "colored." She was not beautiful, but she gave an impression of cleanliness, order, cold, clean hardness, and unusual efficiency. She wore a black crêpe dress, with crisp white organdie collar and cuffs, chiffon hose, and short-trimmed hair. Altogether she was pleasing but a trifle disconcerting to look at. Men always turned to gaze at her, but they did not attempt to flirt—at least not more than once.

Miss Andrews was self-made and independent. She had been born in Indiana of the union of a colored chambermaid in the local hotel and a white German cook. The two had been duly married and duly divorced after the cook went on a visit to Germany and never returned. Then her mother died, and this girl fought her way through school; she forced herself into the local business college, and she fought off men with a fierceness and determination that scared them. It became thoroughly understood in Richmond that you couldn't "fool" with Sara Andrews, Local Lotharios gave up trying. Only fresh strangers essayed, and they received direct and final information. She slapped one drummer publicly in the Post Office and nearly upset evening prayer at St. Luke's, to the discomfiture of a pious deacon who sat beside her and was praying with his hands.

For a long time she was the only "colored" person in town, except a few laborers; and although almost without social life or intimate friends, she became stenographer at the dry goods "Emporium" at a salary which was regarded as fabulous for a young woman. Then Southern Negroes began to filter in as laborers, and the color line appeared, broad and clear, in the town. Sara Andrews could have ignored it and walked across so far as soda fountains and movie theaters were concerned, but she wouldn't. A local druggist wanted to marry her and "go away." She refused and suddenly gave up her job and went to Chicago. There, in 1922, she became secretary to the Honorable Sammy Scott.

The Honorable Sammy was a leading colored politician of Chicago. He was a big, handsome, brown man, with smooth black hair, broad shoulders, and a curved belly. He had the most infectious smile and the most cordial handshake in the city and the reputation of never forgetting a face. Behind all this was a keen intelligence, infinite patience, and a beautiful sense of humor. Sammy was a coming man, and he knew it.

He was, in popular parlance, a "politician." In reality he was a super-business man. In the Second Ward with its overflowing Negro population, Sammy began business in 1910 by selling the right to gamble, keep houses of prostitution, and commit petty theft, to certain men, white and black, who paid him in cash. With this cash he bribed the city officials and police to let these people alone and he paid a little army of henchmen to organize the Negro voters and see that they voted for officials who could be bribed.

Sammy did not invent this system—he found it in full blast and he improved it. He replaced white ward heelers with blacks who were more acceptable to the colored voters and were themselves raised from the shadow of crime to well-paid jobs; some even became policemen and treated Negro prisoners with a certain consideration. Some became clerks and civil servants of various sorts.

Then came migration, war, more migration, prohibition, and the Riot. Black Chicago was in continual turmoil, and the black vote more than doubled. Sammy's business expanded enormously; bootlegging became a prime source of graft and there was more gambling, more women for sale, and more crime. Men pushed and jostled each other in their eagerness to pay for the privilege of catering to these appetites. Sammy became Alderman from

W.E.B. DU BOIS

the Second Ward and committeeman, representing the regular Second Ward Republican organization on the County Central Committee. He made careful alliance with the colored Alderman in the Third Ward and the white Aldermen from the other colored wards. He envisaged a political machine to run all black Chicago.

But there were difficulties—enormous difficulties. Other Negro politicians in his own and other wards, not to mention the swarm of white bosses, had the same vision and ambition as Sammy— they must all be reconciled and brought into one organization. As it was now, Negroes competed with each other and fought each other, and the white party bosses, setting one against the other, got the advantage. It was at this stage of the game that Sara Andrews joined Sammy's staff.

When Sara Andrews applied to the Honorable Sammy for work, he hired her on the spot because she looked unusually ornamental in her immaculate crêpe dress, white silk hose, and short-trimmed hair. She had intelligent, straight gray eyes, too, and Sammy liked both intelligence and gray eyes. Moreover, she could "pass" for white—a decided advantage on errands and interviews.

Sammy's office was on State Street at the corner of Thirty-Second. Most of the buildings around there were old frame structures with living-quarters above and stores below. On each corner were brick buildings planned like the others, but now used wholly for stores and offices. The entrance to Sammy's building was on the Thirty-Second Street side; a dingy gray wooden door opened into a narrow hall of about three by four feet. Thence rose a flight of stairs which startled by its amazing steepness as well as its darkness. At the top of the stairs, the hall was dim and narrow, with high ceilings. At the end was a waiting room facing State Street. It was finished with a linoleum rug that did not completely cover the soft wood floor; its splinters insisted on pulling away as if to avoid the covering of dark red paint. There were two desks in the waiting room, some chairs, and a board upon which were listed "Apartments for rent." Sash curtains of dingy white, held up with rods, were at the windows, and above them in gold letters were painted the names of various persons and of "Samuel Scott, Attorney at Law."

A railing about three feet high made an inner sanctum, and beyond was a closed door marked "Private." Back here in Sammy's private office lay the real center of things, and in front of this and within the rail, Sammy installed Sara. The second day she was there, Sammy kissed her. That was four years ago, and Sammy had not kissed her since. He had not even tried. Just what happened Sammy never said; he only grinned, and all his friends ever really knew was that Sammy and Sara were closeted together for a full half-hour after the kiss and that Sara did most of the talking. But Sara stayed at her job, and she stayed because Sammy discovered that she was a new asset in his business; first of all, that she was a real stenographer. He did not have to dictate letters, which had always been a difficult task. He just talked with Sara and signed what she brought him a few minutes later.

"And believe me," said Sammy, "she writes some letter!"

Indeed Sara brought new impetus and methods into Sammy's business. When that kiss failed, Sammy was afraid he had got hold of a mere prude and was resolved to shift her as soon as possible. Then came her letter-writing and finally her advice. She listened beautifully, and Sammy loved to talk. She drew out his soul, and gradually he gave her full confidence. He discovered to his delight that Sara Andrews had no particular scruples or conscience. Lying, stealing, bribery, gambling, prostitution, were facts that she accepted casually. Personally honest and physically "pure" almost to prudery, she could put a lie through the typewriter in so adroit a way that it sounded better than the truth and was legally fireproof. She recognized politics as a means of private income, and her shrewd advice not only increased the office revenue, but slowly changed it to safer and surer forms. "Colored cabarets are all right," said Sara, "but white railroads pay better."

She pointed out that not only would the World-at-Play pay for privilege and protection, but the World-at-Work would pay even more. Retail merchants, public service corporations, financial exploiters, all wanted either to break the law or to secure more pliable laws; and with post-war inflation, they would set no limit of largesse for the persons who could deliver the goods. Sammy must therefore get in touch with these Agencies in the White World. Sammy was skeptical. He still placed his chief reliance on drunkards, gamblers, and prostitutes. "Moreover," he said, "all that calls not only for more aldermen but more members of the legislature and Negroes on the bench."

"Sure," answered Sara, "and we got to push for Negro aldermen in the Sixth and Seventh Wards, a couple of more members of the legislature, a judge, and a congressman."

"And each one of them will set up as an independent boss, and what can I do with them?"

"Defeat 'em at next election," said Sara, "and that means that you've got to get a better hold on the Negro vote than you've got. Oh, I know you're mighty popular in the policy shops, but you're not so much in the churches. You're corraling the political jobs and ward organizations, but you must get to be popular—get the imagination of the rank and file."

Sammy hooted the suggestion, and Sara said nothing more for a while. But she had set Sammy thinking. She always did that.

In fine, Sara Andrews became indispensable to the Honorable Sammy Scott, and he knew that she was. He would have liked to kiss and cuddle her now and then when they sat closeted together in the den which she had transformed into an impressive, comfortable, and singularly official office. She was always so cool and clean with her slim white hands and perfect clothes. But all she ever allowed was a little pat on the shoulder and an increase in salary. Now and then she accepted jewelry and indicated clearly just what she wanted.

Then for a while Sammy half made up his mind to marry her, and he was about sure she would accept. But he was a little afraid. She was too cold and hard. He had no mind to embrace a cake of ice even if it was well groomed and sleek.

"No," said Sammy to himself and to his friends and even to Sara in his expansive moments, after a good cocktail, "no, I'm not a marrying man."

Sara was neither a prude nor a flirt. She simply had a good intellect without moral scruples and a clear idea of the communal and social value of virginity, respectability, and good clothes.

She saved her money carefully and soon had a respectable bank account and some excellent bonds.

Sammy was born in Mississippi the year that Hayes was elected. He had little education but could talk good English and made a rattling public speech. With Sara's coaching he even attempted something more than ordinary political hokum and on one or two public occasions lately had been commended; even the *Tribune* called him a man of "real information in current events." Sara accordingly bought magazines and read papers carefully. She wrote out his more elaborate speeches; he committed them to his remarkable memory in an hour or so.

Why then should Sammy marry Sara? He had her brains and skill, and nobody could outbid him in salary. Of that he was sure. Why spoil the loyalty of a first-class secretary for the doubtful love of a wife? Then, too, he rather liked the hovering game. He came to his office and his letters with a zest. He discovered the use of letters even in politics. Before Sara's day there was a typewriting machine in Sammy's office, but it was seldom used. Previous clerks had been poor stenographers, and Sammy could not dictate. Besides, why write? Sara showed him why. He touched her finger tips; he brought her flowers and told her all his political secrets. She had no lovers and no prospective lovers. Time enough to marry her if he found he must. Meantime love was cheap in Chicago and secretaries scarce, and, in fine, "I'm not a marrying man," repeated the Honorable Sammy.

Sara smiled coolly and continued:

"I think I see something for us in the Towns case."

Sammy frowned. "Better not touch it," he said. "Bolsheviks are unpopular, especially with railroads. And when it comes to niggers blowing up white folks—well, my advice is, drop it!"

So the matter dropped for a week. Then Sara quietly returned to it: "Listen, Sammy"—Sara was quite informal when they were alone in the sanctum—"I think I see a scoop." Sammy listened. "This Matthew Towns—"

"What Matthew Towns?"

"The man they sent to Joliet."

"Oh! I thought you'd dropped that."

"No, I've just really begun to take it up. This Towns is unusual, intelligent, educated, plucky."

"How do you know?"

"I saw him during the trial, and since then I've been down to Joliet."

"Humph!" said Sammy, lighting his third cigar.

"He is a man that would never forget a service. With such a man added to your machine you might land in Congress."

Sammy laid his cigar down and sat up.

"I keep telling you, Sammy, you've got to be something more than the ordinary colored Chicago politician before you can take the next step. You've got to be popular among respectable people."

"Respectable, hell!" remarked Sammy.

"Precisely," said Sara; "the hell of machine politics has got to be made to look respectable for ordinary consumption. Now you need something to jack you up in popular opinion. Something that will at once appeal to Negro race pride and not scare off the white folks who want to do political business with you. Our weakness as Negro politicians is that we have never been able to get the church people and the young educated men of ability into our game."

"Hypocrites and asses!"

"Quite so, but you'll notice these hypocrites, asses, good lawyers, fine engineers, and pious ministers are all grist to the white man's political machine. He puts forward and sticks into office educated and honest men of ability who can do things, and he only asks that they won't be too damned good and honest to support his main interests in a crisis. Moreover, either we'll get the pious crowd and the educated youngsters in the machine, or some fine day they'll smash it.

"Sammy, have some imagination! Your methods appeal to the same crowd in the same old way. Meantime new crowds are pushing in and old crowds are changing and they want new ways—they are caught by new gags; makes no difference whether they are better or worse than the old-facts are facts, and the fact is that your political methods are not appealing to or holding the younger crowd. Now here's bait for them, and big bait too.

If I am not much mistaken, Towns is a find. For instance: 'The Honorable Sammy Scott secures the release of Towns. Towns, a self-sacrificing hero, now looms as a race martyr. Towns says that he owes all to the Honorable Sammy!'"

"Fine," mocked Sammy, "and niggers wild! But how about the white folks? 'Sam Scott, the black politician, makes a jail delivery of the criminal who tried to wreck the Louisville & Nashville Railway Special. A political shame,' etc., etc."

"Hold up," insisted Sara. "Now see here: the Negroes have been thoroughly aroused and are bitterly resentful at the Klan meeting, the lynching of the porter, and Matthew Towns' incarceration. His release would be a big political asset to the man who pulled it off. And if you are the man and the white political and business world know that your new popularity strengthens your machine and delivers them votes when wanted, and that instead of dealing with a dozen would-be bosses, they can just see you—why, Sammy, you'd own black Chicago!"

"Sounds pretty—but—"

"On the other hand, who would object? I have been talking to the porters and railroad men and to others. They say the judge was reluctant to sentence Towns, but saw no legal escape. The railroad and the Pullman Company owe him millions and were willing to reward him handsomely if he had escaped the law. The Klan owes several hundred lives to him. None of these will actively oppose pardon. It remains only to get one of them actually to ask for it."

"Well—one, which one?" grinned Sammy, touching Sara's fingers as he reached for another cigar.

"The Klan."

"Are you crazy!"

"I think not. Consider; the Klan is at once criminal and victim. Its recent activities have been too open and bombastic. It has suffered political reverses both north and south. It is accused of mere 'nigger-baiting.' Would it not be a grand wide gesture of tolerance for the Klan to ask freedom for Towns? Something like donations to Negro churches, only bigger and with more advertising value."

"Well, sure; if they had that kind of sense."

"They've got all kinds of sense. Now again, there is something funny about that lynching. I've heard a lot of talk. Towns has let out bits of a strange story, and the porters say he was wild and bitter about the lynching. Suppose, now—I'm only guessing—Towns knows more than he has told about this woman and her carrying on. If so, she might be glad to help him. A favor for keeping his mouth shut. I mention this, because she has married since the Klan convention and her husband is a high official of the Klan."

Sammy still didn't see much in the scheme, but he had a great respect for Sara's shrewdness.

"Well—what do you propose?" he asked.

"I propose to go to Joliet again and have a long talk with Towns. Then I'm going to drop down to Washington. I've always wanted to go there. I'll need a letter of introduction from somebody of importance in Chicago to this woman, Mrs. Therwald."

II

It was a lovely February day as Sara walked down Sixteenth Street, Washington—clear, cool, with silvery sunshine. Sara was appropriately garbed in a squirrel coat and hat, pearl-gray hose, and gray suède slippers. Her gloves matched her eyes, and her manner was sedate. She walked down to Pennsylvania Avenue, looked at the White House casually, and then sauntered on to the New Willard. Her color was so imperceptible that she walked in unhindered and strolled through the lobby. Mrs. Therwald was not in, she was informed by the room clerk. She talked with a bell-boy, and when Mrs. Therwald entered, observed her from afar, carefully and at her leisure. She was a big florid woman, boldly handsome, but beginning to show age. About a quarter of an hour after she had taken the elevator, Sara sent up her card and letter of introduction from the wife of a prominent white Chicago politician.

Mrs. Therwald received her. She was a woman thoroughly bored with life, and Sara looked like a pleasant interlude. They were soon chatting easily. Sara intimated that she wrote for magazines and newspapers and that she had come to see the wife of a celebrity.

"Oh, no—we're nothing."

"Oh, yes—the Klan is a power and bound to grow—if it acts wisely."

"I really don't know much about it. My husband is the one interested."

"I know—and that brings me to the second object of my visit— Matthew Towns."

Mrs. Therwald was silent several seconds—and then:

"Matthew Towns? Who—"

"Of course you would not remember," said Sara hastily, for she had noticed that pause, and the tone of the question did not carry conviction. "I mean the porter who was sent to the penitentiary for the attempted wreck of the Klan Special."

"Oh, that—scoundrel."

"Yes. There is, as perhaps you know, a great deal of talk about his silence. He must know—lots of things. I think it rather fine in him to shield—others. I hope he won't break down in jail and talk."

Mrs. Therwald started perceptibly.

"Talk about what?" she asked almost sharply.

Sara was quite satisfied and continued easily. "Well, about the black conspirators against the Ku Klux Klan—or the white ones, because they are more likely to be white. Or he might gossip and just stir up trouble. But I think he's too big for all that. You know, I saw him and talked to him—really handsome, for a colored man. Oh, by the by—but of course not. I was going to ask if by any possibility you had seen him on the train."

"I—I really don't know."

"Of course you wouldn't remember definitely. But to come to the point of my visit: certain highly placed persons are convinced from new evidence, which cannot be published, that Towns is a victim and not a criminal. They are therefore seeking to have Towns pardoned, and I thought how fine it would be if you could induce your husband and someother high officials of the Klan to sign the petition. How grateful he would be! I think it would be the biggest and fairest gesture the Klan ever made, and frankly, many people are saying so. In that case, if he is a conspirator, he could be watched and traced and his helpers found. And then, too, think of his gratitude to *you!*"

Sara left the petition with Mrs. Therwald, and they talked on pleasantly and casually for another half-hour. Miss Andrews "would stay to tea"? "But no—so sorry." Sara said that she had stayed already much longer than she had planned, and hoped she had not bored Mrs. Therwald with her gossip. In truth she did not want to let the lady eat with one who, she might later discover, was a "nigger." They parted most cordially.

Mrs. Therwald happened a week later to say casually to her husband:

"That Towns nigger that they sent to jail—don't you think he'd be safer outside than in? He seemed a decent sort of chap on the trip. I was thinking it might be a shrewd gesture for the Klan to help free him."

Her husband looked at her hard and said nothing. But he did some thinking. That very day the white Democrats of Chicago had complained to the Klan that their small but formerly growing Negro vote was disappearing because of the Klan meeting and the Towns incident. Illinois with its growing Negro vote would be no longer a doubtful state politically unless something was done. How would it do to free Towns?

III

Miss Sara Andrews sat in the anteroom of the office of the Grand Dragon of the Ku Klux Klan in Washington. Several persons looked at her curiously.

"I believe she's a nigger," said a stenographer.

"Italian or Spanish, I would say," replied the chief clerk and frowned, for Sara had decided to wait. She said that she must really see Mr. Green personally and privately. After an hour's wait, she saw him. Mr. Green turned toward her a little impatiently, for she was interrupting a full day.

"What can I do for you?" and he glanced at her card and started to say, "Miss Andrews." Then he looked at her slightly olive skin and the suggestion of a curve in her hair and compromised on "Madam."

Miss Andrews began calmly with lowered eyes. She had on a new midnight-blue tailor-made frock with close-fitting felt hat to match, gay-cuffed black kid gloves, gun-metal stockings, and smart black patent leather pumps. On the whole she was pleased with her appearance.

"I am trying to get a pardon for Matthew Towns, and I want your help."

"Who is Matthew Towns?"

The question again did not carry the conviction that Mr. Green did not really remember. But Sara was discreet and carefully rehearsed the case.

"Oh, yes, I remember—well, he got what he deserved, didn't he?"

"No, he saved the train and got what somebody else deserved."

"Why didn't he reveal the real culprits?"

"That is the point. He may be shielding some persons who we might all agree should be shielded. He may be shielding the dead. He may be shielding criminals now free to work and conspire. But in all probability, he does not know who planned the deed. He was a blind tool. In any case he should go free. For surely, Mr. Green, no one is foolish enough to believe this was the plan of a mere porter."

"Have you any new evidence?"

"Not exactly court evidence," said Sara, "and yet I betray no confidence when I say that we have information and it is much in favor of Towns."

"And what do you want of me?"

"I have come to ask you to sign a request for Matthew Towns' pardon. You see, if you do, it will clear up the whole matter." And she looked Mr. Green full in the face. Her eyes were a bit hard, but her voice was almost caressing.

"I am sure," she said, "that the colored people of America are needlessly alarmed over the Klan, and that you are really their friends in the long run. Nothing would prove this more clearly than a fine, generous action on your part like this."

"But do you think it possible that Towns knows—nothing more of the real perpetrators of the plot?"

"If he did, why didn't he talk? Why doesn't he talk now? Reporters would rush to print his story. Indeed, the longer he stays in jail, the more he may *try* to remember. No, Mr. Green, I am sure that Towns either knows nothing more or will never tell it in jail or out."

Mr. Green signed the petition.

A month later, in Chicago, Sammy was close closeted with his congressman.

"This Towns matter: Pullman people are willing; railroads don't object. Even the Klan is asking for it, and the Republicans better move before the Democrats get credit."

Two weeks later the congressman saw the chairman of the National Republican Committee. The matter got to the Governor a week after that. In April it was very quietly announced that because of certain new evidence and other considerations, and at the request of the Ku Klux Klan, Matthew Towns had been pardoned. The Honorable Sammy Scott and his secretary went to Joliet and took the pardon to the prisoner.

IV

The great Jewish synagogue in Chicago, which the African Methodist Church had bought for half a million dollars in mortgages, was packed to its doors, May first, and an almost riotous crowd outside was demanding admittance. The Honorable Sammy Scott promised them an overflow meeting. Within, all the dignitaries of black Chicago were present. And, in addition, the mayor, the congressman from the black belt, and an unusual outpouring of reporters, represented the great white city. On the platform in the center in a high-backed, heavily-church chair sat the presiding officer, the Right Reverend John Carnes, Presiding Bishop of the District—an inspiring figure, too fat, but black and dignified. At his left sat the mayor, two colored members of the legislature, and several clergymen. At his right sat two aldermen and a congressman, and a tall, thin young man with drawn face and haunted eyes.

Matthew Towns made a figure almost pitiful. He sat drooping forward, half filling the wide chair, and staring blankly at the great audience. At his left was the chairman, and at his right sat the fat old congressman in careless dress, with his shifty eyes; down below the great audience milled and stirred, whispered and quivered.

It was an impressive sight. Every conceivable color of skin glowed and reflected beneath the glare of electricity. There was the strong bronze that burned almost black beneath the light, and the light brown that was a glowing gold. There was every shade of brown, from red oak to copper gold. There were all the shades of gold and cream. And there were yellows that were red and brown; and chalk-like white.

There was every curl and dress of hair. There was every style of clothing, from jewels and evening dress to the rough, clean Sunday coat of the laborer and the blue mohair of his wife. All expressions played on the upturned faces: inquiry, curiosity, eager anticipation, cynical doubt.

The Honorable Sammy was nervous. He did not go on the platform. He hovered back in the rear of the audience, with a hearty handshake here and a slap on the back there.

"*Hel*-lo, old man. Well, well, *well*! And Johnson, as I am alive! My God! But you're looking fit, my boy, *fit*. Well, what's the good word? What do you know? Mother James, as I'm a sinner! Here, Jack! Seat for Mrs. James? *Must* find one. Why, I'd—" etc., etc.

But Sammy was nervous. He didn't "like the look of that bird on the platform." Somehow, he didn't look the part. Why, my God, with that audience he had the cream and pick of black Chicago and the ears of the world. There was one of the *Tribune's* best men, and the *Examiner* and the *News* and the Port had reporters. Good Lord, what a scoop, if they could put it over! He had Chicago in the palm of his hand. But "that bird don't look the part!" and Sammy groaned aloud.

Sara had pushed him into this. She was getting too bossy, too domineering; he'd have to put the reins on her, perhaps get rid of her altogether. Well, not that, of course; she was valuable, but she must stop making him do things against his better judgment. He never had quite cottoned to this jailbird, nohow. Who ever heard of a sane man going to jail to save somebody else? It wasn't natural. Something *must* be wrong with him. Look at those eyes.

Where was Sara? Perhaps she could manage to pump some gumption into him, even at the last moment. If this thing failed, if Towns said the wrong thing or didn't say the right one, he would be knocked into a cocked hat. He had had a hard time bringing the pardon off anyhow. The congressman was skittish; feared the Governor: "Don't like to touch it, Sam. My advice is to drop it."

But Sammy, egged on by Sara, had insisted.

"All right, I'll try it. But look here, nothing else. If I pull this pardon through, that five thousand dollars I promised for the campaign is off. I can't milk the railroads for both."

Sammy had hesitated and consulted Sara.

"Five thousand dollars is five thousand dollars."

W.E.B. DU BOIS

And then he would need the cash this fall. But Sara was adamant.

"Five thousand dollars isn't a drop compared with this if we put it over."

And now Sammy groaned again. If he failed—"God damn it to hell!—*Where* is Sara?"

The exercises had opened. A rousing chorus began that raised the roof and hurled its rhythm against the vibrating audience; an impressive and dignified introduction by the Bishop, and a witty, even if somewhat evasive, speech by the mayor. Sammy began to sweat, and his smile wore off.

The congressman started to introduce the "gentleman whom we all are waiting to hear—the hero, the martyr—Matthew Towns!" There was a shout that rose, gathered, and broke. Then a hush fell over the audience. Matthew seemed to hesitate. He started to rise—stopped, looked helplessly about, and then got slowly to his feet and leaned against the pulpit awkwardly.

"O Lord!" groaned Sammy, "*O Lord*!"

"I am not a speaker," said Matthew slowly.

("It's the God's truth," said Sammy).

"I have really nothing to say." ("And you're sure sayin' it, bo," snarled Sammy). "And if I had I would not know how to." And then he straightened up and added reflectively, "I am—my speech." The audience rustled and Sammy was faint.

"I was born in Virginia—" And then swiftly and conversationally there came the story of his boyhood and youth; of his father and mother; of the cabin and the farm. He had not meant to talk of this. The speech which Sara had at his request prepared for him had nothing of this, but he was thinking of his home. Then followed naturally the story of his student days, of his work and struggles, of the medical school, of the prizes, of his dreams. The audience sat in strained and almost deathly silence, craned forward, scarcely breathing, at the twice-told human tale that touched everyone of them, that they knew by heart, that they had lived through each in its thousand variations, and which was working unconsciously to the perfect climax.

("My God"—whispered Sammy—"he's putting it over—he's putting it over. He's a genius or God's anointed fool!")

Finally Matthew came to that day of return to his junior medical year. He saw the scene again—he felt the surge of hot anger; his voice, his great, full, beautiful voice, rose as again he threw his certificates into the face of the dean. The house roared and rang with applause—the men shouted, the women cried, and up from the Amen corner rose the roll and cadence of the slave song: "Before I'd be a slave I'd be buried in my grave and go home to my God and be free!"

Sammy leaned against the back wall glowing. It was a diamond stickpin for Sara!

Matthew awoke from the hypnotism of his own words, and the fierce enthusiasm died suddenly away. Yet he was no longer afraid of his audience or wanting words. With unconscious artistry he let his climax rest where it was, and he stood a moment with brooding eyes—a lean, handsome, cadaverous figure—and told the rest of his story in even, matter-of-fact tones.

"I ran away from my people and my work. I tried to hide, but I was sent back. I worked as a porter, and I tried to be a good porter. And all the time I wanted to help—to do a great thing for freedom and strike a great blow. I met a man. He was a fanatic; he was sinking into sin, and worse, he was planning a terrible deed. I sensed it and tried to dissuade him from it. I pointed out its impossibility and futility. But he cursed me for a coward and went on. I could have run away; I could have betrayed him. I did instead an awful thing—an awful deed which the death of an innocent man spurred me to. I do not know whether I was right or wrong, but I resolved to die on the train that my brave friend was resolved to wreck—and then—" Matthew paused, and the audience almost sobbed in suspense. "And then on the rushing train, Something would not let me do what I had planned. The credit is not mine. Something hindered; I stopped the train, but I did not betray my terrible friend. I went to jail. My friend—died—" He paused and groped; what was it he must say? What was it to which he must not forget to allude? He stood in silence and then remembered: "And, tonight, through the efforts of Sammy Scott I am free."

That minute the Honorable Sammy Scott reached the apex of his career. The next day Matthew got a job, and Sara Andrews a diamond stickpin.

V

In jail Matthew Towns had let his spirit die. He had become one with the great gray walls, the dim iron gratings, the thud, thud, thud which *was* the round of life, which was life. Bells and marching, work and meals, meals and work, marching and whistles. Even, unchanging level of life, without interest, memory, or hope.

This at first; then, disturbing little things. As the greater life receded, the lesser took on exaggerated importance. The food, the chapel speaker, this whispered quarrel over less than a trifle; the oath and blows of a keeper.

"When I get out!"

Ten years! Ten years was never. If such a space as ten years ever passed, he would come back again to jail.

"They all do," said the keepers; "if not here, elsewhere."

The seal of crime was on him. It would never lift. It could not; it was ground down deep into his soul. He was nothing, wanted nothing, remembered nothing, and even if he did remember the trailing glory of a cloudlike garment, the music of a voice, the kissing of a drooping, jeweled hand—he murdered the memory and buried it in its own blood.

Then came the miracle. First that neat and self-reliant young woman who tried to make him talk. He was inclined to be surly at first, but suddenly the walls fell away, and he saw great shadowed trees and rich grass. He was bending over a dainty tea-table, and he talked as he had talked once before. But he stopped suddenly, angry at the vision, angry at himself. He became mute, morose. He took leave of Sara Andrews abruptly and went back to his bench. He was working on wood.

Then came the pardon. In a daze and well-nigh wordless, he had traveled to Chicago. He sat in the church like a drowning swimmer who, hurled miraculously to life again, breathed, and sank. He had no illusions left.

He knew Sara and Sammy. They wanted to use him. Well, why not? They had bought him and paid for him. All his enthusiasm, all his hope, all his sense of reality was gone. He saw life as a great, immovable, terrible thing. It had beaten him, ground him to the earth and beneath; this sudden resurrection did not make him dizzy or give him any real hope. He gave up all thought of a career, of leadership, of greatly or essentially changing this world. He would protect himself from hurt. He would be of enough use to others to insure this. He must have money—not wealth—but enough to support himself in simple comfort. He saw a chance for this in politics under the command of Sara and Sammy.

He had no illusions as to American democracy. He had learned as a porter and in jail how America was ruled. He knew the power of organized crime, of self-indulgence, of industry, business, corporations, finance, commerce. They all paid for what they wanted the government to do for them—for their immunity, their appetites; for their incomes, for justice and the police. This trading of permission, license, monopoly, and immunity in return for money was engineered by politicians; and through their hands the pay went to the voters for their votes. Sometimes the pay was in cash, sometimes in jobs, sometimes in "influence," sometimes in better streets, houses, or schools. He deliberately and with his eyes closed made himself a part of this system. Some of this money, paid to master politicians like Sammy Scott, would come to him, some, but not much; he would save it and use it.

He settled in the colored workingmen's quarter of the Second Ward—a thickly populated nest of laborers, lodgers, idlers, and semi-criminals. In an old apartment house he took the top-most flat of four dilapidated rooms and moved in with an old iron bed, a chair, and a bureau.

Then he set out to know his district, to know every man, woman and child in it. He was curiously successful. In a few months scarcely a person passed him on the street who did not greet him. The November elections came, and his district rolled up a phenomenal majority for Scott's men; it was almost unanimous.

He deliberately narrowed his life to his village, as he called it. One side of it lay along State Street in its more dreary and dilapidated quarter. It ran along three blocks and then back three blocks west. Here were nine blocks—old, dirty, crowded—with staggering buildings of brick and wood lining them. The streets were obstructed with bad paving, ashes, and garbage. On one corner was a church. Then followed several places where one could buy food and liquor. On State Street were a dance hall, a movie house, and several billiard parlors, interspersed with more or less regular gambling dens. There were a half-dozen halls where lodges met and where fairs and celebrations were carried on. And all over were the homes—good, bad, indifferent.

He was strangely interested in this little universe of his. It had within a few blocks everything life offered. He could find religion—intense, fanatical, grafting, self-sacrificing. He could find prostitutes and thieves, stevedores, masons, laborers, and porters. Thus his blocks were a pulsing world, and in them there was always plenty to do—a donation to the church when the mortgage interest was about due; charity for the old women whose sons and daughters had wandered off; help and a physician for the sick and those who had fallen and broken hip or leg or had been run over by automobile trucks; shoes and old clothes for school children, bail for criminals; drinks for tramps; rent for the dance hall; food for the wild-eyed wastrels; and always, jobs, jobs, jobs for the workers.

When the new colored grocery was started, Matthew had to corral its customers, many of whom he had bailed out for crime. The police were his especial care. He gave them information, and they tipped him off. He restrained them, or egged them on. He warned the gamblers or got them new quarters. He got jobs for men and women and girls and boys. He helped professional men to get off jury duty. He sent young girls home and found older girls in places worse than home. He did not judge; he did not praise or condemn. He accepted what he saw.

Always, in the midst of this he was organizing and coraling his voters. He knew the voting strength of his district to a man. Nine-tenths of them would do exactly as he said. He did not need to talk to them—a few words and a sign. Orators came to his corners and vociferated and yelled, but his followers watched him. He saw this group of thousands of people as a real and thrilling thing, which he watched, unthrilled, unmoved. Life was always tense and rushing there—a murder, a happy mother, thieves, strikers, scabs, school children, and hard workers; a strange face, a man going into business, a girl going to hell, a woman saved. The whole organism was neither good nor bad. It was good and bad. Rickety buildings, noise, smells, noise, work—hard, hard work—

"How's Sammy?" he would hear them say.

"How many votes do you want? Name your man."

Thus he built his political machine. His machine was life, and he stood close to it—lolling on his favorite corner with half-closed eyes; yet he saw all of it. Above it all, on the furthermost corner, on the top floor, were his bare, cold, and dirty rooms. He could not for the life of him remember how people kept things clean. It was extraordinary how dirt accumulated. He never had much money. Sammy handed him over a roll of bills every now and then, but he spent it in his charities, in his gifts, in his bribings, in his bonds. There was never much left. Sometimes there washardly enough for his food.

Long past midnight he usually climbed to his bare rooms—one of them absolutely bare—one with a bed, a chair, and a bureau—one with an oil stove, a chair, and a table.

Then in time the aspect of his rooms began to change. A day came when he went in for his usual talk with the secondhand man. Old Gray was black and bent, and part of his business was receiving stolen goods, the other part was quite legitimate buying and selling secondhand stuff. Towns strolled in there and saw a rug. He had forgotten ever having seen a rug before then. Of course he had—there in Berlin on the Lützower Ufer there was a rug in the parlor—but he shook the memory away with a toss of his head.

This rug was marvelous. It burned him with its brilliance. It sang to his eyes and hands. It was yellow and green—it was thick and soft; but all this didn't tell the subtle charm of its weaving and shadows of coloring. He tried to buy it, but Gray insisted on giving it to him. He declared that it was not stolen, but Towns was sure that it was. Perhaps Gray was afraid to keep it, but Towns took it at midday and laid it on the floor of the barest of his empty rooms. Connors, who was a first-class carpenter when he was not drunk. was out of work again. Towns brought him up and had him put a parquet floor in the bare room. He was afterward half ashamed to take that money from his constituents, but he paid them back by more careful attention to their demands. Then in succeeding months of little things, the beauty of that room grew.

VI

The Honorable Sammy was by turns surprised, dumbfounded, and elated. He could not decide at various times whether Towns was a new kind of fool or the subtlest of subtle geniuses; but at any rate he was more than satisfied, and the efficiency of his machine was daily growing.

The black population of Chicago was still increasing. Properly organized and led, there were no ordinary limits to its power, except excited race rancor as at the time of the riot, or internal jealousy and bickering. Careful, thoughtful manipulation was the program, and this was the Honorable Sammy's long suit. First of all he had to appease and cajole and wheedle his own race, allay the jealousies of other leaders—professional, religious, and political—and get them to vote as they were told.

This was no easy job. Sammy accomplished it by following Sara's advice; first he refused all the more spectacular political offices; he refused to run again as alderman, declined election to the legislature and the like; he secured instead a state commissionership (whence his "honorable") where he still had power but little display; and of course, he was on the State Central Republican committee; then he "played" the clergy, helping with speeches and contributions of large size to lift their mortgages; he stood behind the colored teachers who were edging into the schools; he belonged to every known fraternal order, and at the same time he continued to protect the cabarets, the bootleggers, the gambling dens, and the "lodging" houses. Slowly in these ways his influence and word became well-nigh supreme in the colored world. Everybody "liked" the Honorable Sammy.

And Sammy found Matthew an invaluable lieutenant.

"By gum, Sara, we have turned a trick. To tell the truth, for a long time I distrusted that bird, even after his great speech. I was afraid he'd be a highbrow and start out reforming. Damned if he ain't the best worker I ever had."

"Yes, he'll do for the legislature," said Sara. Sammy scowled.

That was like Sara. Whenever he yielded an inch, off she skipped with an ell.

"Slow, slow," he said frowning; "we can't push a new man and a jailbird too fast."

"Sammy, you're still a fool. Don't you see that this is the only man we can push, because he's tied to us body and soul?"

"I ain't so sure—"

"Sh!"

Matthew came in. He greeted them diffidently, almost shyly. He always felt naked before these two.

They talked over routine matters, and then without preliminaries Matthew said abruptly, "I'd like to take a short vacation. I ought to see my old mother in Virginia."

"Sure," said Sammy cheerfully, and drew out a roll of bills. Matthew hesitated, counted out a few bills, and handed the rest back.

"Thanks!" he said, and with no further word turned and went out.

Sammy's jaw dropped. He stared at the bills in his hand and at the door. "I don't like that handing dough back," he said. "It ain't natural."

"He may be honest," said Sara.

"And in politics? Humph! Wonder just what his game is? I wish he'd grin a little more and do the glad hand act!"

"Do you want the earth?" asked Sara.

It was Christmas time, 1924, when Matthew came back to Virginia after five years of absence. Winter had hardly begun, and the soft glow of Autumn still lingered on the fields. He stopped at the county seat three miles from home and went to the recorder's office. It was as he had thought; his mother's little farm of twenty acres was mortgaged, and only by the good-natured indulgence of the mortgagee was she living there and paying neither interest nor rent.

"Don't want to disturb Sally, you know. She's our folks. Used to belong to my grandfather. So you're her boy, hey? Heard you was dead—then heard you was in jail. Well, well; and what's your business—er—and what's your name? Matthew Towns? Sure, sure, the old family name. Well, Matthew, it'll take near on a thousand dollars to clear that place."

Matthew paid five hundred cash and arranged to pay the rest and to buy the other twenty acres next year—the twenty acres of tangled forest, hill, and brook that he always had wanted as a boy; but his father strove for the twenty smoother acres—strove and failed.

Then slowly Matthew walked out into the country and into the night. He slept in an empty hut beside the road and listened to creeping things. He heard the wind, the hooting of the owls, and saw the sun rise, pale gold and crimson, over the eastern trees. He washed his face by the roadside and then sat waiting—waiting for the world.

He sat there in the dim, sweet morning and swung his long limbs. He was a boy again, with the world before him. Beyond the forest, it lay magnificent—wonderful—beautiful—beautiful as one unforgettable face. He leaped to the ground and clenched his hand. A wave of red shame smothered his heart. He had not known such a rush of feeling for a year. He thought he had forgotten how to feel. He knew now why he had come here. It was not simply to see that poor old mother. It was to walk in *her* footsteps, to know if she had carried his last message.

A bowed old black man crept down the road.

"Good morning, sir."

"Good mo'nin—good mo'nin'. Fine mo'nin'. And who might you be, sah? 'Pears like I know you."

"I am Matthew Towns."

The old man slowly came nearer. He stretched out his hand and touched Matthew. And then he said:

"She said you wuzn't dead. She said God couldn't let you die till she put her old hands on your head. And she sits waitin' for you always, waitin' in the cabin do'."

Matthew turned and went down to the brook and crossed it and walked up through the black wood and came to the fence.

She was sitting in the door, straight, tall, big and brown. She was singing something low and strong. And her eyes were scanning the highway. Matthew leaped the fence and walked slowly toward her down the lane.

VII

Sara Andrews sat in Matthew's flat in the spring of 1925 and looked around with a calculating glance. It was in her eyes a silly room; a man's room, of course. It was terribly dirty and yet with odd bits—a beautiful but uneven parquet floor, quite new; a glorious and costly rug that had never been swept; old books and pamphlets lay piled about, and in the center was a big dilapidated armchair, sadly needing new upholstery. The room was proof that Matthew needed a home. She would invite him to hers. It might lead to something, and Sara looked him over carefully as he bent over the report which she had brought. Outside his haunted eyes and a certain perpetual lack of enthusiasm, he was very good to look at. Very good. He needed a good barber and a better tailor. Sara's eyes narrowed. She didn't quite like the fact that he never noticed *her* tailor nor hairdresser.

They were expecting the Honorable Sammy to breeze in any moment. They formed a curious troika, these three: Sammy, the horse of guidance in the shafts, was the expert on the underworld—the "boys," liquor, prostitution, and the corresponding parts of the white world. He was the practical politician; he saw that votes were properly counted, jobs distributed where they would do his organization most good; and he handled the funds. Sara was intellectually a step higher; she knew the business interests of the city and what they could and would pay for privilege. She was in touch with public service organizations and chambers of commerce and knew all about the leading banks and corporations. Her letters and advice did tricks and brought a growing stream of gold of which Sammy had never before dreamed. Alas, too, it brought interference with some of his practical plans and promises which annoyed him, although he usually yielded under pressure.

Matthew was quite a different element. On the one hand he knew the life of his section of the Chicago black world as no one else. He had not artificially extracted either the good or the evil for study and use—he took it all in with one comprehensive glance and thus could tell what church and school and labor thought and did, as well as the mind of the underworld. At the other end of the scale was his knowledge of national and international movements; his ability to read and digest reports and recent literature was an invaluable guide for Sara and corrective for Sammy.

Much of all this report and book business was Greek to Sammy. Sammy never read anything beyond the headlines of newspapers, and they had to be over an inch high to get his undivided attention. Gossip from high and low sources brought him his main information. Sara read the newspapers, and Matthew the magazines and books. Thus Sammy's political bark skimmed before the golden winds with rare speed and accuracy,

Sammy came in, and they got immediately to business.

"I'm stumped by this legislature business," growled Sammy.

"Smith picked a hell of a time to die. Still, p'raps it was best. There was a lot of stink over him anyhow. Now here comes a special election, and if we ain't careful it'll tear the machine to pieces. Every big nigger in Chicago wants the job. We need a careful man or hell'll be to pay. I promised the next opening to Corruthers. He expects it and he's earned it; Corruthers will raise hell and spill the beans if I fail him."

"Smith was a fool," said Sara, "and Corruthers is a bag of wind when he's sober and an idiot when he's drunk, which is his usual condition. We've got to can that type. We've got to have a man of brains and knowledge in the legislature this fall, or we'll lose out. We're in fair way to make 'Negro' and grafter' synonymous in Illinois office-holding. It won't do, There's some big legislation coming up—street-car consolidation and super-power. Here's a chance, Sammy, to put in our own man, and a man of high type, instead of boosting a rival boss and courting exposure for bribery."

"Well, can't we tell Corruthers how to act and vote? He ought to stay put."

"No. There are somethings that can't be told. Corruthers is a born petty grafter. When he sees a dollar, he goes blind to everything else. He has no imagination nor restraint. We can't be at his shoulder at every turn; he'd be sure to sell out for the flash of a hundred-dollar bill anytime and lose a thousand and get in jail. Then, too, if he should make good, next year Boss Corruthers would be fighting Boss Scott."

Sammy swore. "If I ditch him, I'll lose this district."

"With a strong nomination there's a chance," said Matthew. Sara glanced at him and added: "Especially if I organize the women."

Sammy tore at his hair: "Don't touch 'em," he cried. "Let 'em alone! My God! What'd I do with a bunch of skirts dippin' in? Ain't we got 'em gagged like they ought to be? What's the matter with the State Colored Women's Republican Clubs? And the Cook County organization, with their chairman sitting in on the County Central and women on each ward committee?"

But Sara was obdurate. "Don't be a fool, Sammy. You know these women are nothing but 'me-too's,' or worse, for the men. I'm going to have a new organization, independent of the ward bosses and loyal to us. I'm going to call it the Chicago Colored Woman's Council—no, it isn't going to be called Republican, Democratic, or Socialist; just colored. I'm going to make it a real political force independent of the men. The women are in politics already, although they don't know it, and somebody is going to tell them soon. Why not us? And see that they vote right?"

"The white women's clubs are trying to bring the colored clubs in line for a stand on the street-car situation and new working-women laws," added Matthew.

Sammy brooded. "I don't like it. It's dangerous. Once give 'em real power, and who can hold them?"

"I can."

"Yes, and who'll hold you?"

Sara did not answer, and Sammy switched back to the main matter.

"I s'pose we've got to hunt another man for Smith's place. I see a fight ahead."

Matthew's guests left, and he discovered that he had forgotten to get his laundry for now the second week. He stepped down to the Chinaman's for his shirts and a chat.

Then came a shock, as when an uneasy sleeper, drugged with weariness, hears the alarm of dawn. The Chinaman liked him and was grateful for protection against the police and rowdies. He liked the Chinaman for his industry, his cleanliness, his quiet philosophy of life. Once he tried a pipe of opium there, but it frightened him. He saw a Vision.

Tonight the Chinaman was "velly glad" to see him. Had been watching for him several days—had "a flend" who knew him. Matthew looked about curiously, and there in the door stood his young Chinese friend of Berlin. Several times in his life—oh, many many times, that dinner scene had returned vividly to his imagination, but never so vividly as now. It leapt to reality. The sheen of the silver and linen was there before him, the twinkling of cut glass; he heard the low and courteous conversation—the soft tones of the Japanese, the fuller tones of the Egyptian, and then across it all the sweet I roll of that clear contralto—dear God!—He gripped himself and hurled the vision back to hell.

"How do you do!" he said calmly, shaking the Chinaman's eager hand.

"I am so glad—so glad to see you," the Chinaman said. "I am hurrying home to China, but I heard you were here, and I had to wait to see you. How—"

But Matthew interrupted hastily, "And how is China?"

The yellow face glowed. "The great Day dawns," he said. "Freedom begins. Russia is helping. We are marching forward. The Revolution is on. To the sea with Europe and European slavery! Oh, I am happy."

"But will it be easy sailing?"

"No, no—hard—hard as hell. We are in for suffering, starvation, revolt and reverse, treason and lying. But we have begun. The beginning is everything. We shall never end until freedom comes, if it takes a thousand years."

"You have been living in America?"

"Six months. I am collecting funds. It heartens one to see how these hard-working patriots give. I have collected two millions of dollars."

"God!" groaned Matthew. "Our N. A. A. C. P. collected seventy-five thousand dollars in two years, and twelve million damn near fainted with the effort."

The Chinaman looked sympathetic.

"Ah," he said hesitatingly. "Doesn't it go so well here?"

"Go? What?"

"Why—Freedom, Emancipation, Uplift—union with all the dark and oppressed."

Matthew smiled thinly. The strange and unfamiliar words seemed to drift back from a thousand forgotten years. He hardly recognized their meaning.

"There's no such movement here," he said.

The Chinaman looked incredulous.

"But," he said "but you surely have not forgotten the great word you yourself brought us out of the West that night—that word of faith in opportunity for the lowest?"

"Bosh!" growled Matthew harshly. "That was pure poppycock. Dog eat dog is all I see; I'm through with all that. Well, I'm glad to have seen you again. So long, and goodbye."

The Chinaman looked troubled and almost clung to Matthew's hand.

"The most hopeless of deaths," he said, as Matthew drew away, "is the death of Faith. But pardon me, I go too far. Only one other thing before we part. John here wants me to tell you about some conditions in this district which he thinks you ought to know. Organized crime and debauchery are pressing pretty hard on labor. You have such an opportunity here—I hoped to help by putting you in touch with some of the white laboring folk and their leaders."

"I know them all," said Matthew, "and I'm not running this district as a Sunday School."

He bowed abruptly and hastened away.

VIII

Matthew was uncomfortable. The demon of unrest was stirring drowsily away down in the half-conscious depths of his soul. For the long months since his incarceration he had been content just to be free, to breathe and look at the sunshine. He did not think. He tried not to think. He just lived and narrowed himself to the round of his duties. As those duties expanded, he read and studied, but always in the groove of his work. Sternly he held his mind down and in. No more flights; no more dreams; no more foolishness.

Now, as he felt restless and dissatisfied, he laid it to nerves, lack of physical exercise, some hidden illness. But gradually he began to tell himself the truth. The dream, the woman, was back in his soul. The vision of world work was surging and he must kill it, stifle it now, and sternly, lest it wreck his life again. Still he was restless. He was awakening. He could feel the prickling of life in his thought, his conscience, his body. He was struggling against the return of that old ache—the sense of that void. He was angry and irritated with his apparent lack of control. If he could once fill that void, he could glimpse another life—beauty, music, books, leisure; a home that was refuge and comfort. Something must be done. Then he remembered an almost forgotten engagement.

Soon he was having tea in Sara's flat. He began to feel more comfortable. He looked about. It was machine-made, to be sure, but it was wax-neat and in perfect order. The tea was good, and the cream—he liked cream—thick and sweet. Sara, too, in her immaculate ease was restful. He leaned back in his chair, and the brooding lifted a little from his eyes. He told Sara of a concert he had attended.

"Have you ever happened to hear Ivanoff's 'Caucasian Sketches'?"

Sara had not; but she said suddenly, "How would you like to go to the legislature?"

Matthew laughed carelessly. "I wouldn't like it," he said and sauntered over to look at a new set of books. He asked Sara if she liked Balzac. Sara had just bought the set and had not read a word. She had bought them to fill the space above the writing-desk. It was just twenty-eight inches. She let him talk on and then she gave him some seed-cakes which a neighbor had made for her. He came back and sat down. He tested the cakes, liked them, and ate several. Then Sara took up the legislature again.

"You can talk—you have read, and you have the current political questions at your fingers' ends. Your district will stand with you to a man. Old-timers like Corruthers will knife you, but I can get you every colored woman's vote in the ward, and they can get a number of the white women by trading."

"I don't want the notoriety."

"But you want money—power—ease."

"Yes I want money, but this will take money, and I have none."

"I have," said Sara. And she added, "We might work together with what I've saved and what we both know."

Matthew got up abruptly, walked over and stared out the window. He had had a similar idea, and he thought it originated in his own head. He had not noticed Sara much hitherto. He had not noticed any woman, since—since—

But he knew Sara was intelligent and a hard worker. She looked simple, clean, and capable. She seemed to him noticeably lonely and needing someone to lean on. She could make a home. He never had had just the sort of home he wanted. He wanted a home—something like his own den, but transfigured by capable hands—and devotion. Perhaps a wife would stop this restless longing—this inarticulate Thing in his soul.

Was this not the whole solution? He was living a maimed, unnatural life—no love, no close friendships; always loneliness and brooding. Why not emerge and be complete? Why not marry Sara? Marriage was normal. Marriage stopped secret longings and wild open revolt. It solved the woman problem once and for all. Once married, he would be safe, settled, quiet; with all the furies at rest, calm, satisfied; a reader of old books, a listener to sad and quiet music, a sleeper.

Sara watched him and after a pause said in an even voice:

"You have had a hard shock and you haven't recovered yet. But you're young. With your brains and looks the world is open to you. You can go to the legislature, and if you play your cards right you can go to Congress and be the first colored congressman from the North. Think it over, Mr. Towns."

Towns turned abruptly. "Miss Andrews," he said, "will you marry me?"

"Why—Mr. Towns!" she answered.

He hurried on: "I haven't said anything about love on your side or mine—"

"Don't!" she said, a bit tartly. "I've been fighting the thing men call love all my life, and I don't see much in it. I don't think you are the loving kind—and that suits me. But I do think enlightened self-interest calls us to be partners. And if you really mean this, I am willing."

Matthew went slowly over and took her hand. They looked at each other and she smiled. He had meant to kiss her, but he did not.

It was a grand wedding. Matthew was taken back by Sara's plans. He had thoughts of the little church of his district—and perhaps a quiet flitting away to the Michigan woods, somewhere up about Idlewild. There they might sit in sunshine and long twilights and get acquainted. He would take this lonely little fighting soul in his arms and tell her honestly of that great lost love of his soul, which was now long dead; and then slowly a new, calm communion of souls, a silent understanding, would come, and they would go hand in hand back to the world.

But nothing seemed further from Sara's thought. First she was going to elect Matthew to the legislature, and then in the glory of his triumph there was going to be a wedding that would make black Chicago sit up and even white Chicago take due notice. Thirdly, she was going to reveal to a gaping world that she already owned that nearly new, modern, and beautifully equipped apartment on South Parkway which had just been sold at auction. There was a vague rumor that a Negro had bought it, but none but Sara and her agent knew.

"How on earth did you—" began Matthew.

"I'm not in politics for my health," said Sara, "and you're not going to be, after this. It's got three apartments of seven rooms with sleeping porches, verandas, central heating, and refrigeration. We'll live in the top apartment and rent the other two. We can get easily three thousand a year from them, which will support us and a maid. I've been paying for a car by installments a—Studebaker—and learning to drive, for we can't afford a chauffeur yet."

Matthew sat down slowly.

"Don't you think we might rent the whole and live somewhere—a little more quietly, so we could study and walk and—go to concerts?"

But Sara took no particular notice of this.

"I've been up to Tobey's to select the furniture, and Marshall Field is doing the decorating. We'll keep our engagement dark until after the nomination in the spring. Then we'll have a big wedding, run over to Atlantic City for the honeymoon, and come back fit for the fall campaign."

"Atlantic City? My God!" said Matthew, and then stopped as the door opened to admit the Honorable Sammy Scott.

Sammy was uneasy these days. He was in hot water over this legislature business, and he vaguely scented danger to his power and machine beyond this. First of all he could only square things with Corruthers and his followers by a good lump of money, if Matthew were nominated; and even then, they would try to knife him. Now Sammy's visible source for more money was more laxity in the semi-criminal districts and bribes from interests who wanted bills to pass the legislature. Sammy had given freer rein to the red-light district and doubted if he could do more there or collect much more money without inviting in the reformers. Big business seemed his only resort, but here he was not sure of Matthew. There might be a few nominees who were willing to pay a bit for the honor, but Matthew was not among these. Sara was managing his campaign, and she was too close and shrewd to cough up much. Then, too, Sammy was uneasy about Sara and Matthew. They were mighty thick and chummy and always having conferences. If he himself had been a marrying man—

"Say, Towns," he said genially, "I think I got that nomination cinched, but it's gonna take a pot of dough. Oh, well, what of it? You've got the inside track."

"Unless Corruthers double-crosses us," said Matthew dryly. "That's where the dough comes in. Now see here, I've got a proposition from the traction crowd. They want to ward off municipal ownership and get a new franchise citywide with consolidation. They're going to offer a five-cent car fare and reversion to the city in forty-nine years, and they're paying high for support. They're going to control the nomination in most districts."

"I'll vote against municipal ownership anytime," said Matthew.

Sammy was at once relieved and yet troubled anew. He had an idea that Matthew would get squeamish over this and would thus lose the nomination. That would force Corruthers in.

Sammy still leaned toward Corruthers. But, on the other hand, Corruthers would be sure to do some fool trick even if he were elected, and that or his defeat might ruin Sammy's own plans for Congress next year. He was glad Matthew was tractable, and at the same time he suddenly grew suspicious. Suppose Matthew went to the legislature and made a ripping record? He might himself dare think of Congress. But no—Sara was pledged to Sammy's plan for Congress.

"All right!" said Sammy noisily.

"But look here, Sammy," said Matthew. "Things are getting pretty loose and free down in my district. Casey has opened a new gambling den, and there's a lake of liquor; three policy wheels are running. The soliciting on the streets is open; it isn't safe for a working girl after dark."

"Well, ain't they payin' up prompt?"

"Yes—but—"

"Gettin' squeamish?" sneered Sammy. My God! Was the fool going to cut off the main graft and try to depend on white corporations?

"No—I'm not, but the reformers are. We're just bidding for interference at this rate."

"Hell," said Sammy. "It'll be whore-houses and not Sunday Schools that'll send you to Springfield, if you go." Matthew frowned.

Sara intervened. "I'll see that things are toned down a bit. Sammy will never learn that big business pays better than crime. I'm glad you're going to vote straight on the traction bill."

Matthew still frowned. They both had misunderstood him— curiously. They suspected him of mawkish sentimentality— conscience against gambling, liquor, and prostitution. Nothing of the sort! He had buried all sentiment, down, down, deep down. He was angry at being even suspected. Why was be angry? Was it because he felt the surge of that old bounding, silly self that once believed and hoped and dreamed—that dead soul, turning slowly and twisting in its grave? No, no, not that never. He simply meant to warn Sammy that a district too wide open defeated itself and invited outside interference; it cut off political graft; gamblers were cheating gamblers; the liquor on sale was poison; prostitutes were approaching the wrong people—and, well—surely a girl ought to have the right to choose between work and prostitution, and she ought not to be shanghaied.

And then Sara. She assumed too much. If he had the beginning of the unrest of a new conscience—and he had not—it was over these big corporations. He began to see them from behind and underneath. A five-cent fare was a tremendous issue to thousands. The driblets of perpetual tax on light and air and movement meant both poverty and millions. Surely the interests could pay better than gamblers and prostitutes, but was the graft as honest? Was he going on as unquestioningly? He had promised to vote against municipal ownership quickly and easily. Voters were too stupid or too careless to run big business. Municipal ownership, therefore, would only mean corporation control one degree removed and concealed from public view by election bribery. And after all, traction was not the real question. Super-power was that, and he talked his thought aloud to Sara, half-consciously:

"Oh—traction? Sure—that's only camouflage anyway. Back of it is the furnishing of electric power, cornering the waterfalls of America; paying nothing for the right of endless and limitless taxation, and then at last 'financing' the whole thing for a thousand millions and unloading it on the public! That's the real graft. I am going to think a long time over those bills!"

What did he mean by "thinking a long time"? He did not know what he meant. Neither did Sara. But she knew very clearly what she meant. She was silent and pursed her lips. She was already in close understanding with certain quiet and well-dressed gentlemen who represented Public Service and were reaching out toward Super-Power. They had long been distributing money in the Negro districts, but their policy was to encourage rivalry and jealousy between the black bosses and thus make them ineffective. This kept payments down. Sara had arranged for Sammy to make these payments, while the corporations dealt only with him. Also she had raised the price and promised to deliver four votes in the legislature and three in the Board of Aldermen. Finally, she had just arranged to have Sammy's personal representative occupy an office in the elegant suite of the big corporation attorney who advised Public Service and on his payroll as a personal link between Sammy and the big Public Service czar. It was the biggest single deal she had pulled off, and she hadn't yet told Sammy. The selection of that link called for much thought.

X

The house was finished complete with new and shining furniture, each piece standing exactly where it should. Matthew had particularly wanted a fireplace with real logs. He was a little ashamed to confess how much he wanted it. It was a sort of obsession. As long as he could remember, burning wood had meant home to him. Sara said a fireplace was both dirty and dangerous. She had an electric log put in. Matthew hated that log with perfect hatred.

The pictures and ornaments, too, he did not like, and at last, one day, he went downtown and bought a painting which he had long coveted. It was a copy of a master—cleverly and daringly done with a flame of color and a woman's long and naked body. It talked to Matthew of endless strife, of fire beauty and never-dying flesh. He bought, too, a deliciously ugly Chinese god. Sara looked at both in horror but said nothing. Months afterward when they had been married and had moved home, he searched in vain for the painting and finally inquired.

"That thing? But, Matthew, dear, folks don't have naked women in the parlor! I exchanged it for the big landscape there—it fits the space better and has a much finer frame." Sara let the ugly Chinese god crouch in a dark corner of the library.

The nomination went through smoothly. The "election of Mr. Matthew Towns, the rising young colored politician whose romantic history we all know" (thus *The Conservator*) followed in due and unhindered course, despite the efforts of Corruthers to knife him.

So in June came the wedding. It was a splendid affair. Sara's choice of a tailor was as unerringly correct as her selection of a dressmaker. They made an ideal couple as they marched down the aisle of the Michigan Avenue Baptist Tabernacle. Matthew looked almost distinguished, with that slight impression of remote melancholy; Sara seemed so capable and immaculate.

Sammy, the best man, swore under his breath. "If I'd only been a marrying man!" he confided to the pastor.

W.E.B. DU BOIS

The remark was made to Matthew's young ministerial friend, the Reverend Mr. Jameson, formerly of Memphis. He had come with his young shoulders to help lift the huge mortgages of this vast edifice, recently purchased at a fabulous price from a thrifty white congregation; the black invasion of South Side had sent them to worship Jesus Christ on the North Shore.

"Whom God hath joined together let no man put asunder," rolled the rich tones of the minister. Matthew saw two wells of liquid light, a great roll of silken hair that fell across a skin of golden bronze, and below, a single pearl shining at the parting of two little breasts.

"Straighten your tie," whispered Sara's metallic voice, and his soul came plunging back across long spaces and over heavy roads. He looked up and met the politely smiling eyes of the young Memphis school teacher who once gave him fifteen cents. She was among the chief guests with her fat husband, a successful physician. They both beamed. They quite approved of Matthew now.

"'Tis thy marriage morning, shining in the sun," yelled the choir, with invincible determination. The bridal pair stepped into the new Studebaker with a hired chauffeur and glided away. Matthew looked down at his slim white bride. A tenderness and pity swept over him. He slipped his arm about her shoulders.

"Be careful of the veil," said Sara.

XI

In Springfield, Matthew was again thrust into the world. He shrank at first and fretted over it. Most of the white legislators put up at the new Abraham Lincoln—a thoroughly modern hostelry, convenient and even beautiful in parts. Matthew did not apply. He knew he would be refused. He did try the Leland, conveniently located and the former rendezvous of the members. He had dinner and luncheon there, and after he discovered the limited boarding-house accommodation of colored Springfield, he asked for rooms—a bedroom and parlor. The management was very sorry—but—

He then went down to the colored hotel on South Eleventh Street. The hotel might do—but the neighborhood!

Finally, he found a colored private home not very far from the capítol. The surroundings were noisy and not pleasant. But the landlady was kindly, the food was excellent, and the bed comfortable. He hired two rooms here. The chief difficulty was a distinct lack of privacy. The landlady wanted to exhibit her guest as part of the family, and the public felt free to drop in early and stay late.

Gradually Matthew got used to this new publicity and began to look about. He met a world that amused and attracted him. First he sorted out two kinds of politicians. Both had one object—money. But to some Money was Power. On it they were climbing warily to dazzling heights—Senatorships, Congress, Empire! Their faces were strained, back of their carven smiles. They were walking a perpetual tight rope. Matthew hated them. Others wanted money, but they used their money with a certain wisdom. They enjoyed life. Some got gloriously and happily drunk. Others gambled, riding upon the great wings of chance to high and fascinating realms of desire. Nearly all of them ogled and played with pretty women.

On the whole, Matthew did not care particularly for their joys. Liquor gave him pleasant sensations, but not more pleasant and not as permanent as green fields or babies. He never played poker

W.E.B. DU BOIS

without visioning the joys of playing European politics or that high game of world races which his heart had glimpsed for one strange year—one mighty and disastrous year.

And women! If he had not met one woman—one woman who drew and filled all his imagination, all his high romance, all the wild joys and beauty of being—if she had never lived for him, he could have been a rollicking and easily satisfied Lothario and walked sweet nights out of State Street cabarets. Now he was not attracted. He had tried it once in New York. It was ashes. Moreover, he was married now, and all philandering was over. And yet—how curious that marriage should seem—well, to stop love, or arrest its growth instead of stimulating it.

He had not seen much of Sara since marriage. They had been so busy. And there had been no honeymoon, no mysterious romantic nesting; for Matthew had finally balked at Atlantic City. He tried to be gentle about it, but he showed a firmness before which Sara paused. No, he would not go to Atlantic City. He had gone there once—one summer, an age ago. He had been refused food at two restaurants, ordered out of a movie, not allowed to sit in a boardwalk pavilion, and not even permitted to bathe in the ocean.

"I will not go to Atlantic City. If I must go to hell, I'll wait until I'm dead," he burst out bitterly.

Sara let it go. "Oh, I don't really mind," she said, "only I've never been there, and I sort of wanted to see what it's like. Never mind, we'll go somewhere else." But they didn't; they stayed in Chicago.

So now he was a member of the legislature and in Springfield. The politicians came and went. The climbers avoided Matthew. Colored acquaintances were a debit to rising men. The other politicians knew him—jollied him and liked him—even drew him out for a rollicking evening now and then; but voted that he did not quite "belong." He was always a trifle remote—apart. He never could quite let himself go and be wholly one of them. But he liked them. They lived.

There were several members of the House who were not politicians. They did not count. They fluttered about, uttering shrill noises, and beat their wings vainly on unyielding iron bars.

Then there were men in politics who were not members of the legislature. Grave, well-dressed men of business and affairs. They came for confidential conferences with introductions from and connections with high places, governors, brokers, railway presidents, ruling monarchs of steel, oil, and international finance. And from Sammy; especially from Sammy and Sara. Money was nothing to them, and money was all. A thousand dollars—ten thousand—it was astounding, the sums at their command and the ease with which they distributed it. There was no crude bribery as on State Street—but Matthew soon learned that it was curiously easy to wake up a morning a thousand dollars richer than when one went to bed; and no laws broken, no questions asked, no moral code essentially disarranged. Matthew disliked these men esthetically, but he saw much of them and conferred with one or another of them nearly every week. It was his business. They did not live broadly or deeply, but they ruled. There was no sense blinking that fact. Matthew often forwarded registered express packages to Sara.

And he came to realize that legislating was not passing laws; it was mainly keeping laws from being passed.

Then there were the reformers. He held them—most of them—in respectful pity; palliators, surface scratchers. He listened to them endlessly and gravely. He read their tracts conscientiously, but only now and then could he vote as they asked. They were so ignorant—so futile. If only he, as a practical politician, might tell them a little. Birth control? Mothers' pensions? Restricted hours of labor for women and children? He agreed in theory with them all, but why ask his judgment? Why not ask the Rulers who put him in the legislature? And without the consent of these quiet, calm gentlemen who represented Empires, Kingdoms, and Bishoprics, what could he do, who was a mere member of the legislature?

Yet he could not say this, and if he had said it, they would not have understood. They pleaded with him—he that needed no pleas. One was here now—the least attractive—one stocking awry on her big legs, a terrible hat and an ill-fitting gown.

She was president of the Chicago local of the Box-Makers' Union. Her breasts were flat, her hips impossible, her hair dead straight, and her face white and red in the wrong places.

W.E.B. DU BOIS

"How would you like your daughter down there?" she bleated.

"I haven't one."

"But if you did have?"

"I'd hate it. But I wouldn't be fool enough to think any law would take her away."

"Well, what would?"

"Power that lies in the hands of the millionaire owners of factory stocks and bonds; and the bankers that guide and advise them. Transfer that power to me or you."

"That's it. Now help us to get this power!"

"How?"

"By voting—"

"Pish!"

"But how else? Are you going to sit down and let these girls go to death and hell?"

"I'm not responsible for this world, madam."

"Listen—I know a woman—a *woman*—like you. She's just been elected International President of the Box-Makers. She can talk. She knows. She's been everywhere. She's a lady and educated. I'm just a poor, dumb thing. I know what I want—but I can't say it. But she'll be in Chicago soon—I'm going to bring her to plead for this bill."

"Spare me," laughed Matthew. But he kept thinking of that poor reformer. And slowly and half-consciously—stirred by a thousand silly, incomplete arguments for impossible reform measures—revolt stirred within him against this political game he was playing. It was not moral revolt. It was esthetic disquiet. No, the revolt slowly gathering in Matthew's soul against the political game was not moral; it was not that he discerned anything practical for him in uplift or reform, or felt any new revulsion against political methods in themselves as long as power was power, and facts, facts. His revolt was against things unsuitable, ill adjusted, and in bad taste; the illogical lack of fundamental harmony; the unnecessary dirt and waste—the ugliness of it all—that revolted him.

He saw no adequate end or aim. Money had been his object, but money as security for quiet, for protection from hurt and insult, for opening the gates of Beauty. Now money that did none of these was dear, absurdly dear, overpriced. It was barely possible—and that thought kept recurring—it was barely possible that he was being cheated, was paying too high for money. Perhaps there were other things in life that would bring more completely that which he vaguely craved.

It seemed somehow that he was always passive—always waiting always receptive. He could never get to doing. There was no performance or activity that promised a shining goal. There was no goal. There was no will to create one. Within him, years ago, something—something essential—had died.

Yet he liked to play with words, cynically, on the morals of his situation as a politician. In his office today, he was talking with a rich woman who wanted his vote for limiting campaign funds. He looked at her with narrowed eyes:

"We have got to stop this lying and stealing or the country will die," she said impatiently.

He watched his unlighted cigarette.

"Lying? Stealing? I do not see that they are so objectionable in themselves. Lying is a version of fact, sometimes—often poetic, always creative. Stealing is a transfer of ownership, or an attempted transfer, sometimes from the overfed to the hungry—sometimes from the starving to the apoplectic. It is all relative and conditional—not absolute—not infinite."

"It is laying impious hands on God's truth—it is taking His property."

"I am not sure that God has any truth—that is, any arrangement of facts of which He is finally fond and of which He could not and does not easily conceive better or more fitting arrangement. And as to property, I'm sure He has none. Everytime He has come to us, He has been disgustingly poor."

The woman rose and fled. Matthew sighed and went back to his round of thought. Municipal ownership of transportation in Chicago: he had begun to look into it. He was prejudiced against it by his college textbooks and his political experience. But here somehow he scented something else. Back of the demand made to kill the present municipal ownership was another proposal to

W.E.B. DU BOIS

renew the franchise of the street-car lines with an "Indeterminate Permit," which meant in fact a perpetual charter. There was a powerful lobby of trained lawyers back of this bill, and what struck Matthew was that the same lobby was back of the movement to kill municipal ownership. Were they interested in super-power projects also? Matthew viewed this whole scramble as one who watches a great curdling of waters and begins to sense the current.

He was not evolving a conscience in politics. He was not revolting against graft and deception, but he was beginning to ask just what he was getting for his effort. Money? Some—not so very much. But the thing was not wrong—no—but unpleasant—ugly. That was the word. He was paying too much for money—money might cost too much. It might cost ugliness, writhing, dirty discomfort of soul and thought. That's it. He was paying too much for even the little money he got. He must pay less or get more. Matthew sighed and looked at the next card. It was that of the Japanese statesman whom he had met in Berlin. He arose slowly and faced the door.

XII

I trust I am not intruding," said the Japanese.

Matthew bowed coldly. He gave no sign of recognizing the Japanese, nor did he pretend not to.

"Certainly not—these are my office hours."

The Japanese was equally reticent and yet was just a shade too confidential to be an entire stranger. And again in Matthew's mind flamed and sang that Berlin dinner party.

Even the music floated in his ears. But he put it all rudely and brusquely aside.

"What can I do for you, sir? Be seated. Will you smoke?"

The Japanese took a cigarette, tasted it with relish, and leaned back easily in his chair. He glanced at the office. Matthew was ashamed. If he had been white, he would have had a room in the new Abraham Lincoln Hotel; something fine and modern, clean and smart, with service and light. If he had been black, free, and rich, he would perhaps have received his guest in a house of his own—delicately vaulted and soft with color; something beautiful in brick or marble, with high sweep of a curtain and pillar, a possibility of faint music, and silent deferential service. But being black, half slave, and poor, he had the front room of Mrs. Smith's boarding-house, a show room, to be sure, but conglomerate of jarring styles and tastes, overloaded and thick with furnishings; with considerable dust and transient smells and near the noisy street. Matthew was furious with himself for thinking thus apologetically. Whose business was it how he lived or what he had?

Then the Japanese looked at him.

"I have been much interested in noting the increased political power of your people," he said.

"Indeed," said Matthew, noncommittally.

"When I was in the United States twenty years ago"—(so he had been here twenty years ago and interested in Negroes!)—"you were politically negligible. Today in cities and states you have a voice."

Matthew was silent.

"I have been wondering," said the Japanese with the slow voice of one delicately feeling his way—"I have been wondering how far you have unified and set plans—"

"We have none."

"—either for yourselves in this land, or even further, with an eye toward international politics and the future of the darker races?"

"We have little interest in foreign affairs," said Matthew.

The Japanese shifted his position, asked permission, and lighted a second cigarette. He glanced appraisingly at Matthew.

"Sometime ago," he continued, "at a conference in Berlin, it was suggested that intelligent cooperation between American Negroes and other oppressed nations of the world might sensibly forward the uplift and emancipation of the darker peoples. I doubted this at the time."

"You may continue to doubt," said Matthew. "The dream at Berlin was false and misleading. We have nothing in common with other peoples. We are fighting out our own battle here in America with more or less success. We are not looking for help beyond our borders, and we need all our strength at home."

It would have been difficult for Matthew to say what prompted him to talk like this. Mainly, of course, it was deep-seated and smoldering resentment against this man whose interference, he believed, had wrecked his world. Perhaps, of course, this was not true. Perhaps shipwreck was certain, but—he was determined not to sail for those harbors again, not for a moment even to reconsider the matter; and he repeated as his own the current philosophy of the colored group about him. It sounded false as he spoke, but he talked on. The Japanese watched him as he talked.

"Ah!" he said. "Ah! I am sorry. There were some of us who hoped—"

Matthew's heart leaped. Questions rushed to his lips, and one word clamored for utterance. He beat them back and glanced at his watch.

The Japanese arose. "I am keeping you?" he said.

"No—no—I have a few minutes yet."

The Japanese glanced around, and bending forward, spoke rapidly.

"The Great Council," he said, "of the Darker Peoples will meet in London three months hence. We have given the American Negro full representation; that is, three members on the Board. You are chairman. The other two are—"

Matthew arose abruptly.

"I cannot accept," he said harshly. "I am no longer interested."

"I am sorry," said the Japanese slowly. He paused and pondered, started to speak as Matthew's heart hammered in his throat. But the Japanese remained silent. He extended his hand. Matthew took it, frowning. They murmured polite words, and the visitor was gone.

Matthew threw himself on the couch with an oath, and through his unwilling head tramped all the old pageant of empire with black and brown and yellow leaders marching ahead.

XIII

Matthew was gray with wrath. Sara was quiet and unmoved. "Yes," she said. "I promised them your vote, and they paid for it—a good round sum."

Matthew had been a member of the legislature of Illinois about six months. He had made a good record. Everybody conceded that. Nothing spectacular, but his few speeches were to the point and carried weight; his work on committees had been valuable because of his accurate information and willingness to drudge. His votes, curiously enough, while not uniformly pleasing to all, had gained the praise even of the women's clubs and of some of the reformers, whom he had chided, while at the same time the politicians regarded Matthew as a "safe" man. Matthew Towns evidently had a political future.

Yet Matthew was far from happy or satisfied. Outside his wider brooding over his career, he had not gained a home by his marriage. The flat on South Parkway an immaculate place which must not be disturbed for mere living purposes and which blossomed with dignified magnificence. At repeated intervals crowds burst in for a reception. There was whist and conversation, dancing as far as space would allow; smoking, cocktails, and smutty stories back in the den with the men; whispers and spiteful gossip on the veranda with the ladies; and endless piles of rich food in the dining room, served by expensive caterers.

"Mrs. Matthew Towns' exclusive receptions for the smarter set" (thus the society reporter of *The Lash*) were "the most notable in colored Chicago."

And Sara was shrewd enough, while gaining this reputation for social exclusiveness, to see that no real person of power or influence in colored Chicago was altogether slighted, so that, at least once or twice a year, one met everybody.

The result was an astonishing mélange that drove Matthew nearly crazy. He could have picked a dozen delightful companions— some educated—some derelicts-students—politicians—but all human, delightful, fine, with whom a quiet evening would have been a pleasure. But he was never allowed. Sara always had good reasons of state for including this ward heeler or that grass widow, or some shrill-voiced young woman who found herself in company of this sort for the first time in her life and proclaimed it loudly; and at the same time Sara found excuse for excluding the "nobodies" who intrigued his soul.

Matthew's personal relations with his wife filled him with continual astonishment. He had never dreamed that two human beings could share the closest of intimacies and remain unacquainted strangers. He thought that the yielding of a woman to a man was a matter of body, mind, and soul—a complete blending. He had never forgot—shamefaced as it made him—the way that girl in Harlem had twisted her young, live body about his and soothed his tired, harassed soul and whispered, "There, Big Boy!"

Always he had dreamed of marriage as like that, hallowed by law and love. Having bowed to the law, he tried desperately to give and evoke the love. But behind Sara's calm, cold hardness, he found nothing to evoke. She did not repress passion—she had no passion to repress. She disliked being "mauled" and disarranged, and she did not want anyone to be "mushy" about her. Her private life was entirely in public; her clothes, her limbs, her hair and complexion, her well-appointed home, her handsome, well-tailored husband and his career; her reputation for wealth.

Periodically Matthew chided himself that their relations were his fault. He was painfully conscious of his lack of deep affection for her, but he strove to evolve something in its place. He proposed a little home hidden in the country, where, on a small income from their rents, they could raise a garden and live. And then, perhaps—he spoke diffidently—"a baby." Sara had stared at him in uncomprehending astonishment.

"Certainly not!" she had answered. And she went back to the subject of the super-power bills. The legislature had really done little work during the whole session, and now as the last days drew on the real fight loomed. The great hidden powers of finance had three measures: first, to kill municipal ownership of street-car lines; secondly, to unite all the street transportation interests of Chicago into one company with a perpetual franchise or

W.E.B. DU BOIS

"indeterminate permit"; thirdly, to reorganize, reincorporate, and refinance a vast holding company to conduct their united interests and take final legislative steps enabling them to monopolize electric and water power in the state and in neighboring states.

To Matthew the whole scheme was clear as day. He had promised to vote against municipal ownership, but he had never promised to support all this wider scheme. It meant power and street-car monopoly; millions in new stocks and bonds unloaded on the public; and the soothing of public criticism by lower rates for travel, light, and power, and yet rates high enough to create several generations of millionaires to rule America. He had determined to oppose these bills, not because they were wrong, but because they were unfair. For similar reasons he had driven Casey's gambling den out of business in his district; the roulette wheel and most of the dice were loaded.

But Sara was keen on the matter. Lines were closely drawn; there was strong opposition from reformers, Progressives, and the labor group. Money was plentiful, and Sara had pledged Matthew's votes and been roundly paid for it.

She and Sammy were having a conference on the matter and awaiting Matthew. Sara sensed his opposition; it must be overcome. Sammy was talking.

"Don't understand their game," said Sammy, "but they're lousy with money."

"I understand it," said Sara quietly, "and I've promised Matthew's vote for their bills."

Sammy's eyes narrowed.

Just then, Matthew came in.

"What have you promised?" he asked, looking from one to the other. Sara quietly gathered up her papers.

"Come home to lunch," she said, "and I'll tell you."

She knew that she had to have this thing out with Matthew, and she had planned for it carefully. Sammy whistled softly to himself and did a little jig after his guests had left. He thought he saw light.

"I didn't think that combination could last long," he said to his new cigar. "Too perfect."

Sara steered her Studebaker deftly through the traffic, bowing to deferential policemen at the traffic signals and recognizing well-dressed acquaintances here and shabby idlers there, who raised their hats elaborately. Matthew sat silent, mechanically lifting his hat, but glancing neither right nor left. They glided up to the curb at home, at exactly the right distance from it, and stopped before the stepping-stone. Sara flooded the carburetor, turned off the switch, and carefully locked it. Matthew handed her down, and with a smile at the staring children, they entered the lofty porch of their house. They opened the dark oaken door with a latchkey and slowly mounted the carpeted stairs. Sara remarked that the carpet was a little worn. She feared it was not as good as Carson-Pirie had represented. She would have to see about it soon.

A brown maid in a white apron smilingly let them into the apartment and said that lunch was "just ready—yes'm, I found some fine sweet potatoes after you phoned, and fried them." Matthew loved fried sweet potatoes. They had a very excellent but rather silent lunch, although Sara talked steadily about various rather inconsequential things. Then they went to the "library," which Matthew never used because its well-bound and carefully arranged books had scarcely a volume in which he had the slightest interest. Sara closed the door and turned on the electric log. "I promised the super-power crowd," she said, "that you would vote for their bills."

It was then that Matthew went pale with wrath. "How dared you?"

"Dared? I thought you expected me to conduct your campaign? I promised them your vote, and they paid a lot for it. Of course, it was cloaked in a real-estate transaction, but I gave them a receipt in your name and mine and deposited the money."

Matthew felt for the flashing of a moment that he could kill this pale, hard woman before him. She felt this and inwardly quailed, but outwardly kept her grip.

"I don't see," she said, "any great difference between voting for these bills and against municipal ownership. It is all part of one scheme. I hope," she added, "you're not going to develop a conscience suddenly. As a politician with a future, you can't afford to."

The trouble was that Matthew himself suddenly knew that there was no real difference. It was three steps in the same direction instead of one. But the first was negative and tentative, while the three together were tremendous. They gave a monopoly of transportation and public service in Chicago to a great corporation which aimed at unlimited permission to exploit the water power of a nation forever at any price "the traffic would bear." Of course it was no question of right and wrong. It was possible to buy privilege, as one bought votes; he himself bought votes, but—well, this was different. This privilege could be bought, of course—but not of him. It was cheating mental babies whom he did not represent—whom he did not want to represent.

He was a grafting politician. He knew it and felt no qualms about it. But he had always secretly prided himself that his exchanges were fair. The gamblers who paid him got protection; prostitutes who were straight and open need not fear the police; workers in his district could not be "shaken down" by thieves. Even in the bigger legislative deals, it was square, upstanding give and take between men with their eyes open. But this—there was no use explaining to Sara. She knew the difference as well as he. Or did she? That rankling shaft about "conscience." He was a politician who was directly and indirectly for sale. He had no business with a conscience. He had no conscience. But he had limitations. By God! Everybody had some limitations. He must have them. He would sell himself if he wished, but he wouldn't be sold. He was not a bag of inert produce. He refused to be compelled to sell. He was no slave. He must and would be free. He wanted money for freedom. Well, he'd been sold. Where was the money? He wanted money. He must have it. There and there alone lay freedom, and his chains were becoming more than he could bear.

"Where is the money you got?" he said abruptly.

"I've invested it."

"I want it."

"You can't get it—it's tied up in a deal, and to disturb it would be to risk most of our fortune."

"I've put some money in our joint account."

"That's invested too. What's the use of money idle in a savings bank at four percent when we can make forty?"

"How much are we worth?"

"Oh, not so much," said Sara cautiously. "Put the house minus the first mortgage at, say, fifty thousand—we may have another ten or fifteen thousand more." Thus she figured up.

"Matthew," she added quickly, "be sensible. In a couple of years you'll be in Congress—the greatest market in the land, and we'll be worth at least a hundred thousand. Oppose these bills, and you go to the political ashpile. Sammy won't dare to use you. My mortgagees will squeeze me. The city will come down on us for violations and assessments, and first thing we know we'll be penniless and saddled with piles of brick and mortar. As a congressman you can ignore petty graft and get in 'honestly,' as people say, on big things; in less than ten years, you'll be rich and famous. Now for God's sake, don't be a fool!"

Matthew Towns voted for the traction group of bills, but they were defeated by an aroused public opinion which neither Republicans nor Democrats dared oppose. Matthew at the same time saved from defeat at the last moment four bills which the Progressives and Labor group were advocating. They were not radical but were entering wedges to reduce the burden on working mothers, lessen the hours of work for women, and establish the eight-hour day. One bill to restrict the power of injunctions in labor disputes failed despite Matthew's efforts.

The result was curious. Matthew was commended by all parties. The machine regarded him as safe but shrewd. The Farmer-Labor group regarded him as beginning to see the light. The Democrats regarded him as approachable. Sara was elated. She determined to begin immediately her campaign to send Matthew to Congress.

XIV

The Honorable Sammy Scott was having the fight of his life and he knew it. It almost wiped the genial smile from his lips, but he screwed it on and metaphorically stripped for the fray. He knew it was the end or a glorious new beginning for Sammy Scott.

Sammy's first real blow had been Sara's wedding. He had settled down to the comfortable fact that if Sara ever married anybody it would be Sammy Scott. At whom else had she ever looked—of whom had she ever thought? He was her hero in shrewdness and accomplishment, and hepreened himself before her. There hung the fruit—the ripe, sleek, dainty fruit at his hand. He had only to reach out and pluck it. He was not a marrying man. But—who could tell? He might want a change. He might make his pile and retire. Or go traveling abroad. Then? Well, he might marry Sara and take her along. Time would tell.

And then—then without warning—without a flash of suspicion, the blow fell. Of course, others had talked and hinted and winked. Sammy laughed and pooh-poohed. He knew Sara. Nobody could take his capable secretary off the Honorable Sammy Scott. No, sir!

After the announcement and through the marriage, Sammy bore up bravely. He never turned a hair, at least to the public. He was best man and general manager at the wedding, and his present of a grand piano, with Ampico attachment, made dark Chicago gasp.

Gradually, Sammy got an idea into his head. Sara was a cool and deep one. Perhaps, perhaps, mused Sammy, as she left him after a long and confidential talk, perhaps this husband business was all a blind. Perhaps after the marriage with a rather dull husband for exhibition purposes, Sara was going to be more approachable. In her despair at not inveigling Sammy himself into marriage—so Sammy argued, waving his patent-leather shoes on their high perch—after her wiles failed, then perhaps she'd decided to have her cake and eat it too. All right—all the same to Sammy. Of course, he might have preferred—but women are curious.

He hinted something of this to Sara and got a cryptic response—a sort of prim silence that made him guffaw and slap his thigh. Of course, he had upbraided her first with disloyalty and quitting; but all this she disclaimed with pained surprise. She gave Sammy distinctly to understand—she did not say it—that she was loyally and eternally his steward forever and ever.

So Sammy was shaken but hopeful, and matters went on as usual until the second blow fell from a clear sky. Sara proposed to resign as his secretary! This brought him to his feet with deep suspicion. Was she double-crossing him? Was she playing him for a sucker? She had been in fact no more approachable to his familiarities since than before marriage—if anything, less. She actually seemed to be putting on airs and assuming a place of importance. If Sammy had dared, he would have dropped her entirely the moment she resigned. But he did not dare, and he knew that Sara knew it. He caught the glint in her gray eyes and almost felt the steel grip of her dainty hand.

Moreover, Sara explained it all very clearly. As the wife of a member of the legislature, it did not look quite the correct thing for her to be just a secretary. She proposed, therefore, to have an office of her own next Sammy's where the work of her women's organization could be done. At the same time, with an assistant, she could still take charge of Sammy's business. Sammy had hopes of that assistant, but before he had anyone to propose, Sara had one chosen. She was nothing to look at, but she certainly could make a typewriter talk. Business went as smoothly as ever, and Sammy couldn't complain.

No, evidently Sara could not be dropped. She knew too much of facts and methods. So, ostensibly, Sammy and Sara were in close alliance and almost daily consultation, and they were at the same time watching each other narrowly.

The trouble culminated over the nomination for Congress. For thirty years, Negroes, deprived of representation in Congress, after White of North Carolina had been counted out, had planned and hoped politically for one end—to put a black man in Congress from the North. The necessary black population had migrated to New York, Philadelphia, and St. Louis; but in Chicago alone did they have not only the numbers but the political machine capable of engineering the deal. It had long been the plan of Sammy's machine to have the white congressman, Doolittle, retire at the end of his present term and Sammy nominated in his stead. This was the ambition of Sammy's life, the crowning of his career. He and Sara had discussed it for years in every detail. Every step was surveyed, every contingency thought out. It was only necessary to wait for enough political power in Sammy's machine to dictate the nomination of one colored candidate among the myriad of aspirants. That time had now come.

Sammy was the recognized colored state boss; three aldermen and three colored members of the legislature took his orders; the colored judge owed his place to Sammy, and, while independent, was friendly. The public service corporations were back of Sammy with money and influence. Four "assistant" corporation counsels named by Sammy were receiving five thousand dollars a year each for duties that, to say the least, were not arduous; while the Civil Service, the Post Office, and the schools had hundreds of colored employees who owed or thought they owed their chance to make a decent living to the Honorable Sammy Scott. Finally, there was Sara's Colored Women's Council, through which for the first time the Negro women loomed as an independent political force.

Thus Sammy was dictator and candidate, and the party machine had definitely and categorically promised. The Negro majority in the First Congressional District was undoubted.

Now, however, and suddenly, matters changed. Since Matthew's success, Sara had definitely determined to kill off Sammy and send Matthew to Congress. Sammy sensed this, and these politicians began to stalk each other. Sara's task was hardest, and she knew it. Sammy was Heir Apparent by all the rules of the game. But there were pitfalls, and Sara knew them. She was going to make no mistake, but she was watching.

Gradually Sammy became less communicative. He had a number of secret conferences in the early spring of 1926, to which Sara, contrary to custom, was not invited; and his accounts of these meetings were vague.

"Oh, just a get-together—talkee, talkee; nothing important."

But Sara wasn't fooled. She knew that Sammy was in trouble and struggling desperately. The fact was that Sammy was sorely puzzled. First and weightiest, the white party bosses wanted Doolittle for "just one more term." Doolittle held exceedingly important committee places in Congress, and especially as chairman of the Ways and Means Committee of the House, he was a power for tariff legislation. Millions depended on the revision which exporters, farmers, and laborers were demanding more and more loudly. Then there was legislation for the farmers and on the railroads and above all certain nationwide super-power plans at Niagara, at Muscle Shoals and Boulder Dam. It was no question of "color," the white leaders carefully explained. It was a grave question of party interests. Two years hence, the nomination was Sammy's with bands playing. This year, Doolittle simply *must* go back, and money was no object.

That was reason Number One, and as money always was an object with Sammy, it loomed large in his thought. But that wasn't all. Sammy did not trust Sara, and Sara, by efficiently organizing the colored women, had quietly become the biggest single political force in his colored constituency. Indeed, her new Colored Women's Council was the most perfect piece of smoothly running political machinery that Sammy knew. He couldn't touch it, and he had tried. Now Sara had an uncomfortably popular husband. Matthew was a successful member of the legislature, young and intelligent, with some personal popularity. His very faults—aloofness, absentmindedness, indifference to money or fame—increased his vogue. If Doolittle were forced to resign, could Sammy land the nomination without Sara's help? And with the knifing of men like Corruthers, who was still sore with Sammy; and particularly without the party slush fund?

Sammy hesitated and all but lost. He pocketed twenty-five thousand dollars for campaign expenses within a few days and consented to Doolittle's renomination. But he did not dare announce it. Sara scented a crisis. She looked over his papers—

always kept carelessly—and ran across his bank book. She noticed that twenty-five thousand dollar cash deposit. Then she got busy on the Doolittle end. She knew a maid long connected with the congressman's family. Soon she had inside news. It was going to be announced that Doolittle was not to resign. His health (which was to have been the excuse) had been "greatly improved by a trip to Europe," and the honor of another and strictly final term was to be given this "friend and champion of our race!"

Sara immediately took the high hand. She walked into Sammy's office without knocking and closed the door. She was brief, inaccessible, and coldly indignant. She reminded Sammy of his solemn promise to refuse Doolittle another term; she accused him of being bribed and announced distinctly her withdrawal from all political alliance with the Scott machine!

Sammy was aghast. It was the coldest hold-up he had ever experienced. He promised her office, influence, money, and anything in reason for Matthew. She was adamant. She expressed great sorrow at this breaking of old ties.

"Oh, go to hell!" growled Sammy and slammed the door after her. He knew her game, of course. She was going to run Matthew for Congress, and, by George, she had a chance to win, unless he could kill Matthew off.

Sara immediately gave her story to the newspapers, colored and white, and called meetings of all her clubs. Bedlam broke loose about Sammy's devoted head. He was accused of "Betraying and Selling out his Race to White Politicians!" The Negro papers, by secret information or astonishingly lucky guess, named the exact sum he received—twenty-five thousand dollars. The white papers sneered at Negro grafting politicians and praised the upright and experienced Doolittle. Sammy's appointees and heads of his political machine sat securely on the fence and said and did nothing. They were glad that Sammy had missed the nomination. They were waiting to know just what their share of the slush fund was to be. They were afraid of the popular uproar against Sammy. Above all, they feared Sara. It looked perilously like Sammy's finish.

Sammy was no quitter. When he was "down, he was never out." And now he really began to fight. Sammy turned to the gang he could best trust for underground dirty work. The very respectability which Sara had forced on him in his chief appointments greatly cramped his style. He had to go back to his old cronies and his old methods. He made peace with the Gang. Soon he had around him Corruthers and a dozen like him. Sammy promised the utmost liberality with funds and began by distributing scores of new hundred-dollar bills. They all decided that the case was by no means desperate. Towns could, at worst, defeat Doolittle at the election only by dividing the Republican vote. He himself had small chance for the Republican nomination. And even if he got it, Sammy could also split the vote and defeat him. As long then as the bosses stood pat for Doolittle, Towns' only hope was to run on an independent ticket. Could he win? Probably not. Negroes did not like to scratch a straight Republican ticket. Meantime, however, in order to insure Doolittle's election and keep their machine intact, Towns must be put out of the running altogether. As Sammy said: "We've gotta frame Towns."

"Publish him as a jailbird."

"What, after I got him pardoned as an innocent hero and worked that gag all over the country?"

"Knock him on his fool head," sneered an alderman.

"There's only one thing to do with a bozo like him, and that is to trip him up with a skirt."

"Can't he steal something?"

They went over his career with a fine-tooth comb until at last they came back to that lynching and train wreck and his jail record.

"I remember now," said Sammy thoughtfully, "that Sara unearthed a lot of unpublished stuff."

"We've got to discover new evidence and admit that we were fooled."

Corruthers had been lolling back in his chair, smoking furiously and saying nothing. His red hair blazed, and his brown freckles grew darker. Suddenly now he let the two front legs of his chair down with a bang.

"Oh, to hell with you all!" he snarled. "You don't have to get no new evidence. I've had the dope to kill Towns for six months."

Sammy did not appear to be impressed. He had little faith in Corruthers.

"What is it?" he growled, with half a sneer in his tone.

"It is this. Towns made that attack on the woman for which another porter was lynched on the Klan Special last year."

Sammy sat up quickly. "Like hell!" he snapped.

"Yes, like hell! Towns confessed it to the executive committee of the porters. Said he was in the woman's compartment when the husband discovered them. He knocked the husband down and escaped. The husband thought it was the regular car porter, and he got his friends and lynched him. Towns offered to tell this story to the general meeting of the porters and in court, but the committee wouldn't let him. They let him say only that he knew the lynched porter was innocent, because he wasn't in the car. They figured it would be bad policy to admit that the woman had been attacked by anyone. I got this story from the secretary of the committee. After you ditched me for the nomination to the legislature, I tried to get him to come out with it and swear to it, but he wouldn't. He was backing Towns. Then I tried to find the widow of the guy who was lynched. I knew she would tell the truth fast enough. Well, I couldn't get her until the election was over, but I've got her now fast enough. She's in New York, and I've been writing to her.

"And that ain't all. Remember, there was another colored woman mixed up in this. Called herself an Indian princess and got away with it. Princess nothing! I figure she was in the blackmailing game with Towns, double-crossed him, and left him holding the bag. Slip me five hundred for expenses, and I'll go to New York tonight and round up both of these dames. We'll bury Towns so deep he'll never see the outside of jail again."

Sammy hesitated. He didn't like this angle of attack. It was— well, it was hitting below the belt. But, pshaw! Politics was politics, and one couldn't be too squeamish. He peeled off five one-hundred-dollar bills.

That night Corruthers went east.

XV

Sara was delighted at Sammy's move in the Doolittle nomination. If he had stuck to his original plan, it would have been difficult for her to refuse him her support. As it was, the chorus of denunciation at Sammy's apostasy was easily turned to a chorus demanding the nomination of Matthew Towns to Congress, before the rival politicians in Sammy's machine could prevent it. It was suggested that if the Republicans refused to nominate him and insisted on Doolittle, he might run independently and get support from the mass of the Negro vote, all the reformers, and, possibly, even the Democrats, in a district where they otherwise had no chance. Sara followed up the suggestion quickly. Club after club in her Colored Women's Council nominated Matthew by acclamation, until almost the solid Negro women's vote apparently stood back of him.

Matthew was astounded. He had never dreamed that Sara could effect his nomination to Congress. He resented her means and methods. He half resolved to refuse utterly, but, after all, it was a great chance, a door to freedom, power. But he would have to pay. He would have to strip his soul of all self-respect and lie and steal his way in. He knew it. What should he do? What could he do?

Sara had immediately taken the matter of Matthew's nomination to the white women's clubs and to the reformers. Here she struck a snag; Matthew had gained applause from the Farmer-Labor group for his support of some of their bills in the legislature; but after all, he was well known as a machine man and had voted at the dictation of big interests in the traction deal. How then could they nominate Towns, unless, of course, he was prepared to cut away from the machine and take a new progressive stand?

It was Mr. Cadwalader, leader of the Progressive group, speaking to Sara. She agreed that Matthew must take a stand. In her own mind it was a first step before she could coerce the Republicans. But how could she induce Matthew to play her game? It would be fairly easy for a trained politician. He would simply say that he was not opposed to municipal ownership but simply to this particular bill, and point out its defects. Defects were always easy to find. Then he would say that he knew that the "indeterminate permit" bill was doomed to defeat and that he could only get support for the other measures by promising to vote for it. This he could say and then make promises for the future, but not too many. But would Matthew do this? Of course not. He had no such subtlety. On the other hand, if he got up and tried to tell the straightforward truth, Sara had a plan that might work. Yes, it was worth trying. She did not see how she could avoid a trial.

"Matthew," she said that night, "I want you to come with me Tuesday and explain frankly to a committee of the Women's City Club your attitude on the super-power projects."

Matthew stared: "And how shall I explain my vote?"

"By telling the truth. Then I'll say a word."

Matthew made no comment. Gradually in his own soul he had made a declaration of independence. He would not in the future, more than in the past, be hemmed in by petty moral scruples. He still honestly believed that burglary was ethically no worse than Big Business. But thereafter in each particular instance he was going to be the judge. He would buy and sell if he so wished, but he would not be bought and sold. He was glad to go before that club and talk openly and cleanly of traction and Super-Power.

The scene inspired him. They sat high up above the roaring city, in a softly beautiful and quiet room. There rose before him intelligent faces—well-groomed and well-carried bodies, mostly of women. He saw clearly, behind their ease and poise, the toiling slavery of colored millions. He was not deceived into assuming that their show of interest would easily survive any real attack on their incomes or comforts. And yet they were willing to listen. Within limits, they wanted reform and the uplift of men.

Matthew knew his subject. He knew it even better than many experts who had spoken there, because he brought in and made real and striking the point of view and the personal interest not simply of the skilled worker, but of the laborer, the ditch-digger, the casual semi-criminal. They listened to him in growing astonishment. Here was a machine politician who had voted deliberately against his own knowledge and convictions, and yet who explained their own belief and aims much better than they could, and who nevertheles—

"Why then did I vote as I did?"

He was about to say frankly that he voted at the dictation of the machine, but that he did not propose to do this again. He would hereafter use his own judgment. His judgment might not always agree with theirs. It might sometimes agree with the machine politicians'. But it would always be his judgment. Before, however, he could say anything, Sara arose. He saw her and hesitated in astonishment.

Sara arose. She looked almost pretty—simply but well gowned, self-possessed and nervously expectant. Matthew never was sure afterward whether she actually was nervous or whether this was not one of her poses.

She arose and said, "May I interrupt right here?" What could Matthew say? He could hardly tell his own wife in public to shut up, although that was what he wanted to say. He had to bow grimly, even if not politely. The chairman smiled, looked a little astonished, and then explained: "This is perhaps not exactly the place where we would expect an interruption, but as most of you know, this is Mr. Towns' wife, and she wants to say a word right here if he and you are willing."

Many had thought Sara white. Now they all "could see that she was colored!" At least they pretended never really to have been in doubt that slight curl in her hair—the delicate tint of her skin—the singular gray eyes, etc. But she was unusually well dressed—"yes, quite intelligent, too, they say—yes." But what a singular point at which to interrupt! It would be especially interesting to hear the speaker proceed just here. But Matthew bowed abruptly and sat down. He was curious to see what Sara was up to. Her nimble mind always outran his in unguessed directions.

"He voted as he did because I had promised the politicians that he would, and he was too chivalrous to make me break my word, as he should have."

W.E.B. DU BOIS

Matthew gasped and glanced to the door. It was too far off and blocked with silk and fur.

"I know now I was quite wrong, but I did not realize it then. I received my political education, as many of you know, as a member of a political machine, where the first commandment is, Obey. I was and am ambitious for my husband. I was a little scared at his liberal views before I understood his reasons and until we had talked them over. The machine asked his vote against municipal ownership. He gave it. He explained to me as he has to you the case for and against municipal ownership in the present state of Chicago politics. He believed this bill meant indirect corporation control. Then the Interests—the same Interests—came to me about the other two bills. You see," said Sara prettily, "we're partners, and I act as a sort of secretary to the combination and write the letters and see the visitors."

Matthew groaned in spirit, and one lady whispered to another that here was, at least, one ideal family.

"I promised them our support," continued Sara, "without further thought. I probably assumed I knew more than I did, and perhaps I was too eager to curry favor for my husband in high places—"

"And perhaps," whispered Mr. Cadwalader in the rear, "you got damned well paid for it."

Sara proceeded: "I was wrong and my husband was angry, but I pleaded with him. Since then I have come to a clearer realization of the meaning and function of political machines. But I argued then that without the machine, colored people would get no recognition even from respectable and intelligent people; that the machine had elected my husband, and that he owed it support. Finally, he promised to support the bills in loyalty to me, but only on condition that afterward we resign from Sammy Scott's organization. This we have done."

There was prolonged applause. They did not all believe Sara's explanation, but they were willing to forget the past in the face of this seemingly definite commitment for the future. But Matthew gasped. It was the smoothest, coolest lie he had ever heard, and yet it was so near the truth that he had to rub his own inner eyes. He was literally dumb when members of the committees congratulated this ideal couple and promised to turn the support of reformers toward Matthew's independent nomination. Some saw also the wisdom of Sara's delicate suggestion that this—almost domestic misfortune—be not broadcast yet to the public press, and that it only be intimated in a general way that Mr. Towns' attitude was on the whole satisfactory.

XVI

There was war in Chicago—silent, bitter war. It was part of the war throughout the whole nation; it was part of the World War. Money was bursting the coffers of the banks—poor people's savings, rich people's dividends. It must be invested in order to insure principal and interest for the poor and profits for the rich. It had been invested in the past in European restoration and American industry. But difficulties were appearing—far-off signs of danger which bankers knew. European industry could only pay large dividends if it could sell goods largely in the United States. High tariff walls kept those goods out. American industry could pay large dividends only if it could sell goods abroad or secure monopoly prices at home. To sell goods abroad it must receive Europe's goods in payment. This meant lower tariff rates. To keep monopoly at home, prices must be kept up by present or higher tariff rates. It was a dilemma, a cruel dilemma, and bankers, investors, captains of industry, scanned the industrial horizon, while poor people shivered from cold and unknown winds.

There was but one hope in the offing which would at once ward off labor troubles by continued high wages and yet maintain the fabulous rate of profit; and that was new monopoly of rich natural resources. Imperial aggressiveness in the West Indies, Mexico, and Africa held possibilities, when public opinion was properly manipulated. But right here in the United States was White Coal! Black coal, oil, and iron were monopolized and threatened with diminishing returns and world competition. But white coal—the harnessing of the vast unused rivers of the nation; monopolizing free water power to produce dear electricity! Quick! Quick! Act silently and swiftly before the public awakes and sees that it is selling something for nothing. Keep Doolittle in Congress. Keep all the Doolittles in Congress. Let the silent war against agitators, radicals, fools, keep up. Hold the tariff citadel a little longer—then let it crash with the old savings gone but the new investments safe and ready to take new advantage of lower wages and less impudent workers. So there was war in Chicago—World War, and the Republican machine of Cook County was fighting in the van. And in the machine Sammy and Sara and Matthew were little cogs.

A Michigan Avenue 'bus was starting south from Adams Street in early March when two persons, rushing to get on at the same time, collided. Mrs. Beech, president of the Women's City Club, was a little flustered. She ought to have come in her own car, but she did not want to appear too elegant on this visit. She turned and found herself face to face with Mr. Graham, the chairman of the Republican County Central Committee. They lived in the same North Shore suburb, Hubbard Woods, and had met before.

"I beg your pardon," said Mr. Graham hastily. "One has to rush so for these 'buses that it is apt to be dangerous."

Mrs. Beech smiled graciously. She was rather glad to meet Mr. Graham, because she wanted to talk somethings out with him. They sat on top and began with the weather and local matters in their suburb. Then Mrs. Beech observed:

"The colored folks are certainly taking the South Side."

"It is astonishing," answered Mr. Graham. "What would the ghosts of the old Chicago aristocracy say?"

"Well, it shows progress, I suppose," said Mrs. Beech.

"I am not so sure about that," said Mr. Graham. "It shows activity and a certain ruthless pushing forward, but I am a little afraid of results. We have a most difficult political problem here."

"So I understand; in fact, I am going to a meeting of one of their women's clubs now."

"Indeed! Well, I hope we may count on your good offices," and Mr. Graham smiled. "I don't mind telling you that we are in trouble in this district. We have got a big Negro vote, well organized under Sammy Scott, of whom perhaps you have heard. Scott and his gang are not easily satisfied. They have been continually raising their demands. First, they wanted money, and indeed they have never got over that; but they demanded money first for what I suspect amounted to direct bribery. This, of course, was coupled with protection for gambling and crime, a deplorable situation, but beyond control. This went on for a while, although the sums handed them from the party coffers were larger and larger. Then they began to want offices, filling appointments as janitors and cleaners at first; then higher and higher until at last the Negroes of Chicago have two aldermen, three members of the legislature, a state senator, a city judge and several commissionerships."

"They are proving apt politicians," smiled Mrs. Beech.

"And they are not through," returned Mr. Graham, "Today they are insisting upon a congressman."

"Well, they deserve some representation, don't they, in Congress?"

"Yes, that's true; but neither they nor we are ready for it just yet. Membership in Congress not only involves a certain social status and duties, but just now in the precarious economic position of the country, we need trained and experienced men in Congress and not mere ward politicians."

"Is Doolittle a man of such high order and ability?"

"No, he is not. Doolittle is an average politician, but he is a white man; he has had long experience; he holds exceedingly important places on the House committees because of his long service; and above all he is willing to carry out the plans of his superiors."

"Or in other words," said Mrs. Beech tartly, "he takes orders from the machine."

"Yes, he does," said Graham, turning toward her and speaking earnestly. "And how are we going to run this country unless thoughtful men furnish the plans and find legislators and workers who are willing to carry them out? We are in difficulties, Mrs. Beech. If the tariff is tinkered with by amateur radicals, your income and mine may easily go to smash. If securities which are now good and the basis of investment are attacked by Bolsheviks, we may have an industrial smash such as the world has seldom seen. We haven't paid our share for the World War yet, and we may have to foot a staggering bill.

"Now, we have farsighted plans for guiding the industrial machine and keeping it steady; Doolittle is a cog, nothing more than a cog, but a dependable cog, in the machine. Now here come the Negroes of this district and demand the fulfillment of a promise, carelessly, and to my mind foolishly given several years ago, that after this term Doolittle was to be replaced in Congress by the head of the black political machine, Sammy Scott. Well, it's impossible. I think you see that, Mrs. Beech. We don't want Scott in Congress representing Chicago. He has neither the brains nor the education—"

Mrs. Beech interrupted. "But I understand," she said, "that there is a young college-bred man who is candidate and who is intellectually rather above the average of our Congressmen."

"There certainly is," said Mr. Graham, bitterly, "and he's got a wife who is one of the most astute politicians in this city."

"Yes," said Mrs. Beech, "I am on my way to one of her meetings. It is at her home on Grand—I mean, South Parkway. I wonder where I should transfer?"

"I will show you," said Mr. Graham. "We have still a little way to go. It would be just like Mrs. Towns to pull all strings in order to get you to her house. She has social aspirations and is the real force behind Towns."

"But Towns himself?" asked Mrs. Beech.

"Towns himself is a radical and has a shady record. He was once in the penitentiary. His wife is trying to keep him in hand, but his appeal is to the very elements among white people and colored people which mean trouble for conservative industry in the United States. He cannot for a moment be considered. I have talked frankly to you, Mrs. Beech. We are coming to your corner now, but I wish we could come to some sort of understanding with the liberal elements that you represent. I do not think that you, Cadwalader, and myself are so far apart. I hope you will help us."

Mrs. Beech descended and Graham rode on.

It was some hours later that Mr. Cadwalader and Mrs. Beech had dinner together. They represented various elements interested in reform. Mr. Cadwalader was the official head of the Farmer-Labor Party in Chicago, while Mrs. Beech represented one element of the old Progressive Party and looked toward alliance with Mr. Cadwalader's group.

"But," Mr. Cadwalader complained over his fish, "we've got an impossible combination. We cannot get any real agreement on anything. You and I, for instance, cannot stand for free trade as a present policy. It would ruin us and our friends. On the other hand, we cannot advocate a high tariff. We and our manufacturing friends want gradual reduction rather than increase of duties. Then, too, our friends among the farmers and the laborers want high and low tariff at the same time, only on different things. The farmers want cheap foreign manufactured goods and high rates on food; the laborers want free food and high manufacturing wages. Finally, we have all got to remember the Socialists and Communists who want to scrap the whole system and begin anew."

"I was talking with Mr. Graham yesterday," said Mrs. Beech, "and he believes that the Republicans and the Farmer-Labor Party could find some common aims."

"I am sure we could, if the Republicans would add to their defense of sound business and investment some thought of the legitimate demands of the farmer and laborer, and then would restrain legislation which directly encourages monopoly."

"True," said Mrs. Beech, "but wouldn't any rapprochement with the Republicans drive out of your ranks the radicals who swell the potential reform vote? And in this case would we not leave them to the guidance of demagogues and emphasize the dangerous directions of their growth?"

"Precisely, precisely. And that is what puzzles me. You know, only last night I was visiting a meeting of one of the newer trade unions, the Box-Makers. It was organized locally in New York in 1919 and now has a national union headquarters there. The union here is only a year old, but it is the center of dangerous radicalism, with lots of Jews, Russians, and other foreigners. They want paternalism of all sorts, with guaranteed wages, restricted ages and hours of work, pensions, long vacations and the like; not to mention wild vaporings about absolute free trade; 'One Big Union'; government ownership of industry, and limitation of wealth. And the trouble also," continued Mr. Cadwalader, "is that this union has some startlingly capable leaders; two representatives from New York were there last night, and a letter from the National President was read which was dangerous in its sheer ability, appeal, and implications.

"I was aghast. I wanted to repudiate the whole thing forthwith, but I was afraid, as you say, that I would drive them bodily over to the Socialists and Communists. In general, I'm beginning to wonder if we could try to marshal this extreme movement back of Matthew Towns. I don't exactly trust him, and I certainly do not trust his wife. But Towns has got sense. He is a practical politician. And it may be that with his leadership we can restrain these radicals and keep them inside a normal liberal movement."

Mrs. Beech pushed her dessert aside and sat for a while in a brown study.

"I am wondering too just how much can be done in this one Chicago congressional district, to use Towns and his wife in order to unite Republicans and Progressives, so as to begin a movement which should liberalize the Republican Party and stabilize the radicals. Unless we do this, or at least begin somewhere to do it, I see little hope for reform in politics. A third party in the United States is impossible on account of the Solid South. They are a dead weight and handicap to all political reform. They have but one shibboleth, and that is the Negro."

"Yes," said Mr. Cadwalader, "and the Democrats play their usual role in this campaign. Their positive policies are exactly the same as the Republicans'. They, of course, have no chance of winning in this political district, unless the Republicans split. Now with Towns' revolt, the Republican machine is split and the Democrats are just waiting. If Towns should be nominated they would raise the question of the color line and yell 'nigger.' They might in this way elect one of their own number or some independent. If Doolittle is nominated, it is going to be hard to elect him if Towns runs as an independent; and in that case it might be good politics for the Democrats to back Towns and beat the Republican machine. So there they are on the fence, waiting."

"On the other hand," said Mrs. Beech, "down in the black trenches the war is bitter, as I gathered from my attendance at the meeting this afternoon. Sammy Scott, the boss, and Sara

Towns were formerly close associates and know each other's personalities, political methods, and secrets. They are watching each other narrowly and are utterly unhindered by scruples. What sort of personality has this man Matthew Towns? Do you know anything about him?"

"I've been looking up his record. He intrigues me. He had, I find, an excellent record in medical school. Then in silly pique he became a Pullman porter and, I judge, sank pretty low. He does not seem to have committed any crime, but went to jail on a technicality because he wouldn't betray some of his friends. Scott rescued him and used him. He's got brains and education, but he's queer and not easily approachable."

"Well, if I were you," said Mrs. Beech as she arose, "I'd get in touch with Towns and cultivate him. He may be worth while. His wife is a shrewd climber, but even that might be an asset."

And so they parted.

XVII

The Honorable Sammy Scott was carefully planning his lines of battle and marshaling his forces. First he threw out certain skirmish lines—feints to veil his main action. Of course they might unearth or start something, but he was not putting his main dependence upon them. Of such a nature was Corruthers' trip to the East. It flattered Corruthers and gave him something to do, and it left Sammy unhindered to arrange his main campaign. And, of course, it was also possible that something would come out of this visit.

Among his other skirmishing efforts, Sammy kept looking for the weak spots in Matthew's armor, but was unable to find many. Matthew's obvious faults rather increased his popularity. He drank liquor, but not much, and Sammy saw no chance to make him or keep him drunk. He tried bribery on Towns from every point of view, but personal graft had not attracted Towns even when he was in the machine, and Sammy had little hope that it would now. Nevertheless, he saw to it that Towns was offered a goodly lump sum to withdraw his candidacy. Of course, Towns refused. The trouble was, as Sammy argued, that his machine could not afford to offer enough. He did not dare make the offer to Sara. She was capable of pocketing cash and candidate too.

Sammy's main dependence was to regain or split the Negro vote by careful propaganda; to reorganize his own machine and drive his leaders into line by the free use of money; and to alienate the church and the women from Towns by digging up scandals. Of course that second establishment that Matthew kept down where he used to live was a hopeful bit of scandal, only Sammy couldn't discover the woman. Naturally there must be a woman, or why should he keep the rooms?

Finally Sammy would try, wherever possible, strong-arm methods to intimidate the independents. Beyond this he believed that in some way he might split the Progressive support back of Matthew by making Matthew say or do something that was too radical for men like Cadwalader, or by making him bind himself to a program which was too reactionary for the radical Laborites.

Sammy envisaged the situation thus: If all efforts failed and Matthew received the Farmer-Labor nomination and the support of the majority of the colored vote, nevertheless, a huge sum of money spent at the polls might even then defeat him. If bribery failed and the Negro vote stood solid, the Progressives gave full support and the Democrats secret aid, Matthew would be elected, but Sammy would emerge from the campaign able to tell the party bosses that the fault was theirs; they should have kept their promise and nominated him. After that, with a large campaign fund, he could reorganize his machine and keep watch on Matthew in office. If Matthew failed to do as the machine told him, and this would probably happen, Sammy would succeed to his job. If Matthew succeeded, he could and must be brought back into the Republican fold, which meant into Sammy's machine.

Of course, all these possibilities which hinged on Matthew's successful election were wormwood to Sammy, and he concentrated fiercely on forestalling such success. He was sitting alone in his office this night and thinking things out when there came a 'phone call. It was Corruthers.

Corruthers came in a half hour later. Corruthers was a cadaverous blond, red-headed and freckled, a drunkard, a dope fiend, and a spellbinder, with brains and no self-control, thoroughly dishonest and extremely likable. He claimed to be a nephew of Frederick Douglass. He looked distinctly glum.

Corruthers was one of those who are dangerous only when they are successful. Once he began to lose he gave up. Sammy was quite different. He was most dangerous losing. It was then that he fought furiously and to the last ditch. Evidently Corruthers had been disappointed and was ready to surrender.

"Didn't do a thing," he said, "not a thing. Sure, I found the widow of that porter who was lynched. She's working in New York. But, my God! She thinks Towns is Jesus Christ and won't hear a word against him. Swears that the story that he attacked anybody is a lie and threatens to go to court if anybody says that Towns was responsible for her husband's death. I can't figure her out at all. I know the story that I got was the truth, but I can't prove it.

"Then I tried to get a line on that dead man in the wreck. He may have been a fellow named Perigua. Some say he was, but others declare that Perigua went back to Jamaica and has been seen there since. I don't know how it was. Then I was all wrong about that brown woman. She was an Indian princess, sure enough, a high muck-a-muck and fabulously rich. Probably got interested in Towns because he was a good porter. At any rate, she's gone back to India, so everybody says, although there again some declare that she has returned."

"Well, what did you do about that?" asked Sammy impatiently.

"Well, I found out the address of her bankers and went down to inquire about her. Seems that her little country, Bwodpur, has some sort of commercial agency which I was referred to. It didn't look like much. Mean little office, with two or three Indians sitting around. All I could do was to leave my address and say that I had some news for the lady about Matthew Towns; then I came home."

"Hell!" said Sammy, lighting another cigar.

"But today," continued Corruthers, "an East Indian called at my place and asked about Towns. Said he'd been sent."

"What did you do with him?" asked Sammy.

"He's outside," said Corruthers.

"Well, for God's sake! And gassing about nothing all this time! Bring him in."

"Wait a minute," said Corruthers. "What are we going to say to him? I couldn't think of anything. Of course we might pinch him for a little cash."

"Nix," said Sammy, "leave him to me."

The Indian entered. He looked thin and was poorly dressed. Sammy was disappointed, but he handed him one of his cheap cigars, which the Indian refused.

"I understand," said the Indian in very good English, "that you have some message from or about Matthew Towns."

"Ah," said Sammy. "Not from him, but about him. Er'r, I believe the lady with whom you are connected is friendly with Mr. Towns."

"Her Royal Highness in the past has deigned to express something like that."

"And—still interested?"

"I do not know."

"I mean, she wouldn't let him suffer or get into trouble, and she wouldn't want to get in trouble herself on account of him?"

"Perhaps not, but what is the case?"

Sammy paused thoughtfully and then started.

"You see, it is this way. This fellow Towns got in jail for not peaching on a pal. I got him out. He made a good record in the legislature and his friends persuaded him to run for Congress. I'd be glad to see him go, but his enemies and the enemies of his race are threatening to bring up this old jail case, and they say that your Princess is involved. It would be a nasty mess to have her name dragged in publicly now. The only way out, as I see it, is for somebody to persuade Towns to withdraw. Can you or your lady manage this?"

"Very well," said the Indian, arising.

"But can you do anything?"

"I do not know, I will report."

And then Sammy said: "What! 'way to India?"

"Her Royal Highness is represented in this country. Good day."

Sammy glowered after him.

"Royal Highness! Hell!" said Corruthers. "And see all the time wasted on that guy. We ought to have asked him straight for money."

"Looks like a mare's nest," said Sammy, "but my rule is to try everything. Well, enough of that. Now my plan is to see what we can do to split the Progressives and this Farmer-Labor bunch, which is promising to support Towns. I know Sara's game; she's playing both ends against the middle. But I'm going to break it up."

XVIII

Sara had, of all concerned, the most difficult road and the most brilliant prospects. She saw wealth, power, social triumph ahead if she could elect Matthew to Congress. But she knew just how difficult it would be to beat the Republican machine with its money and organization. Her first task was to hold the Negro vote back of Matthew. That was easy so long as he was a regular Republican. When he bolted Sammy's machine, Sara had to capitalize race pride and resentment against Doolittle and Sammy. She continued to insist that Matthew was a good Republican but not a Sammy Scott henchman. For a while her success here was overwhelming, but could she hold it three months with hungry editors and grafting henchmen?

She concentrated on *The Lask*, whose editors had sharp tongues and wide pockets and kept them flaying Sammy and the Republicans. She went after her women's clubs and cajoled and encouraged them by every device to stand strong. She made every possible use of the women's organizations connected with the fraternal societies. She already belonged to everything that she could join, and was Grand Worthy Something-or-other in most of them. She pushed the idea of uniforms and rituals, for these things appeal naturally to folk whose lives are gray and uneventful. She had a uniformed Women's Marching Club and a Flying Squadron with secret ritual which she used for political spy work.

All these things carried new dimensions to the lives of a class of colored women who had been hitherto bound chiefly to their kitchens and their churches. Woman's "new sphere," of which they had read something in the papers, had hitherto meant little to them. They were still under the spell of the old housework, except as they raised money in the churches. Here was work newer and more interesting than church work. The colored ministers protested, but were afraid to protest too much, because many of Sara's political followers were still their best church workers, and they dared not say or do too much to alienate them.

Sara worked feverishly during March because she knew perfectly well that the real difficulty lay ahead. The election of Matthew might involve voting not only against Sammy's machine but against the Republican ticket and with the Farmer-Labor group, and possibly even voting with the Democrats. Casual white outsiders cannot understand what this problem is. These colored women were born Republicans, even more than their fathers and brothers, because they knew less of the practical action of politics. Republicanism was as much a part of their heritage as Methodism or the rites of baptism. They were enthusiastic to have a colored man nominated by the Republican Party. But could she so organize and concentrate that enthusiasm that it would carry these women over into the camp of hereditary political and economic enemies?

They looked upon the white labor unions as open enemies because the stronger and better-organized white unions deliberately excluded Negroes. The whole economic history of the Negro in Chicago was a fight for bread against white labor unions. Only in the newer unions just organized chiefly among the foreign-born—and fighting for breath among the unskilled or semi-skilled laborers—only here were colored people welcomed, because they had to be. Of course, the very name of the Democratic Party was anathema to black folk. It stood for slavery and disfranchisement and "Jim Crow" cars. Well, Sara knew that she had a desperate task, and she was fighting hard.

She was in touch with the labor unions and soon sensed their right and left wings. The right wing was easy to understand. They were playing her game and compromising here and there to obtain certain selfish advantages. Sara was sure she could take care of them. The extreme left group was more difficult to understand. She did not know what it was they really wanted, but she quickly sensed that they had astute leadership. The international president of the Box-Makers, who lived in New York, was evidently well educated and keen. Sara had written her in the hope of avoiding contact with the local union. Her answers showed her a desperately earnest woman. Sara did everything to induce her by letter to wield her Chicago influence for Matthew, but so far had seen no signs of success. This left group was meantime clamoring, pushing their claims and asking promises and making inconvenient suggestions. So far Sara had avoided meeting them.

One thing, one very little thing, Sara kept in her mind's eye, and that was Doolittle and his health. If anything happened to Doolittle before the primary election—well, if it happened, Sara wanted to know it and to know it first. And it was precisely here that Sammy made his second mistake. He calculated that the news of any change in Doolittle's health would reach him first, because Doolittle's valet was a staunch member of his machine. Indeed, he got him the job. Now Sara knew this as well as Sammy, and she worked accordingly. Doolittle lived officially on the South Side but actually in Winnetka, away up on the North Shore, in a lovely great house overlooking the blue lake. Sara had careful and minute knowledge of his household. Of course, his servants were all colored. That was good politics. Sara again had recourse to that maid who had told her first of the plan to renominate Doolittle. She had the maid at tea on one of her Thursday "at homes," and was careful to have in some of her most expensive friends—the doctor's wife, the banker's daughter, the niece of the vice-president of Liberty Life.

Sara did not say that the quiet and well-behaved stranger was simply a maid, and by this very reticence tied the maid to her forever. Also, Sara pumped her assiduously about Doolittle's health without directly asking after it. She easily learned that it was much more precarious than the public believed. Immediately, through the maid, Sara got in touch with the valet. She picked him up downtown in her car and brought him to luncheon one day, when Matthew was away from home.

"I do not want you to think, Mr. Amos, that I have anything against the excellent Mr. Doolittle."

"No, ma'am, no, ma'am, I'm sure you ain't. I am sorry he's running again. He oughtn't to done it. He ain't in no fit condition to make a campaign. He wouldn't of done it if he had been left alone; but there's his wife full of ambition and the big bosses full of plans."

"I do wish Sammy had stood pat and insisted on the nomination," said Sara thoughtfully.

W. E. B. DU BOIS

"I'll never forgive him," said Mr. Amos. "It was sheer lack of backbone and an itching palm."

"You are a great friend of his, I know."

"Well," said Mr. Amos, "I don't like him as well as I use to, although I know he got me my job. Tell you what, ma'am, I wish your husband could get the nomination." They talked on. When finally he stood at the front door, Sara was saying:

"I hope, of course, that all will go well, for Doolittle is a deserving old man, but if anything *should* change in his physical condition I'd like to know it *before* anybody else, Mr. Amos; and I'm depending on you." And her dependence was expressed in the shape of a yellow bill which she slipped in Mr. Amos' hand. He took occasion to examine it under the electric light as he was waiting for the bus. It was a bank note for five hundred dollars. Mr. Amos missed two buses looking at it.

Less than a week later, while Sara was at her desk one morning, about to send out notes for one of her innumerable committee meetings, the telephone rang. The low voice of Mr. Amos came over it:

"Mr. Doolittle has had an attack. He is quite ill."

She thanked him softly and hung up.

The next morning Sara went down to Republican headquarters, where she used to be well known. She was regarded with considerable interest this morning, but remained unperturbed. She asked for a certain gentleman who was always busy, but Sara wrote a note and sent it in to him with a card. He found time to see her.

"Mr. Graham," she said, "what do you think of Congressman Doolittle's health?"

Mr. Graham looked at her sharply, took off his glasses, and polished them carefully, as he continued to look. "I have every reason to suppose," he said slowly, "that Mr. Doolittle's health is excellent."

"Well, it isn't," said Sara.

"I suppose your source of information—" But Sara interrupted him.

"Frankly, Mr. Graham—suppose that Congressman Doolittle should die before the primary election."

"We'd be in a hell of a muddle," blurted out Mr. Graham.

"You would," said Sara. "You could hardly nominate Sammy, because Sammy is very unpopular just now among colored voters."

"Thanks to you," said Mr. Graham.

"No, Mr. Graham, thanks to you. Now my husband, Mr. Matthew Towns, is both popular and—intelligent."

"Especially," added Mr. Graham, "with the Farmer-Labor reformers and the Bolsheviks."

"Not a bad bunch of votes to bring to the Republican Party just now."

"Well, any colored candidate would have to bring in something to offset the hullabaloo which the Klan would raise in this town if we nominated a Negro and a—one with your husband's record, to Congress."

"Precisely, and I am calculating that the support of the reform groups and the solidarity of the colored vote would much more than offset this and make the election certain."

"In any case, Mrs. Towns, I take it that your husband has been promised the support of the Farmer-Labor group only on condition that he stand on their platform."

"He has given them to understand," said Sara carefully, and with a smile, "that he sympathizes with their ideals."

"Well," said Mr. Graham crisply, "that puts him out of the running for the Republican nomination, even in the extremely unlikely event that Mr. Doolittle for any reason should not or could not receive it."

"I wonder," said Sara. "You know quite well that the intellectuals in the Farmer-Labor group are bound to support Republican policies up to a certain point. Their financial interests compel them; now it would be good politics for the Republicans to go a step beyond that point in order to attract, by some show of liberality, as large a group as possible of the liberals. Then, having split off their leaders and their thinkers, we might let the rest of the radicals go hang. What I am proposing in fine, Mr. Graham, is this: that the nomination of my husband (in the unlikely event that Mr. Doolittle should not be well enough to accept) might be a piece of farsighted politics on your part and bring you the bulk of the liberal vote, while at the same time paralyzing and splitting up the power of the radicals."

Mr. Graham fingered his mustache. "I will not forget this visit, Mrs. Towns," he said.

Sara walked out; taking a taxi, she quietly slipped over to the Democratic headquarters. She asked to see Mr. Green of Washington.

"Mr. Green?" asked the porter, doubtfully.

"Yes, he is in town temporarily and making his headquarters here. I will not keep him long. Here is my card. I have met him."

After a while another gentleman came out.

"Mr. Green is only calling at this office. Just what is your business with him?"

"Please tell him that once in Washington he signed a petition for me that helped release Matthew Towns from Joliet. Mr. Towns is my husband and is now running for Congress."

A few minutes later Sara was closeted with Mr. Green, a high official of the Klan. He looked at her with interest.

"And what can I do for you this time, madam?"

"You remember me?"

"Perfectly."

"I trust you have not regretted helping me."

"No."

"Have you followed Mr. Towns' career?"

"I know something of it."

"Well, he may be nominated for Congress by the Republicans, and he may not. If he does not get the nomination, he will run independently on the Farmer-Labor ticket. Any help that the Democrats could give us in such a campaign would greatly impede the Republicans." Mr. Green smiled, but Sara proceeded:

"In the unlikely event that he should be nominated by the Republicans I have come to ask you if it would not be possible for you to restrain any anti-Negro campaign against him or any undue reference to his jail sentence. You see, with the Republican and Farmer-Labor support he would probably be elected, and if that election came with your silent help, he would be even more disposed to look with favor upon you and your help than he is now. And he feels now that he owes you a great deal."

Mr. Green looked at her curiously. Finally, as he arose, he shook hands with her and said:

"I am glad you came to me."

Sara was a little exhausted when she reached home, but she still had some letters to write. The maid said that the telephone had rung and that some Mr. Amos would call her later. Sara sat down by her well-ordered desk and inserted a new pen-point. Soon the telephone rang. Mr. Amos' voice came over the wire:

"Mr. Doolittle is some better, but still in bed."

Sara looked at the clock. It was four. She ordered dinner and went back to her writing. The hours passed slowly. At half-past five Matthew came in, and they ate silently at six. While they were eating the telephone rang again.

"Mr. Doolittle has gone out for a short drive. He is better, but far from well."

They finished dinner. Matthew stood about restlessly a while, smoking. Then with a muttered word he went out. Sara sat down beside the telephone and waited. The messages came at intervals, each shorter than the other.

"Mr. Doolittle has returned."

"He has taken a chill."

"The physicians are working over him."

"He is sinking."

Eight, nine, and ten o'clock chimed on Sara's gilt desk clock, and then:

"Congressman Doolittle is dying."

Sara waited no longer. It was March 20. The primary election was to take place April 8. She took a taxi for Republican headquarters.

XIX

S ammy's campaign was progressing. Its progress was not altogether satisfactory, but Sammy was encouraged. Most of the best colored newspapers had been "seen" and were acting satisfactorily. *The Conservator* had one week a strong defense of the "Grand Old Man and Friend of Our Race, the Honorable Calvin Doolittle!" The next week, it featured a lynching, scored the Democrats, and pointed to Doolittle's vote on the anti-lynching bill. *The Lash*, when Sara refused its last exorbitant demand for cash, started a series of scathing attacks on the white trade unions and accused them of being filled with "nigger-haters" and Catholics. Other smaller sheets followed suit, with regrets that Mr. Towns was being misled into opposition to the Republican leaders who had always been friends, etc. Only one paper, *The Standard*, stood strong for Matthew at a price which Sara could afford; but even that paper avoided all attacks on the Republican Party.

The local clubs and political centers of Sammy's machine gave every evidence of prosperity, while police interference with gambling and prostitution ceased. The prohibition officials apparently stopped all efforts in the main black belt, and there were wild and ceaseless rumors that the Klan was back of a widespread effort to beat the Republicans.

Only the women stood strong. And so strong did they stand under Sara's astute leadership and marshaling care that Sammy was still worried. They were difficult to reach. Sluggers could not break up their meetings. They could easily out-gossip Sammy's sensation-mongers, and against their hold on the churches, the colored newspapers availed nothing. It remained true, therefore, after two months' campaign, that the great majority of Negro voters were still apparently opposed to Sammy and strongly in favor of Matthew's nomination. Nevertheless, with time and money, Sammy was sure he could win. The trouble was, time was pressing. Only two weeks was left before the primary elections.

Reflecting on all this, Sammy Scott after dinner one day took a stroll, smoking and greeting his friends. He dropped in at some of the clubs and had a word of advice or of information. He took drinks in a couple of cabarets; watched a little gambling. As he sat in one of the resorts, he listened to the talk of a young black radical. The fellow was explaining at length what Negroes ought to demand in wages and conditions of labor, how they ought to get into the trade unions, and how they were welcomed by unions like that of the Box-Makers. Sammy sidled over to him. He struck Sammy as the sort of man who might carry on a useful propaganda among some of the colored voters and strengthen the demands made on Matthew to take so radical a position that the Republicans could not accept him.

Sammy talked with him and finally invited him to supper. He was undoubtedly hungry. Then he invited Sammy to come with him to a meeting of the Box-Makers. They went west to that great district where the black belt fades into the white workingmen's belt. In a dingy crowded hall, a number of people were congregated. They were discussing the demands of the Box-Makers, and Sammy listened at the door.

"How many of us," yelled one man, "make as much as fifteen dollars a week, and how can we live on that?"

"Yes," added a woman, "how can we live, even if we women work too? We can make only five or six dollars, and out of work a third of the time."

"Oh, you got it easy even at that. You ought to see where we work, down in damp and unventilated cellars. No porters to keep the shops and the washrooms clean; the stink and gloom and dirt all about us."

"In my shop we never get sunlight a day in the year."

Another one broke in. "And we're working twelve or thirteen hours a day with clean-up on Sunday. It ain't human, and we won't stand it no longer."

Sammy edged in and sat down. Pretty soon the speakers gathered on the stage—the young colored man whom he had met, another colored man whom he did not at first recognize, and several white organizers and delegates. There were long speeches and demands and fiery threats, but Sammy waited because he wanted to talk to that young fellow again. When the meeting was over, the young man came down accompanied by the other colored man, and Sammy noted with a start that it was the Indian with whom he had had conference concerning Matthew.

Sammy was puzzled. What was that Indian doing there on the stage? Especially when he represented aristocracy, at least if what he said about the Princess was to be believed. "Or is it that they are on to me?" thought Sammy. "Is the Princess interfering or not?" Then suddenly he saw a possibility. The Princess or her friends might want Matthew nominated for Congress, but nominated on this radical platform. Good, so did he. Oh, boy! So did he. He got hold of the young colored man and walked away. They had a long conversation about the platform of the radicals and about putting this platform up to Matthew Towns and insisting that he stand on it. Also, Sammy lent the young man twenty-five dollars and told him to come to see him again.

XX

It was late when Sammy got back to his office, after midnight, in fact. As he rushed in hurriedly he saw to his astonishment that Sara Towns was sitting in the outer room. A number of his cronies and henchmen were grouped about, staring, laughing, and smoking. Sara was elaborately ignoring them. She had arranged herself quite becomingly in the best chair with her trim legs in evidence, the light falling right for her costume and not too strongly on her face. The fact was that her face showed some recent signs of wear, despite the beauty parlors. Sammy stopped, swore softly under his breath, and glared. What did it mean? Thought Sammy rapidly. Surrender or attack? But he quickly recovered his poise and soon was his smiling, debonair self.

"May I see you a few moments alone?" asked Sara.

"Sure! Excuse me, boys, ladies first."

They went into the inner sanctum and drove out some more of Sammy's lieutenants. Sara closed the door and looked around the inner office with disgust.

"My, but you're dirty here!"

Sammy apologized. "It ain't exactly as clean as it was in your day," he grinned. She dusted a chair, arranged her skirt and tilted her hat properly, looking into the mirror opposite. Sammy waited and lighted another cigar.

"Sammy, I came to suggest that we join forces again."

Sammy looked innocent, but did some quick calculations. Aha! He knew that combination wouldn't last. Wonder what broke first?

"Well, I don't know," he drawled finally. "You broke it up yourself, you remember."

"Yes, I did. You see, I thought at the time you were going to nominate Doolittle for congressman."

"Yes," said Sammy. "And I still am."

"No, you're not," answered Sara. "He just died."

Sammy dropped his cigar. He fumbled for it and got to his feet. Then he sat down again limply.

"Well, I'll be God damned," he remarked and grabbed the telephone.

As a matter of fact, Sara had left the house and rushed to Republican headquarters before Doolittle was actually dead. Mr. Graham had, of course, been warned of Doolittle's sudden illness, but he had not heard of his death for the simple reason that it had not yet taken place. When, therefore, this self-possessed, gray-eyed little woman came in and announced Doolittle's death, Graham did not believe it. Five minutes later it was confirmed on the phone. But still the thing looked uncanny, because Sara had only been there five minutes and must have announced the death at exactly the minute it actually took place. But she had been quite matter-of-fact and had gone right to business.

"Can't we get together?" she had said. "Under the circumstances you cannot nominate a white man now. You have no excuse for doing it after your past promises. Then, too, you can't nominate Sammy Scott. He is too unpopular, thanks to you. Even if you try to nominate him, Matthew Towns can beat him in the primary. If you buy up the primary vote with a big slush fund, as Sammy plans, Towns, with the support of the Liberals and perhaps the Democrats, together with the bolting Negroes, can be elected."

The chairman had sneered in his confusion: "Negroes don't bolt."

"Not usually," Sara replied, "but they may this time. In fact," she said, "I think they will."

In his own mind the chairman was afraid she was right.

"Why not nominate Towns?" she asked.

"Well," said the chairman, sparring for time, "first there is Sammy; and secondly, there is the question as to what Towns will do in Congress."

"He will promise to do anything you say," said Sara. "And I am going to see Sammy now." Thus she came and told Sammy the news.

Sammy struggled at the phone. The operator was evidently asleep, but he got through to Graham at last. Sure enough,

Doolittle was dead! Sammy stared into the instrument. It certainly looked bad for him. Here he had got the most important news of the campaign from headquarters through Sara. Very well. Evidently he must tie up with Sara again. In such an alliance he had everything to gain and nothing to lose. As his political partner, at least she could not continue to attack him. The matter of the nomination would not be settled until the primary was held in April. He had twelve days to work in. He had seen a president made in less time.

Sammy put down the telephone and turned to Sara with a smile, but underneath that smile was grim determination, and Sara, of course, knew it. He was going to fight to the last ditch, but he extended his hand with the most disarming of smiles.

"All right, partner," he said, "we'll start again. Now what's your plan?"

"My plan is," said Sara coolly, "to have you work with me for the nomination of Matthew to Congress."

"Where do I come in?" said Sammy.

"You come in at the head of a united machine with a large campaign fund."

"That wasn't the old plan," said Sammy.

"No, it wasn't," answered Sara, "but who broke up the old plan?"

"Graham tried to," said Sammy, "but God didn't let him."

"True," answered Sara, "and naturally somebody has got to pay for not stopping Graham, and that somebody is you. Still," she said, "the price need not be prohibitive. After Matthew has had a term in Congress, why not Sammy Scott?"

Sammy smiled wryly. "All right," said Sammy. "I'm set. Now what are we going to do?"

"We are going to try and get the Republican and the Farmer-Labor people to unite on the nomination of Matthew."

"Good!" said Sammy. "Here goes."

"Of course," added Sara, "we must be careful not to make our new alliance too open and scare off the Liberals. We must drift together apparently as fast and no faster than these two wings come to an understanding. That understanding I'm going to engineer, and I want your help. First you go to Graham and tell

W.E.B. DU BOIS

him you'll support Matthew. I've told him you're coming. As soon as I've heard from him that you've seen him, I'll get hold of Cadwalader and tell him the news. We'll work on this toward a final conference just before the primaries."

XXI

Neither to Sammy nor to Sara did their new alliance make any real difference. It healed the open and public split, but Sammy continued to bore into Matthew's support, and Sara continued to strengthen his popularity and defenses. Beyond that, Sammy and Sara had always admired each other. Each was a little at a loss without the other. Neither had many intimate associates or confidants whom they wholly trusted. Both had the highest respect for each other's abilities. They knew that their new alliance was a truce and not a union. Each suspected the other, and each knew the other's suspicions. At the same time, they needed each other's skill and they wanted desperately to confide in each other, as far as they dared.

Sara had suggested that just before the primaries, a conference of Republicans and Liberals might be held in order to come to a final understanding and unite on Matthew's nomination. Sammy had to assent. He had plans of his own for this conference, which he hoped to make a last desperate effort at Matthew's undoing. He knew just what kind of conference would best serve his ends, but he did not dare let Sara know what he wanted.

On one point Sara had of course made up her mind: no agreement between Matthew, Graham, and Cadwalader was going to depend on the chances of a single conference or even of several conferences. She was going to conduct secret negotiations with all parties, until the final conference should find them in such substantial agreement that definitive action would be easy; that is, all except the left-wing labor unions. The surer she became of the main groups, the less did Sara think of these common laborers and foreigners. They could come in at last, when agreement or protest would make little real difference.

Sara hoped that she might come to this agreement by mere verbal fencing. She hoped so, but she knew better. Sooner or later there must be a definite understanding with Graham.

Very well, when the crisis came she would meet it. With her mind then on this closing conference as merely the ratification of agreements practically made, Sara at first settled on something big and impressive: a church or hall mass meeting of all parties and interests, making an overwhelming demand for the election of Matthew Towns as congressman. Sammy listened, his head on one side, his cigar at an impressive angle, his feet elevated, perhaps a bit higher than usual; his coat laid aside.

"Um-um!" he nodded. "Fine; fine big thing. If it could be put over. Smashing publicity." Then he took a long pull at his cigar and looked intently at the glowing end.

"Of course," he said reflectively, "there is one thing: would Matthew make the right kind of speech?" Sammy was really afraid he would; Sara not only did not know whether or not Matthew would make the right kind of speech; she did not even know if he would try. In fact, he might deliberately make the wrong kind of speech, even after agreement had already been reached. Sara's doubt rested on the fact that she and Matthew had had a tilt this very morning, and she at least had had it out. She put the situation before him, frank and stark, with no bandying of words.

"Now see here. You have got this nomination in your hands and on a silver salver, if you want it. But in order to get it you've got to make the kind of statement that will satisfy the Republicans backed by big business, the Democrats backed by big business, and the Farmer-Labor party led by reformers and union labor. You've even got to cater to the radical wing of the trade unions. It will mean straddling and twisting and some careful lying. It will mean promises which it is up to you to fulfill after election, if you want to, and to break if you want to—after election. It will mean half promises and double words and silences to make people think what you are going to do, what you are not going to do, or what you do not know whether you are going to do or not. Unless you do something like this you will lose the nomination.

"Or, what's just as bad, you will lose the Republican nomination. Perhaps you have kidded yourself into thinking that you can make a winning fight with the Farmer-Labor nomination and the independent Negro vote. Well, listen to me. You can't. There isn't such a thing as an independent Negro vote. Or at any rate it is so small as to be negligible. The Negroes are going to fight and yell before election. At the election they are going to trot to the polls and vote the Republican ticket like good darkies. If you want to go to Congress, you have got to get the Republican nomination.

"On the other hand, nothing will clinch this nomination, the election, and the wholehearted future support of the Republican machine like your ability to poll not simply the Republican vote, but the Farmer-Labor vote and the vote of the independent Democrats and at least a part of the radical vote. You can do this if you don't act like a fool."

Matthew had pushed his breakfast aside and looked out of the window. He saw a few trees and the gray apartment houses beyond. Above lay the leaden sky.

"Suppose," he said, "that instead of making this campaign, I should ask for the part of the money we have made which is mine and give up this game?" Sara's little mouth settled into straight, thin lines. "You wouldn't get it," she said, "because it doesn't belong to you. You didn't earn it; I did. You haven't saved any. You have squandered money, even recently; I don't know what for, and I don't care. But I have drawn out all the money in our joint account and put it in my own account. Everything we have got stands in my name, and it is going to stand there until you get into Congress. And that's that."

Matthew had looked at Sara solemnly with brooding eyes. She was always uncomfortable when he looked at her like that. He seemed to be quite impersonal, as though he were entering lone realms where she could not follow. Soon, some of her assurance had fallen away and her language became less precise:

"Well, what's the idea? What ya glaring at? D'ye think I am going to fail or let you fail after climbing all this distance?"

Apparently he had not heard her. He seemed to be judging her in a far-off sort of way. He was thinking. In a sense Sara was an artist. But she failed in greatness because she lacked the human element, the human sympathy. Now if she had had the abandon, that inner comprehension, of the prostitute who once lived opposite

Perigua—but no, no, Sara was respectable. That meant she was a little below average. She was desperately aware of the prevailing judgment of the people about her. She would never be great. She would always be, to him—unendurable. He got up suddenly and silently and walked three miles in the rain. He ended up at his own lodging with its dust and gloom and stood there in the cold and damp thinking of his marriage, six months—six centuries ago.

Again and for a second, for a third, time in his life, he was caught in the iron of circumstance. And he wasn't going to do anything. He couldn't do anything. He was going to be the victim, the sacrifice. Although this time it seemed different from the others. In the first case, of the wreck, he had saved his pride. In the second, the nomination to the legislature, he had sold his body but ransomed his soul, as he hoped. But this time, pride, soul, and body were going.

He looked about at these little trappings of the spirit within him that had grown so thin: gold of the Chinese rug, beneath its dim Chicago dirt; the flame of a genuine Matisse. He had never given up the old rooms of his in the slums, chiefly because Sara would not have the things he had accumulated there in her new and shining house; and he hated to throw them all away. He had always meant to go down and sort them out and store the few things he wanted to keep. But he had been too busy. The rent was nominal, and he had locked the door and left things there.

Only now and then in desperation he went there and sat in the dust and gloom. Today, he went down and waded in. He sat down in the old, shabby easy-chair and thought things out. He was, despite all, more normal and clearer-minded than when he came here out of jail. He was not so cynical. He had found good friends—humble everyday workers, even idlers and loafers whom he trusted and who trusted him. Life was not all evil. He did not need to sell his soul entirely to the devil for bread and butter. Life could be even interesting. There were big jobs, not to be done, but to be attempted, to be interested in. He was not yet prepared to let Sara spoil everything. He began to look upon her with a certain aversion and horror. He planned to live his life by himself as much as possible. She had her virtues, but she was too hard, too selfish, utterly unscrupulous.

He searched his pockets for money. He went downtown and paid two hundred dollars for a Turkish rug for the bedroom—a silken thing of dark, soft, warm coloring. He lugged it home on the street car and threw it before his old bed and let it vie with the dusky gold of its Chinese mate. He had searched for another Matisse and could not find one, but he had found a copy of a Picasso a wild, unintelligible, intriguing thing of gray and yellow and black. He paid a hundred dollars for it and hung it on another empty wall. He was half-consciously trying to counteract the ugliness of the congressional campaign.

Long hours he sat in his room. There was no place in Sara's house it was always Sara's house in his thought—for anything of this, for anything of his: for this big, shabby armchair that put its old worn arms so sympathetically about him. For his pipe. For the books that his fingers had made dirty and torn and dog-eared by reading. For the pamphlets that would not stand straight or regular or in rows. He sat there cold and dark until three o'clock in the morning. Then he stood up suddenly and went to a low bootlegger's dive, a place warm with the stench of human bodies. He sought there feverishly until he found what he wanted—a soul to talk with. There was a mason and builder who came there usually at that hour, especially when he was half drunk and out of work. He was a rare and delicate soul with a whimsical cynicism, with easily remembered tales of lost and undiscovered bits of humanity, with exquisite humor. He played the violin like an angel. Matthew found him. He sat there until dawn. He ordered him to build a fireplace and bathroom in his apartment—something beautiful.

As he sat silently listening to the luscious thrill of the "Spanish Fandango" he determined to do one thing: he would resign from the legislature. Then if he failed in the nomination to Congress, he would be left on the road to freedom. If he gained the nomination, be would gain it with that much less deception and double-crossing. Of course Sara would be furious. Well, what of that?

At daybreak he went back to his rooms and started cleaning up. He swept and dusted, cleaned windows, polished furniture. He sweated and toiled, then stopped and marveled about Dirt. Its accumulation, its persistence was astonishing. How could one attack it? Was it a world symptom? Could machines abolish it, or only human weariness and nausea? Late in the afternoon he went out and bought a new big bed with springs and a soft mattress, a bath robe, pajamas, and sheets and some crimson hangings. He hid in the wall some of his money which remained. He knew what he was doing; he was surrendering to Sara and the Devil and soothing his bruised soul by physical work and the preparation of a retreat where he would spend more and more of his time. He would save and hide and hoard and some day walk away and leave everything. But he wrote and mailed his resignation as member of the legislature. That at least was a symbolic step.

From her interview with Matthew, Sara emerged shaken but grim. She had no idea what Matthew was going to do. She had put the screws upon him more ruthlessly than she had ever dared before. She had cut off his money, his guiding dream of a comfortable little fortune. She had told him definitely what he had to think and promise, and he had silently got up and gone his way. Suppose he never came back, or suppose he came back and eventually went to this final conference and "spilled the beans"; threw everything up and over and left her shamed and prostrate before black and white Chicago? No, she couldn't risk a mass meeting.

"No," she said in answer to Sammy's query, and looked at him with a frankness that Sammy half suspected was too frank.

"I don't know what Matthew is going to say or do. And I am afraid we can't risk a mass meeting."

Sammy was silent. Then he said:

"That resignation was a damn shrewd move." Sara glanced up.

"What—" She started to ask "What resignation?" but she paused. "What, do you think will be its effect?" She would not let Sammy dream she did not know what he was talking about.

"Well—it'll mollify the boys. Give me a chance to run Corruthers in at a special election—convince the bosses that Towns is playing square."

Sara was angry but silent. So that fool had resigned from the legislature! Surrendered a sure thing for a chance. Did the idiot think he was already elected to Congress, or was he going to quit entirely?

She took up the morning *Tribune* to hide her agitation and saw the editorial—"a wise move on the part of Towns and shows his independence of the machine."

Sara laid down the paper carefully and thought—tapping her teeth with her pencil. Was it possible that after all—

Then she came back to the matter in hand. Sammy would have liked to suggest a real political conference: a secret room with guarded door; cigars and liquor; a dozen men with power and decision, and then, give and take, keen-eyed sparring, measuring of men, and—careful compromise. Out of a conference like that anything might emerge, and Sammy couldn't lose entirely.

But he saw that Sara had the social bee in her head. She wanted a reception, a luncheon, or a dinner. Something that would celebrate a conclusion rather than come to it. He was not averse to this, because he was convinced it would be disastrous to Sara. No social affair of whites and Negroes could come to any real conclusion. It could only celebrate deals already made. Sammy meant to block such deals. But he didn't suggest anything; he let Sara do that, and Sara did. After profound thought, and still clicking her pencil on her teeth, she said: "A meeting at my home would be the best. A small and intimate thing. A luncheon. No, a dinner, and a good dinner. Let's see, we'll have—"

And then Sara and Sammy selected the personnel. On this they quite agreed. If all went well, Sara suggested that the mass meeting might follow. Sammy cheerfully agreed—if all went well.

Immediately Sara began to prepare for this conference. First she made a number of personal visits, just frank little informal talks with Mr. Graham, with Mr. Cadwalader, with Mrs. Beech and others. Mr. Cadwalader and Mrs. Beech both began by congratulating Sara on Matthew's resignation from the legislature.

"Statesmanlike!" said Cadwalader. "It proves to our people that the reported understanding between him and Scottis untrue."

"Very shrewd," said Mrs. Beech, "to make this open declaration of independence."

"He often takes my advice," said Sara with a cryptic smile, and she explained that when Sammy had approached her, offering cooperation after Doolittle's death, they had, of course, to accept—"to a degree and within limits."

"Of course, of course!" it was agreed.

By her visits she got acquainted with these leaders, measured their wishes, and succeeded fairly well in making them interested in her. She let them do as much talking as possible but also talked herself, clearly and with as much frankness as she dared. She was trying to find out just what the Republicans wanted and just what the reformers demanded.

From time to time she wrote these things down and put the formulas and statements before Matthew, writing them out carefully and precisely in her perfect typewriting. He received them silently and took them away, making no comment. Only once was the resignation from the legislature referred to:

"I'm glad you took my hint about the legislature," said Sara sweetly, one night at dinner.

Matthew stared. When had she hinted, and what?

Sara proceeded further with her plans. She put before Mr. Graham a suggested platform which contained a good many of the Republican demands but even more of the Progressive demands. Mr. Graham immediately rejected it as she expected. He pointed out just how much more he must have and what things he could under no circumstances admit.

Sara tried the same method with Mr. Cadwalader; only in his case she submitted a platform with less of the Progressive demands and more of the Republican. She had more success with him. She could easily see that Mr. Cadwalader after all really leaned considerably toward Republican policies and was Progressive in theory and by the practical necessity of yielding something to the Labor group. But the question Sara quickly saw was, Which Labor group? There were, for instance, the aristocrats in the Labor world; the skilled trade unions connected with the American Federation of Labor; and on the other hand, there was the left wing, the Communist radicals, and there was a string of uncommitted workers between. Mr. Cadwalader consulted the conservative labor unionists and evolved a platform which was not so far from Sara's, and indeed as she compared them, Mr. Graham and Mr. Cadwalader seemed easily reconcilable, at least in words. Sara tried again and brought another modified platform to Mr. Graham. Mr. Graham read it and smiled. So far as words went, there was really little to object to, but he laid it aside and looked Sara squarely in the eye, and Sara looked just as squarely at him. It had come to a showdown, and both knew it. Sara attempted no further fencing. She simply said:

"What is it specifically that you want Matthew to do in Congress? Write it out, and I'll see that he signs it."

He took a piece of paper and wrote a short statement. It had reference to specific bills to be introduced in the next Congress, on the tariff, on farm relief, on railroad consolidation, and on super-power. He even named the persons who were going to introduce the bills. Then he handed the slip to Sara. She read it over carefully, folded it up, and put it in her bag.

"You'll receive this, signed, at or before the final conference."

"Before will be better," suggested Mr. Graham.

"Perhaps," answered Sara, "but on the night of the conference it will be time enough."

Mr. Graham looked almost genial. Sara was the kind of politician that he liked, especially as he saw at present no way to escape a colored candidate, and on the whole he preferred Matthew Towns to Sammy Scott.

"But how about the Radical wing?" he asked. "Are they going to accept this platform?"

"That is the point," said Sara. "I am trying to make the platform broad enough to attract the bulk of the Labor group, but I have not consulted the radicals yet. If they accept what I offer, all right; but even if they do not, we have made sure of the majority of the third party's support."

In this way and by several consultations with Mr. Cadwalader, Mrs. Beech, and their friends, Sara evolved a statement which seemed fair, especially when most of the persons involved began to realize that Matthew Towns on this platform was pretty sure of election.

Sara then turned to the Labor group. Mr. Cadwalader had smoothed the way for her to meet the labor-union heads, and it took Sara but a short time to learn how the land lay there. Eight-hour laws, and anti-injunction legislation, of course; but above all "down with Negro scabs!" Negroes should be taught never to take white strikers' jobs.

"Even if white unions bar them before and after the strike," thought Sara. But she did not say so. She agreed that scabbing was reprehensible, and in turn the union leaders unctuously asserted the "principle" of no color line in the Federation of Labor. It was quite a love feast, and both Sara and Mr. Cadwalader were elated.

Then Sara finally plucked up courage and visited the headquarters of the left-wing trade unionists. She had anticipated some unpleasantness, and she was not disappointed. Her earlier contact with the group had been by letter, and she had been impressed by the shrewd leadership and evidence of wide vision. She was prepared for careful mental gymnastics and careful play of word and phrase. Instead she found a rough group of painfully frank folk. The surroundings were dirty, and the people were rude. It was much less attractive than her visits to the well-furnished headquarters of the Republicans or to the rooms of the Woman's City Club. But if Sara was disgusted with the people and surroundings, she was even more put out with their demands. They came out flat-footed and assumed facts that were puzzling. She did not altogether understand them, chiefly because she had not taken time to study them; it was words and personalities that she had come to probe. The flat demands therefore seemed to her outrageous, revolutionary.

"Overthrow capital? What do you mean?" she said. "Do you want to stop industry entirely and go back to barbarism?"

Then all talked at once in that little crowded room, and she did not pretend to understand:

"What's Towns going to do for municipal ownership of public services? For raising the income taxes on millionaires? For regulating and seizing the railroads? For curbing labor injunctions? For confiscating the unearned increment? For abolishing private ownership of capital?"

Sara stared; then she gathered up her papers.

"I shall have to ask Mr. Towns," she said, crisply. "We will have another consultation next week." And she swept out, vowing to have nothing to do with this gang again. She told Sammy about it and suggested that he hold all further consultations with them.

"It is no place for a lady," she said.

"Lots of them down there," said Sammy.

"You mean those working-women?" said Sara with disgust.

It suited Sammy very well to take charge of further conferences with the Laborites. He had already been engaged in stiffening the demands of the Republicans on the one hand and arousing the suspicion of the colored voters against the trade unionists on the other: and now he was more than willing to push the left wing toward extreme demands. He worked through his young radical friend and now and then saw and talked with the Indian.

Sara was quite sure that he would do something like this, but she did not care. The more radical the left wing was, the fewer votes it would poll and the stronger would be Matthew's hold upon the main bloc of the Progressive group. She was sure of Graham unless Matthew got crazy and went radical. And Matthew seemed to be obeying the whip and bit.

It seemed to Sara the proper time to put Graham's ultimatum before Matthew. She did not argue or expatiate; she simply handed him the statement with the remark:

"Mr. Graham expects to receive this, signed by you, at the conference or before. Your nomination depends upon it."

Then she powdered her nose, put on her things, patted her hat in shape, and walked out. Matthew walked up and down the room. Up and down, up and down, until the walls were too narrow. Then he went out and walked in the streets. It was the last demand, and it was the demand that left him no shred of self-respect. What crazed him was the fact that he knew that he was going to sign it, and that in addition to this, he was going to promise to the Progressives, and perhaps even to the left-wing Laborites, almost exactly opposite and contradictory things. He had reached his nadir. Then he held up his head fiercely. From nadir he would climb! But even as he muttered this half aloud, he did not believe it. From such depths men did not climb. They wallowed there.

Finally, about April first, a week before the primary election, Sara decided that it was time for her final conference. She gave up entirely the idea of a mass meeting. That could come after the primary, when Matthew's nomination was accomplished.

What she really wanted was a dinner conference. There again she hesitated. She was afraid that some of the people whom she was determined to have present, some of the high-placed white folk, might hesitate to accept an invitation to dinner in a colored home. Gradually she evolved something else; a small number of prominent persons were invited to confer personally with Mr. Towns at his home. After the conference, "supper would be served." Sara put this last. If anyone felt that they must, for inner or outer compulsions, leave after the conference, they could then withdraw; but Sara proposed to keep them so long and to make the dinner-supper so attractive that it would be, in fact, quite an unusual social occasion. "Quite informal" it was to be, so her written invitations on heavy paper said. But that was not the voice of her dining room.

XXII

Sara looked across that dining room and was content. The lace over-cover was very beautiful. The new china had really an exquisite design, and her taste in cut glass was quite vindicated. The flowers were gorgeous. She would have preferred Toles, the expensive white caterer, but, of course, political considerations put that beyond thought. The colored man, Jones, was, after all, not bad and had quite a select white clientele in Chicago. It was a rainy night, but so far not one person invited had declined, and she viewed the scene complacently. She doubted very much if there was another dining room in Chicago that looked as expensive. Bigger, yes, but not more expensive, in looks at least.

Sara was in no sense evil. Her character had been hardened and sharpened by all that she had met and fought. She craved wealth and position. She got pleasure in having people look with envious eyes upon what she had and did. It was her answer to the world's taunts, jibes, and discriminations. She was always unconsciously showing off, and her nerves quivered if what she did was not noticed. Really, down in her heart, she was sorry for Matthew. He seemed curiously weak and sensitive in the places where he should not have been; she herself was furious if sympathy or sorrow seeped through her armor. She was ashamed of it. All sympathy, all yielding, all softness, filled her with shame. She hardened herself against it. Tonight she looked upon as a step in her great triumph.

There were twenty people in all besides Matthew and Sara. Of these, six were white. There was Mr. Graham, the Republican city boss, and with him a prominent banker and a high state official; Mrs. Beech, the president of the Woman's City Club, was there, and a settlement worker from the stockyard district; and, of course, Mr. Cadwalader. Sara regarded the banker and the president of the City Club as distinct social triumphs for herself. It was something unique in colored Chicago. And especially on a cold and rainy night like this!

W.E.B. DU BOIS

Besides these there were fourteen colored persons. First, Sammy and Corruthers. Sara had violently objected to the thin, red-headed and freckled Corruthers, but Sammy solemnly engaged to see that he arrived and departed sober and that he was kept in the background. He made up for this insistence by bringing two of his most intelligent ward leaders with their wives, who were young and pretty, although not particularly talkative, having, in truth, nothing to say. Sara had insisted upon the physician and his wife from Memphis and the minister and his wife. All of these were college-trained and used to social functions. Two colored editors had to be included, and two colored women representing Sara's clubs.

The president of the Trade Unions' City Central was at first included among the guests, but when he heard that the meeting was to be at a colored home and include a supper, he reneged. Mr. Murphy habitually ate with his knife and in his shirt sleeves and he didn't propose "to have no niggers puttin' on airs over him." At the same time the unions must be represented; so the settlement worker was chosen at Mrs. Beech's suggestion.

Sammy had pointed out rather perfunctorily that it might be a mistake not to include some radicals and that in any event they might send a delegation if they heard of the conference. Sara merely shrugged her shoulders, but Sammy saw to it that the left-wing unions *did* hear of the conference and of their exclusion.

The stage was set deftly in the large reception room opening in front on the glass-enclosed veranda. There was a little orchestra concealed here behind the ferns, and it was to play now and then while the company was gathering and afterward while they were eating. There were cigarettes and punch, and as Mr. Corruthers soon discovered, there were two kinds of punch. In the main reception room were soft chairs and a big couch, while thick portières closed off the dining room and the entrance hall. To the right was the door to the little library, and here Matthew held his interviews, the door standing ajar.

Matthew sat beside a little table in a straight chair. There were pens, blotters, and writing materials, and all over, soft reflected lights. Sara and Sammy had general charge, and both were in their element. The company gathered rather promptly. Sara stood in the main parlor before the portières that veiled the dining room, where she could receive the guests, entertain them, and send them to consultation with Matthew. Sammy stood between the hall and the reception room where he could welcome the guests, overlook the assembly, and keep his eye on Corruthers.

Everybody was overanxious to please, but the difficulties were enormous. There was no common center of small talk to unite black and white, educated and self-made. The current tittle-tattle of the physician's and minister's wives was not only Greek to the banker and the president of the City Club, but not at all clear to the wives of the colored politicians. The conversation between Mr. Cadwalader and the Republican bosses was a bit forced. Perhaps only in the case of the intelligent white settlement worker and the colored representatives of the Women's Clubs was a new, purely delightful field of common interest discovered.

In Chicago as elsewhere, between white and colored, the obvious common ground was the Negro problem, and this both parties tried desperately to avoid and yet could not. They were always veering toward it. The editor and the banker sought to compare their respective conceptions of finance. But they never really got within understanding distance. Even Sara was at times out of her depth, in a serious definite conversation. With a particular person whom she knew or had measured she could shine. But the light and easy guidance of varied conversation in an assembly of such elements as these was rather beyond her. She hurried here and there, making a very complete and pleasing figure in her flesh-colored chiffon evening frock. But she was not quite at ease.

Sammy's finesse helped to save the day, or rather the night. He had real humor of a kindly sort, and shrewd knowledge of practically everybody present. He supplied the light, frank touch. He subtly separated, grouped, entertained, and reseparated the individuals with rare psychology. He really did his best, and with as little selfishness as he was capable of showing.

The Republican boss, the banker, and the state official were among the earliest arrivals. They sat down with Matthew and entered into earnest conversation. Evidently, they were reading over the latest draft of the proposed platform. Sara was taut and nervous. She tried not to listen, but she could not help watching. She saw Matthew shift the papers until he exposed one that lay at the bottom. The two gentlemen read it and smiled. Quite carelessly and after continued conversation, Mr. Graham absently put the paper in his pocket. By and by they arose and mingled with the other guests. They were all smiling. The boss whispered to Sara that he was satisfied, perfectly satisfied. She knew Matthew had signed the paper.

Sara was radiant. She personally escorted the banker to a seat beside the president of the City Club. She did not know that these two were particularly uncongenial, but they were both well-bred and kept up polite conversation until Mrs. Beech excused herself to talk with Matthew. Matthew was a figure distraught and absentminded. His dress was much too negligent and careless to suit Sara, although he had put on his dinner jacket. Still, as Sara looked him over now and then, he did not make an altogether bad appearance. There was a certain inherent polish, an evidence of breeding which Sara always recognized with keen delight. It seemed easily to rise to the surface on occasions of this sort. Mr. Cadwalader and Mrs. Beech were now talking with Matthew. They seemed at first a little disturbed, but Sara was pleased to note that Matthew had aroused himself and was talking rather quickly and nervously but impressively. Evidently the two representatives of the liberal groups liked what he said. They called in the settlement worker. When at last they arose, all of them seemed pleased.

"I think," said the president of the City Club, "we have come to a good understanding."

"Really," said Mr. Cadwalader, "much better than I hoped for. You can count on us."

Sara sighed. The thing was done. Of course, there was the difficulty of those radical Labor people, but these she regarded as on the whole the least difficult of the three groups. She would perhaps approach them again tomorrow. Even if she had failed they could not do much harm now.

Sammy had about given up. It looked as though Matthew was going to be triumphantly nominated. In fact, he had just learned that Matthew had made one unexpected move, and whether it was stupid or astute, Sammy was undecided. Corruthers had told him that during that very afternoon the left-wing Labor people had got at Matthew and told him that they had not been included in the negotiations after that first visit of Sara, and that none of their representatives were invited to the conference tonight. Matthew had been closeted with them a couple of hours, but just what was said or done Sammy was unable to learn. Apparently his henchman, the young colored radical, was not present, and he could not find the Indian. His hope then that the radicals would burst in on this conference and make trouble at the last moment seemed groundless. Perhaps Matthew by some hocus-pocus had secured their silent assent. The Labor delegation would probably not arrive at all. Meantime, this conference must get on. If success was sure, he must be in the band wagon. He gradually gathered his colored politicians out into the dining room, where there was good liquor. He got the white women and the colored women on the porch in earnest conversation on settlement work for the South Side. The younger women and men, including the Republican boss and his friends, he brought together in the main reception room and started some sprightly conversation. All this was done while Sara had been arranging carefully and not too obviously the personal conferences with Matthew. Well, it was all over.

Then he noticed Corruthers beckoning to him furtively from the half-raised portières that led to the hall. He looked about. Various members of the colored group were talking with the whites, and Matthew had emerged from the little library and seemed to be having a pleasant chat with the minister. Sammy slipped out.

"Say," said Corruthers, "that Labor delegation is here and they want to come in." Sammy pricked up his ears. Aha! It looked as though something might happen after all.

He walked over to Sara and imparted his news.

"Well, they are not coming in here," said Sara.

"But," expostulated Sammy, "they have evidently been invited."

"Not by me," snapped Sara. "But I suspect by Matthew. He was with them this afternoon."

Sara started and tapped her foot impatiently. But Sammy went on:

"Don't you think it would be good politics to let them have their say? We don't need to yield to them in anyway."

Sara was unwilling, but she saw the point. It was a shame to have this love feast broken into. Then a plan occurred to her. They need not come in here; they could meet Matthew in the little library. The door to the reception room could be closed, and they could enter from the hall. Meantime, Sammy saw Corruthers again beckoning excitedly from the door. He walked over quickly, and Corruthers whispered to him.

"My God!" said Sammy. "Hush, Corruthers, and don't say another word. Here, come and have a drink!"

Then he hurried back to Sara. Sara interrupted him before he could speak.

"Take them into the library. I will have Matthew receive them." She sauntered over to Matthew. "Matthew, dear, some of the Bolsheviks are here and want to talk to you. I have had them taken from the hall directly to the library. You can close the door. They will probably feel more at ease then."

Matthew rose and said a little impatiently: "Why not have them in here?"

"They preferred the smaller room," said Sara. "They are not exactly—dressed for an evening function."

And then, turning, she ordered the portières which concealed the dining room to be thrown open, and as Matthew stepped into the small library, the blaze of Sara's supper fell upon the company in the reception room.

The table was a goodly sight. The waiters were deft and silent. The music rose sweetly. The company was hungry, for it was nearly nine. Even Mrs. Beech, who had meant to dine in Hubbard Woods, changed her mind. Little tables with lace, linen, china, and silver were set about, and soon a regular dinner of excellent quality was being served. Tongues loosened, laughter rose, and a feeling of good fellowship began to radiate, Mr. Cadwalader and Mrs. Beech agreed *sotto voce* that really this was quite average in breeding and as a spectacle; they glowed at the rainbow of skins—it was positively exciting.

Sammy was almost hilarious. He could not restrain a wink at Corruthers, and both of them simultaneously bolted for the hall in order to laugh freely and get some more of that other punch. Meantime, Sara's unease increased. Her place and Matthew's had been arranged at the edge of the dining room at a table with Mrs. Beech and Mr. Graham. The banker, the state official, and the two pretty young politicians' wives were at a table next, and the other tables were arranged as far as possible with at least one bit of color.

But where was Matthew? Thought Sara impatiently. It was time for the toast and the great announcement—the culmination of the feast and conference. Mrs. Beech asked for Mr. Towns.

"He's having a last word with the Communists," laughed Sara.

"Oh, are they here?" asked Mr. Cadwalader uneasily—"at the last moment?"

"They wouldn't come in—they are asking about some minor matters of adjustment, I presume."

But Sara knew she must interfere. She distrusted Matthew's mushy indecision. To reopen the argument now might spoil all. She could stand it no longer. She arose easily, a delicate coffee cup in hand, and said a laughing word. She moved to the library door. Sammy watched her. The others sensed in different ways some slight uneasiness in the air.

"Well, Mr. Towns," said Sara, pushing the door wide, "we—"

The light of the greater room poured into the lesser—searching out its shadows. The ugly Chinese god grinned in the corner, and a blue rug glowed on the floor. In the center two figures, twined as one, in close and quivering embrace, leapt, etched in startling outline, on the light.

XXIII

Matthew had turned and started for the library. He had glanced at the reception room. He would not have been human not to be impressed. He was going to be a member of the Congress of the United States. He was going to be the first Negro congressman since the war. No—really the first; all those earlier ones had been exceptions. He was real power. Power and money. Sara should not fool him this time. He understood her. He would have his own funds. He would, of course, follow the machine. He must. He must keep power and get money. But he would have some independence—more and more as time flew. Until—

He squared his shoulders, opened the door, and closed it behind him. The room was dimly lighted save the circle under the reading-light on the table. He looked about. No one was there. But there were voices in the hall. He waited.

Then slowly shame overwhelmed him. He was paying a price for power and money. A great, a terrible price. He was lying, cheating, stealing. He was fooling these poor, driven slaves of industry. He had listened to their arguments all this afternoon. He had meant now to meet the delegation brusquely and tell them railingly that they were idiots, that he could do little— something he'd try, but first he must get into Congress.

But he couldn't find the words. He walked slowly over to the table and stood facing the door. It was all done. It was all over. He had sold his soul to the Devil, but this time he had sold it for something. Power? Money? Nonsense! He had sold it for beauty; for ideal beauty, fitness and curve and line; harmony and the words of the wise spoken long ago. He stood in his dinner jacket, sleek but careless, his shirt front rumpled, the satin of his lapel flicked with ash, his eyes tired and red, his hair untidy. He stood and looked at the door. The door opened; he dropped his eyes. He could not look up. He heard not the clumping tramp of a delegation, but the light step of a single person. He almost knew that it was the national president of the Box-Makers, come to make their last appeal. Somehow he had a desperate desire to defend himself before the merciless logic and wide knowledge of this official whom he had never met. She had never even written or answered his letters directly, but only through that dumpy stupid state president. She was to have been present this afternoon. She was not; only her pitiless written arraignment of his platform had been read. He had expected her tonight when he heard the delegation had arrived. But he could not look up. He simply took the paper which was handed to him, sensing the dark veil-like garments and the small hand in its cheap cotton glove. He took the paper which the woman handed him. On it was written:

Our labor union, in return for its support, asks if you will publicly promise them that on every occasion you will cast your vote in Congress for the interests of the poor man, the employee, and the worker, whenever and wherever these interests are opposed to the interests of the rich, the employer, and the capitalist. For instance—

Thus the paper began, and Matthew began slowly to read it. It was an absurd request. Matthew almost laughed aloud. He had thought to carry it off with a high hand, to laugh at these oafs and jolly them, insisting that first he must *get* to Congress, and then, of course, he would do what he could. Naturally, he was with them. Was he not a son of generations of workers? Well, then, trust him. But they had not come to argue. They were asking him to sign another paper, and to sign on the line. They could never be trusted to keep such a pledge silent. No, they would publish it to the world. Ha, ha, ha! What ghastly nonsense all this lying was! He stopped and went back to the paper and began reading it again. Something was gripping at him. Some tremendous reminder, and then suddenly the letters started out from the page and burned his gaze, they flamed and spread before him. He saw the strong beauty of the great curves, the breadth and yet delicate uplifting of the capitals, the long, sure sweep of the slurred links. Great God! That writing! He knew it as he knew his own face. His hand had started to his inner pocket—then he tried to whisper, hoarsely—

"Where—who wrote this? Who—" He looked up.

A dark figure stood by the table. An old dun-colored cloak flowed down upon her, and a veil lay across her head. Her thin dark hands, now bare and almost clawlike, gripped each other. They were colored hands. Quickly he stepped forward. And she came like a soft mist, unveiled and uncloaked before him. Always she seemed to come thus suddenly into his life. And yet perhaps it was he himself that supplied the surprise and sudden wonder. Perhaps in reality she had always come quite naturally to him, as she came now.

She was different, yet every difference emphasized something eternally marvelous. Her hair was cut short. All that long, cloudlike hair, the length and breadth of it, was gone; but still it nestled about her head like some halo. Her gown was loose, ill-fitting, straight; her hands, hard, wore no jewels, but were calloused, with broken nails. The small soft beauty of her face had become stronger and set in still lines. Only in the steadfast glory of her eyes showed unchanged the Princess. She watched him gravely as he searched her with his eyes; and then suddenly Matthew awoke.

Then suddenly the intolerable truth gripped him. He lifted his hands to heaven, stretched them to touch the width of the world, and swept her into his tight embrace. He caught her to him so fiercely that her little feet almost left the ground, and her arms curled around his neck as their lips met.

"Kautilya," he sobbed. "Princess of India."

"Matthew," she answered, in a small frightened whisper.

There was a silence as of a thousand years, a silence while again he found her lips and kept them, and his arms crept along the frail, long length of her body, and he cried as he whispered in her ears. Perhaps some murmur from the further rooms came to them, for suddenly they started apart. She would have said the things she had planned to say, but she did not. All the greater things were forgotten. She only said as he stared upon her with wild light in his eyes:

"I am changed." And he answered:

"The Princess that I worshiped is become the working-woman whom I love. Life has beaten out the gold to this fine stuff." And then with hanging head he said: "But I, ah, I am unchanged. I am the same flying dust."

She walked toward him and put both hands upon his shoulders and said, "Flying dust, that is it. Flying dust that fills the heaven and turns the sunlight into jewels." And then suddenly she stood straight before him. "Matthew, Matthew!" she cried. "See, I came to save you! I came to save your soul from hell."

"Too late," he murmured. "I have sold it to the Devil."

"Then at any price," she cried in passion, "at any price, I will buy it back."

"What shall we do—what can we do?" he whispered, troubled, in her hair.

"We must give up. We must tell all men the truth; we must go out of this Place of Death and this city of the Face of Fear, untrammeled and unbound, walking together hand in hand."

And he cried, "Kautilya, darling!"

And she said, "Matthew, my Man!"

"Your body is Beauty, and Beauty is your Soul, and Soul and Body spell Freedom to my tortured groping life!" he whispered.

"Benediction—I have sought you, man of God, in the depths of hell, to bring your dead faith back to the stars; and now you are mine."

And suddenly there was light.

And suddenly from Matthew dropped all the little hesitancies and cynicisms. The years of disbelief were not. The world was one woman and one cause. And with one arm almost lifting her as she strained toward him, they walked shoulder to shoulder out into that blinding light. And as they walked there seemed to rise above the startled, puzzled guests some high and monstrous litany, staccato, with moaning monotones, bearing down upon their whisperings, exclamations, movements, words and cries, across the silver and crystal of the service:

"I will not have your nomination."

(What does he mean—who is this woman?)

"I'd rather go to hell than to Congress."

(Is the man mad?)

"I'm through with liars, thieves, and hypocrites."

(This is insulting, shameless, scandalous!)

"The cause that was dead is alive again; the love that I lost is found!"

(A married man and a slut from the streets!) "Have mercy, have mercy upon us!" whispered the woman.

The company surged to its feet with hiss and oath.

Sara, white to the lips, her hard-clenched hand crushing the fragile china to bits, walked slowly backward before them with blazing eyes.

"I am free!" said Matthew.

The low voice of the Princess floated back again from the crimson curtains of the hall:

"Kyrie Eleison."

The high voice of Sara, like the final fierce upthrusting of the Host, shrilled to a scream:

"You fool—you God-damned fool!"

XXIV

The hall door crashed. The stunned company stared, moved, and rushed hurriedly to get away, with scant formality of leave-taking. It was raining without, a cold wet sleet, but the beautiful apartment vomited its guests upon the sidewalk while taxis rushed to aid.

The president of the Woman's City Club rushed out the door with flushed face.

"These Negroes!" she said to the settlement worker. "They are simply impossible! I have known it all along, but I had begun to hope; such persistent, ineradicable immorality! And flaunted purposely in our very faces! It is intolerable!"

The settlement worker murmured somewhat indistinctly about the world being "well lost" for something, as they climbed into a cab and flew north.

The Republican boss, the state official, and the banker loomed in the doorway, pulling on their gloves, adjusting their coats and cravats, and hailing hurrying taxis.

"Well, of all the damned fiascos," said the banker.

"Niggers in Congress! Well!" said the official.

"It is just as well," said the boss. "In fact it is almost providential. It looked as though we had to send a Negro to Congress. That unpleasant possibility is now indefinitely postponed. Of course, now we'll have to send you."

"Oh!" said the banker softly and deprecatingly.

"It is going to cost something," said the boss shrewdly. "You will have to buy up all these darky newspapers and grease Sammy's paw extraordinarily well. The point is, buying is possible now. They have no comeback, Sammy may have aspirations, but I think we can make even him see that it will be unwise to put up another colored candidate now. No, the thing has turned out extraordinarily well; but I wonder what the devil got hold of Towns, acting as though he was crazy?"

The physician's wife and the lawyer's lingered a little, clustering to one side so as to avoid meeting the white folks; they stared and whispered.

"It is the most indecent thing I have heard of," said the physician's wife. The lawyer's wife moaned in her distress:

"To think of a Negro acting that way, and before these people! And after all this work. Won't we ever amount to anything? Won't we ever get any leaders? I am simply disgusted and discouraged. I'll never work for another Negro leader as long as I live."

And they followed their husbands to the two large sedans that stood darkly groaning, waiting.

The physician snarled to the minister, "And with the streets full of women cheaper and prettier."

The Labor delegation had pushed into the library as Mathew and Kautilya left, and entered the reception room. They stood now staring at the disheveled room and the guests rushing away.

"What's happened?"

"Has he told them what's what?"

"Are they deserting us? Are they running away?"

But the colored club women walked away in silence in the rain. They parted at the corner and one said:

"I'm proud of him, at last."

But the other spit:

"The beast!"

XXV

S ammy's world was tottering, and looking upon its astonishing ruins he could only gasp blankly:

"What t' hell!" Never before in his long career and wide acquaintanceship with human nature had it behaved in so fantastic and unpredictable a manner. Never had it acted with such incalculable and utter disregard of all rules and wise saws. That a man should cheat, lie, steal, and seduce women, was to Sammy's mind almost normal; that he should tell the truth, give away his money, and stick by his wife was also at times probable. These things happened. He'd seen them done. But that a man with everything should choose nothing: that a man with high office in his grasp, money ready to pour into his pocket, a home like this, and both a wife *and* a sweetheart, should toss them all away and walk out into the rain without his hat, just for an extra excursion with a skirt—

"What t' hell!" gasped Sammy, groping back into the empty house. Then suddenly he heard the voice of Sara.

He found her standing stark alone, a pitiful, tragic figure amid the empty glitter of her triumph, with her flesh-colored chiffon and her jewels, her smooth stockings and silver slippers. She had stripped the beads from her throat, and they were dripping through her clenched fingers. She had half torn the lace from her breast, and she stood there flushed, trembling, furious with anger, and almost screaming to ears that did not hear and to guests already gone.

"Haven't I been decent? Haven't I fought off you beasts and made me a living and a home with my own hands? Wasn't I married like a respectable woman, and didn't I drag this fool out of jail and make him a man? And what do I get? *What do I get?* Here I am, disgraced and ruined, mocked and robbed, a laughing-stock to all Chicago. What did he want? What did the jackass want, my God? A cabaret instead of a home? A whore instead of a wife? Wasn't I true to him? Did I ever let a man touch me? I made money—sure, I made money. I *had* to make money. *He* couldn't. I made money out of politics. What in hell is politics for, if it isn't for somebody to make money? Must we hand all the graft over to the holy white folks? And now he disgraces me! Just when I win, he throws me over for a common bawd from the streets, and a mess of dirty white laborers; a common slut stealing decent women's husbands. Oh—"

Sammy touched her hesitatingly on the shoulder and pleaded: "Don't crack, kid. Stand the gaff. I'll see you through."

But she shrank away from him and screamed:

"Get out, don't touch me. Oh, damn him, damn him! I wish I could horsewhip them; I wish I could kill them both."

And suddenly Sara crumpled to the floor, crushing and tearing her silks and scattering her jewels, drawing her knees up tight and gripping them with twitching hands, burying her hair, her head and streaming eyes, in the crimson carpet, and rolling and shaking and struggling with strangling sobs.

WHILE WITHOUT GRAY MISTS LAY thin upon a pale and purple city. Through them, like cold, wet tears dripped the slow brown rain. The muffled roar of moving millions thundered low upon the wind, and the blue wind sighed and sank into the black night; and through the chill dripping of the waters, hatless and coatless, moved two shapes, hand in hand, with uplifted heads, singing to the storm.

PART IV

THE MAHARAJAH OF BWODPUR

1926, APRIL–APRIL, 1927

The miracle is Spring. Spring in the heart and throat of the world. Spring in Virginia, Spring in India, Spring in Chicago. Shining rain and crimson song, roll and thunder of symphony in color, shade and tint of flower and vine and budding leaf. Spring–two Springs, with a little Winter between. But what if Spring dip down to Winter and die, shall not a lovelier Spring live again? Love is eternal Spring. Life lifts itself out of the Winter of death. Children sing in mud and rain and wind. Earth climbs left and sits astride the weeping skies.

I

The rain was falling steadily. One could hear its roar and drip and splash upon the roof. All the world was still. Kautilya listened dreamily. There was a sense of warmth and luxury about her. Silk touched and smoothed her skin. Her tired body rested on soft rugs that yielded beneath her and lay gently in every curve and crevice of her body. She heard the low music of the rain above, and the crimson, yellow, and gold of a blazing fire threw its shadows all along the walls and ceiling. The shadows turned happily and secretly, revealing and hiding the wild hues of a great picture, the reflections of a mirror, the flowers and figures of the wall. In silence she lay in strange peace and happiness—not trying to think, but trying to sense the flood of the meaning of that happiness that spread above her. Her head lifted; slowly, noiselessly, with infinite tenderness, she stretched her arms toward Matthew, till his head slipped down upon her shoulder. Then, on great, slow, crimson islands of dream, the world floated away, the rain sang; and she slept again.

Long hours afterward in the silence that comes before the dim blue breaking of the dawn, Matthew awoke with a start. The rain had ceased; the fire was dim and low; a vague sense of terror gripped him. His breath struggled dizzily in his throat, and then a little shaft of sunshine, pale, clear, with a certain sweetness from the white dampness of sky and earth, wandered down from the high window and leapt and lay on the face of happiness. She lay very still, so still that at first he scarce could see the slow rise and fall of the soft silk that clung to her breast. And then the surge of joy shook him until he had to bite back the sob and wild laughter.

Hard had been their path to freedom. In his first high courage, Matthew had pictured themselves walking through that door and into the light; a powerful step, a word of defiance against the indignant, astonished, angry wave of the world. Yet in truth they had walked out with hands clasped and faces down, and he never knew what words he said or tried to say. Phrases struck upon their ears.

"—knifed his race—a common hawd—a five-minute infatuation—primitive passion—"

Across the endless length of the parlor they had toiled, and down by the blazing dinner table; out far, far out into the narrowing hall; they had brushed by people who shrank away from them. Coatless, hatless, they had walked into the cold and shivering storm. And then somehow they were warm again. Then happiness had fallen softly upon them. Hand in hand they walked singing through the rain.

"Where are we going, Matthew?" she had whispered long hours later, as her tired feet faltered.

And he lifted her in his arms and raised his face to the water and answered:

"We are going down the King's highway to Beauty and Freedom and Love. I can hear life growing down there in the earth and pulling beneath the hard sidewalks and white bones of the dead. Listen, God's darling, to the singing of the rain; hear the dawn coming afar and see the white wings of the mist, how they beat about us."

And so they had come home and slept in his attic nest.

Slowly Matthew lifted himself, arranged the golden glory of the Chinese rug again around her, tucking in her little feet and drawing it close at the side. Noiselessly he slipped to the fireplace and made the golden flames hiss and sputter and swirl up to the sun-drenched sky, and then he came back and stretched himself beside her, slipping, as she slept on, her head upon the curve of his elbow and looking down upon her face.

It was a magnificent face. Something had come and something had gone since the day when he saw it first. Something had gone of that incomprehensible beauty of color, infinite fineness of texture, richness of curve, loveliness of feature, which made her then to his eyes the loveliest thing in the world. But in its place there lay upon her peaceful, sleeping countenance a certain strength and nobility; a certain decision and calm, that was like beauty swept with life, like sunshine softened with mist. The heavy coils of purple hair had been cut away, and yet the hair still lay thick and strong upon her forehead.

Suddenly he wanted to see her eyes, the eyes that he had never forgotten since first he looked into them, eyes that were pools at once of mystery and revelation, misty with half-sensed desire, and calm with power. He wanted to see her eyes again and see them at once with the high consciousness of birth that belonged to the Princess of the Lützower Ufer and with that look of surrender and selfless love that he had caught in the little room behind the parlor. He wanted again desperately to see those eyes which said all these things; yet he lay very still lest for a single moment he should disturb her. And then he looked down, and her eyes were looking up to him. Slowly and happily she smiled.

"Krishna," she murmured. His mind went racing back through the shadows and he whispered back, "Radha." And again they slept.

When Kautilya awoke again, there was a slow music stealing in from the inner room. It was the andante from Beethoven's Fifth Symphony, infinite in tenderness, triumph, and beauty; and it came from afar so that no scratch of the phonograph or creak of mechanism spoiled its sweet melody. She sat up suddenly with a little cry of joy, throwing aside the great Chinese rug and swathing herself in the silk of the white mandarin's robe that lay ready for her. With this music in her ears she found the bathroom with its tub of steaming water and with its completeness, half plaintive with neglect.

A half hour later she found new silken things in the dressing room. The rug lay upon the floor, and the old worn easy-cha was drawn before the fire. Beside the flaming dance of the fire was a low, white Turkish taboret; toward it Matthew came, clad in an old green bathrobe which hung carelessly along his tall body. There was a tarboosh with faded tassel upon his head. The hot coffee steamed on the salver, with toast and butter and cream. There was an orange in halves and a little yellow rosebud. She laughed in the sheer delight of it all, and held him long and close before they turned to their eating. The morning sun poured in.

The music was changed to that largo of Dvorák built on the echoing pain of the Negro folksong, which is printed on the other side of the Victor record. Matthew would not let her stir, and after a while from the kitchen came a brave splashing of dishes and a song. He came back soon, bringing an old volume of poems. Without a word, only a long look, they nestled in the chair near the fire and read. And so the day passed half wordless with beauty and sound, full of color and content, until the sunlight went crimson and blue upon the walls and the fire shadows danced again.

"There are so many things I would ask you," said Matthew. And then Kautilya took his head between her hands and laid the breadth of his shoulders upon her knees and said:

"And there are so many things I want to tell you of myself. I want to tell you all the story of my life; of my falling and rising; of my love for you; and of that mother of yours who lives far down in Virginia in the cabin by the wood. Oh, Matthew, you have a wonderful mother. Have you seen her hands? Have you seen the gnarled and knotted glory of her hands?" And then slowly with wide eyes: "Your mother is Kali, the Black One; wife of Siva, Mother of the World!"

II

M atthew was talking in the darkness as they lay together closely entwined in each other's arms.

"You will tell me, dear one, all about yourself? How came you here, masquerading as a trade union leader?"

"It must be a long, long story, Matthew—a Thousand Nights and a Night?"

"So short a tale? Talk on, Scheherazade!"

So Kautilya whispered, nestling in his arms: "But first, Matthew, sing me that Song of Emancipation—sing that Call of God, 'Go down, Moses!' I believe, though I did not then know it—I believe I began to love you that night."

Matthew sang. Kautilya whispered:

"When you left me and went to jail, I seemed first to awake to real life. From clouds I came suddenly down to earth. I knew the fault was mine and the sacrifice yours. I left the country according to my promise to the government. But it was easy to engineer my quick return from London in a Cunard second cabin, without my title or real name.

"And then came what I shall always know to have been the greatest thing in my life. I saw your mother. No faith nor religion, Matthew, ever dies. I am of the clan and land that gave Gotama, the Buddha, to the world. I know that out of the soul of Brahma come little separations of his perfect and ineffable self and they appear again and again in higher and higher manifestations, as eternal life flows on. And when I saw that old mother of yours standing in the blue shadows of twilight with flowers, cotton, and corn about her, I knew that I was looking upon one of the ancient prophets of India and that she was to lead me out of the depths in which I found myself and up to the atonement for which I yearned. So I started with her upon that path of seven years which I calculated would be, in all likelihood, the measure of your possible imprisonment. We talked it all out together. We prayed to God, hers and mine, and out of her ancient lore she did the sacrifice of flame and blood which was the ceremony of my own great fathers and which came down to her from Shango of Western Africa.

"You had stepped down into menial service at my request—you who knew how hard and dreadful it was. It was now my turn to step down to the bottom of the world and see it for myself. So I put aside my silken garments and cut my hair, and, selling my jewels, I started out on the long path which should lead to you. I did not write you. Why did I need to? You were myself, I knew. But I sent others, who kept watch over you and sent me news.

"First, I went as a servant girl into the family of a Richmond engineer."

Matthew started abruptly, but Kautilya nestled closer to him and watched him with soft eyes.

"It was difficult," she said, "but necessary. I had known, all my life, service, but not servants. I had not been able to imagine what it meant to be a servant. Most of my life I had not dreamed that it meant anything; that servants meant anything to themselves. But now I served. I made beds, I swept, I brought food to the table, sometimes I helped cook it. I hated to clean kitchens amid dirt and heat, and I worked long hours; but at night I slept happily, dear, by the very ache of the new muscles and nerves which my body revealed.

"Then came the thing of which your mother had warned me, but which somehow I did not sense or see coming, until in the blackness of the night suddenly I knew that someone was moving in my room; that someone had entered my unlocked door."

Matthew arose suddenly and paced the floor. Then he came and sat down by the couch and held both her hands.

"Go on," he said.

"I sat up tense and alert and held in my hand the long, light dagger with its curved handle and curious chasing; a dagger which the grandfathers of my grandfather had handed down to me. That night, Matthew, I was near murder, but the white man, my employer, slipped as I lunged, and the dagger caught only the end of his left eye and came down clean across cheek, mouth, and chin, one inch from the great jugular vein, just as the mistress with her electric torch came in.

W.E.B. DU BOIS

"Instead of arrest which I thought I surely faced, the man was hurried out and off and the woman came to me in the still morning, worn and pale, and said, 'I thank you. This is perhaps the lesson he needed.'

"She paid me my little wage and I walked away."

"But, Kautilya, why, why did you go through all this? What possible good could it do?"

"Matthew, it was written. I went to Petersburg and worked in a tobacco factory, sitting cramped at a long bench, stripping the soft fragrant tobacco leaf from those rough stems. It was not in itself hard work, but the close air, the cramped position, the endless monotony, made me at times want to scream. And there were the people about me: some good and broken; some harsh, hard, and wild. Leering men, loud-mouthed women. I stayed there three endless months until it seemed to me that every delicate thought and tender feeling and sense of beauty had been bent and crushed beyond recognition. So I took the train and came to Philadelphia.

"I worked in two restaurants; one on Walnut Street, splendid and beautiful. The patrons usually were kind and thoughtful with only now and then an overdressed woman who had to express her superiority by the loudness of her tones, or a man who was slyly insulting or openly silly. Only the kitchen and the corridors bruised me by their contrast and ugliness. Singularly enough in this place of food and plenty, the only proper food we waitresses could get to eat was stolen food. I hated the stealing, but I was hungry and tired. From there I went down to South Street to a colored restaurant and worked a long time. It was an easy-going place with poor food and poor people, but kind. They crowded in at all hours. They were well-meaning, inquisitive; and if a busy workingman or a well-dressed idler sought to take my hand or touch my body he did it half jokingly and usually not twice."

"Servant, tobacco-hand, waitress; mud, dirt, and servility for the education of a queen," groaned Matthew.

"And is there any field where a queen's education is more neglected? Think what I learned of the mass of men! I got to know the patrons: their habits, hardships, histories. I was the friend of the proprietors, woman and husband; but the enterprise didn't pay. It failed. I cried. But just as it was closing I learned of your release, and after but a year, suddenly I was in heaven. I thought I had already atoned.

"But I knew that yet I must wait. That you must find your way and begin to adjust your life before I dared come into it again. And so I went to New York, that my dream of life and of the meaning of life to the mass of men might be more complete.

"I discovered a paper box-making factory on the lower East Side. It was a non-union shop and I worked in a basement that stank of glue and waste, ten and twelve hours a day for six dollars a week. It was sweated labor of the lowest type, and I was aghast. Then the workers tried to organize—there was a strike. I was beaten and jailed for picketing, but I did not care. That which was begun as a game and source of experience to me became suddenly real life. I became an agent, organizer, and officer of the union. I knew my fellow laborers, in home and on street, in factory and restaurant. I studied the industry and the law, I traveled, made speeches, and organized. Oh, Matthew—it was life, life, real life, even with the squalor and hard toil."

"Yes, it was life. And the Veil of Color lifted from your eyes as it is lifting even from my blindness. Those people there, these here—they are all alike, all one. They are all foolish, ignorant, and exploited. Their highest ambition is to escape from themselves—from being black, from being poor, from being ugly—into some high heaven from which they can gaze down and despise themselves."

"True, my Matthew, and while I was learning all this which you long knew, you seemed to me striving to unlearn. Oh, how I watched over you! You came down to Virginia. Hidden in the forest, I watched with wet eyes. Hidden in the cabin, I heard your voice. I caught the sob in your throat when your mammy told of my coming. I knew you loved me still, and I wanted to rush into your arms. But, 'Not yet—not yet!' said your wise old mother.

"I was working busily and happily when the second blow fell, the blow that came to deny everything, that seemed to say that you were not self of my own self and life of the life which I was sharing in every pulse with you. You married. I gave up."

"You did not understand, Kautilya. You seemed lost to me forever. I was blindly groping for some counterfeit of peace. If I had only known you were here and caring!"

"I went down again to Virginia and knelt beside your mother, and she only smiled. 'He ain't married,' she said. 'He only thinks he is. He was wild like, and didn't know where to turn or what to do. Wait, wait.'

"I waited. You would not listen to my messengers whom continually I sent to you—the statesmen of Japan, the Chinese, the groping president of the Box-Makers. Like Galahad you would not ask the meaning of the sign. You would not name my name. How could I know, dearest, what I meant to you? And yet my thought and care hovered and watched over you. I knew Sammy and Sara and I saw your slow and sure descent to hell. I tried to save you by sending human beings to you. You helped them, but you did not know them. I tried again when you were sitting in the legislature down at Springfield. You knew, but you would not understand. You sneered at the truth. You would not come at my call."

"I did not know it was your voice, Kautilya."

"You knew the voice of our cause, Matthew—was that not my voice?"

Matthew was silent. Kautilya stroked his hand.

"We met in London, the leaders of a thousand million of the darker peoples, with, for the first time, black Africa and black America sitting beside the rest. I was proud of the Negroes we had chosen after long search. There were to be forty of us, and, Matthew, only you were absent. I looked for you to the last. It seemed that you must come. We organized, we planned, and one great new thing emerged—your word, Matthew, your prophecy: we recognized democracy as a method of discovering real aristocracy. We looked frankly forward to raising not all the dead, sluggish, brutalized masses of men, but to discovering among them genius, gift, and ability in far larger number than among the privileged and ruling classes. Search, weed out, encourage; educate, train, and open all doors! Democracy is not an end; it is a method of aristocracy. Some day I will show you all we said and planned.

"All the time, until I left for this great meeting I had expected that somehow, some way, all would be well. Sometime suddenly you would come away. You would understand and burst your bonds and come to us—to me. But as I left America fear entered my heart—fear for your soul. I began to feel that I must act—I must take the step, I must rescue you from the net in which you were floundering. "I remember the day. Gloom of fog held back the March spring in London. The crowded, winding streets echoed with traffic. I heard Big Ben knelling the hour of noon, and a ray of sunlight struggled dizzily on the mauve Thames. A wireless came. You were selling your soul for Congress.

"Before, you had stolen for others. You had upheld their lies—but your own hands were clean, your heart disclaimed the dirty game. Now you were going to lie and steal for yourself. I saw the end of our world. I must rescue you at any cost—at any sacrifice. I rushed back across the sea. Five days we shivered, rolled, and darted through the storm. Almost we cut a ship in two on the Newfoundland banks, but wrenched away with a mighty groan. I landed Friday morning, and left at two-fifty-five—at nine next morning I was in Chicago. That night I led your soul up from Purgatory—free!

"And here we are, Matthew, my love; and it is long past the hour of sleep; and you are trembling with apprehension at things which did not happen, at pits into which I did not fall, at failures over which we both have triumphed."

The Princess paused, and Matthew started up. There was a loud insistent knocking at the door.

"Go," said the Princess. "Have we not both expected this?"

Matthew hesitated a moment and then walked to the door and opened it. A colored police officer and two white men in citizens' clothes stepped in quickly and started as if to search, until they saw the Princess sitting on the disheveled bed.

"Well?"

"We were hunting for you two," said one of the plainclothes men.

"And you have found us?" asked Matthew.

"Yes, evidently. We wondered where you were spending the night."

"We were spending the night here, together," said Matthew.

"Together," repeated the Princess. The other man began to write furiously.

"You admit that," said the first man.

"We admit it," said Matthew, and the Princess bowed her head.

"Perhaps we had better look around a little," said the other man tentatively. But the policeman protested.

"You got what you wanted, ain't ya? Mr. Towns is a friend of mine, and I don't propose to have no monkey business. If you're through, get out." And slowly they all passed through the door.

III

May, and five o'clock in the morning. The sun was whispering to the night, and the mist of its words rose above the park. Matthew and Kautilya swung rapidly along through the dim freshness of the day. They both had knapsacks and knickerbockers, and shoulder to shoulder, hand in hand, and singing low snatches of song, they hurried through Jackson Park. It was such a morning as when the world began: soft with breezes, warm yet cold, brilliant with the sun, and still dripping with the memory of sweet, clean rain. There was no dust—no noise, no movement. Almost were the great brown earth and heavy, terrible city, still. Singing, quivering, tense with awful happiness, they went through the world. Far out by the lake and in the drowsy afternoon, when they had eaten sausage and bread and herbs and drunk cool water, after Kautilya had read the sacred words of the Rig-veda, she laid aside the books and talked again, straining his back against her knees as they sat beneath a black oak tree, her cheek beside his ear, while together they stared out upon the waving waters of Lake Michigan.

Matthew said:

"Now tell me beautiful things, Scheherazade. Who you are and what? And from what fairyland you came?"

"I cannot tell you, Matthew, for you do not know India. Oh, my dear one, you must know India.

"India! India! Out of black India the world was born. Into the black womb of India the world shall creep to die. All that the world has done, India did, and that more marvelously, more magnificently. The loftiest of mountains, the mightiest of rivers, the widest of plains, the broadest of oceans—these are India.

"Man is there of every shape and kind and hue, and the animal friends of man, of every sort conceivable. The drama of life knows India as it knows no other land, from the tragedy of Almighty God to the laugh of the Bandar-log; from divine Gotama to the sons of Mahmoud and the stepsons of the Christ.

"For leaf and sun, for whiff and whirlwind; for laughter, and for tears; for sacrifice and vision; for stark poverty and jeweled wealth; for toil and song and silence—for all this, know India. Loveliest and weirdest of lands; terrible with flame and ice, beautiful with palm and pine, home of pain and happiness and misery—oh, Matthew, can you not understand? This is India—can you not understand?"

"No, I cannot understand; but I feel your meaning."

"True, true! India must be felt. No man can know India, and yet the shame of it, that men may today be counted learned and yet be ignorant, carelessly ignorant, of India. The shame, that this vast center of human life should be but the daubed footstool of a stodgy island of shopkeepers born with seas and hearts of ice."

"But you know India, darling. Tell India to the world."

"I am India. Forgive me, dearest, if I play with words beyond meaning—beyond the possibility of meaning. Now let me talk of myself—of my little self—"

"That is more to me than all India and all the world besides."

"I was born with the new century. My childhood was a dream, a dream of power, beauty, and delight. Before my face rose every morning the white glory of the high Himalayas, with the crowning mass of Gaurisankar, kissing heaven. Behind me lay the great and golden flood of Holy Ganga. On my left hand stood the Bo of Buddha and on my right the Sacred City of the Maghmela.

"All about me was royal splendor, wealth and jewels and beautiful halls, old and priceless carpets, the music of tinkling fountains, the song and flash of birds; and when I clapped my childish hands, servants crawled to me on their faces. Of course, much that I know now was missing—little comforts of the West; and there were poverty, pain, sickness, and death; but with all this, around me everywhere was marble, gold and jewels, silk and fur, and myriads who danced and sang and served me. For I was the little Princess of Bwodpur, the last of a line that had lived and ruled a thousand years.

"We came out of the black South in ancient days and ruled in Rajputana; and then, scorning the yoke of the Aryan invaders, moved to Bwodpur, and there we gave birth to Buddha, black Buddha of the curly hair. Six million people worshiped us as divine, and my father's revenue was three hundred lakhs of rupees. I had strange and mighty playthings: elephants and lions and tigers, great white oxen and flashing automobiles. Parks there were and palaces, baths and sweet waters, and amid it all I walked a tiny and willful thing, curbed only by my old father, the Maharajah, and my white English governess, whom I passionately loved.

"I had, of course, my furious revolts: wild rebellion at little crossings of my will; wild delight at some of the efforts to amuse me; and then came the culmination when first the flood of life stopped long enough for me to look it full in the face.

"I was twelve and according to the ancient custom of our house I was to be married at a great Durbar. He was a phantom prince, a pale and sickly boy who reached scarcely to my shoulder. But his dominion joined with mine, making a mighty land of twelve million souls; of wealth in gold and jewels, high mineral walls, and valleys fat with cream. All that I liked, and I wanted to be a crowned and reigning Maharanee. But I did not like this thin, scared stick of a boy whose pearls and diamonds seemed to drag him down and make his dark eyes shine terrorstricken beneath his splendid turban.

"I enjoyed the magnificent betrothal ceremony and poked impish fun at the boy who seemed such a child. A tall and crimson Englishman attended him and ran his errands and I felt very grand, riding high on my silken elephant amid applauding thousands. The 'Fringies,' as we called the English, were here in large numbers and always whispering in the background, nodding politely, playing with me gravely, and yielding to my whims. I confess I thought them very wonderful. I set them, unconsciously, above my own people.

"I remember hearing and but half understanding the talk of my guardian and counselors. They were apparently vastly surprised that the English had allowed this marriage. It would seem the English had long resisted the wishes of the people of Sindrabad. They had, you see, more power in his land than in ours. Our land was independent—or at least we thought so. To be sure we sent

W.E.B. DU BOIS

no ministers to foreign lands—but what did we know or care of foreign lands? To be sure our trade was monopolized by the English, but it was good and profitable trade. Internally we were free and unmolested, save that an unobtrusive Englishman was always at court. He was the Resident. He 'advised' us and spied upon us, as I now know.

"Now it was different in Sindrabad, where my little prince ruled under English advisers. Sindrabad was in the iron grip of the English. They long frowned upon the power of Bwodpur, a native, half-independent Indian state. They refused to countenance a marriage alliance with Sindrabad and continued to refuse; then suddenly something happened. A new English Resident appeared, a commissioner magnificent with medals, well trained, allied to a powerful English family of the nobility, and backed by new regiments of well-armed men. He had lived long in the country of my phantom prince; now be came to us smiling and bringing the little Maharajah by the hand and giving consent and benediction to our marriage.

"I heard my father ask, aside, hesitating and frowning:

"'What is back of all this?'

"But I only half listened to this talk and intrigue. I wanted the Durbar and the glory of the pageant of this marriage. So in pomp and magnificence beyond anything of which even 1, a princess, had dreamed, we were married in the high hills facing the wide glory of the Himalayas; the drums boomed and the soldiers marched; the elephants paraded and the rajahs bowed before me and I was crowned and married, her Royal Highness, the Maharanee of Bwodpur and Sindrabad. There was, I believe, some dispute about this 'royal,' but father was obdurate."

"You mean that you were really a wife, while yet a child?" asked Matthew.

"Oh, no, I was in reality only a betrothed bride and must return to my home for Gauna, that is, to wait for years until I was grown and my bridegroom should come and take me to his home. But he never came. For somehow, I do not remember why, there came a time of darkness and sorrow, when I could not go abroad, when I was hurried with my nurse from palace to palace and got but fleeting glances of my phantom prince even on his rare calls of ceremony. Once I came upon him in a long, cold and marble corridor as, running, I escaped from Nurse. He was standing, thin, pale, and in tears. His brown skin was gray and drawn; he looked upon me with great and frightened eyes and whispered: 'Flee, flee! The English will kill you too.' That was all.

"I do not know how it happened. I know that the English commissioner was transfixed with horror. This bronze boy, just as he had started home, was found in the forest, his face all blood, dead. My father was wan with anger, and, it seemed, all against the English. He did not accuse them directly of this awful deed, but he knew that the death of both these married children, the last of their line, would throw both countries into the control of England. There were wild rumors in the air of the court. In strict compliance with ancient custom, I as a widow should have died with my little bridegroom, but even the priests saw too much power for England in this, and suddenly my father summoned my English companion and sent me with her to England, while he reigned in my name in Sindrabad and in his own right in Bwodpur.

"My governess was a quiet, clear-eyed woman, with a heart full of courage and loyalty. Sometimes I thought that she and my father had loved each other and that because of the hopelessness of this affection she was suddenly sent home and I with her.

"Then came beautiful days. I loved England. I loved the work of my tutors and the intercourse with the new world that spread before me. I stayed two full years, until I was fourteen, and then again came clouds. There was a tall English boy of whom I saw much. We had ridden, run, and played together. He told me he loved me. I was glad. I did not love him, but I wanted him to love me because the other girls had sweethearts. But he was curiously fierce and gruff about it all. He wanted to seize and embrace me and I hated the touch of his hands, for after all he was not of royal blood, which then meant so much to me.

"One day he suddenly asked me to run away and marry him. I laughed.

"'Yes, I mean to marry you,' he said. 'I am going to have you. I don't care if you are colored.' I gasped in amazement. He didn't *care*. He, a low-born shopman's brat, and I, a princess born. I, '*colored*'! I wanted to strike him with my croquet mallet. I rushed away home.

"It seemed that the scales had fallen from my eyes. I understood a hundred incidents, a dozen veiled allusions and little singular happenings. I suddenly realized that these dull, load, ugly people actually thought me inferior because my skin was browner than their bleached and roughened hides. They were condescending to me—me, whose fathers were kings a thousand years before theirs were ragpickers.

"I rushed in upon my governess. I opened my lips to rage. She stopped me gently: my father was dead in Bwodpur. I was summoned to India to marry and reign. But I did not go. The news of my father's death came on August first, 1914. When I reached London and the India Office, August fourth, the world was at war.

"There ensued a series of quick moves followed by protracted negotiations; the English explained that it would never do to start their royal charge for India in time of war. Bwodpur retorted that it would never do to have their Maharanee far away in England in time of war. The India Office delicately suggested that the presence in England of an Indian princess of high birth and influence would do much to cement the empire and win the war for civilization, and secretly they whispered that it would be unwise to send to India, when English power was weak, a person who might become a rallying center for independence.

"Bwodpur pointed out that my presence in India was precisely the thing needed to arouse a feeling favorable to England and oppose the disruptive forces of *Swaraj*, which were undermining native dynasties as well as imperial power.

"But after all, England had the advantage in that argument, because I was in England; and while I probably would not have been allowed to return home had I wished, official England put forth every effort to make me want to stay. At first, I was imperious and discontented, remembering that I was 'colored.' But official England took no notice, and with deep-laid plans and imperturbable self-possession proceeded to capture my imagination and gain my affection. England became gracious and kind. London opened its heart and arms to this dark and difficult charge. Even royalty held out a languid hand, and I was presented at court in 1916 and formally received in society.

"I did not yield easily. I sat back upon my rank. I used my wealth. When I was invited out I took the pas from Duchesses as the child of a reigning monarch. I made the county aristocracy cringe and the city snobs almost literally hold my train. All this until my poor foster mother was filled with apprehension. Slowly but surely, however, my defenses were beaten down and I capitulated.

"In the midst of war hysteria, I became the social rage, and I loved it. I forgot suspicion and intrigue. I liked the tall and calm English men, the gracious and well-mannered English women. I loved the stately servants, so efficient, without the eastern servility to which I had been born. I knew for the first time what comfort and modern luxury meant.

"I danced and knitted and nursed and studied. I spent weekends in storied castles, long days in museums and nights at theaters and concerts, until the War grew harder. Money like water flowed through my careless hands. I gave away gold and jewels. I was a darling of the white gods, and I adored them. I even went to the front in France for temporary duty as a nurse—carefully guarded and pampered.

"Can I make you realize how I was dazed and blinded by the Great White World?"

"Yes," said Matthew. "I quite understand. Singularly enough, we black folk of America are the only ones of the darker world who see white folk and their civilization with level eyes and unquickened pulse. We know them. We were born among them, and while we are often dazzled with their deeds, we are seldom drugged into idealizing them beyond their very human deserts. But you of the forest, swamp, and desert, of the wide and struggling lands beyond the Law—when you first behold the glory that is London, Paris, and Rome, I can see how easily you imagine that you have seen heaven; until disillusion comes-and it comes quickly."

"Yes," sighed Kautilya, with a shudder, "it came quickly. It approached while I was in France in 1917. Suddenly, a bit of the truth leapt through. There, at Arras, an Indian stevedore, one of my own tribe and clan, crazed with pain, bloody, wild, tore at me in the hospital.

"'Damn you! Black traitor. Selling your soul to these dirty English dogs, while your people die—your people die.'

"I hurried away, pale and shaken, yet heard the echo: 'Your people die!'

"Then I descended into hell; I slipped away unchaperoned, unguarded, and in a Red Cross unit served a month in the fiery rain before I was discovered and courteously returned to England.

"Oh, Vishnu, Incarnate, thou knowest that I saw hell. Dirt and pain, blood and guts, murder and blasphemy, lechery and curses; from these, my eyes and ears were almost never free. For I was not serving officers now in soft retreats, I was toiling for 'niggers' at the front.

"Sick, pale, and shaken to my inmost soul, I was sent back to the English countryside. I was torn in sunder. Was this Europe? Was this civilization? Was this Christianity? I was stupefied—I—"

Shuddering, she drew Matthew's arms close about her and put her cheek beside his and shut her eyes.

Matthew began to talk, low-voiced and quickly, caressing her hair and kissing her closed eyes. The sun fell on the fiery land behind, and the waters darkened.

"We must go now, dearest," she said at length; "we have a long walk." And so they ate bread and milk and swung, singing low, toward the burning city. At Hyde Park she guided him west out toward the stockyard district. In a dilapidated street they stopped where lights showed dimly through dirty windows.

"This is the headquarters of the Box-Makers' Union," he said suddenly and stared at it as at a ghost.

"Will you come in with me?" she asked.

It was a poor, bare room, with benches, a table, and a low platform. Several dozen women and a few men, young and old, white, with a few black, stood about, talking excitedly. A quick blow of silence greeted their entrance; then a whisper, buzz, and clatter of sound.

They surged away and toward and around them. One woman—Matthew recognized the poor shapeless president—ran and threw her arms about Kautilya; but a group in the corner hissed low and swore. The Princess put her hand lovingly on the woman who stood with streaming eyes, and then walked quietly to the platform.

"I am no longer an official or even a member of the international union. I have resigned," she said simply in her low, beautiful voice. A snarl and a sigh answered her.

"I am sorry I had to do what I did. I have in a sense betrayed you and your cause, but I did not act selfishly, but for a greater cause. I hope you will forgive me. Sometime I know you will. I have worked hard for you. Now I go to work harder for you and all men." She paused, and her eyes sought Matthew where he stood, tall and dark, in the background, and she said again in a voice almost a whisper:

"I am going home. I am going to Kali. I am going to the Maharajah of Bwodpur!"

She walked slowly out, but paused to whisper to the president: "That bag—that little leather bag I asked you to keep—will you get it?"

"But you took it with you that—that night."

"Oh, did I? I forgot. I wonder where it is?" and Kautilya joined Matthew and they walked out.

Behind them the Box-Makers' Union sneered and sobbed.

IV

I do not quite understand," said Matthew. "You have mentioned twice—the Maharajah of Bwodpur. Did he not die?"

"The King is dead, long live the King! But do not interrupt—listen!" They were sitting in his den on one side of a little table, facing the fire that glowed in the soft warmth of evening.

They had had their benediction of music—the overture to *Wilhelm Tell*, which seemed to picture their lives. Together they hummed the sweet lilt of the music after the storm.

Before them was rice with a curry that Kautilya had made, and a shortcake of biscuit and early strawberries which Matthew had triumphantly concocted. With it, they drank black tea with thin slices of lemon.

"I think," said Kautilya, "that there was nothing in this century so beautiful as the exaltation of mankind in November, 1918. We all stood hand in hand on the mountain top, upon some vaster Everest. We were all brothers. We forgot the horror of that blood-choked interlude. I forgot even the front at Arras. I remember tearing like a maenad, cypress-crowned, through Piccadilly Circus, hand in hand with white strangers.

"I had just had an extraordinary conversation with an Englishman of highest rank. He had bowed over my hand.

"'Your Highness,' he said, 'when the Emperor saw fit to urge your stay in England, he had hopes that your influence and high birth would do much to win this war for civilization." I was thrilled. England! Actually to be necessary to this land of enjoyment and power! Perhaps to go back in triumph from this abode of Supermen! To help them win the war, and bring back, as reward, freedom for India!

"Long this member of the cabinet talked while my hostess and chaperon guarded us from interruption. We surveyed the policies and hopes and fears of India. One hour later as he kissed my hand, he whispered: 'Who knows! Your Highness may take back an English Maharajah to share your throne!' I looked at him in dumb astonishment; then slowly I saw light. Long months I pondered over that hint.

"And when the Armistice actually came I had had a glorious vision. I was ready to forgive England and Europe. They were but masses of shortsighted fallible men, like all of us. We had all slept. Now the world was awake.

"There was no real line of birth or race or color. I loved them all. The nightmare was ended. The world was free. The world was sane. The world was good. The world was Peace. For the first time in my life and the last, I was English; a loyal subject of the Emperor then in Buckingham Palace—I with a thousand years of royalty behind me. I saw New India, a proud and free nation in the great free sisterhood of the British Raj."

"Yes, yes, I understand," said Matthew. "There was a moment then when I loved America. I cannot conceive it now."

"It was so natural that that which happened should happen just then as I was exalted, blind with ideal fervor, and set to see God and love everywhere. I saw the man first in Piccadilly on that night of nights. He was my knight in shining armor: tall, spare, and fair, with cool gray eyes, his arm in a sling, his khaki smooth and immaculate, his long limbs golden-booted and silver-spurred. I turned and lighted the cigarette for him when I saw him fumbling. Then I looked up at him in startled wonder, unconsciously held out my hand to him, and he kissed it gravely. I did not then dream that he knew me and my station.

"We met weeks later and were presented at that country estate down in Surrey where I had convalesced from my excursion to the front. It was so typically an English traditional setting—so quiet, sweet, and green; so gracious, restful, and comforting, cushioned for every curve and edge of body and soul. Evil, poverty, cruelty seemed so far removed as to be impossible—some far-off half-mythical giant and ogre about which one could argue and smile and explain, while deft servants and endless land and wealth made life a beautiful and a perfect thing.

"He came down for a weekend. His arm had been amputated above the elbow and I was desperately sorry for this maimed fellow, scarcely thirty-five, broken in his very morning of life.

He was neither handsome, witty, nor really educated in any broad way; but his silence and self-repression, his stiff formality, his adherence to his social code, became him. One could imagine depth of thought, fire of emotion, power of command, all sealed and hidden in that fine body. He wooed me in the only way that I was then accessible—not by impetuous word or attempted array of learning, but by silent deference. He was always waiting; always bowing gravely; always rising to his feet and standing at attention with his poor maimed arm, and always insistently arranging my cushions and chairs with his lone hand.

"Then too, to complete the setting and push me by my own pride into what I might otherwise have paused before, there was the young Marchioness of Thorn. She was penniless, plain but stately; and, as everyone knew and saw, hopelessly in love with my cavalier, Captain the Honorable Malcolm Fortescue-Dodd. As an earl's youngest son, Malcolm also had naught but his commission. Once I thought he loved her as she loved him. Then I decided not. Perhaps my decision was easier because of her evident dislike for me.

"At first I literally did not notice the Marchioness of Thorn. Then when I sought to atone and be gracious, I realized with astonishment that she was actually trying to be distant and patronizing with me! Patronizing, mind you, to a Maharanee of Bwodpur and Sindrabad! I was at first amused and then half angry, and finally, as guest of honor, I completely ignored this haughty lady and in sheer revenge annexed as my knight Captain the Honorable Malcolm.

"Even then I was startled when with scant delay he formally asked my hand in marriage. It was in a way a singular sort of innovation. Native Indian Princesses were recognized as reigning monarchs by England, but there had never been formal marital alliances, because it would have involved difficulties of rank and religion on both sides; and then, too, our princesses were usually married long before they saw England or knew Englishmen. In this case, however, a scion of ancient English nobility, albeit but a penniless and untitled younger son, was asking a reigning Indian princess in marriage. Should I—could I—accept? Was I lowering my rank? Was I helping or hindering India?

"A discreet emissary of the India Office came down and discussed matters with me. It seemed that in the new world that was dawning, much of the old order was changing. Indian affairs must soon assume a new status. Should India emerge with new freedom and self-determination as a country entirely separate in race, religion, and politics from Mother England? Or as one allied by interest and even intermarriage? It was an astonishing argument, and—was it not natural?—I was flattered. I saw myself as the first princess of a new order, and while theoretically I held myself the equal of British royalty itself and certainly would have preferred a duke or marquis or even an earl in his own right, yet—and even this was discreetly hinted—earldoms and marquisates were often created for loyal and ambitious servants of the state.

"This very intention again made my head go up in pride. Why should a Maharanee of Bwodpur stoop to English strawberry leaves? I would lift him to my own royal throne, if I so wished. Did I wish it? I felt strangely alone, far from my people and their advice. What would my counselors think? Would they be gratified or alarmed, uplifted or estranged? And then again, was this a high affair of state or a triumph of romantic love? I did not know.

"Yet I was curiously drawn to this tall, silent soldier, with his maimed arm and cold, gray eyes. If only I could draw a light of yearning and passion into those eyes it might bring the answering lightning from my heart and let me, the princess, know such love as peasants only can afford! And so I hesitated and then finally when, through the India Office, the formal assent of my family was handed me, I consented. Formal announcement of the engagement was gazetted and became a nine days' wonder; at Haslemere, some of the great names of England, including British royalty itself, gathered at my betrothal ball.

"I was quite happy. Happy at the gracious reception of my royal blood into the noble blood of England; happy at my consciousness of power. I stood, with my English maidens in attendance, and looked across the ballroom floor—beautiful women, flashing uniforms, stately personages, soft-footed servants; the low hum of word and laughter, the lilt of music.

"Suddenly tears rose in my throat. I was happy, of course, but I wanted love. I had been repressed and cool and haughty toward this wounded man of my choice. I was suddenly yearning to let my naked heart look unveiled into his eyes and see if I would flame and his tense cold face kindle in reply. Where was he? I searched the hall with my glance. He had been beside me but a quarter of an hour since. A mischievous-eyed young maiden of my train blushed, smiled, and nodded. I smiled an answer and turned. There was a draped passage to the supper room behind us, and looming at the end was that easily recognized form. I waved my maidens back, and turning, entered noiselessly. I wanted to be alone with love for one moment, if perchance love were there.

"He was talking to someone I could not see. I stepped forward and his voice held me motionless.

"It was the Marchioness of Thorn. I froze. I could not move. His voice came low and tense, with much more feeling in it than I had ever heard before:

"'What else is there for me, a poor and crippled younger son? Can you not see, dearest, that this is a command on the field of battle? Think what it means to have this powerful buffer state, which we nearly lost, in the hands of a white English ruler; a wall against Bolshevik Russia, a club for chaotic China; a pledge for future and wider empire.'

"'But you'll only be her consort.'

"'I shall be Maharajah in my own right. The India Office has seen to that. I can even divorce her if I will, and I can name my own successor. Depend upon it, he'll be white.'

"Then came the answering voice, almost shrill:

"'Malcolm, I can't bear the thought of your mating with a nigger.'

"'Hell! I'm mating with a throne and a fortune. The darky's a mere makeweight.'

"In those words I died and lived again. The world crashed about me, but I walked through it; turning, I beckoned my maidens, who came streaming behind.

"'Malcolm, this is our waltz,' I said as I came into the light. He stood at attention, and the Marchioness, bowing slightly, began talking to the women, as we two glided away. I went through ball and supper, speeded my guests, and let the Captain kiss my hand in farewell. He paused and lingered a bit over it and came as near looking perturbed as I ever saw him; he was not sure how much I had overheard; but I bit blood from my lips and looked at him serenely. The next day I left for London and India to prepare for the intra-Imperial and interracial wedding."

Matthew and Kautilya had long been walking through the night lights of the crowded streets downtown, hand in hand as she talked. Now she paused and at Michigan and Van Buren they stood awhile shoulder to shoulder, letting the length of their bodies touch lightly. As they waited a chance to cross Michigan, a car snorted and sought to slip by, then came to a wheezy halt.

"Well, well, well!" said the Honorable Sammy, holding out a fat hand and eyeing them quizzically. They greeted him with a smile.

"Say, can't we have a talk?" he asked finally.

"Sure," said Matthew. "Come to my den."

Sammy could not keep his eyes off Kautilya, although there was frank puzzlement in them rather than his usual bold banter. They rode north rapidly in his car, seated together in the rear with close clasped hands. Once at home, Kautilya made Sammy silently welcome and said little. She arranged the small table as Matthew lighted the fire, warmed up a bit of the curry, and brought out a decanter of dark, old crimson wine.

The Honorable Sammy gurgled and expanded.

"What ya gonna do?" he asked. "Gee, this stuff's great—what is it?"

"Indian curry.—We don't know yet."

"Want a job?"

"No," said Matthew slowly, and Kautilya walked over to him softly and slipped an arm about his shoulder.

"Can't coo on air," said Sammy with some difficulty, his mouth being pretty full. "See here! 'Course you and Sara couldn't make it. I never expected you to. She's—well, you're different. Now suppose you just get a divorce. My friend, the judge, will fix it up in a month, and then I can hand you a little job that will help with the bread and butter."

"She can have the divorce," said Matthew.

"But," said Sammy, "you get it, and get it first." Matthew did not answer.

"You see," explained Sammy elaborately, "Sara's funny. Just now she's filled full with hating your lady. She thinks it will hurt you worse to keep you married to her. She thinks you'll tire of this dame and perhaps then come crawling back, so she can kick you good and plenty. See? Now if you begin action for divorce first, for—ah—cruelty—incompatibility—that goes in Illinois why she'd fight back like a tiger and divorce you for adultery. See?"

There was an awkward silence. Then Matthew ventured: "And you, Sammy. I hope you are going to Congress?"

Sammy scowled and shoved his plate back.

"No—not this year. You sure mussed that up all right. But wait till we put Bill Thompson back as mayor. Then we'll shuffle again and see."

"I'm sorry," said Matthew.

"Oh, it's all right. 'Course Sara is sore—damned sore and skittish. But it's all right. You just push that divorce and we'll stand together, see?"

Sammy arose, pulled down his cuffs, straightened his tie, and lit a new, long, black cigar.

"Well—so long!" he said, teetering a moment on heel and toe. Then he leered archly at Kautilya, winked at Matthew, and was gone.

For a minute the two stood silently gripping each other close and saying no word. It was as though some evil wind from out the depths of nowhere had chilled their bones.

V

"I want to sit in a deep forest," said Kautilya, "and feel the rain on my face." So they went furtively and separately down the long lanes of men, stepping softly as those who would escape wild beasts in a wilderness. They met in the Art Gallery beside the lake and walked here and there like strangers, and yet happily and deliciously conscious of each other. At last by elaborate accident they sat down together before a great red dream of sun and sky and air and rolling, tossing waters.

Then they went out and climbed on a bus and happened in the same seat and rode wordlessly north. At Evanston they took the electric train and fared further north. Kautilya slipped off her skirt and was in knickerbockers. Matthew slung his knapsack and blankets on his shoulders. The gray clouds rolled in dark arrows on the lake, and at last they sat alone in the dim forest, huddled beneath a mighty elm, and the rain drifted into their faces. They spent the night under the scowling sky with music of soft waters in their ears. At midnight Kautilya turned and nestled and spoke:

"I stopped in London on my way to India, ostensibly for last-minute shopping, but in reality to explore a new world. In that week in the trenches I had met a new India—fierce, young, insurgent souls irreverent toward royalty and white Europe, preaching independence and self-rule for India. They affronted and scared and yet attracted me. They were different from the Indians I knew and more in some respects like the young Europeans I had learned to know. Yet they were never European. I sensed in them revolution—the change long due in Asia. I had one or two addresses, and in London I sought out some of the men whom I had nursed and helped for a month. They knew nothing of my rank and history. They received me gladly as a comrade and assumed my sympathy and knowledge of their revolutionary propaganda. Ten days I went to school to them and emerged transformed. I was not converted, but my eyes and ears were open.

"I was nineteen when I returned to India and found the arrangements for my English wedding far advanced. My people were troubled and silent. The land was brooding. Only the English were busy and blithe. New native regiments appeared with native line officers. New fortifications, new cities, new taxes were planned. New cheap English goods were pouring in, and the looms and hands of the native workers were idle. The trail of death, leading from the far World War, marched through the land and into China, and thence came the noise of upheaval, while from Russia came secret messages and emissaries.

"The four years of my absence had been years of change and turmoil; years when this native buffer state, breasted against Russia and China and in the path of the projected new English empire in Thibet and secured to English power by the marriage of two children, maimed dolls in the thin white hand of the commissioner, was seething with intrigue.

"My own people were split into factions and divided counsels. After all I was a woman, and in strict law a widow. As such I had no rights of succession. On the other hand, I was the last of a long and royal line. I was the only obstacle between native rule and absorption by England in Sindrabad, and the only hope of independence in Bwodpur. I was the foremost living symbol of home rule in all India. The struggle shook the foundations of our politics and religion, but finally, contrary to all precedent, I had been secretly confirmed as reigning Maharanee after the death of my father. Everything now depended on my marriage, which the most reactionary of my subjects saw was inevitable if my twelve million subjects were to maintain their independence against England.

"Immediately I was the center of fierce struggle: England determined to marry me to an English nobleman; young India determined to rally around me, to strip me of wealth, power, and prerogatives, and to set up here in India the first independent state.

"My phantom prince, poor puppet in the hands of England, I soon saw had probably been murdered by the Indian fanatics of Swaraj, whom then I hated, although I realized that perhaps Englishmen with ulterior motives had egged them on. Two suitors for my hand and power came forward—a fierce and ugly old rajah from the hills who represented the Indians' determination for self-rule under the form of monarchy, and a handsome devil from the lowlands, tool and ape of England: I hated them both. I could see why in desperation my family had consented to my marriage with Fortescue-Dodd.

"I looked about me and realized my wealth and power from my twelve million subjects and from the pathway of my kingdom between India and China. Widowed even before I was a wife, bearing all the Indian contempt for widowhood; child with the heavy burden of womanhood and royal power, I was like to be torn in two not only by the rising determination of young India to be free of Europe and all hereditary power, but also by the equal determination of England to keep and guard her Indian empire.

"I looked on India with new and frightened eyes. I saw degradation in the cringing of the people, starvation and poverty in my own jewels and wealth, tyranny and ignorance in the absolute rule of my fathers, harsh dogmatism in the transformed word of the great and gentle Buddha and the eternal revelation of Brahma."

"But," cried Matthew, "was there no one to guide and advise this poor child of nineteen?"

"Not at first. My natural advisers were fighting against those who threatened my throne, and young India alone was fighting England. I called my family in counsel. Boldly I took the side of young India against England and called the young educated Indians together, many of them cousins and kinsmen, and offered the weight of my wealth and power to forward their aims. The result was miraculous. Some of my old and reactionary kinsmen stood apart, but they did not actively oppose us. Some very few of the most radical of the advocates of *Swaraj* refused to cooperate with royalty on any terms. But I gathered a great bloc of young trained men and women. Long we planned and contrived and finally with united strength turned on England.

"My own mind was clear. I was to be the visible symbol of the power of New India. With my new council I would rule until such time as I married a prince of royal blood and set my son on the throne as Maharajah of Bwodpur. But I postponed marriage.

I wanted light. I wanted to hear what other dark peoples were doing and thinking beneath the dead, white light of European tyranny.

"I called a secret council of the Durbar and laid my plans before them. The splendid wedding ceremony of the proposed English alliance approached. The bridegroom and a host of officials arrived, and from the hills arrived too that ancient and ugly Rajah who was old when he sought my hand in vain seven years before and now had grandchildren older than I.

"The hosts assembled, the ceremony gorgeous in gold and ivory and jewels began: the elephants, painted and caparisoned, marching with slow, sedate, and mighty tread; the old high chariots of the rajahs, with huge wheels and marvelous gilding, drawn by great oxen; the curtained palanquins of the women; the clash of horns and drums and high treble of flutes.

"Then at the height and culmination of the ceremony and before the world of all India and in the face of its conquerors, I took my revenge on the man and nation that had dared to insult a Maharanee of Bwodpur. As Captain the Honorable Malcolm Fortescue-Dodd kneeled in silver and white to kiss my hand, the ancient Rajah from the hills stepped forward and interposed. As the eldest representative of my far-flung family, he announced that this marriage could not be. A plenary council of the chief royal families of India had been held, and it had been decided that it was beneath the dignity of India to accept as consort for a princess of the blood a man without rank or title—unless, he added, 'this alliance was by the will and command of the Maharanee herself.'

"All the world turned toward me and listened as I answered that this marriage was neither of my will nor wish but at the command of my family. Since that command was withdrawn—

"'I do not wish to marry Captain the Honorable Malcolm Fortescue-Dodd.'

"England and English India roared at the insult. There were a hundred conjectures, reasons, explanations, and then sudden silence. After all it was no time for England to take the high hand in India. So it was merely whispered in select circles that the family of Fortescue-Dodd had decided that the women of India were not fit consorts for Englishmen and that they had therefore allowed me gracefully to withdraw. But we of India knew that England was doubly determined to crush Bwodpur.

"Four years went by. Although ruling in my own right, I made that ancient Rajah my guardian and regent and thus put behind my throne all the tradition of old India. Meantime with a growing council of young, enthusiastic followers I began to transform my kingdoms. We mitigated the power of the castes and brought Bwodpur and Sindrabad nearer together. We contrived to spend the major part of the income of the state for the public welfare instead of on ourselves, as was our ancient usage. We began to establish public schools and to send scholars to foreign lands.

"Only in religion and industry were my hands tied—in religion by my own people; in industry by England. We had Hindus and Mohammedans, Buddhists of every shade, and a few more or less sincere Christians. I wanted to clean the slate and go back to the ancient simplicity of Brahma. But, ah! Who can attack the strongholds of superstition and faith!"

"Who indeed!" sighed Matthew. "Our only refuge in America is to stop going to church."

"The church comes to us in India and seizes us. I could only invoke a truce of God to make Allah and Brahma and Buddha sit together in peace, to respect each other as equals.

"In industry my hands were tied by the English power to sell machine goods and drive our artisans from the markets. In vain I joined Mahatma Gandhi and tried to force the boycott over my land. My people were too poor and ignorant. Yet slowly we advanced and there came to us visitors from Egypt, Japan, China, and at last from Russia down across that old and secret highway of the Himalayas, hidden from the world.

"Sitting there in the white shadow of Gaurisankar we conferred with young advanced thinkers of all nations and old upholders of Indian faith and tradition. We conceived a new Empire of India, a new vast union of the darker peoples of the world.

"To further this I started on the Grand Tour of the Darker Worlds. I went secretly by way of Thibet and New China; saw

Sun Yat-sen in Pekin. I was three months in Japan, where the firm foundation of our organization of the darker peoples was laid. Then I spent three months in Russia, watching that astonishing experiment in a land which had suffered from tyranny beyond conception. I tried to learn its plans, and I received every assurance of its sympathy. Down by Kiev I came to Odessa and sailed the Black Sea.

"I saw the towers of Constantinople shining in the sun and stood in that great center where once Asia poured the light of her culture into the barbarism of Europe and made it a living soul. I walked around those mighty walls, where Theodosius held back the Nordic and the Hun. I went by old Skutari and its vast city of the dead; down by a slow and winding railway, three hundred and fifty miles westward to Angora. There I sat at the feet of Kemal and heard his plans. Thence overland by slow and devious ways I came through Asia Minor and Syria. Down by the Kizilirmak and the great blue waters of the Tuz Tcholli Gol; over to Kaisapieh and through the dark passes of the Anti-Taurus; then skirting the shining Mediterranean, I saw French Syria at Aleppo, Hamah, and Damascus; I saw Zion and the new Jerusalem and came into the ancient valley of the Nile and into the narrow winding streets of Cairo."

"You have seen the world, Kautilya, the real and darker world. The world that was and is to be."

"It was a mighty revelation, and it culminated fittingly in Egypt, where in a great hall of the old university hung with rugs to keep out both the eavesdropper and the light, the first great congress of the darker nations met under the presidency of Zahglul Pasha. We had all gathered slowly and unobtrusively as tourists, business men, religious leaders, students, and beggars, and we met unnoticed in a city where color of skin is nothing to comment on and where strangers are all too common. We were a thousand strong, and never were Asia, Africa, and the islands represented by stronger, more experienced, and more intelligent men.

"Your people were there, Matthew, but they did not come as Negroes. There were black men who were Egyptians; there were black men who were Turks; there were black men who were Indians, but there were no black men who represented purely and simply the black race and Africa.

"Of all the things we did and planned and said in a series of meetings, I will tell you in other days. Let it suffice now to say that I came back to Europe by Naples and Paris and then went to Berlin. There I sat and planned with a small special committee, and there it was that I brought up the question of American Negroes, of whom I had heard much in Russia. The committee was almost unanimously opposed. They thought of Negroes only as slaves and half-men, and were afraid to risk their cooperation, lest they lose their own dignity and place; but they were not unwilling to let American Negroes, if they would, start some agitation or overt act. Even if it amounted to nothing, as they expected, it would at least focus attention. It would intensify feeling. It would help the coming crisis.

"But who could do this?

"The curious and beautiful accident of our meeting, after my committee had discussed and rejected the Negroes of America as little more than slaves, deeply impressed me. And in the face of strong advice, as you know, I helped you to return to America and report to me on the rumored uprising which had been revealed to me by curious and roundabout ways.

"I was not thinking of you then, Matthew, at least not consciously. I was thinking of the great Cause and I wanted information. I looked at America and tried to understand it. There was here a mystery of the art of living that the world must have in order to have time for life. I saw America and lost you. Almost, in the new intensity of my thinking, I forgot you as a physical fact. You remained only as a spirit which I recognized as part of me and part of the universe. And then suddenly the blow came, falling through open skies, and I saw you facing disgrace and death and locked for ten years in jail.

"Before I saw you, I, with most of the others except the Chinese, had thought of our goal as a substitution of the rule of dark men in the world for the rule of white, because the colored peoples were the noblest and best bred. But you said one word that night at dinner."

"I did not say it—it was said. I opened my mouth and it was filled."

"You remember it! It was a great word that swung back the doors of a world to me. You said that the masses of men of all races might be the best of men simply imprisoned by poverty and ignorance.

"It came to me like a great flash of new light, and you, the son of slaves, were its wonderful revelation. I determined to go to America, to study and see. I began to feel that my dream of the world based on the domination of an ancient royal race and blood might not be all right, but that as Lord Buddha said, and as we do not yet understand, humanity itself was royal.

"Then things happened so rapidly that I lost my grip and balance and sense of right and wrong. I sent you on a wild chase to almost certain death. I planned to go with you to watch and see. The secret, powerful hand of the junta sought to threaten us both and save the great cause. How singularly we fought at cross purposes! They wanted you to go and stir up any kind of wild revolt, but they wanted to keep me and themselves from any possible connection with it in thought and deed. They almost threatened you with death. They pushed you out alone. They tried to keep me from sailing. And finally you went down into the depths, dear heart, almost to the far end." Her voice fell away, and they lay and watched the birth of the new and sun-kissed day.

All that day they wandered and talked and finally late at night came home. Kautilya was almost ready for bed when she said drowsily:

"Oh, Matthew—the little leather bag I brought—where did you put it, dear?"

"Leather bag? I saw none."

"But it was not at the union headquarters. They said I took it with me to—to Sara's."

"Then you must have left it there. We carried nothing away. Nothing."

"Oh, dear—I must have left it—what shall I do?"

"Was it valuable or just clothes?"

"It was—valuable. Very valuable, intrinsically and—in meaning."

"I am so sorry—may I ask—?"

"Yes—it has many of the crown jewels of Bwodpur."

"The crown jewels!"

"Yes. Some of them always travel with the heir to the throne. I have carried these since father's death. Some of the jewels are beautiful and priceless. Others, like the great ruby, are full of legends and superstitious memory. The great ruby is by legend a drop of Buddha's blood. It anoints the newborn Maharajah. It is worn on his turban. It closes his eyes in death."

"Oh, Kautilya, Kautilya! We must find these things—I will go to Sara's myself. What do you think them worth—I mean would they be worth stealing?"

"Oh, yes, they must be worth at least a hundred lakhs of rupees. Matthew paused, then started up.

"What—you mean—you don't mean—a million dollars?"

"At least that—but don't be alarmed. They are mostly too large and unusual for sale. They are insured and I have a description. Probably the bag is sitting somewhere unnoticed. Oh, I am so careless; but don't worry. Let me write a note and call a messenger. I have faithful helpers. The bag will soon be found."

The note was dispatched, and Kautilya was soon making a mysterious Indian dish for supper and singing softly.

Matthew was still thinking with astonishment, "The crown jewels of Bwodpur—a million dollars!"

VI

Sammy was uneasy. He had a telegram from Sara announcing her sudden return from New York. She was arriving in the morning. But there was no letter in answer to several urgent ones from Sammy, a bit misspelled and messy, but to the point, He had suggested among other things that Sara remain east until September.

Sara, after the tragic failure of her long-laid plans, had taken a trip to New York. She put on her best clothes and took plenty of funds. She wired to the Plaza for a suite of rooms—a sitting room, bedroom, and bath. She arrived in the morning of April 10 on the Twentieth Century, had a good lunch, and went to a dressmaker whose name and ability she had learned. She ordered a half-dozen new gowns. She secured, at the hotel, orchestra seats for two good shows—Ziegfeld's Follies and a revue at the Winter Garden, and she also got a seat for *The Jewels of the Madonna* at the Metropolitan. She hired a car with a liveried chauffeur and drove through the park and down the avenue to Washington Square and back to the Plaza and had tea there; she took a walk, went to the Capitol, and dined at the Ritz.

For four or five days Sara tried the joys of free spending and costly amusement. She was desperately lonesome. Then she struck up acquaintance with a lady and her husband whom she met at the Plaza by the accident of sitting at the same table. They were from Texas. Sara was a bit dismayed, but did not flinch. They were as lonesome and distraught as she and grabbed like her at the novelty of a new voice. They played together at theater and dinner, rides to Westchester and Long Island, and at night they went to Texas Guinan's club, accompanied by an extra man whom the husband had picked up somewhere. Sara was sleepy and bored, and the drinks which she tasted made her sick. Her escort when sober danced indifferently and was quite impossible as he got gradually drunk.

Next morning Sara arose late with a headache, reserved a berth to Chicago, and wired Sammy:

"Arrive tomorrow morning at nine."

Sammy had not been expecting this. In fact he had made up his mind that she would be away at least three months and was laying his plans. This sudden turn upset him. He looked about the office helplessly. When the Fall campaign began, he would want Sara back in harness; but he was not ready for her now. First of all, that damned Towns had made no move toward a divorce. There were his belongings which Sara bad bundled up hastily and sent to him when she left. They were in the corner of his office now, and Sammy rose and aimlessly looked them over. There was a bundle of clothes, two boxes of books, and two bags. What had Sara written about these bags? Yes, here was the note.

"This smaller bag is not his and doesn't belong in the house. It was sitting in the library. It may belong to some of the guests or to that woman. If it is inquired for, return it. If not, throw it away."

Sammy lifted it. It seemed rather solid. He picked it up and examined it. It was of solid thick leather and tarnished metal, which looked like silver. It was securely locked. There was a small crest stamped on the silver. Yes, it undoubtedly belonged to the Princess. It would be an excuse for another visit to her.

Then Sammy sat down, eyeing the bag idly, and returned to his thoughts. Neither Sara nor Matthew had made the slightest movement toward a divorce. Now it was Sammy's pet idea that Sara should not begin proceedings. He wanted her to pose for sometime as the injured victim. He wanted Towns to kill himself beyond redemption by not only deserting Sara but brazenly seeking legal separation. Now that neither made a move Sammy got uneasy. What was the big idea? Was Sara going to hold on to him because she wanted him back or just to thwart the other woman? Did Matthew want his freedom, or was he playing around and ready to return to Sara later? Sammy was stumped. He had spoken to Matthew before the lady, and yet Matthew had neither answered nor taken any steps. Didn't the woman want Matthew divorced?

Then Sammy looked at the bag again. Queer woman—queer bag. Didn't look or feel like a toilet case. No—contents weren't soft enough for clothing. Well—he must get rid of this junk and clean up his office and Sara's and get ready for her tomorrow. Then Sammy looked at that bag again. What was this "Princess," anyhow? What was her game? Here was a chance to find out. He tried to open the bag. It was securely locked. The lock was very curious and was probably a combination and not a key lock, in spite of certain holes. Sammy again felt carefully of the contents—shook the bag, tamed around and upside down. Then suddenly he shut and lo the door and drew the curtain and took out his knife. He attempted to slit the leather. It was very heavy, and once cut, after considerable difficulty, it revealed a fine steel mesh below Sammy was aroused and beset with curiosity. He got a wire ripper and soon had a hole about two inches long. Through this he drew a small Russian leather box fastened with a gold gilded clasp. He opened this and found a dozen or more large transparent unset stones that looked like diamonds.

Sammy began to perspire. Then he wiped the sweat from his brow and sat down to think. He examined his own diamond ring. These stones certainly looked genuine. They scratched the window glass. But—it couldn't be! If these were diamonds they'd be worth—Hell! Sammy took out one, closed the box, and inserted it in the bag. He closed the aperture carefully and started with it to the safe. No, suppose Sara asked for it! No, he turned it around and set it carelessly and in full sight in the corner. Then he unlocked the office door and 'phoned Corruthers.

"Say," he said when Corruthers appeared, "take this to Bea and see if it's worth anything."

Corruthers ran his fingers through his red hair.

"Phony," he declared. "Who stuck you with it?"

"Shut up," said Sammy, "and ask Ben and don't try no monkey business neither."

Corruthers was back in a half hour.

"Say," he began excitedly. "Where'd you get this—?"

Sammy interrupted. "Send them clothes and books to Towns."

"Sure—but—"

"What's the stone worth?"

"Five thousand dollars."

Sammy bit his cigar in two but managed to keep from swallowing the stub and dropping the end—

"Oh—er—that all?"

"Well—you might get more if you could prove ownership. He says it's an unusual stone. How—"

"'Tain't mine," said Sammy. "Probably stolen. A bird wanted to sell it, but I don't know—" and he shooed wanted to Corruthers out.

Five thousand! And one of a dozen! And that bag. Again Sammy locked up carefully, drew the shades, and turned on the electric lights. Then he brought the bag to the desk and with a knife and improvised tools, tore it entirely open. There were a half-dozen boxes, several paper bundles, and two or three chamois bags. He spread the contents out on the desk and literally gasped. Such jewels he had never seen. Not only smaller uncut diamonds in profusion, but several large stones in intricate settings, beautiful emeralds, two or three bags of lovely matched pearls, and above all, a great crimson ruby that looked like a huge drop of blood.

Sammy gasped, sat down, stood up, whistled, and whirled about; and whirling, faced, sitting quietly in his own chair, a person who seemed at first an utter stranger. Then Sammy recognized him as the Indian with whom he had had several conferences during the campaign and whom he had met together with the young radical Negro down at the radical Box-Makers' Union.

Sammy suddenly grew furious.

"How the hell—" he began; but the Indian interrupted suavely.

"Through the window there," he said. "You pulled the shade down, but you didn't lock the window. I have been watching there several days."

"Well, by God," and Sammy half turned toward the desk; but the Indian still spoke very quietly.

"I wouldn't if I were you," he said.

Sammy didn't. On the other hand he sat down in another chair and faced the Indian.

"Well, what about it?" he said.

"These jewels," said the Indian, "are, as I presume you suspect, the property of her Royal Highness, the Princess of Bwodpur. In fact they are part of the crown jewels which always accompany the heir to the throne wherever he or she goes. Her Royal Highness is unfortunately very careless. She had the jewels with her when she started to interview Mr. Towns that night, and in the turmoil of the evening, evidently forgot them. Yesterday she sent me a note asking that I find them. I went to the residence of Mrs. Towns and found it locked on account of her absence, but I secured entrance."

"That kind of thing sometimes lands people in jail," said Sammy dryly.

"Yes," said the Indian, "and the theft of jewels like these might land one further in jail and for a longer time."

Sammy didn't answer, and the Indian continued: "I searched the house and was satisfied that the bag was not there, and then I learned that certain things had been delivered at your office. I came down here and saw the bag sitting here. That was early yesterday morning, while the janitor was sweeping."

"Damn him!" said Sammy.

"It wasn't his fault," said the Indian. "I forget what excuse I gave him, but you may be sure it was a legitimate one. Yesterday and today I have spent watching you to be sure of your attitude."

"Well?" said Sammy.

"Well," returned the Indian, "I had hoped that the proof which I have would secure the bag, untampered with and without question or delay."

"What proof?" asked Sammy.

"A careful description of the jewels made by the well-known firm which has insured them and which would at the slightest notice put detectives on their track. Also, a letter from her Royal Highness directing that these jewels be delivered to me."

"And you expect to get these on such trumped-up evidence?"

"Yes," said the Indian.

"And suppose I refuse?"

"I shall persuade you not to."

Sammy thought the matter over. "Say," said he, "can't you and I come to some agreement? Why, here is a fortune. Is there any use wasting it on Matthew and that Princess?"

"We can come to an agreement," said the Indian.

"What?" asked Sammy.

"You have," said the Indian, "an unset diamond in your pocket which, with a certificate of ownership that I could give you, would easily be worth ten thousand dollars. You may keep it."

Sammy rose in a rage. "I can not only keep that," he said, "but I can keep the whole damn shooting-match and—" But he didn't get any further. The Indian had arisen and showed in the folds of his half-Oriental dress a long, wicked-looking dagger.

"I should regret," he said, "the use of violence, but her Royal Highness' orders are peremptory. She would rather avoid, if possible, the police. I am therefore going to take these jewels to her. If afterward you should wish to prosecute her, you can easily do it."

Sammy quickly came to his senses: "Go ahead," he said.

The Indian deftly packed the jewels, always managing to face Sammy in the process. Finally, with a very polite goodnight, he started to the door.

"Say," said Sammy, "where are you going to take those jewels?"

"I have orders," said the Indian slowly, "to place them in the hands of Matthew Towns."

The door closed softly after him. Sammy seated himself and thought the matter over. He had a very beautiful diamond in his pocket which he examined with interest. His own feeling was that it would make a very splendid engagement ring for Sara. Then he started. . . suppose these jewels were given to Matthew, or part of them, and suppose Sara got wind of it? Would she ever give Matthew up? That was a serious matter a very serious matter. In fact, she must not get wind of it. Then Sammy frowned. Good Lord! He had actually had his hands on something that looked like at least one million dollars. Ah, well! It was dangerous business. Only fools stole jewels of that sort.

A messenger boy entered with a telegram.

> I have decided to go to Atlantic City. Do not expect me until I write.
>
> SARA

W.E.B. DU BOIS

VII

I've got a job," said Matthew, early in June.

Kautilya turned quickly and looked at him with something of apprehension in her gaze. It was a beautiful day. Kautilya had been arranging and cleaning, singing and smiling to herself, and then stopping suddenly and standing with upturned face as though listening to inner or far-off voices. Matthew had been gone all the morning and now returned laden with bundles and with a sheaf of long-stemmed roses, red and white, which Kautilya seized with a low cry and began to drape like cloud and sun upon the table.

Then she hurried to the phonograph and put a record on, singing with its full voice a flare of strange music, haunting, alluring, loving. It poured out of the room, and Matthew joined in, and their blended voices dropped on the weary, dirty street. The tired stopped and listened. The children danced. Then at last:

"I've got a job," said Matthew; and answering her look and silence with a caress, he added: "I got it myself—it's just the work of a common laborer. I'm going to dig in the new subway. I shall get four dollars a day."

"I am glad," said Kautilya. "Tell me all about it."

"There is not much. I've noticed the ads and today I went out and applied. There was one of Sammy's gang there. He said I wouldn't like this—that he could get me on as foreman or timekeeper. I told him I wanted to dig."

"To dig, that's it," said Kautilya. "To get down to reality, Matthew. For us now, life begins. Come, my man, we have played and, oh! Such sweet and beautiful play. Now the time of work dawns. We must go about our Father's business. Let's talk about it. Let's stand upon the peaks again where once we stood and survey the kingdoms of this world and plot our way and plan our conquests. Oh, Matthew, Matthew, we are rulers and masters! We start to dig, remaking the world. Too long, too long we have stood motionless in darkness and dross. Up! To the work, in air and sun and heaven. How is our world, and when and where?"

They sat down to a simple lunch and Matthew talked.

"We must dig it out with my shovel and your quick wit. Here in America black folk must help overthrow the rule of the rich by distributing wealth more evenly first among themselves and then in alliance with white labor, to establish democratic control of industry. During the process they must keep step and hold tight hands with the other struggling darker peoples."

"Difficult—difficult," mused Kautilya, "for the others have so different a path. In my India, for instance, we must first emancipate ourselves from the subtle and paralyzing misleading of England—which divides our forces, bribes our brains, emphasizes our jealousies, encourages our weaknesses. Then we must learn to rule ourselves politically and to organize our old industry on new modern lines for two objects: our own social uplift and our own defense against Europe and America. Otherwise, Europe and America will continue to enslave us. Can we accomplish this double end in one movement?"

"It is paradoxical, but it must be done," said Matthew. "Our hope lies in the growing multiplicity and worldwide push of movements like ours; the new dark will to self-assertion. China must achieve united and independent nationhood; Japan must stop aping the West and North and throw her lot definitely with the East and South. Egypt must stop looking north for prestige and tourists' tips and look south toward the black Sudan, Uganda, Kenya, and South Africa for a new economic synthesis of the tropics."

"And meantime, Matthew, our very hope of breaking the sinister and fatal power of Europe lies in Europe itself: in its own drear disaster; in negative jealousies, hatreds, and memories; in the positive power of revolutionary Russia, in German Socialism, in French radicalism and English labor. The Power and Will is in the world today. Unending pressure, steadying pull, blow on blow, and the great axis of the world quest will turn from Wealth to Men."

"The mission of the darker peoples, my Kautilya, of black and brown and yellow, is to raise out of their pain, slavery, and humiliation, a beacon to guide manhood to health and happiness and life and away from the morass of hate, poverty, crime, sickness, monopoly, and the mass-murder called war."

Kautilya sat with glowing eyes. She looked at Matthew and whispered:

"Day dawns. We must—start."

Matthew hesitated and faltered. He talked like one exploring the dark:

"I had thought I might dig here in Chicago and that you might write and study, and that we together might live far out somewhere alone with trees and stars and carry on—correspondence with the world; and perhaps—"

"If we only could," she said softly; and in the instant both knew it was an impossible idyl.

A week went by. There grew a certain stillness and apprehension in the air. The hard heat of July was settling on Chicago. Each morning Matthew put on his overalls and took his dinner-pail and went down into the earth to dig. Each night he came home, bathed, and put on the gorgeous dressing gown Kautilya had bought him and sat down to the dinner Kautilya had cooked—it was always good, but simple, and he ate enormously. Then there was music, a late stroll beneath the stars, and bed. But always in Kautilya's eyes, the rapt look burned.

And little things were beginning to happen. At first Matthew's old popularity in his district had protected him. He always met nods and greetings as he and Kautilya fared forth and back. Then came reaction—the social tribute of the half-submerged to standards of respectability. Here and there a woman sneered, a child yelled, and a policeman was gruff. As weeks went by, Sammy interfered, and active hostility was evident. Jibes multiplied from chance passersby who recognized them; the sneers of policemen were open. Then came the question of money, which never occurred to Kautilya, but drove Matthew mad when he tried to stretch his meager wage beyond the simple food to American Beauty roses and new books and bits of silk and gold.

Tonight as they returned from a silent but sweet stroll a bit earlier than their wont, they met a crowd of children, those children who seem never to have a bedtime. The children stared, laughed, jeered, and then stoned them. Matthew would have rushed upon them to tear their flesh, but Kautilya soothed him, and they came breathless home.

They stood awhile clinging in the dark. Then slowly Matthew took her shoulders in his hand and said:

"We have had the day God owed us, Kautilya, and now at last we must face facts frankly. Here and in this way I cannot protect you, I cannot support you, and neither of us can do the great work which is our dream."

"It was brave and good of you, Matthew, to speak first when you knew how hard the duty was to me and how weak I am in presence of our love. Yes, we have had the day God owed us— and now, Matthew, the day of our parting dawns. I am going away."

He knew that she was going to say this, and yet until it was said he kept trying to believe it would not come. Now when it did come it struck upon his ears like doom. The brownness of his face went gray, and his cheeks sagged with sudden age. He looked at her with stricken eyes, and she, sobbing, smiled at him through tears.

"You are a brave man," she went on steadily. "In this last great deed, I will not fear. I go to greet the ghosts of all my fathers, the Maharajahs of Bwodpur. India calls. The black world summons. I must be about my fathers' business. Tomorrow, I go. This night, this beautiful night, is ours. Behold the good, sweet moon and the white dripping of the stars. There shall be no fire tonight, save in our twined bodies and in our flaming hearts."

But he only whispered, "Parted!"

"Courage, my darling," she said. "Nothing, not even the high Majesty of Death, shall part us for a moment. There is a sense—a beautiful meaning—in which we two can never part. To all time, we are one wedded soul. The day may dawn when in cries and tears of joy we shall feel each other's arms again. But we must not deceive ourselves. It is possible that now and from this incarnate spirit we part forever. Great currents and waves of forces are rolling down between. It may not lie in human power to breast them. But, Matthew, oh, Matthew, always, always wherever I am and no matter how dark and drear the silence—always I am with you and by your side."

Matthew was calm again and spoke slowly: "No, we will not deceive each other," he said; "I know as well as you that we must part. I am ready for the sacrifice, Kautilya. There was a time when I did not know the meaning of sacrifice, when I interpreted it as surrendering an ounce to get a pound, exchanging a sunrise for a summer. But now, I know that if I am asked to give up you forever, and nothing, nothing can come in return, I shall do it quietly and with no outcry. I shall work on, doing the very best I know how. I shall keep strong in body and clear in mind and clean in soul. I shall play the great game of life as we have conceived and dreamed it together, and try to dream it further into fact. But in all that living, working, doing, dear Kautilya, I shall be dead. For without you—there is no life for me.

"I suppose that all this feeling is based on the physical urge of sex between us. I suppose that other contacts, other experiences, might have altered the world for us two. But the magnificent fact of our love remains, whatever its basis or accident. It rises from the ecstasy of our bodies to the communion of saints, the resurrection of the spirit, and the exquisite crucifixion of God. It is the greatest thing in our world. I sacrifice it, when I must, for nobler worlds that others may enjoy."

"I did not mistake you, Matthew; I knew you would understand. The time is come for infinite wisdom itself to think life out for us. This honeymoon of our high marriage with God alone as priest must end. It was our due. We earned it. But now we must earn a higher, finer thing."

Then hesitatingly she continued and spoke the yet unspoken word:

"First comes your duty to Sara. Even if you had not miraculously returned to me, you would have been forced to let Sara know by some unanswerable cataclysm that you would no longer follow her leading—either this, or your spiritual death; for you knew it, and you were planning revolt and flight. You were frightened at the thought of poverty and unlovely work; but now that you are free and have known love, you must return to Sara and say:

"'See, I am a laborer: I will not lie and cheat and steal, but I will work in any honest way.' If it still happens that she wants you, wants the *real* you, whom she knows now but partially and must in the end know fully—a man honest to his own hurt, not greedy for wealth; loving all mankind and rejoicing in the simple things of life—if she wants this man, I—I must let you go. For she is a woman; she has her rights."

Matthew answered slowly:

"But she will not want me; I grieve to say it in pity, for I suffer with all women. Sara loves no one but herself. She can never love. To her this world-tangle of the races is a lustful scramble for place and power and show. She is mad because she is handicapped in the scramble. She would gladly trample anything beneath her feet, black, white, yellow, if only she could ride in gleaming triumph at the procession's head. Jealousy, envy, pride, fill the little crevices of her soul. No, she will not want me. But—if you will—as you have said, hers shall be the choice. She must ask divorce, not I. And even beyond that I will offer her fully and freely my whole self."

"And in the meantime," said Kautilya, "there are greater things—greater issues to be tested. We will wait on the high gods to see if maybe they will point the way for us to work together for the emancipation of the world. But if they decide otherwise, then, Matthew—"

"Then," continued Matthew gently, "we are parted, and forever."

"Yes," she whispered. "You and I, apart but eternally one, must walk the long straight path of renunciation in order that the work of the world shall go forward at our hands. We must work. We must work with our hands. We must work with our brains. We must stand before Vishnu; together we will serve.

"For, Matthew, hear my confession. I too face the horror of sacrifice. All is not well in Bwodpur, and each day I hearken for the call of doom across the waters. The old Rajah, my faithful guardian and ruler in my stead, is dead. Tradition, jealousy, intrigue, loom. For of me my people have a right to demand one thing: a Maharajah in Bwodpur, and one—of the blood royal!"

W.E.B. DU BOIS

Matthew dropped his hands suddenly. Suddenly he knew that his own proposal of sacrifice was but an empty gesture, for Sara did not want him—would never want him. But Bwodpur wanted—a King!

Kautilya spoke slowly, standing with hanging hands and with face upraised toward the moon.

"We widows of India, even widows who, like me, were never wives, must ever face the flame of Sati. And in living death I go to meet the Maharajah of Bwodpur."

"Go with God, for after all it is not merely me you love, but rather the world through me."

"You are right and wrong, Matthew; I would not love you, did you not signify and typify to me this world and all the burning worlds beyond, the souls of all the living and the dead and of them that are to be. Because of this I love you, you alone. Yet I would love you if there were no world. I shall love you when the world is not."

She continued, after a space:

"I did not tell you, but yesterday my great and good friend, the Japanese baron whom you have met and dislike because you do not know him, came to see me. He knows always where I am and what I do, for it is written that I must tell him. You do not realize him yet, Matthew. He is civilization—he is the high goal toward which the world blindly gropes; high in birth and perfect in courtesy, filled with wide, deep, and intimate knowledge of the world's past—the world, white, black, brown, and yellow: knowing by personal contact and acquaintanceship the present from kings to coolies. He is a man of lofty ideal without the superstition of religion, a man of decision and action. He is our leader, Matthew, the guide and counselor, the great Prime Minister of the Darker World.

"He brought me information—floods of facts: the great conspiracy of England to re-grip the British mastery of the world at any cost; the titanic struggle behind the scenes in Russia between toil and ignorance defending the walls against organized stupidity and greed in Western Europe and America. He tells me of the armies and navies, of new millionaires in Germany and

France, of new Caesarism in Italy, of the failing hells of Poland and dismembered Slavdom. The world is a great ripe cherry, gory, rotten—it must be plucked lest it fall and smash.

"My friend talked long of Asia—of my India, of poor Bwodpur. The Dewan who now rules for me, for all his loyalty and ability and his surrounding of young and able men, is distraught with trouble. It is unheard of that a Maharanee without a Maharajah should rule in Bwodpur. Some will not believe that the old Rajah is dead, but say that, shut up within his castle in High Himalaya, that ancient and unselfish man, who was my King in name, still lives as the reincarnate Buddha—lives and rules, and they would worship him. Around this and other superstitions, the continued and inexplicable absence of the Maharanee, the innovations of schools, health training, roads, and mysterious machinery, the neglect of the old religion, looms the intrigue of the English on every side—money, cheap goods, titles, decorations, hospitality, and magnificent Durbars—oh, all is not well in Bwodpur; even the throes of revolution threaten: Moslem and Hindu are at odds, Buddhist and Christian quarrel. Bwodpur needs me, Matthew, but she needs more than me: she needs a Maharajah.

"Facing all this, Matthew, my man, with level eye and clear brain we must drain the cup before us: if return to India severs me from the western world and you—if the dropping of oceanwide dreams into the little lake of Bwodpur is my destiny—the will of Vishnu prevail. If your reunion with Sara is the only step toward the real redemption and emancipation of black America, then, Matthew, drain the cup. But after all, the day of decision is not yet. And whatever comes, Love our love is already eternal."

Matthew pondered and said:

"The paradox is amazing: the only thing that was able to lift me from cynical selfishness, organized theft and deception, was that finest thing within me—this love and idealization of you. If I had not followed it at every cost, I should have sunk beneath hell. And yet now I am anathema to my people. I am the Sunday School example of one who sold his soul to the devil. I am painted as punished with common labor for following lust and desecrating the home. People who recognize me all but spit upon me in the street. Oh, Kautilya, what shall we do against these forces that are pushing, prying, rending us apart? Is it possible that the great love of a man for a woman—the perfect friendship and communion of two human beings—can ever be mere evil?"

They turned toward the room and looked at it. "I cannot keep these things," he said. "They mean you. They meant you unconsciously before I knew that I should ever see you again. The Chinese rug was the splendid coloring of your skin; the Matisse was the flame of your high spirit; the music was your voice. I am going to move to one simple, bare room where again and unhindered by things, I can see this little place of beauty with you set high in its midst. And I shall picture you still in its midst. I could not bear to see anyone of these things without you."

She hesitated. "I understand, I think, and the rug and picture shall go with me," she said. "And yet I hate to think of your living barely and crudely without the bits of beauty you have placed about you. Yet perhaps it is well. In my land, you know, men often, in their strong struggle with life, go out and leave life and strip themselves of everything material that could impede or weight the soul, and sit naked and alone before their God. Perhaps, Matthew, it would be well for you to do this. A little space—a little space."

"How long before we know?" he said, turning toward her suddenly and taking both her hands.

"I cannot say," she answered. "Perhaps a few weeks, perhaps a little year. Perhaps until the spirit Vishnu comes down again to earth."

He shivered and said, "Not so long as that, oh, Radha, not so long! And yet if it must be—let it be."

And so they dismantled the room and packed and baled most of the things therein. At last in full day they went down to the Union Station and walked slowly along toward the gates with clasped hands. A beautiful couple, unusual in their height, in the brownness of their skins, in their joy and absorption in each other.

A porter passed by, stopped, and glanced back. He whispered to another: "That's him; and that's the woman." Then others whispered, porters and passengers. A knot of the curious gathered and stared. But the two did not hurry; they did not notice. Someone even hissed, "Shameless!" and someone else said, "Fool!" and still they walked on and through the gates and to the train. He kissed her lips and kissed her hands, and without tears or words she stepped on the train and looked backward as it moved off. Suddenly he lifted both hands on high, and tears rolled down his cheeks.

VIII

Matthew wrote to Kautilya at the New Willard in Washington, and in one of his letters he said: "I am digging a Hole in the Earth. It is singular to think how much of life is and has been just digging holes. All the farmers; all the miners; all of the builders, and how many many others have just dug holes! The bowels of the great crude earth must be pierced and plumbed and explored if we would wrest its secrets from it. I have a sense of reality in this work such as I have never had before—neither in medicine nor travel, neither as porter, prisoner, nor lawmaker. What I am actually doing may be little, but it is indispensable. So much cannot be said of healing nor writing novels. I am digging not to plant, not to explore, but to make a path for walking, running, and riding; a little round tunnel through which man may send swiftly small sealed boxes full of human souls, from Dan even unto Beersheba.

"Yes, just about that. Just about fifty miles of tunnel we will have before this new Chicago subway is finished. And you have no idea of the problems—the sweat, the worry, the toil of digging this little hole. For it is little, compared to the vast and brawny body of this mighty earth. It is like the path of some thin needle in a great football of twine. The earth resists, frantically, fiercely, tenaciously. We have to fight it; to outguess it; to know the unknown and measure the unmeasured.

"There lies the innocent dust and sand of a city street held down from flying by bits of stone and pressed asphalt. So pliant and yielding, so vulnerable. But it is watching—watching and waiting. I can feel it; I can hear it. It will make a bitter struggle to hide its heart from prying eyes. Its very surrender is danger; its resistance may be death. I go down girded for a fight with a hundred others in jersies and overalls and thick heavy shoes. We are like hard-limbed Grecian athletes, but less daintily clad. One can see the same ripple and swelling of muscles, and I felt at first ashamed of my flabbiness. But this thing is real, not mere sport: we are not playing. There is no laughing gallery with waving colors and triumphant cries. For us this thing is life and death, food and drink, commerce, education, and art. I am in deadly earnest. I am bare, sweating, untrammeled. My muscles already begin to flow smooth and unconfined. I have no stomach, either in flesh or spirit. My body is all life and eagerness, without weight.

"Rain, sun, dust, heat and cold; the well, the sick, the wounded, and the dead. I saw a man make a little misstep and jump forward; his head struck the end of a projecting beam and cracked sickeningly. In fifteen minutes he was forgotten and the army closed ranks and went forward; I just heard the echo of the cry of his woman as it sobbed down to the mud underneath the ground. Yes, it is War, eternal War from the beginning to the end. We plumb the entrails of the earth.

"The earth below the city is full of secret things. Voices are there calling day and night from everywhere to everybody. I did not know before the paths they chose, but now I see them whispering over long gray bones beneath the streets. Lakes and rivers flow there, pouring from the hills down to the kitchen sinks with steady pulse beneath the iron street. Thin blue gas burns there in leaden pockets to cook and heat, and light is carried in steel to blaze in parlors above the dark earth. There is a strange world of secret things—of wire pipes, great demijohns and caverns, secret closets, and long, silent tunnels here beneath the streets.

"The houses sag, stagger, and reel above us, but they do not fall: we hold them, force them back and prop them up. A slimy sewer breaks and drenches us; we mend it and send its dirty waters on to the canal, the river, and the sea. Gas pipes leak and stifle us. Electricity flashes; but we are curiously armed with such power to command and such faith like mountains that all nature obeys us. Lamps of Aladdin are everywhere and do their miracles for the rubbing: great steel and harnessed Genii, a hundred feet high, lumber blindly along at our beck and call to dig, lift, talk, push, weep, and swear. Yesterday, one of the giants died; fell forward and crumpled into sticks and bits of broken steel; but it shed no blood; it only hissed in horror. We strain in vast contortions underneath the ground. We perform vast surgical operations with

W.E.B. DU BOIS

insertions of lumber and steel and muscle; we tear down stone with thunder and lightning; we build stone up again with water and cement. We defy every law of nature, swinging a thousand tons above us on nothing; taking away the foundations of the city and leaving it delicately swaying on air, afraid to fall. We dive and soar, defying gravitation. We have built a little world down here below the earth, where we live and dream. Who planned it? Who owns it? We do not know.

"And right here I seem to see the answer to the first question of our world-work: What are you and I trying to do in this world? Not merely to transpose colors; not to demand an eye for an eye. But to straighten out the tangle and put the feet of our people, and all people who will, on the Path. The first step is to reunite thought and physical work. Their divorce has been a primal cause of disaster. They that do the world's work must do it thinking. The thinkers, dreamers, poets of the world must be its workers. Work is God."

Matthew laid down the pen and wrote no further that day. He had a singular sense of physical power and spiritual freedom. There was no doubt in his heart concerning the worth of the work he was doing—of its good, of its need. Never before in his life had he worked without such doubt. He felt here no compulsion to pretend; to believe what he did not believe; or to be that which he did not want to be.

IX

To the woman riding alone into an almost unknown world, all life went suddenly black and tasteless. In a few short years and without dream of such an end, she had violated nearly every tradition of her race, nearly every prejudice of her family, nearly every ideal of her own life. She had sacrificed position, wealth, honor, and virginity on the altar of one far-flaming star. Was it worth it? Was there a chance to win through, and to win to what? What was this horrible, imponderable, unyielding mask of a world which she faced and fought?

The dark despair of loneliness overwhelmed her spirit. The pain of the world lay close upon her like a fitted coffin, airless, dark, silent. Why, why should she struggle on? Was it yet too late? A few words on this bit of yellow paper, and lo! Could she not again be a ruling monarch? One whose jewels and motor-cars, gowns and servants, palaces and Durbars would make a whole world babble?

What if she did have to pay for this deep thrill of Life with submission to white Europe, with marriage without love, with power without substance? Could she not still live and dance and sing? Was she not yet young, scarce twenty-six, and big with the lust for life and joy? She could wander in wide and beautiful lands; she could loll, gamble, and flirt at Lido, Deauville, and Scheveningen; she could surround herself with embodied beauty: look on beautiful pictures; walk on priceless carpets; build fairytales in wood and stone!

On all this she was trying to turn her back, for what? For the shade of a shadow. For a wan, far-off ideal of a world of justice to people yellow, black, and brown; and even beyond that, for the uplift of maimed and writhing millions. Dirty people and stupid, men who bent and crawled and toiled, cringed and worshiped snakes and gold and gaudy show. What, where, and whither lay the way to all this? It was the perfect love and devotion of one human soul, one whose ideals she tried to think were hers, and hers, his.

Granting the full-blown glory of the dream, was it humanly possible? Was there this possibility of uplift in the masses of men? Was there even in Matthew himself, with all his fineness of soul, the essential strength, the free spirit, the high heart, and the understanding mind? Had he that great resolve back of the unswerving deftness of a keen brain which could carry through Revolution in the world? He was love. Yes, incarnate love and tenderness, and delicate unselfish devotion of soul. But was there, under this, the iron for suffering, the thunder for offense, and the lightning for piercing through the thick-threaded gloom of the world, and for flashing the seething crimson of justice to it and beyond? And if in him there lay such seed of greatness, would it grow? Would it sprout and grow? Or had servility shriveled it and disappointment chilled it and surrender to the evil and lying and stealing of life deadened it at the very core?

Oh, Matthew, Matthew! Did he know just what she had done and how much she had given and suffered? Did he still hold the jewel of her love and surrender high in heaven, or was she after all at this very moment common and degraded in his sight? Gracious Karma, where was she in truth now? She of the sacred triple cord, a royal princess of India and incarnate daughter of gods and kings! She who had crossed half the world to him, fighting like a lioness for her own body. Where was she now in the eyes and mind of the man whom she had raised in her soul and set above the world? Only time would tell. Time and waiting—bitter, empty waiting. Waiting with hanging hands. And then one other thing, one thing above all Things, one mighty secret which she had but partially breathed even to Matthew. For there was a King in India who sued for her hand. He willed to be Maharajah of Bwodpur. He would lead Swaraj in India. He would unite India and China and Japan. He pressed for an answer. Bwodpur pressed. Sindrabad pressed. All the world pressed down on one lone woman.

Then as she sat there crumpled and wan, with tear-swept eyes and stricken heart, slowly a picture dissolved and swam and grew faint and plain and clear before her: a little dark cabin, swathed in clinging vines, nestling beneath great trees and beside a singing brook; flowers struggled up beside the door with crimson, blue, and yellow faces; hot sunshine filtered down between the waving leaves, and winds came gently out of sunset lands. In the door stood a woman; tall, big, and brown. Her face seemed hard and seamed at first; but upon it her great cavernous eyes held in their depths that softness and understanding which calls to lost souls and strengthens and comforts them. And Kautilya rose with wet eyes and stumbled over time and space and went half-blind and groping to that broad, flat bosom and into those long, enfolding arms. She strained up into the love of those old, old eyes.

"Mother," she sobbed, "I've come home to wait."

W.E.B. DU BOIS

X

"I am tired," wrote Matthew in August, "but I am singularly strong. I think I never knew before what weariness was. At the day's end I am often dead on my feet, drugged and staggering. I can scarcely keep awake to eat, and I fall to bed and die until sudden dawn comes like crashing resurrection. Yet I have a certain new clearness of head and keenness of vision. Dreams and fancies, pictures and thoughts, dance within my head as I work. But I half fear them. They seem to want to drag me away from this physical emancipation. I try to drown and forget them. They are in the way. They may betray and subdue me.

"Where is the fulcrum to uplift our world and roll it forward? More and more I am convinced that it lies in intelligent digging; the building of subways by architects; the planning of subways and skyscrapers and states by workingmen.

"Curiously enough, as it is now, we do not need brains here. Yes, here in a work which at bottom is Thought and Method and Logic, most of us are required not to think or reason. Only the machines may think. I wrote of the machines as our Slaves of the Lamp, but I was wrong. We are the slaves. We must obey the machines or suffer. Our life is simply lifting. We are lifting the world and moving it. But only the machines know what we are doing. We are blindfolded. If only they did not blindfold us! If we could see the Plan and understand; if we could know and thrust and trace in our mind's eye this little hole in the ground that writhes under Chicago; how the thrill of this Odyssey would nerve and hearten us! But no, of the end of what we are doing we can only guess vaguely. The only thing we really know is this shovelful of dirt. Or if we dream of the millions of men this hole will shoot in and out, up and down, back and forth—why will it shoot them and to whom and from what into what Great End, whither, whither?

"I could not finish this, and three days have gone. Yesterday I arose with the dawn before work and began reading. It was a revelation of joy. I was fresh and rested and the morning was bright and young. I read Shakespeare's *Hamlet*. I am sure now that

I never have read it before. I told people quite confidently that I had. I looked particularly intelligent when *Hamlet* was discussed or alluded to. But if this was the truth, I must have read *Hamlet* with tired mind and weary brain; mechanically, half-comprehendingly. This morning I read as angels read, swooping with the thought, keen and happy with the inner spirit of the thing. Hamlet lived, and he and I suffered together with an all too easily comprehended hesitation at life. I shall do much reading like this. I know now what reading is. I am going to master a hundred books. Nothing common or cheap or trashy, but a hundred master-thoughts. I do not believe the world holds more. These are the days of my purification that I may rise out of selfishness and hesitation and unbelief and depths of mental debauchery to the high and spiritual purity of love.

"Now I must go. I shall walk down to the morning sunlight which is soft and sweet before its midday dust and heat; others gradually will join me as I walk on. On some few faces I shall catch an answering gleam of morning, some anticipation of a great day's work; but on most faces there will be but sodden grayness, a sort of ingrained weariness which no sleep will ever last long enough to drive away—save one sleep, and that the last.

"These faces frighten me. What is it that carves them? What makes my fellow men who work with their hands so sick of life? What ails the world of work? In itself, it is surely good; it is real; it is better than polo, baseball, or golf. It is the Thing Itself. There is beauty in its movement and in the sunshine, storm, and rain that walk beside it. Here is art. An art singularly deep and satisfying. Who does not glow at the touch of this imprisoned lightning that lies inert above the hole? We touch a bit of metal: the sullen rock gives up its soul and flies to a thousand fragments. And yet this glorious thunder of the world strikes on deaf ears and eyes that see nothing. At morning most of us are simply grim; at noon, we are dull; at night, we are automata. Even I cannot entirely escape it. I was free and joyous this morning. Tonight I shall be too tired to think or feel or plan. And after five, ten, fifteen years of this—what?

W.E.B. DU BOIS

"I am trying to think through some solution. I see the Plan—our Plan, the great Emancipation—as clearly and truly as ever. I even know what we must aim at, but now the question is where to begin. It's like trying to climb a great mountain. It takes so long to get to the foothills.

"This problem of lifting physical work to its natural level puzzles me. If only I could work and work wildly, unstintingly, hilariously for six full, long hours; after that, while I lie in a warm bath, I should like to hear Tschaikowsky's Fourth Symphony. You know the lilt and cry of it. There must be much other music like it. Then I would like to have clean, soft clothes and fair, fresh food daintily prepared on a shining table. Afterward, a ride in green pastures and beside still waters; a film, a play, a novel, and always you. You, and long, deep arguments of the intricate, beautiful, winding ways of the world; and at last sleep, deep sleep within your arms. Then morning and the fray.

"I would welcome with loud Hosannas the dirt, the strain, the heat, the cold. But as it is, from the high sun of morning I rush, lurch, and crumple to a leaden night. The food in my little, dirty restaurant is rotten and is flung to me by a slatternly waitress who is as tired as I am. My bed is dirty. I'm sorry, dear, but it seems impossible to keep it clean and smooth. And then over all my neighborhood there hangs a great, thick sheet of noise; harsh, continuous, raucous noise like a breath of hell. It seems never to stop. It is there when I go to sleep; it rumbles in my deepest unconsciousness, and thunders in my dreams; it begins with dawn, rising to a shrill crescendo as I awake. There is no beauty in this world about me—no beauty. Or if these people see beauty, they cannot know it. They are not to blame, poor beeves; we are, we are!

"I grow half dead with physical weakness and sleep like death, but my body waxes hard and strong. I refused a clerk's job today, but I have been made a sort of gang foreman. I know the men. There are Finns and Italians, Poles, Slovaks, and Negroes. We do not understand each other's tongues; we have our hates and fancies. But we are one in interest: we are all robbed by the contractors. We know it and we are trying to organize and fight back. I do not know just what I should do in this matter. I never before realized that a labor union means bread, sleep, and shelter. Can we build one of this helpless, ignorant stuff? I do not know. But this at least I do know: Work is God."

Matthew wrote no more. He was alone, but he was trying to think things out. What could really be done? If the task of the workers were cut in half, would they all work correspondingly harder? Of course they would not. Some would; he would. Most of them would sit around, dull-eyed, and loaf. Profits would dwindle and disappear. There might even be huge deficits. And could one get the men who knew and thought and planned all this to guide and to lead without the price of profit?

Oh, yes, some could be got for the sheer joy of fine effort. They would work gladly for board, clothes, and creation, Some men would do it because they love the game. But the kind of men who were spending profits today on the North Shore, on Fifth Avenue, Regent Street, and the Rue de la Paix—no! It would call for a kind of man different from them, with a different scheme of values. Yes, to work without money profit would demand a different scheme of values in a different kind of man; and to do full work on half-time in the ditch would need a different kind of man, with a new dream of living: perhaps there lay the world's solution: in men who were—different.

He sat alone and tried to think it all out; but he could think no further because he was too lonely. He needed the rubbing of a kindred soul—the answering flash of another pole. His loneliness was not merely physical; his soul was alone. Kautilya was not answering his letters, and she had been gone two great months. Far down within him he was sick at heart. He could not quite understand why it had seemed to Kautilya so inevitable that they must part. He kept coming back to the question as to whether the excuse she gave was real and complete.

Could it be possible that she must sacrifice herself to a strange and unloved husband for reasons of state? What after all was little lost Bwodpur in the great emancipation of races? What difference whether she ruled as Princess or worked as worker? What was "royal blood," after all?

W.E.B. DU BOIS

And then, too, why this illogical solicitude for Sara's right to him, after that supreme and utter betrayal and denial of all right? Was it not possible, more than possible, that he had disappointed Kautilya, just as he had disappointed himself and his mother and his people and perhaps some far-off immutable God?

Kautilya had built a high ideal of manhood and crowned it with his likeness, and yet when she had seen it face to face, perhaps it had seemed to crash before her eyes.

Perhaps—and his mind writhed, hesitated; and yet he pushed it forward to full view—perhaps, after all, there was unconsciously in Kautilya some borrowed, strained, and seeping prejudice from the dead white world, that made her in her inner soul and at the touch, shrink from intimate contact with a man of his race; and perhaps without quite realizing it, they had faced the end and she had seen life and love and dreams die; then softly but firmly she had put him by and gone away.

Thus Matthew's dull and tired brain dropped down to clouds of weariness. But he did not surrender. The old desolation and despair seemed underlaid now by harsher iron built on sheer physical strength. He did not even rise and undress lest the ghosts of doubt grip him as he walked and moved. He slept all night dressed and sitting at his empty deal table, his head upon his hands. And he dreamed that God was Work.

XI

Sara had at last arrived. Sammy had met her. It was early in September, and he had not seen her for five months. They had a good breakfast at the Union Station, and Sammy had retailed so much news and gossip that Sara was happier and more alive than she had felt for a long time. She was very calm and sedate about it, but after all she knew that the Black Belt of Chicago with its strife, intrigue, defeats, and triumphs was, for her, Life.

"And where have you been?" asked Sammy.

"New York, Atlantic City, Boston, Newport, and a few places like that."

"Have a good time?"

"Fair."

Sammy whirled her home in a new Lincoln that was a dream, and a black chauffeur in brown livery who knew his spaces to the tenth of an inch and glided up Michigan Avenue like smooth and unreverberating lightning.

"New car?" asked Sara.

"Yep! Celebrating."

"Celebrating—what?"

"Saw the old man last Wednesday down at Springfield." And then Sammy adroitly switched into a long and most interesting account of the latest and biggest Jewish tabernacle which her pastor had bought with liberal political donations.

Sara said nothing further about the car and that Springfield interview. Sammy knew she was curious, but just how deeply and personally curious she was, he was not certain. So he waited. In Sara's apartment he wandered about, a bit distrait, while she took her usual good time to dress. The apartment was immaculate and in perfect order. Sammy saw no trace of that scene five months ago. And as for Sara, when she emerged, her simple, close-fitting tailor-made costume was all Sammy could ask or imagine.

"I say, kid, don't you think we might talk this thing out and come to some understanding?"

Sara opened her eyes. "Talk what out?"

"Well, about you and me. You see, you had me going, and I had to do something. I couldn't just stand by and lose everything. So I got busy. I hated to do it, but I had to."

"You didn't do it—God did."

"God nothing! I remembered the woman on that train wreck and I found her."

"It is a lie. She found you," said Sara.

"Well, it was a little like that, but the minute I laid eyes on her I knew she was the woman I had heard about. And I told her all about Matthew; how queer he was, and how he was hesitating, and how no man like him could ever make a politician. Then she laid low, but she came that night. I didn't think she would."

"You're a pretty friend."

"Say, kid, don't be hard. It was a bit tough, I own, for you. But I had you in the plan. Now listen to reason. Matthew was no good. He was going flabby. He's no real politician. He didn't know the game, and he had fool Reform deep in his system. He was just waking up, and he'd 'a' raised Hell in Congress. We never could have controlled him. Now when I get in Congress—"

"Congress!" sneered Sara. "Do you think any nigger has a chance now?"

But Sammy talked on.

"—and when you are my wife—"

"Wife!"

"Sure, I've never been a marrying man, as I have often explained—"

"Not retail," said Sara.

"And wholesale don't count in law; but I need you, I see that now, and I'm damned if I am going to lose you to another half-baked guy."

"I am not divorced yet, and I am not sure—"

"You mean you ain't sure you ain't half in love with him still?"

"I hate the fool. I'd like to horsewhip her in City Hall."

"Too late, kid, she's left him."

"Left him?"

"Sure—gone bag and baggage, and what do you know! He's digging in the subway—a common laborer. Oh, he's up against it,

I'll tell the world. Reckon he wouldn't mind visiting the old roost just now." And Sammy glanced about with approval.

Sara looked him over. Sammy was no Adonis. He was approaching middle age and was showing signs of wear and tear. But Sara was lonesome, and between her and Sammy there was a common philosophy, a common humor, and a common understanding. Neither quite trusted the other, and yet they needed each other. Sara had missed Sammy more than she dared acknowledge, while without Sara, Sammy felt one-armed.

Sammy continued:

"No, kid. Your lay is still the quiet, injured wife, shut up at home and in tears, until after the next election. See? A knockout! Matthew is politically dead this minute. Right here I come in. The bosses know that they got to take a dose of black man for Congress sooner or later. They came near getting a crank. But even your fine Italian hand couldn't make him stay put. He never would have been elected."

"Oh, I don't know."

"You got it right there, kid, you *don't* know, and you know you don't. And now here I am. The bosses will have to take me sooner or later. All I need is you."

"But I hear that the governor and Thompson are at outs."

"Sure."

"And you're hitched up with the governor."

"Sure again. I'm opposing Thompson. But after he's elected by a smashing majority, the governor and the Washington crowd will need him, he'll need the governor, and they'll both need me!"

"H'm—I see. Well, you'll have to do some tight-rope walking, my friend."

"Precisely, and that's where you come in."

"Indeed! Now listen to me. Don't think, Sammy, you're going to get both money and office out of these white politicians at the same time. When they pay big they take the big jobs. If you want to go to Congress you'll pay. The only exception to that rule was the game I played and won and then that fool threw away."

Sammy smiled complacently. "Did you see my new Lincoln?"

"Yes, and wondered."

"Four thousand bucks, and the shuffer's gettin' thirty-five per. And say! Remember that big white stone house at Fiftieth and Drexel Boulevard?"

"You mean at Drexel Square, with the big oaks and a fountain?"

"Yep!"

"Yes, I remember it—circular steps, great door with beveled glass, and marble lobby!"

"No different! Driveway and garage; sun parlor, twenty rooms, yard, and big iron fence. Well, that's where we're gonna live. I've bought it."

"Sammy! Why, you must be suddenly rich or crazy!"

"Kid, I've made a killing! While you were leading me a dance for Congress, I got hold of all the dough I could grab and salted it away. Oh, I spent a lot on the boys, but I had a lot to spend. Graham and the Public Service was wild to return Doolittle. I spent a pile, but I didn't spend all by a long shot. I put a hunk into two or three good deals—real estate, bootlegging, and—well—other things. Then when Matthew flew the coop I rushed at the gang and put up such a yell that they let me in on something big: and listen, sister! Little Sammy is on Easy Street and sittin' pretty! Believe me, I ain't beggin'—I'm going to buy my way into Congress if it takes a hundred thousand simoleons."

Sara looked Sammy over.

"And you're counting on me, are you?"

"Sure thing! As soon as election is over, we can have proceedings for a divorce on foot quietly, and it will be over in a week or so. Meantime, you're my secretary again, and you're going to name your own salary."

Sara arose and smoothed her frock. She looked so unmoved and unapproachable that Sammy half lost his nerve.

"Don't let him get you, Sara. Don't let black Chicago think you're down and out because of one man. What do you say, kid? You know, I—I always liked you. I was crazy about you the minute you stepped through that door five years ago. I figured that nobody but me was ever going to marry you. But you were so damned standoffish—I sorta wanted you to melt a little first and be human. But now, Lord, kid, I'm crawlin' and beggin' you on any terms. What do you say? See here! I'll bet you a diamond as big as a hen's egg against a marriage license that you'll be happier as my wife than you've been in ten years. What d'ya say, kid?"

Sara still stood looking at Sammy thoughtfully as she reached for her vanity case. She turned to the mantel mirror and was sometime powdering her nose. Then she obeyed an impulse, a thing she had not done for ten years. She turned deliberately, walked over to Sammy, and kissed him.

"You're on, Sammy," she said.

XII

D earest Matthew, my man," wrote Kautilya in September, "forgive my silence. I am in Virginia with your mother. I could not stay in Washington. I wanted to sit a space apart and in quiet to think and hearken and decide. The wind is in the trees, the strong winds of purpose, the soft winds of infinite desire; the wide black earth around me is breathing deep with fancies. There is rain and mud and a certain emptiness. But somehow I love this land, perhaps because mother loves it so. I seem to see salvation here, a gate to the world. Here is a tiny kingdom of tree and wood and hut. Oh, yes, and the brook, the symphony of the brook. And then there are the broad old fields as far as we can look toward the impounding woods.

"Beloved, I am beginning to feel that this place of yours may be no mere temporary refuge. That it may again be Home for you. I see this as yet but dimly, but life here seems symbolic. Here is the earth yearning for seed. Here men make food and clothes. We are at the bottom and beginning of things. The very first chapter of that great story of industry, wage and wealth, government, life.

"On such deep founding-stones you may perhaps build. I can see work transformed. This cabin with little change in its aspect can be made a place of worship, of beauty and books. I have even planned a home for you: this old and black and vine-clad cabin undisturbed but with an L built behind and above. The twin cabin must run far back and rise a half story for a broad and peaceful chamber—for life with music and color floating in it. Perhaps a little lake to woo the brook; and then, in years, of course, a tower and a secret garden! Yes, I should like to see a tower, where Muezzins call to God and His world.

"And this world is really much nearer to our world than I had thought. This brook dances on to a river fifty miles away—next door only for a little Ford truck. And the river winds in stately curve down Jamestown-of-the-Slaves. We went down the other day, walking part of the way through woods and dells, toward the great highway of the Atlantic. Think, Matthew, take your geography and trace it: from Hampton Roads to Guiana is a world of colored folk, and a world, men tell me, physically beautiful beyond conception; socially enslaved, industrially ruined, spiritually dead; but ready for the breath of Life and Resurrection. South is Latin America, east is Africa, and east of east lies my own Asia. Oh, Matthew, think this thing through. Your mother prophesies. We sense a new age.

"This is the age of commerce and industry—of making, shaping, carrying, buying and selling. We have made manufacturers, railroad men, and merchants rich because we ranked them highest, and we have helped them in cities for convenience, and they are white and in white cities. Just suppose we change our ranking. Suppose in our hearts we rate the colored farmers and all discoverers, poets, and dreamers high and even higher and give them space outside of white cities? We would widen the world. It is simply a matter of wanting to. We have bribed white factories with tariffs and monopoly. We are going to bribe black agriculture and poetry. And, Matthew, Work is not God—Love is God and Work is His Prophet."

Hurriedly Matthew wrote back: "No, no, Kautilya of the World, no, no! Think not of home in that breeder of slaves and hate, Virginia. I shudder to find you there even for a season. There is horror there which your dear eyes are not yet focused to see and which the old blindness of my mother forgets. There is evil all about you. Oh, sister, you do not know—you do not dream. Down yonder lurk mob and rape and rope and faggot. Ignorance is King and Hate is High Prime Minister. Men are tyrants or slaves. Women are dolls or sluts. Industry is lying, and government stealing.

"The land is literally accursed with the blood and pain of three hundred years of slavery. Ask mother. Ask her to tell you how many years she has fought and clawed for the honor of her own body. There is a little weal on her breast, a jagged scar upon her knee, a broken finger on one hand. Ask her whence these came. Ask her who imprisoned and killed my father and why and where her other children are buried. Come away, come away, my crumpled bird, as soon as may be, lest they despoil you. You may hide there until our wounds are healed, but then come away to the midst of life. Only in the center of the world can our work be done. We must stand, you and I, even if apart, where beats down the fiercest blaze of Western civilization, and pushing back this hell, raise a black world upon it.

"I ought not to write tonight, for I am in the depths; the sudden change of Chicago's Fall has dropped upon me. I caught cold and was ill a day, and then I arose and did not go to work. Instead, I went down to the art gallery. There was a new exhibit of borrowed paintings from all ends of the world. After mud and filth and grayness, my soul was starving for color and curve and form. I went. And then went back again, day after day. I literally forgot my work for a week and bathed myself in a new world of beauty.

"I saw in Claude Monet what sunrise and sunset on the old cathedral at Rouen might say to a human soul, in pale gold, white, and purple, and in purple, yellow, and gold. I felt the mists of London hiding Big Ben. Rich somber peace and silence fell on me and on the picnic party beneath spreading branches. I walked with that lady about the red flowers of her garden. I reveled in blue seas, faint color-swept fields, riot of sweet flowers, poppies and grain, brooks and villages.

"I saw Pisano's Paris; the colors of Matisse raged in my soul, deluging all form, unbeautiful with rhythm. I delighted in the luscious dark folk of Paul Gaugin, in sun and shade, fruit and sea, palm and totem, and in the color that melts and flows and cries. Then there were the mad brown-gray-green lines of Picasso which swerved and melted into strange faces, forms, and figures, haunting things like their African prototypes; there was a dark little girl by Derain floating in a field of blue with a yellow castle, square and old.

"As from a far flight into the unknown I came back to the lovely coloring of Brangwyn and Cottet. I discovered the lucent blue water of Cézanne, his plunging landscapes and the hard truth of his faces. I saw how lovely Mrs. Samari looked to Renoir and vineyards to Van Gogh.

"At the end of the week I emerged half-ashamed, uncertain in judgment, and yet with added width to my world. I dimly remembered how you all talked of painting there in Berlin; then I knew nothing, nothing. Or rather now I know nothing, and then I did not know how ignorant I was. And, withal, mentally breathless, I returned with a certain peace and slept to dreams of clouds of light. I rose the next morning lightheaded, rested and strong, and went down blithely to that hole in the ground, to the grim, gigantic task. I was a more complete man—a unit of a real democracy.

"Even as I reached for my shovel the boss yelled at me. 'Away a week. You're fired!' Well, somehow I got back again after a few days. After all, I reckon, I am a good worker. But there was still trouble, and the boss had taken a dislike to me. It was like a groom incurring the displeasure of some high lackey in the court of Louis XIV. As I have said, we subway laborers were not yet organized, and emissaries from the trade unions were working among us. I never knew what unions meant before. I think I was a bit prejudiced against them. They were organizations, to my mind, which took food from the mouths of black men.

"Now suddenly I saw the thing from the other side. Unless we banded ourselves together and as one body against this Leviathan which 'hires and fires,' we were helpless, crushed piecemeal, having no voice as to ourselves and our work. And so I went in for the union. We struck: our hours of work were too long; the overtime was too poorly paid; we were being maimed by accidents and cheated of our insurance; we had no decent luncheon time or place. Well, we struck and we were roundly beaten. There were five hungry men eager to take every place we left vacant; mostly black men—they were hungriest. There were the police and politics against us.

"Again I was 'fired,' and this time for good. It was strange in this great, busy, and rich city, actually to be among the unemployed, and so much work to be done! I never believed in the unemployed before. To me the unemployed were the lazy, the shiftless, the debauched. But I am not lazy. I am eager for work; I am strong and willing and for a week I actually did not know how I was going to earn my bread.

"Several times and in several places I applied for work, and then at last I found a new reason staring in my face. It was

W. E. B. DU BOIS

Sammy. He strutted over to me as I came out of one employment office, and stood with his legs apart, scowling at me. He had neither smile nor handshake. 'Say, bo,' he blustered, 'why didn't you come around and fix up them divorce papers? See here, I'm tired of your damned stallin!' Think you're going to crawl back to Sara one of these days because your fancy woman has jilted you? Well, by God, you ain't. You're going ahead with this divorce, or I'll damn well drive you out of Chicago.'

"I made no answer. I think I smiled at him a little because he did appear to me pathetically funny; and then I went and got a job. I knew one place where workers were scarce, but I had always shrunk from going there. But that morning I went out to the stockyards and got a job. The world stinks about me. I am lifting rotten food. I am helping to murder things that live. The continual bleating of death beats on my ears and heart. I am drugged with weariness and ugliness. I seem to know as never before what pain and poverty mean. In the world there is only you—only you and that halo about your head which is the worldwide Cause.

"But Sammy's command set me thinking. I dimly see what must be done to restore the balance and cooperation of the white and black worlds: Brain and Brawn must unite in one body. But where shall the work begin? I begin to believe right here in Chicago, crossroads of the world—midway between Atlantic and Pacific, North and South Poles. This is the place. How shall I begin?"

XIII

There had been a long silence. Matthew had set his teeth and written regularly and methodically, words that did not say or reveal much. And then at last out of the South there came one morning a long, clear cry from Kautilya.

"Oh, Matthew, Matthew. The earth here in this October is full with fruit and harvest. The cotton lies dark green, dim crimson, with silver stars above the gray earth; my own hand has carried the cotton basket, and now I sit and know that everywhere seed that is hidden dark, inert, dead, will one day be alive, and here, here! And Matthew, my soul doth magnify the Lord. Within the new twin cabin above the old (for I have built it already, dear—I *had* to) sitting aloft, apart, a bit remote, is low, dark, and beautiful room of Life, with music and with wide windows toward the rising and the setting of the sun. Outside the sun today is beaten shimmering copper-gold. The corn shocks and the fields are dull yellow; the bare cotton stalks are burning brown. But the earth is rich and full, and Love sits wild and glorious on the world. I have been reading to dear mother. She sits beside me, silent, like some ancient priestess. I read out of the Hebrew scriptures words of cruelty and war, and then in the full happiness of my heart I found that passage in Luke: 'My soul doth magnify the Lord!' And now my spirit is rejoicing, and the ineffable Buddha, blood of the blood of my fathers, seems bowing down to his low and doubting handmaiden. Well-beloved, shall not all generations call us Blessed and do great things for us, and we for them? All children, all mothers, all fathers; all women and all men? Thus do I bend and kiss all the lowly in the name of Him who 'hath put down the Mighty from their seats and exalted them of low degree!'

"We will build a world, Matthew, you and I, where the Hungry shall be fed, and only the Lazy shall be empty. Oh, I am mad, mad, Matthew, this day when the golden earth bows and falls into the death of Winter toward the resurrection of Spring! Life seems suddenly clear to me. I see the Way. Matthew, I am not afraid of Virginia or the white South. I know more of it than you think and mother has told me. It is crude and cruel, but, too, it is warm and beautiful. It is strangely, appealingly human. Nothing so beautiful as Virginia can be wholly hellish. I have my troubles here, mother and I, but we have faced it all and beaten them back with high and steady glance. I see the glory that may come yet to this Mother of Slavery.

"I will not, I cannot, be sorry for you, Matthew, for your poor bruised soul and for the awful pit in which your tired feet stand. Courage, my man. Drain the cup. Drain it to the dregs, and, out of this crucifixion, ascend with me to heaven."

XIV

I am glad, dear Kautilya," wrote Matthew at Christmas time, "that you are happy and content. But I am curious to understand that Way which you see so clearly. As for me, I am sorely puzzled. I believe in democracy. Hitherto I have seen democracy as the corner stone of my new world. But today and with the world, I see myself drifting logically and inevitably toward oligarchy. Baseball, movies, Spain, and Italy are ruled by Tyrants. Russia, England, France, and the Trusts are ruled by oligarchies. And how else? We Common People are so stupid, so forgetful, so selfish. How can we make life good but by compulsion? We cannot choose between monarchy and oligarchy or democracy—no—we can only choose the objects for which we will enthrone tyrannical dictators; it may be dictators for the sake of aristocrats as in Czarist Russia, or dictators for the sake of millionaires as in America, or dictatorship for the factory workers and peasants as in Soviet Russia; but always, everywhere, massed and concentrated power is necessary to accomplish anything worth while doing in this muddled world, hoping for divine Anarchy in some faraway heaven.

"Whether we will or not, some must rule and do for the people what they are too weak and silly to do for themselves. They must be made to know and feel. It is knowledge and caring that are missing. Some know not and care not. Some know and care not. Some care not and know. We know and care, but, oh! How and where? I am afraid that only great strokes of force—clubs, guns, dynamite in the hands of fanatics—that only such Revolution can bring the Day.

"I wish I could see the solution of world misery in a little Virginia cottage with vines and flowers. I wish I could share the surging happiness which you find there; but I cannot, I am too far from there. I am far in miles, and somehow I seem insensibly to grow farther in spirit. I agree that America is the place for my work, and if America, then Chicago; for Chicago is the epitome of America. New York is a province of England. Virginia, Charleston, and New Orleans are memories, farming and industrial hinterlands. California is just beyond the world. Chicago is the American world and the modern world, and the worst of it. We Americans are caught here in our own machinery; our machines make things and compel us to sell them. We are rich in food and clothes and starved in culture. That fine old accumulation of the courtesies of life with its gracious delicacy which has flowered now and again in other lands is gone-gone and forgotten. We push and shoulder each other on the streets, yell, instead of bowing; we have forgotten 'Please,' 'Excuse me,' 'I beg your pardon,' and 'By your leave' in one vast comprehensive 'Hello!' and 'Sa-ay!'

"Courtesy is dead—and Justice? We strike, steal, curse, mob, and murder, all in the day's work. All delicate feeling sinks beneath floods of mediocrity. The finer culture is lost, lost; maybe lost forever. Is there beauty? Is there God? Is there salvation? Where are the workers so rich and powerful as here in America, and where so arid, artificial, vapid, so charmed and distracted by the low, crude, gawdy, and vulgar? I can only hope that after America has raped this land of its abundant wealth, after Africa breaks its chains and Asia awakes from its long sleep, in the day when Europe is too weak to fight and scheme and make others work for her and not for themselves—that then the world may disintegrate and fall apart and thus from its manure, something new and fair may sprout and slowly begin to grow. If then in Chicago we can kill the thing that America stands for, we emancipate the world.

"Yes, Kautilya, I believe that with fire and sword, blood and whips, we must fight this thing out physically, and literally beat the world into submission and a real civilization. The center of this fight must be America, because in America is the center of the world's sin. There must be developed here that world-tyranny which will impose by brute force a new heaven on this old and rotten earth."

It was almost mid-January when Kautilya's reply to this letter came. It was as ever full of sympathy and love, and yet Matthew thought he saw some beginnings of change.

"If the world is aflame," said Kautilya, "and I feel it flaming—the place of those who would ride the conflagration is truly within and not behind or in front of the Holocaust. Where then is this center, and what shall we who stand there do? Here are my two disagreements with you, dear Matthew. America is not the center of the world's evil. That center today is Asia and Africa. In America is Power. Yonder is Culture, but Culture gone to seed, disintegrated, debased. Yet its re-birth is imminent. America and Europe must not prevent it. Only Asia and Africa, in Asia and Africa, can break the power of America and Europe to throttle the world.

"And, oh, my Matthew, your oligarchy as you conceive it is not the antithesis of democracy—it is democracy, if only the selection of the oligarchs is just and true. Birth is the method of blind fools. Wealth is the gambler's method. Only Talent served from the great Reservoir of All Men of All Races, of All Classes, of All Ages, of Both Sexes—this is real Aristocracy, real Democracy—the only path to that great and final Freedom which you so well call Divine Anarchy.

"And yet this, dear Matthew, you yourself taught me—you and your struggling people here. In Africa and Asia we must work, and yet in Africa and Asia we are outside the world. That is the thing I always felt at home. Outside, and kept outside, the centers of power. Even to us in Europe, the closed circle of power is narrow and straitly entrenched; the stranger can scarce get foothold, and when he gets in, Power is no longer there. It is flown. In America your feet are further within the secret circle of that power that half-consciously rules the world. That is the advantage of America. That is the advantage that your people have had. You are working within. They are standing here in this technical triumph of human power and can use is as a fulcrum to lift earth and seas and stars.

"But to be in the center of power is not enough. You must be free and able to act. You are not free in Chicago nor New York. But here in Virginia you are at the edge of a black world. The black belt of the Congo, the Nile, and the Ganges reaches by way of Guiana, Haiti, and Jamaica, like a red arrow, up into the heart of white America. Thus I see a mighty synthesis: you can work in Africa and Asia right here in America if you work in the Black Belt. For a long time I was puzzled, as I have written you, and hesitated; but now I know. I am exalted, and with my high heart comes illumination. I have been sore bewildered by this mighty America, this ruthless, terrible, intriguing Thing. My home and heart is India. Your heart of hearts is Africa. And now I see through the cloud. You may stand here, Matthew—here, halfway between Maine and Florida, between the Atlantic and the Pacific, with Europe in your face and China at your back; with industry in your right hand and commerce in your left and the Farm beneath your steady feet; and yet be in the Land of the Blacks.

"Dearest, in spite of all you say, I believe, I believe in men; I believe in the unlovely masses of men; I believe in that prophetic word which you spoke in Berlin and which perhaps you only half believed yourself. And why should I not believe? I have seen slaves ruling in Chicago and they did not do nearly as badly as princes in Russia. Gentle culture and the beauty and courtesies of life—they are the real end of all living. But they will not come by the dreaming of the few. Civilization cannot stand on its apex. It must stand on a broad base, supporting its inevitable and eternal apex of fools. The tyranny of which you dream is the true method which I too envisage. But choose well the Tyrants—there is Eternal Life! How truly you have put it! Workers unite, men cry, while in truth always thinkers who do not work have tried to unite workers who do not think. Only working thinkers can unite thinking workers.

"For all that we need, and need alone, Time; the alembic, Time. The slow majestic march of events, unhurried, sure. Do not be in a hurry, dear Matthew, do not be nervous, do not fret. There is no hurry, Matthew, your mother's Bible puts it right: 'A day unto the Lord is as a thousand years, and a thousand years as one day.'"

XV

Endless time! Matthew laughed and wept. Endless time! He was almost thirty. In a few years he would be forty, and creative life, real life, would be gone; gone forever. But he knew; he saw it all; he faced grimly and without flinching the terrible truth that for seven months he had sought to hide and veil away from himself. Kautilya did not plan for him in her life. Almost she did not want him, although perhaps this last fact she had not quite realized. She had tried him and his people and found them wanting. It was a sordid mess, sordid and mean, and she was unconsciously drawing the skirts of her high-bred soul back from it. She missed—she must miss—the beauty and wealth, the high courtesy and breath of life, which was hers by birth and heritage. And she must have searched in vain and deep disappointment in this muck of slavery, servility, and make-believe, for life. She had bidden him drain the cup. He would.

More and more was he convinced that the parting of himself and Kautilya was forever; that he must look this eventuality squarely in the face. And looking, he was sure that he had found himself. With his new physical strength had come a certain other strength of soul and purpose. Once he had sought knowledge and fame; once he had sought wealth; once he had sought comfort. Now he would seek nothing but work, and work for work's own sake. That work must be in large degree physical, because it was the physical work of the world that had to be done as prelude to its thought and beauty. And then beyond and above all this was the ultimate emancipation of the world by the uplift of the darker races. He knew what that uplift involved. He knew where he proposed to work, despite the ingenuity of Kautilya's argument. He did not yet see how physical toil would bring the spiritual end he sought, save only in his own soul. Perhaps—perhaps that would be enough. No, no! He still rejected such metaphysics.

Meantime one step loomed closer and clearer. He would follow the word of Kautilya, because there was a certain beauty and completeness in her desire that he offer himself back to

Sara. He saw that it would not be a real offer if it were not really meant. First, of course, Sara must see him as he was and realize him; a man who worked with his hands; a man who did his own thinking, clear and straight, even to his own hurt and poverty. A man working to emancipate the lowest millions. And, because of this and for his own salvation, certain cravings for beauty must be satisfied: simple, clear beauty, without tawdriness, without noise and meaningless imitation. Seeing him thus, perhaps, after all, in her way, in her singular, narrow way, Sara might realize that she had need of him. It was barely possible that, with such love as still oozed thinly in the hard crevices of her efficient soul, she loved him. Very well. If she wanted him as he was, realizing that he had loved someone else as he never could love her, well and good. He would go back to her; he would be a good husband; he would be, in the patois of the respectable, "true," but in a higher and better sense, good.

Matthew saw, too, with increasing clearness, something that Kautilya, he thought, must begin to realize, and that was that her freedom from him and his people—her freedom from this entanglement from which the thoughtful Japanese and Indians had tried to save her—would mean an increased and broader chance for her own work in her own world. And she had a work if she could return to it untrammeled by the trademark of slavery and degradation. She had tried to see a way in America for herself and Matthew to tread together. But all this was self-deception.

Matthew saw clearly, however, that he must give Kautilya no inkling of his own understanding and interpretation of herself. He knew that in her high soul there was that spirit of martyrs which might never let her surrender him voluntarily, that she would seek to stand by him just as long as it seemed the honorable thing to do. And so he would not "wince nor cry aloud," but he would "drain the cup."

That night he telephoned the maid at Sara's house, and learning that Sara was in, went down to see her. It was a hard journey. It was like walking back in time. He went through all the writhings of that period of groping revolt and yearning. He walked up the steps with the same feeling of revulsion and entered that prim and cold atmosphere, that hard, sharp grinding of life. He rang the bell. The maid stared, grinned, fidgeted.

"Yes—she's in—but I don't think—she said never to—"

She wanted Matthew to push past and go in unannounced, and he meant to, but he couldn't. He stood hesitating.

Sara's clear voice came from within:

"Who is it, Eliza?"

"It is Matthew Towns," said Matthew. "I would like—"

There were quick steps. The maid withdrew. The door banged in his face. Matthew wrote to Kautilya nothing of this, but only to continue that argument about work and wealth and race. He said:

"Art is long, but industry is longer. Revolution must come, but it must start from within. We must strip to the ground and fight up. Not the colored Farm but the white Factory is the beginning; and the white Office and the Street stand next. The white artisan must teach technique to the colored farmer. White business men must teach him organization; the scholar must teach him how to think, and the banker how to rule. Then, and not till then, will the farmer, colored or white, be the salt of the earth and the beginning of life."

Then in a postscript he added:

"I have had notice of Sara's action for divorce. I shall go in person to the hearing and answer, and I shall assent to whatever she may wish. I hope sincerely you are well. I have feared you might be sick and keep it from me. But even in sickness there is one consolation. Life at its strongest and longest is short. Bad as it is and beautiful as it has been for us, it is soon over. I kiss the little fingers of your hand."

Kautilya replied with a little note that came in early March, scribbled on wrapping paper, with uncertain curves:

"Matthew, I am afraid. Suddenly I am desperately afraid. Just what I fear I do not know—I cannot say. Perhaps I am ill. I know I am ill. Oh, Matthew, I am afraid. Life is a terrible thing. It looms in dark silence and threatens. It has no bowels of compassion. Its hidden soul neither laughs nor cries—it just is, is, *is*! I am afraid, Matthew—I am in deadly fear. The terror of eternal life is upon

W.E.B. DU BOIS

me—the Curse of Siva! Come to me, Matthew, come! No, no—do not come until I send. I shall be all right."

Matthew's heart paused in sudden hurt. He knew what must have happened: the Great Decision must be made. She had been summoned to India and must go. He started to pack his suitcase. He telephoned about trains. Then he hesitated, "No, no—do not come until I send." That was her decision. Against her will he must not go. But perhaps already she had changed her mind. Perhaps she was physically ill. Perhaps already Death, cloaked in black, stood in the shadows behind her writhing bed! Or, worse, perhaps she was going away and could not pause to say goodbye.

He telegraphed—"May I—" No, he tore that up: "Shall I come?"

The answer came in a few hours.

"No, all is well. I have been very ill, but I am better and I shall be out soon in the sweet springtime. I am going to walk and sew; I am going to be happy: infinitely happy. I want to see the heavy earth curling up before the shining of my plowshare. I want to feel the gray mule dragging off my arms, with the sky for heaven and the earth for love. I want to see seed sink in the dead earth. How can you say that life is short? Life is not short, my darling Matthew, it is endless. You and I will live for a thousand years and then a thousand years more; and then ten thousand years shall be added to that. Oh, man of little faith! Do you not see, heart of me, that without infinite life, life is a joke and a contradiction? Wish and Will are prisoned and manacled in Fact, whatever that fact may be; but with life built on life here on earth, now and not in your silly Christian parlor heaven, the tiny spark that is God thrills through, thrills through to triumph in a billion years; so vast, and vaster, is the Plan."

Matthew humored her mood. She saw the end of their earthly happiness here in time, and she was straining toward eternity. He could not deceive himself or her, and he wrote with a certain sad smile in his heart:

"Infinite and Eternal? Yes, dear Princess of the Winds; the Moonlight Sonata, snow on a high hill, the twitter of birds on boughs in sunlight after rain, health after sickness—God! Are not these real, true, good, beautiful, infinite, eternal? Whether Immortal Life, dearest and best, is literal truth or not, I do not care. No one knows whether anything in life or larger than life bursts through to some inconceivable triumph over death. None knows, none can know. But, ah, dear heart, what difference? There is, after all, sunrise and rain, starlight, color, and the surge and beat of sound. And on that night when my body kissed yours, a billion years lived in one heartbeat. What more can I ask? What more have I asked or dreamed, Queen of the World, than that? Already I am Eternal. In thy flesh I have seen God."

And Kautilya answered:

"I know, I know, heart's-ease, but that is not enough: back of it all, back of the flesh, the mold, the dust, there must be Reality; it must be there; and what can reality be but Life, Life Everlasting? If we, we our very selves, do not live forever, Life is a cruel joke."

Yes, Life *was* a cruel joke, and Matthew turned to write of everyday things:

"As I sat last night huddled over my supper—a very greasy pork chop, sodden potatoes, oleomargarine, soggy cornbread, partly cooked cabbage, and weak, cold coffee—as I sat in my grimy overalls and guzzled this mess, someone came and sat at my table with its dirty oil-cloth cover. I did not look up, but a voice, a rather flat, unusual voice, ordered rice. 'Just rice.' Then I looked up at a Chinese woman, and she smiled wanly back.

"I prefer," she said, "don't you, the cuisine of the Lützower Ufer?"

"It was one of our Chinese friends. I was glad and ashamed to see her. She seemed to notice nothing—made no comment, asked no awkward questions. Principally she talked of China.

"Oh, China, China, where shall we find leaders! They rise, they fall, they die, they desert. The men who can do, the men of thought and knowledge, the men who know technique, the unselfish and farseeing—how shall we harness these to the greatest chariot in the world and not have them seduced and stolen by Power, Pleasure, Display, Gluttony? Oh, I know it is the old story of human weakness, but if only we had a little more strength and unity now and then at critical moments, we could climb a step and lift the sodden, smitten mass.

"'There was Chiang Kai-Shek, so fine and young a warrior! I knew him well. I saw once his golden face alight with the highest ideals, his eyes a Heaven-in-Earth. Today, what is he? I do not know. Perhaps he does not. Oh, why was it that Sun Yat Sen must die so soon? But'—she rose from the half-eaten, mushy rice—'we must push on always on!' And then pausing she said, timidly, 'And you, my friend. Are you pushing—on?'

"I hesitated and then arose and stood before her: 'I am pushing on!' I said. She looked at me with glad eyes, and touching her forehead, was gone. And I was right, Kautilya, I am pushing on."

And turning from Kautilya's sealed letter, he took another sheet and laboriously wrote a long letter to Sara, saying all there was to be said; explaining, confessing, offering to return to her if she wanted him, but on the conditions which she must already know. He received no answer. Yet once again he wrote and almost pleaded. Again he had no word.

XVI

There was a little court scene on State Street in April, 1927. It looked more like an intimate family party, and everybody seemed in high good humor. The white judge was smiling affably and joking with the Honorable Sammy Scott. Two or three attorneys were grouped about. Hats, canes, and briefcases were handy, as though no one expected to tarry long. Mrs. Sara Towns came in. Mrs. Towns was a quiet and thoroughly adequate symphony in gray. She had on a gray tailor-made suit, with plain sheath skirt dropping below, but just below, her round knees. There was soft gray silk within and beneath the coat. There were gray stockings and gray suède shoes and gray chamoisette gloves. The tiny hat was gray, and pulled down just a trifle sideways so as to show sometimes one and sometimes two of her cool gray eyes. She looked very competent and very desirable. The Honorable Sammy's eyes sparkled. He liked the way Sara looked. He did not remember ever seeing her look better.

He felt happy, rich, and competent. He just had to tell Corruthers, aside:

"Yes, sir! She just got up of her own accord and gave me a kiss square on the beezer. You could 'a' bowled me over with a feather."

"Oh, she always liked you. She just married Towns for spite."

Sammy expanded. Things were coming very nicely to a head. The new Mayor had just been elected by a landslide; at the same time the Mayor's enemy, the Governor, knew that while Sammy had fought the Mayor in the primaries according to orders, he had nevertheless come out of the election with a machine which was not to be ignored. The pending presidential election was bound to set things going Sammy's way. The Mayor's popularity was probably local and temporary. The Governor had his long fingers on the powerful persons who pull the automata which rule the nation. These automata had been, in Sammy's opinion, quite convinced that no one would do their will in Congress better than the Honorable Sammy Scott. Moreover, the Governor and Mayor were not going to be enemies long. They could not afford it.

In other words, to put it plainly, the slate was being arranged so that after the presidential election of 1928, the succeeding congressional election would put the first colored man from the North in Congress, and it was on the boards that this man was to be Sammy. Meantime and in the three years ensuing, the prospective Mrs. Sara Scott and her husband were going to have a chance to play one of the slickest political games ever played in Chicago. Above all, Sammy was more than well-to-do, and Sara was no pauper. He wasn't merely asking political favors. He was demanding, and he had the cash to pay. Sammy rubbed his hands and gloated over Sara.

A clerk hurried in with a document. The judge, poising his pen, smiled benevolently at Sara. Sara had seated herself in a comfortable-looking chair, holding her knees very close together and yet exhibiting quite a sufficient length of silk stocking of excellent quality.

"Does the defendant make any reply?" asked the judge. And then, without pausing for an answer, he started to write his name. He had finished the first capital when someone walked out of the gloom at the back of the room and came into the circle of the electric light which had to shine in the office even at noontime.

Matthew came forward. He was in overalls and wore a sweater. Yet he was clean, well shaven, and stood upright. He was perhaps not as handsome as he used to be. His face seemed a bit weather-beaten, and his hair was certainly thinner. But he had an extraordinarily strong face, interesting, intriguing. He spoke with some hesitancy, looking first at the judge, then at Sara, to whom he bowed gravely in spite of the fact that after a startled glance, she ignored him. He only glanced at Sammy. Sammy was literally snarling with his long upper lip drawn back from his tobacco-stained teeth. He almost bit through his cigar, threw it away, and brought out another, long, black, and fresh. His hand trembled as he lit it, and he blew a furious cloud of smoke.

"I did not come to answer," said Matthew, "but simply to state my position."

("My God!" thought Sammy. "I'll bet he's got that bag of diamonds!")

"Have you got a lawyer?" asked the judge, gruffly.

"No, and I do not need one. I merely want to say—"

"What's all this about, anyway?" snapped Sammy.

Sara sat stiff and white and looked straight past Matthew to the wall. On the wall was a smirking picture of the late President Harding. An attorney came forward.

"We are willing that the defendant make any statement he wants to. Is there a stenographer here?"

The judge hesitated and then rang impatiently. A white girl walked in languidly and sat down. She stared at the group, took note of Sara's costume, and then turned her shoulder.

"I merely wanted to say," said Matthew, "that the allegations in the petition are true."

"Well, then, what are we waitin' for?" growled Sammy.

"I ran away from my wife and lived with another woman. I did this because I loved that woman and because I hated the life I was living. I shall never go back to that life; but if by any chance Mrs. Towns—my wife needs me or anything I can give or do, I am ready to be her husband again and to—"

He got no further. Sara had risen from her chair.

"This is intolerable," she said. "It is an insult, a low insult. I never want to see this, this—scoundrel, again."

"Very well, very well," said the judge, as he proceeded to sign the decree for absolute divorce. Sara and Sammy disappeared rapidly out the door.

Matthew walked slowly home, and as he walked he read now and then bits of his last letter from Kautilya. He read almost absentmindedly, for he was meditating on that singularly contradictory feeling of disappointment which he had.

One has a terrible plunge to make into some lurking pool of life. The pool disappears and leaves one dizzy upon a bank which is no longer a bank, but just arid sand.

In the midst of this inchoate feeling of disappointment, he read:

"Are we so far apart, man of God? Are we not veiling the same truth with words? All you say, I say, heaven's darling. Say and feel, want, and want with a want fiercer than death; but, oh, Love, our bodies will fade and grow old and older, and our eyes dim, and our ears deaf, and we shall grope and totter, the shades of shadows, if we cannot survive and surmount and leave decay and death. No, no! Matthew, we live, we shall always live. Our children's children living after us will live with us as living parts of us, as we are parts of God. God lives forever—Brahma, Buddha, Mohammed, Christ—all His infinite incarnations. From God we came, to God we shall return. We are eternal because we are God."

Matthew sat down on the curb, while he waited for the car, and put his back against the hydrant, still reading:

"My beloved, 'Love is God, Love is God and Work is His Prophet'; thus the Lord Buddha spoke."

The street car came by. He climbed aboard and rode wearily home. He could not answer the letter. The revulsion of feeling and long thought-out decision was too great. He had drained the cup. It was not even bitter. It was nauseating. Instead of rising to a great unselfish deed of sacrifice, he had been cast out like a dog on this side and on that. He stared at Kautilya's letter. What had she really wanted? Had she wanted Sara to take him back? Would it not have eased her own hard path and compensated for that wild deed by which she had rescued his soul? Did not her deed rightly end there with that week in heaven? Was not his day of utter renunciation at hand? And if one path had failed, were there not a thousand others? What would be more simple than walking away alone into the world of men, and working silently for the things of which he and Kautilya had dreamed?

XVII

As Matthew reached the landing of his room, four long flights up, he saw a stranger standing in the gloom. Then he noted that it was an East Indian, richly garbed and bowing low before him. Matthew stared. Why, yes! It was the younger of the two Indians of Berlin. Matthew bowed silently and bade him enter. The room looked musty and dirty, but Matthew made no excuses, merely throwing up the window and motioning his guest to a seat. But the Indian bowed again courteously and stood.

"Sir," he said, "I bear a rescript from the Dewan" and High Council of State of the Kingdom of Bwodpur, containing a command of her Royal Highness, the Maharanee, and addressed, sir, to you. Permit me to read:

> To Matthew Towns, Esquire, of Chicago
> Honored Sir:
> By virtue of the Power entrusted to us and by command of our sovereign lady, H.R.H. Kautilya, the reigning Maharanee, we hereby urge and command you to present yourself in person before the Maharanee, at her court to be holden in Prince James County, Virginia, U.S.A., at sunrise, May 1, 1927, there to learn her further pleasure.
>
> > Given at our capital of Khumandat
> > this 31st day of March, 1927,
> > at the Maharanee's command.
> >
> > > BRABAT SINGH,
> > > Dewan

"March 31?" asked Matthew.

"Yes," returned the Indian. "It was placed in my hands this week with the command that it should be presented to you as soon as the order of divorce was entered. In accordance with these orders I now present the rescript." Again he bowed and handed the document to Matthew. Then he straightened again and said: "I bear also a personal letter from her Royal Highness which I am charged to deliver."

Matthew excused himself, and opening, read it:

"Matthew, Day has dawned. Of course a little Virginia farm cannot bound your world. Our feet are set in the path of moving millions.

"I did not—I could not tell you all, Matthew, until now. The Great Central Committee of Yellow, Brown, and Black is finally to meet. You are a member. The High Command is to be chosen. Ten years of preparation are set. Ten more years of final planning, and then five years of intensive struggle. In 1952, the Dark World goes free—whether in Peace and fostering Friendship with all men, or in Blood and Storm—it is for Them—the Pale Masters of today—to say.

"We are, of course, in factions—that ought to be the most heartening thing in human conference—but with enemies ready to spring and spring again, it scares one.

"One group of us, of whom I am one, believes in the path of Peace and Reason, of cooperation among the best and poorest, of gradual emancipation, self-rule, and worldwide abolition of the color line, and of poverty and war.

"The strongest group among us believes only in Force. Nothing but bloody defeat in a worldwide war of dark against white will, in their opinion, ever beat sense and decency into Europe and America and Australia. They have no faith in mere reason, in alliance with oppressed labor, white and colored; in liberal thought, religion, nothing! Pound their arrogance into submission, they cry; kill them; conquer them; humiliate them.

"They may be right—that's the horror, the nightmare of it: they may be right. But surely, surely we may seek other and less costly ways. Force is not the first word. It is the last—perhaps not even that.

"But, nevertheless, we have started forward. Our chart is laid. Our teeth are set, our star is risen in the East. The 'one far-off divine event' has come to pass, and now, oh, Matthew, Matthew, as soon as both in soul and body you stand free, hurry to us and take counsel with us and see Salvation.

"Last night twenty-five messengers had a preliminary conference in this room, with ancient ceremony of wine and blood and fire. I and my Buddhist priest, a Mohammedan Mullah, and a Hindu leader of Swaraj, were India; Japan was represented by an artisan and the blood of the Shoguns; young China was there and a Lama of Thibet; Persia, Arabia, and Afghanistan; black men from the Sudan, East, West, and South Africa; Indians from Central and South America, brown men from the West Indies, and—yes, Matthew, Black America was there too. Oh, you should have heard the high song of consecration and triumph that shook these rolling hills!

"We came in every guise, at my command when around the world I sent the symbol of the rice dish; we came as laborers, as cotton pickers, as peddlers, as fortune tellers, as travelers and tourists, as merchants, as servants. A month we have been gathering. Three days we have been awaiting you—in a single night we shall all fade away and go, on foot, by boat, by rail and airplane. The Day has dawned, Matthew—the Great Plan is on its way."

Matthew folded the letter slowly. She had summoned him—but to what? To love and marriage? No, to work for the Great Cause. There was no word of personal reunion. He understood and slowly looked up at the Indian. The Indian spoke again: "Sir, with your permission, I have a final word."

"Proceed."

"I have delivered my messages. You have been summoned to the presence of the Princess. I now ask you—beg of you, not to go. Let me explain. I am, as you know, in the service of her Royal Highness, the Maharanee of Bwodpur. Indeed my fathers have served hers many centuries."

"Yes," said Matthew, without much warmth.

"You will naturally ask why I linger now. I will be frank. It is to make a last appeal to you—to your honor and chivalry. To me, sir, the will of the Maharanee of Bwodpur is law. But above and beyond that law lies her happiness and welfare and the destiny of India. When her Royal Highness first evinced interest in you and your people, we of her entourage foresaw trouble. Our first efforts to forestall it were crude, I admit, and did not take into account your character and ideals. We seriously underrated you. Yet yourself must admit the subsequent events proved us right.

"Once you were in trouble, and, as the Princess rather quixotically assumed, by her fault, it was her nature to dare anything in order to atone. She gave up everything and went down into the depths. It was only with the greatest difficulty that she was prevailed upon not to surrender the Crown itself. As it was, she gave up wealth and caste and accepted only barest rights of protection and guardianship of her person, upon which we had to insist.

"Finally in a last wild excess of frenzy, sir, she sacrificed to you her royal person. Sir, that night I was near murder, and you stood in the presence of death. But duty is duty, and the Princess can do no wrong. To us she is always spotless and forever right. But, sir, I come tonight to make a last plea. Has she not paid to the uttermost farthing all debts to you, however vast and fantastic they may appear to her? Can you—ought you to demand further sacrifice?"

"Sacrifice?"

"Do you realize, sir, the meaning of this summons?"

"I thought I did. It is to attend a meeting which she has called."

"What I say is from no personal knowledge I have not seen her Royal Highness since she left here; but the reason is indubitable. The day of the coronation of a Maharajah in Bwodpur is at hand."

Matthew started. "Her Royal Highness is—married?"

"She is to be married."

"And she is summoned to India?"

"She is. Three Indians of highest rank have arrived in this country, and I believe they have come to fetch her and the royal ruby."

"And why, then, has she summoned me?"

"Perhaps she still hesitates between—"

"Love and duty?" said Matthew, dreamily.

"Between self-indulgent phantasy and the salvation of Bwodpur," cried the Indian passionately.

"And I," said Matthew slowly, "can seal her choice."

"To few it is given to make a higher, finer sacrifice. You are free. You have but to hint and you can be rich—pardon me—I know. Well, what more? Will you not, in turn, free the Princess? Do the fine and generous act; let her go back to her people."

"Does the Princess wish this freedom?"

"She is one who would not admit it if she did. And yet her very solicitude concerning Mrs. Towns—did it not suggest to you that she saw in your reunion with Sara, on a higher and more congenial plane, a chance for her to renew her own life and work? Is it possible that she cannot yearn for something beyond anything you can offer?"

"Yes, that occurred to me, and I made the offer to my former wife—perhaps too crassly and ungraciously, but with full sincerity."

"True—and now why not follow further and write the Princess, definitely and formally withdrawing from her life, and doing it with such decision that there shall be no doubt in her mind?" The Indian bent forward with strained and eager face.

"You seem—anxious," said Matthew.

"I am," said the Indian. "You do not realize how our hopes for Bwodpur center on the Princess: an independent sovereignty about which a new Empire of India might gradually gather. Then, her eager and inexperienced mind, reaching out, leapt beyond to All India and All Asia; gradually there came a vision of all the Darker Races in the World—everybody who was not white, no matter what their ability or history or genius, as though color itself were merit.

"And now, now finally, God preserve us, the Princess is stooping to raise the dregs of mankind; laborers, scrubwomen, scavengers, and beggars, into some fancied democracy of the world! It is madness born of pity for you and your unfortunate people.

"With every dilution of our great original idea, the mighty mission of Bwodpur fades. The Princess is mad—mad; and you are the center of her madness. Withdraw—for God's sake and your own go! Leave us to our destiny. What have you to do with royalty and divinity?"

The Indian was trembling with fervor and excitement, and his black eyes burned into Matthew's heart. "You will forgive me, sir. I have but done my duty as I saw it," he said.

Matthew looked at the Indian thoughtfully.

"I believe you are right," he said. "Quite right. I believe that you and your friends were right from the beginning and that I was—headstrong and blind. Now the problem is to find a way out."

"For the brave," said the Indian, slowly and distinctly, "there is always a way—out."

XVIII

Matthew stood awhile looking at the door where the Indian with low salaam had disappeared. Then, turning hastily, he put a few things into his handbag, and going out, closed the door. He left a note and key under the doormat and started downstairs, almost colliding with a boy who was racing up, two steps at a time.

"Looking for a man named Towns—know where he stays?"

"I'm Matthew Towns."

"Long distance wants you—quick—drugstore—corner." And he flew down, three steps at a time. Matthew stood still a long minute. He could not go away leaving her standing, waiting, listening. No. This thing must be faced, not dodged. He must talk to her. If she asked, he must even go to her. She, too, was no coward. Eye to eye and face to face, she would say the last word: she was summoned home to India. And then the final parting? He could say it—he would. They must work for the world—but she in her high sphere, and he in his, more lowly: forever parted, forever united in soul.

And more: this meeting which she had announced was of the highest importance. He must attend it and make it successful. He must show Kautilya that her return to India need not hinder nor in the slightest degree retard the Great Plan.

He descended slowly and went into the drugstore and into the little booth. How curious that he had never thought of evoking this miracle before in his heavy loneliness! Yet it was well. There was, there could be, but this ending; out of time and space he was calling a memory.

"Hello—hello! New York—hello, Richmond—go ahead."

At first the voices came strained, far-off, unnatural, interrupted with hissings and brazen echoes. Then at last, real, clear, and close, a voice came pouring over the telephone in a tumult of tone:

"Matthew, Matthew! I have heard the great good news. I am happy, very, very happy. And, Matthew, the friends are waiting. They want you here at sunrise."

W.E.B. DU BOIS

"But, Kautilya—is it necessary that I come? Is it wise? I have been thinking long, Kautilya—"

"Matthew, Matthew, what is wrong? Why would you wait? Are you ill? Has something happened?"

"No, no, Kautilya, I am well—and if you wish me, I am coming—if the friends insist. But I have been wondering if I could not meet them elsewhere, a little later?"

"Later! Matthew—what do you mean?"

"I mean, Kautilya, that I have a duty to perform toward you and the world."

"Matthew, do you mean that you have changed toward me?"

"Changed? No, never. But I see more clearly—as clearly as you yourself saw when you bade me drain the cup."

"What have you feared, Matthew?"

"Nothing but myself. And now that fear is gone—I have drained the cup."

"Yes, dear one. And yet you knew that never and to no one could I give you up?"

"Rather I knew that each must surrender the other."

"To whom, Matthew?"

"To God and the Maharajah of Bwodpur."

A sound that was a sigh and a sob came over the phone.

"Oh, God!" it whispered—"the Maharajah of Bwodpur!"

"Listen, Kautilya—I know—all."

"All?" she gasped. "All! A Maharajah is to be crowned in Bwodpur."

A little cry came over the wire.

"And you have been summoned to the coronation—is it not true?"

"Yes."

"And you must go. Bwodpur—the darker peoples of the world call you. Would it not be easier if—if with this far farewell you left me alone to meet the committee and draft the Plan?"

"No—no—no, Matthew—you do not—you cannot understand. You must come—unless—"

"Kautilya, darling, then I will come—of course I will come. I will do anything to make the broad straight path of your duty easier to enter. Only one thing I will not do, neither for Wealth nor Power nor Love; and that is to turn your feet from this broad and terrible way. And so to bid you Godspeed—to greet you with farewell and to hold you on my heart once more ere I give you up to God—I come, Kautilya."

Her voice sang over the wires:

"Oh, Matthew—my beautiful One—my Man—come—come!—And at sunrise."

"I am coming."

"And at sunrise?"

"But—impossible."

"Have you read the rescript? By sunrise, the first of May."

"But, dear, it is April 30. It takes a train—"

"Nonsense. There is an airplane fueled, oiled, and waiting for you at the Maywood flying field. Stop for nothing—go now; quickly, quickly, oh, my beloved."

Click. Silence. Slowly he let the receiver fall and turned away. He would not falter, and yet almost—almost he wished the truth otherwise. It would have been hard enough to surrender a loved one who wanted to be free, but to send away one who clung to him to her own hurt called for bitter, bitter courage; and dark and bitter courage stood staunch within him as he took out his watch. Or, perhaps, she too was full of courage and blithe and ready to part? He shivered. It was ten o'clock at night. The field was far away. He glanced up at his room, then paused no longer.

"Taxi—Maywood flying field. And quick!"

"Good Lord, boss, that's forty miles—it'll cost you near—"

"It's worth twenty—five dollars for me to get there in two hours."

The taxi leapt and roared. . .

The pilot glanced scowling at the brown face of his lone passenger and climbed aloft. Matthew crawled into the tiny cabin. It was entirely closed in with glass save where up a few steps at the back perched the hard-faced pilot. There were seats for three other passengers, but they were empty.

There arose a roar—a roar that for seven hours never ceased, never hesitated, but crooned and sang and thundered. They

W.E.B. DU BOIS

moved. The lights of Chicago hurried backward. It was midnight. The lights swayed and swam, and suddenly, with a sick feeling and a shiver of instinctive fright, Matthew realized that they were in the air, off the earth, in the sky—flying, flying in the night.

Slowly and in a great circle they wheeled up and south. The earth lay dark beneath in dim and scattered brilliance. They left the great smudge of the crowded city and swept out over flat fields and sluggish rivers. Fires flew in the world beneath and dizzily marked Chicago. Fires flew in the world above and marked high heaven. Between, the gloom lay thick and heavy. It crushed in upon the plane. The plane roared and rose. Matthew could hear the beating and singing of wings rushing by in the night as though a thousand angels of evil were battling against the dawn. He shrank in his strait cabin and stared. His soul was afraid of this daring, heaven-challenging thing. He was but a tossing, disembodied spirit. There was nothing beneath him—nothing. There was nothing above him, nothing; and beside and everywhere to the earth's ends lay nothing. He was alone in the center of the universe with one hard-faced and silent man.

Then the strange horror drew away. The stars, the "ancient and the everlasting stars," like old and trusted friends, came and stood still above him and looked silently down: the Great Bear, the Virgin, and the Centaur. East curled the Little Bear, Hercules, and Bootes; west swung the Lion, the Twins, and the Little Dog. Vega, Arcturus, and Capella gleamed in faint brilliance.

The plane rocked gently like a cradle. Above the clamor of the engine rose a soft calm. Below, the formless void of earth began to speak with the shades of shadows and flickering, changing lights. That cluster of little jewels that flushed and glowed and dimmed would be a town; that comet below was an express train tearing east; that blackness was a world of farms asleep. In an hour Indianapolis was a golden scintillating glory with shadowy threads of smoke. In another hour Cincinnati—he groped at the map yes, Cincinnati—lay in pools of light and shade, and the Ohio flowed like ink.

Suddenly the whole thing became symbolic. He was riding Life above the world. He was triumphant over Pain and Death.

He remembered death down there where once the head of Jimmie thumped, thumped, on the rails. He heard the wail of that black and beautiful widowed wife. "They didn't show me his face!" He saw Perigua lying still in death with that smile on his lips, and he heard him say, "He didn't have no face!" Then came the slippers, her white and jeweled feet that came down from heaven and opened the gates of hell. Someone touched his shoulder. He knew that touch. It was arrest; arrest and jail. But what did he care? He was flying above the world. He was flying to her.

A soft pale light grew upon the world—a halo, a radiance as of some miraculous virgin birth. Lo! In the east and beneath the glory of the morning star, pale, faintly blushing streamers pierced the dim night. Then over the whole east came a flush. The dawn paused. Mountains loomed, great crags, gashed and broken and crowned with mighty trees. The wind from the mountains shrieked and tore; the plane quivered. A moment it stood still; then it dipped and swerved, swayed and curved, dropped, and shot heavenward like a bird. It pierced the wind-wound mists and rose triumphant above the clouds. The sun sprayed all the heavens with crimson and gold, and the morning stars sang in the vast silence above the roar, the unending roar of the airplane.

Matthew's spirit lifted itself to heaven. He rode triumphant over the universe. He was the God-man, the Everlasting Power, the eternal and undying Soul. He was above everything—Life, Death, Hate, Love. He spurned the pettiness of earth beneath his feet. He tried to sing again the Song of Emancipation—the Call of God—"Go down, Moses!"—but the roar of the pistons made his strong voice a pulsing silence.

The clouds parted, melted, and ran before the gleaming glory of the coming sun. The earth lay spread like a sailing picture—all pale blue, green, and brown; mauve, white, yellow, and gold. He faintly saw cities and their tentacles of roads, rivers like silver ribbons, railroads that shrieked and puffed in black and silent lines. Hill and valley, hut and home, tower and tree, flung them swift obeisance, and down, down, away down on the flat breast of the world, crawled men—tiny, weak, and helpless men: some men, eyes down, crept stealthily along; others, eyes aloft, waved and ran and disappeared.

Out of the golden dust of morning a city gathered itself. Its outstretched arms of roads moved swiftly, violently apart, embracing the countryside. The smudge of its foul breath darkened the bright morning. The living plane circled and spurned it, roared to its greeting thousands, swooped, whirled to a mighty curve, rose, and swooped again. Matthew's heart fell. He grew sick and suddenly tired with the swift careening of the plane. The sorrows of earth seemed to rise and greet him. He was no longer bird or superman; he was only a helpless falling atom—a deaf and weary man. They circled a bare field and fell sickeningly toward it. They dropped. His heart, his courage, his hopes, dropped too. They swooped again and circled, rose, and swooped, until dizzy and deaf they landed on an almost empty field and taxied lightly and unsteadily to a standstill. The engine ceased, and the roar of utter silence arose.

Matthew was on earth again, and on the earth where all its pettiest annoyances rose up to plague him. A half-dozen white men ran out, ager, curious. They greeted the pilot vociferously. Then they stared. Matthew climbed wearily down and stood dizzy, dirty, and deaf. They whispered, laughed, and swore, and turning, took the pilot to his steaming bath and breakfast and left Matthew alone.

Matthew stood irresolute, hatless, coatless in the crisp air, clad only in his jersey and overalls. Then he took a deep breath and walked away. In a wayside brook he bathed. He walked three miles to Richmond and boarded a train at six for his home. He found the Jim Crow car, up by the engine, small, crowded, and dirty. The white baggage men were washing up in it, clad in dirty undershirts. The newsboy was dispossessing two couples of a double seat and piling in his wares, swearing nobly. Matthew found a seat backward by a window. Leaning out, he spied a boy with lunches hurrying up to the white folks' car, and he induced him to pause and bought a piece of fried chicken and some cornbread that tasted delicious. Then he looked out.

The Spring sang in his ears; flowers and leaves, sunshine and shade, young cotton and corn. He could not think. He could not reason. He just sat and saw and felt in a tangled jumble of thoughts and words, feelings and desires, dreams and fears. And above it all lay the high heart of determination.

They rolled and bumped along. He sat seeing nothing and yet acutely conscious of every sound, every movement, every quiver of light, the clamor of hail and farewell, the loud, soft, sweet, and raucous voices. The movement and stopping, the voices and silence, grew to a point so acute that he wanted to cry and sing, walk and rage, scream and dance. He sat tense with half-closed eyes and saw the little old depot dance up from the far horizon, slip near and nearer, and slowly pause with a sighing groan. No one was there. Yes—one old black man who smiled and said:

"Mornin', Matthew, mornin'. How you comin' on?"

But Matthew with a hurried word had stridden on, his satchel in hand, his eyes on the wooded hill beyond. He passed through the village. Few people were astir:

"Hello, Matthew!"

"By God, it's Mat!"

The sounds fell away and died, and his feet were on the path—his Feet were on the Path! And the surge of his soul stifled his breath. He saw the wood, the broached the gate. Beyond was the blur of the dim old cabin looking wider and larger.

XIX

He saw her afar; standing at the gate there at the end of the long path home, and by the old black tree—her tall and slender form like a swaying willow. She was dressed in eastern style, royal in coloring, with no concession to Europe. As he neared, he sensed the flash of great jewels nestling on her neck and arms; a king's ransom lay between the naked beauty of her breasts; blood rubies weighed down her ears, and about the slim brown gold of her waist ran a girdle such as emperors fight for. Slowly all the wealth of silk, gold, and jewels revealed itself as he came near and hesitated for words; then suddenly he sensed a little bundle on her outstretched arms. He dragged his startled eyes down from her face and saw a child—a naked baby that lay upon her hands like a palpitating bubble of gold, asleep. He swayed against the tall black tree and stood still.

"Thy son and mine!" she whispered, "Oh, my beloved!"

With strangled throat and streaming eyes, he went down upon his knees before her and kissed the sandals of her feet and sobbed:

"Princess—oh, Princess of the wide, wide world!"

Then he arose and took her gently to his breast and folded his arms about her and looked at her long. Through the soft and high-bred comeliness of her lovely face had pierced the sharpness of suffering, and Life had carved deeper strong, set lines of character. An inner spirit, immutable, eternal, glorious, was shadowed behind the pools of her great eyes. The high haughtiness of her mien was still there, but it lay loose like some unlaced garment, and through it shone the flesh of a new humility, of some half-frightened appeal leaping forth to know and prove and beg a self-forgetting love equal to that which she was offering.

He kissed the tendrils of her hair and saw silver threads lurking there; he kissed her forehead and her eyes and lingered on her lips. He hid his head in the hollow of her neck and then lifted his face to the treetops and strained her bosom to his, until she thrilled and gasped and held the child away from harm.

And the child awoke; naked, it cooed and crowed with joy on her soft arm and threw its golden limbs up to the golden sun. Matthew shrank a little and trembled to touch it and only whispered:

"Sweetheart! More than wife! Mother of God and my son!" At last fearfully he took it in his hands, as slowly, with twined arms, they began to walk toward the cabin, their long bodies and limbs touching in rhythm. At first she said no word, but always in grave and silent happiness looked up into his face. Then as they walked they began to speak in whispers.

"Kautilya, why were you silent? This changes the world!"

"Matthew, the Seal was on my lips. We were parted for all time except your son was born of me. That was my fateful secret."

"Yet when first the babe leapt beneath your heart, still you wrote no word!"

"Still was the Silence sealed, for had it been a girl child, I must have left both babe and you. Bwodpur needs not a princess, but a King."

"And yet even with this our Love Incarnate, you waited an endless month!"

"Oh, silly darling, I waited for all—all; for his birth, for news to India, for your freedom. Do you not see? There had to be a Maharajah in Bwodpur of the blood royal; else brown reaction and white intrigue had made it a footstool of England. If I had not borne your son, I must have gone to prostitute my body to a stranger or lose Bwodpur and Sindrabad; India; and all the Darker World. Oh, Matthew—Matthew, I know the tortures of the damned!"

"And without me and alone you went down into the Valley of the Shadow."

"I arose from the dead. I ascended into heaven with the angel of your child at my breast."

"And now Eternal Life makes us One forever."

"Immortal Mission of the Son of Man."

"And its name?" he asked.

"'Madhu,' of course; which is 'Matthew' in our softer tongue."

Crimson climbing roses, bursting with radiant bloom, almost covered the black logs of wide twin cabins, one rising higher than the other; the darkness of the low and vine-draped hall between caught and reflected the leaping flames of the kitchen within and beyond. Above and behind the roofs, rose a new round tower and a high hedge; the fields were green and white with cotton and corn; the tall trees were softly singing.

Old stone steps worn to ancient hollows led up to the hall and on them loomed slowly Matthew's mother, straight, immense, white-haired, and darkly brown. She took the baby in one great arm, infinite with tenderness, while the child shivered with delight. She kissed Matthew once and then said slowly with a voice that sternly held back its tears:

"And now, son, we'se gwine to make dis little man an hones' chile—Preacher!"

A short black man appeared in the door and paused. He looked like incarnate Age; a dish of shining water lay in one hand and a worn book in the other. He was clad in rusty black with snowy linen, and his face was rough and hewn in angry lineaments around the deep and sunken islands of his eyes.

The preacher read in the worn book from the seventh chapter of Revelation:

"After these things I saw four Angels standing on the four corners of the earth"—stumbling over the mighty words with strange accent and pronunciation—"and God shall wipe away all tears from their eyes!"

Then in curious short staccato phrases, with pauses in between, he lined out a hymn. His voice was harsh and strong, and his breath whistled; but the voice of the old mother rose clear and singularly sweet an octave above, while at last the baritone of Matthew and the deep contralto of Kautilya joined to make music under the trees:

> *Shall I—be car—*
> *ried to-oo—the skies*
> *on flow-ry be-eds*
> *of ease!*

Thus in the morning they were married, looking at neither mother nor son, preacher nor shining morning, but deep into each other's hungry eyes. The voice of the child rose in shrill sweet obbligato and drowned here and again the rolling periods:

"—you, Kautilya, take this man. . . love, honor and obey—"

"Yes."

"—Towns, take this woman. . . until death do you part."

"Yes—yes."

"—God hath joined together; let no man put asunder!"

THEN THE ANCIENT WOMAN STIFFENED, closed her eyes, and chanted to her God:

"Jesus, take dis child. Make him a man! Make him a man, Lord Jesus—a leader of his people and a lover of his God!

"Gin him a high heart, God, a strong arm and an understandin' mind. Breathe the holy sperrit on his lips and fill his soul with lovin' kindness. Set his feet on the beautiful mountings of Good Tidings and let my heart sing Hallelujah to the Lamb when he brings my lost and stolen people home to heaven; home to you, my little Jesus and my God!"

She paused abruptly, stiffened, and with rapt face whispered the first words of the old slave song of world revolution:

"I am seekin' for a City—for a City into de Kingdom!"

Then with closed and streaming eyes, she danced with slow and stately step before the Lord. Her voice lifted higher and higher, outstriving her upstretched arms, shrilled the strophe, while the antistrophe rolled in the thick throat of the preacher:

THE WOMAN: "Lord, I don't feel no-ways *tired*—"

THE MAN: "*Children!* Fight Christ's fury, *Halleluiah!* "

THE WOMAN: "*I'm*—a gonta shout glory when this world's on *fire!* "

THE MAN: "*Children!* Shout God's glory, Hallelu!"

THERE FELL A SILENCE, AND then out of the gloom of the wood moved a pageant. A score of men clothed in white with shining swords walked slowly forward a space, and from their midst came three old men: one black and shaven and magnificent in raiment; one yellow and turbaned, with a white beard that swept his burning flesh; and the last naked save for a scarf about his loins. They carried dishes of rice and sweetmeats, and they chanted as they came.

One voice said, solemn and low:

> *"Oh, thou that playest on the flute, standing by the*
> *water-ghats on the road to Brindaban."*

A second voice, still lower, sang:

> *"Oh, flower of eastern silence, walking in the path of stars,*
> *divine, beautiful, whom nothing human makes unclean:*
> *bring sunrise, noon and golden night and wordless*
> *intercession before the wordless God."*

And a third voice rose shrill and clear:

> *"Oh, Allah, the compassionate, the merciful! who sends his*
> *blessing on the Prophet, Our Lord, and on his family and*
> *companions and on all to whom he grants salvation."*

They gave rice to Matthew and Kautilya, and sweetmeats, and all blessed them as they knelt. Then the Brahmin took the baby from his grandmother and wound a silken turban on its little protesting head—a turban with that mighty ruby that looked like frozen blood. Swaying the babe up and down and east and west, he placed it gently upon Kautilya's outstretched arms. It lay there, a thrill of delight; its little feet, curled petals; its mouth a kiss; its hands like waving prayers. Slowly Kautilya stepped forward and turned her face eastward. She raised her son toward heaven and cried:

"Brahma, Vishnu, and Siva! Lords of Sky and Light and Love! Receive from me, daughter of my fathers back to the hundredth name, his Majesty, Madhu Chandragupta Singh, by the will of God, Maharajah of Bwodpur and Maharajah dhirajah of Sindrabad."

Then from the forest, with faint and silver applause of trumpets:

"King of the Snows of Gaurisankar!"
"Protector of Ganga the Holy!"
"Incarnate Son of the Buddha!"
"Grand Mughal of Utter India!"
"Messenger and Messiah to all the Darker Worlds!"

Envoy

The tale is done and night is come. Now may all the sprites who, with curled wing and starry eyes, have clustered around my hands and helped me weave this story, lift with deft delicacy from out the crevice where it lines my heavy flesh of fact, that rich and colored gossamer of dream which the Queen of Faërie lent to me for a season. Pleat it to a shining bundle and return it, sweet elves, beneath the moon, to her Mauve Majesty with my low and fond obeisance. Beg her, sometime, somewhere, of her abundant leisure, to tell to us hard humans: Which is really Truth—Fact or Fancy? The Dream of the Spirit or the Pain of the Bone?

A Note About the Author

W.E.B. Du Bois (1868–1963) was an African American sociologist, historian, civil rights activist, and socialist. Born in Massachusetts, he was raised in Great Barrington, an integrated community. He studied at the University of Berlin and at Harvard, where he became the first African American scholar to earn a doctorate. He worked as a professor at Atlanta University, a historically black institution, and was one of the leaders of the Niagara Movement, which advocated for equal rights and opposed Booker T. Washington's Atlanta compromise. In 1909, he cofounded the NAACP and served for years as the editor of its official magazine *The Crisis*. In addition to his activism against lynching, Jim Crow laws, and other forms of discrimination and segregation, Du Bois authored such influential works as *The Souls of Black Folk* (1903) and *Black Reconstruction in America* (1935). A lifelong opponent of racism and a committed pacifist, Du Bois advocated for socialism as a means of replacing racial capitalism in America and around the world. In the 1920s, he used his role at *The Crisis* to support the artists of the Harlem Renaissance and sought to emphasize the role of African Americans in shaping American society in his book *The Gift of Black Folk* (1924).

A Note from the Publisher

Spanning many genres, from non-fiction essays to literature classics to children's books and lyric poetry, Mint Edition books showcase the master works of our time in a modern new package. The text is freshly typeset, is clean and easy to read, and features a new note about the author in each volume. Many books also include exclusive new introductory material. Every book boasts a striking new cover, which makes it as appropriate for collecting as it is for gift giving. Mint Edition books are only printed when a reader orders them, so natural resources are not wasted. We're proud that our books are never manufactured in excess and exist only in the exact quantity they need to be read and enjoyed. To learn more and view our library, go to minteditionbooks.com

bookfinity & MINT EDITIONS

Enjoy more of your favorite classics with Bookfinity,
a new search and discovery experience for readers.
With Bookfinity, you can discover more vintage
literature for your collection, find your Reader Type,
track books you've read or want to read,
and add reviews to your favorite books.
Visit www.bookfinity.com, and click on
Take the Quiz to get started.

Don't forget to follow us
@bookfinityofficial and @mint_editions